Into the Light

Book 3 of the Rocky Creek Series

KATHRYN ASCHER

Virginia

Into the Light

Published in the United State by BQB Publishing

(Boutique of Quality Books Publishing, Inc.)
www.bqbpublishing.com

978-1-937084-89-9 (p)
978-1-937084-90-5 (e)

Library of Congress Control Number: 2016910212

Book design by Robin Krauss, www.bookformatters.com
Cover design by Valerie Tibbs, www.tibbsdesign.com

Other Books

in The Rocky Creek Series

What It Takes
On the Line

Praise for What It Takes

"Kathryn Ascher has written a truly entertaining story with wonderful and loveable characters."

-Bella Lee from Bella's Little Book Blog

"What It Takes by Kathryn Ascher is one of these brilliant debut works that make me want for more."

-Claudia B. from My Little Avalon Book reviews

"What It Takes has all of the elements in a classic romance novel which appeal to me; believable main characters, a great storyline and a well-crafted villain."

-Sue G. from Lady Celeste Reads Romance reviews

Praise for On the Line

Five stars. "Kathryn Ascher presents an intriguing, well-written story of two women, Janelle and her sister actress Kelsey Morgan . . . The characters are multi-faceted and realistic—the author writes a great villain and a nasty mother—and the plot had enough intrigue and twists to keep me invested in the story."

-Lady Celeste Reads Romance

"A very realistic story with characters that one can relate to. There is just the right amount of drama, romance, and suspense. There was a lot of thought put into developing all the supporting characters as well and it made the book very enjoyable."

-Sumina K. for NetGalley

Dedication

For Matt, my sounding board and occasional punching bag (not literally). Thank you for still being willing to give advice and direction, even if I don't like it, and thank you for giving me the occasional kick in the pants (not literally) when I need it.

Acknowledgments

When writing, I always come across a question or two that I don't have the answer for. I would like to thank Angie, again, for having the answers I needed. Thank you, Bridget, for your knowledge of all things French (even though most of them didn't make it into the book). Thank you Cyn, Creah, and Tamara for your wonderful advice. Many thanks to Pearlie and Terri, my BQB Publishing team, for working with me to make this story the best it can be.

And, as always, thank you, reader, for buying this book. I hope you enjoy reading it as much as I enjoyed writing it.

Prologue

Jackson Harris threw his leg over the branch and leaned back against the trunk of the old oak tree outside of the house of his best friend, Charlie Dodd. He'd climbed that tree at least a dozen times—usually when he needed to hide from his parents for some reason and going in the front door of the Dodd house wasn't an option—but it never got easier. It didn't help that today, he was dressed for a funeral. He looked over his dress pants and undershirt for holes or snags he might have gotten on the climb up and breathed a sigh of relief when he found none. His mother would kill him if he put a hole in his best Sunday suit, which was why the matching coat, shirt, tie, and shoes were laid neatly over the back of a chair on the patio below.

With a frown, he stared at the second story window directly in front of him.

It was the window of Kerri Dodd, Charlie's younger sister, and she had locked herself in her room. Not that Jackson could blame her.

Her parents had just died and it was time to go to the funeral.

After their visit to the funeral home the night before, she'd locked herself in her bedroom and hadn't come out since. Her brother was starting to worry.

Jackson had been at their home every day since the night of the accident, offering Charlie and Kerri support and sharing in their grief. He had watched Kerri gradually withdraw from everyone. This morning, with her silent refusal to come out of her room, he was particularly concerned about her. She was a sensible girl. She wouldn't do anything stupid. But still, he knew he'd feel better if he could see her for himself.

He focused on her window as he inched closer to the house along the branch, hoping the window would be unlocked and easy to open from the outside. Thankfully he had no problems gently pushing up the framed glass as his eyes searched the room.

Sixteen-year-old Kerri was seated at her vanity, dressed in a plain black dress. When he saw her reflection in the mirror, his heart thudded against his chest. Her sorrow was etched on her tear-streaked cheeks. Her red-rimmed, steel-colored eyes were hollow, devoid of the joy and lightness he was so familiar with. He hated the emptiness he saw and wanted more than anything to take that pain and sadness from her.

He swallowed the lump in his throat as he pulled himself through her window, landing on her floor with a suppressed grunt.

Surprised, she quickly pivoted on her seat to face him. "Jackson?" Her words escaped on a wobbly breath. "Did you climb the tree?"

Brushing dirt from the knees of his pants, he lifted the corners of his lips in a half-smile. "Well, I didn't fly," he replied, hoping to get a laugh from her.

Her mouth fell open a fraction and she nodded. "Oh."

A pounding on her door had both of them turning to look at it. "Kerri, c'mon," came Charlie's voice from the other side. "We need to leave."

Jackson glanced over his shoulder at Kerri and saw the tears fill her eyes just before her shoulders slumped and she turned away. He strode to the door and unlocked it, then eased it open wide enough to meet Charlie's red-rimmed stare. He tried to hide it, but Jackson knew how much Charlie had cried over the last few days. He also knew that Charlie's impatience was fueled mostly by the fact he wanted to have the funeral over and done with. Charlie hoped that once his parents were buried, the grief would somehow be easier to bear.

Jackson knew better.

"Give us a few minutes," Jackson said.

Charlie pressed his lips together as if he might argue, but he simply nodded and tapped his watch.

Jackson closed the door and turned to see Kerri sitting on the edge of the bed, hugging her arms to her body.

"Please don't make me go," she softly begged as she began rocking back and forth.

His heart broke for her.

He silently studied her, his worry for her well-being tightening his chest. Even as she swayed on the bed, she was still poised and graceful. Her black dress was simple, but he noticed how it hugged her waist, accentuating the curves he had only recently recognized.

He had known her since she was two and he was five, when her family had moved to Rocky Creek. He'd become instant friends with Charlie and, for Jackson who was the youngest of three boys, Kerri was the sister he never had. He realized now she was no longer the girl he'd grown up with. She was developing into a beautiful woman that he was happy to know. It seemed cruel that her parents would miss seeing her continue to mature.

"I should have been with them," she mumbled.

Her suggestion made him nauseous and Jackson was on his knees in front of her before he realized he was moving. Her eyes were focused on the wall behind him and he laid his hands on either side of her on the bed.

"Kerri," he calmly stated. "No."

"I should have been in the car with them." Her gaze was still somewhere over his shoulder. "It's my fault they're dead. I could have . . ."

Jackson moved to sit on the bed beside her and slipped an arm around her. Her eyes met his and immediately filled with tears before she crumpled against his chest.

"It's not your fault," he said softly into her lemon-and-honeysuckle-scented hair as his other arm rose to surround her and she sobbed violently into his T-shirt. "You couldn't have prevented the accident."

Five nights ago, Kerri had stayed home alone while her parents had gone out for dinner. Charlie had just returned to college for his sophomore year and Kerri would be starting her junior year in high school soon. As they were driving home, Mr. Dodd had suffered a massive heart attack and crashed the car in a heavily wooded area. Both passenger and driver had died at the scene.

"I could have been driving them myself," Kerri muttered, still sobbing. She laid her small palm against his chest and turned her face away.

Jackson remained still, afraid that she might mistake a nod of understanding as one of agreement. She'd only had her driver's license for a month and her parents would have wanted her to practice, but he wasn't convinced that scenario would have turned out the way she thought.

"Or I should have tried harder to get them to stay home." Her voice was drained and tired.

"Don't do this to yourself," he murmured, with his arm still around her. "The 'what ifs' will drive you crazy."

"How do you know?"

"I did the same thing when my father died."

She tilted her face upward to look at him. "But you were twelve and he died in the line of duty, right?"

"True," he agreed, thinking back to the last time he saw his father.

"You couldn't have stopped it," she added in a matter-of-fact tone that made his lips twitch. At least she seemed to be calming down.

"No, I couldn't have stopped it." Jackson blew out a shaky breath. He hadn't shared these memories about his father's death with anyone else before. "But I hadn't been a very good son for several days leading up to his death. I had argued with him about everything. I had been skimping on my chores and then back-talked when he'd called me on it."

She sat up and lifted her face to his. He couldn't meet her gaze, afraid of what he might see in her eyes.

"That last morning, just before he left for work, we had the biggest fight we'd ever had." Jackson said in a small voice. He could hear her breathing beside him and feel the warmth of her gaze on his face as they sat in silent commiseration.

"What was the fight about?" she finally asked.

His gaze dropped to the floor. He could still picture his father in his crisp police uniform as he'd stood over Jackson and expressed his disappointment with his youngest son's behavior.

"He'd heard me sass my mother. He yelled at me about treating women the right way. He lectured me about respecting women, said he would not have me being disrespectful to my mother in his house, and if he heard about me disrespecting any woman while I was out of his house, I would get the worst whippin' I'd ever had."

Jackson closed his eyes.

"That was our last conversation. I hated myself for months because of it." He opened his eyes and looked into hers. "Still do sometimes," he added as he took her hand. "I can't help but think, what if I'd behaved better that morning? Maybe he would have been more focused on doing his job. Or what if I'd been a model son, like my brothers, for the weeks before? Maybe he wouldn't have been as angry with me that morning. The truth is, I know I couldn't have stopped what happened to him, but I still wish I could have changed our final moments together."

"Oh, Jackson." Kerri sighed as she raised her palm to his cheek. The warmth of it reached his toes and he felt weak in the knees.

He cleared his throat. "My point is, you can't give in to the 'what ifs.' You won't be able to grieve properly or move on." He took her hand from his cheek and lowered it to the mattress between them, holding it tightly.

Her brow furrowed. "Do you think you can ever move on?"

It had been seven years since his father died. "No," he answered honestly. "Not really."

Her lids lowered over her eyes as she leaned her head onto his shoulder again. She took a few deep breaths as he stared at their clasped hands.

"I can't do it, Jackson," she whispered as he felt her tears soaking through his shirt.

"Yes, you can."

She pushed away from him and shook her head. Her brow puckered and she looked toward the bedroom door. "I keep hoping I'll wake up and realize this was all a nightmare," she murmured, and he wasn't sure if she was talking to herself or to him. "If I go to their funeral," she choked on the word, "I'll have to accept this is real." She turned to him again, fresh tears trailing down her cheeks. "I'm not ready for that."

He nodded and slid his arm around her back again and pulled her against his chest. He understood what she was feeling. He still had moments when it didn't seem real to him that his dad was gone. Still had moments when he hated seeing his oldest brother, Nathan, sitting in their father's place at the table or in other roles that had once been their dad's.

"I know." Jackson laid his cheek on the top of her head. "I can't promise that it will be easy. But I can promise to be by your side."

One

Kerrigan Dodd nervously walked into the conference room of the Memphis hotel and stiffly reached for the outstretched hand of her new boss.

"Jacob, it's nice to finally meet you," she said as she noticed the glint of the red stone and the sparkle of the diamond-studded "G" on the large ring he wore.

"Kerrigan, it's a pleasure to meet you as well," Jacob Goldberg replied with a smooth, Southern accent. With a wave of his arm, he motioned her further into the room.

He was a partner in an up-and-coming recording company and the producer of several bands. She had just been hired to manage the one he found most troublesome, Malhypnus. He'd told her he thought they had the highest potential and he didn't want to see it wasted because they were the worst behaved of all the bands he produced. On top of their bad behavior, they were also terrible at managing their money.

Managing money was one of Kerrigan's strong suits. Marketing, accounting, and financial planning had been her majors in college, and she'd spent the past three years in Zurich, Switzerland, sharpening her skills and working for various banks.

"Thank you for coming on such short notice." Jacob tossed his briefcase onto the table then turned to face her.

She met his bright blue gaze, taking in his long nose, high cheekbones, square jaw, and full lips, all topped off with a full head of black hair, much like her own. She was certain any other woman would find him handsome enough to swoon over. But Kerrigan felt nothing for Jacob.

"I'll have to admit, I was a little hesitant when I first saw your resume," Jacob continued. "You have no experience in the music industry, but you come highly recommended in the financial field. Have you had a chance to look over the budget and familiarize yourself with the issues?"

Kerrigan nodded. "I already have ideas on how to fix some of the problems."

She laid her binder, filled with printed copies of the files he'd emailed her the day before, on the table next to his briefcase, then folded her arms across her chest. The music industry may be unfamiliar to her, but she knew money. Besides, she'd been looking for something different, something that could expand her horizons as well as her resume, which was one of the reasons she'd taken the job.

What had started as a year of studying abroad in Paris during her junior year in college had ended up taking her to London, and then Zurich. She'd been in Europe for four years and had been starting to miss home when an invitation to a wedding arrived in the mail. Still, she'd been hesitant to come home to Rocky Creek, but the groom was one of her brother's best friends, and also her best friend's brother, and she hadn't wanted to miss the wedding. With a little arm-twisting from her brother and best friend, she'd decided to quit her job in Switzerland and make the trip home permanent.

Three months later, the excitement of the wedding had worn off and she was over her homesickness.

Even eight years after their death, the reminders of her happy life with her parents quickly returned to make her miserable in her hometown. Trying to avoid the memories had been one of the reasons she'd taken the opportunity to study in Paris.

Another reason she'd left home and lingered in Europe longer than she'd planned was Jackson Harris. She'd developed a crush on him when she was fourteen, but realized she was in love with her brother's friend when she was sixteen, just after the grief of her parents' deaths had subsided enough to not be overwhelming. She had tried for two years to get him to notice her, but he hadn't felt the same, and he'd proven it by walking out of her life when she was eighteen. Now, she had no idea where Jackson was or what he was doing, and she feared seeing him around Rocky Creek unexpectedly, so she'd started to look for a job that would take her away.

When Jacob's offer had come the day before, she'd seen the perfect escape. She turned her focus back to her new boss.

"In my experience, I've discovered the problems aren't always just with the money. Sometimes there are underlying issues. Could you give me some background on the band members? That might help me better understand how to approach some of the problems."

"In this case, your observations would be correct. Most of the problems stem from Sebastian's spoiled behavior," Jacob said with a shake of his head, tension lines forming around his lips. "He expects everything to be done his way, spends more money nightly than the band brings in weekly, and is pretty much single-handedly responsible for running off the last four managers."

"Four managers? Since the tour started four months ago?" Kerrigan frowned.

Jacob nodded. "After he ran the last one off, I decided that the next manager I hired would be the band's last chance." He casually stepped toward her, and out of habit she stiffened. "When I spoke with your references, I knew you were the best last chance I could give them. My partners are ready to cut them loose right now."

Kerrigan tapped her fingers lightly against her upper arm as she digested Jacob's revelations. She couldn't say she was surprised by this information. Most rock bands were famous for having at least one prima donna, and it sounded as if that role in Malhypnus belonged to Sebastian.

"What about the other band members—what can you tell me about them?"

"I don't expect you'll have too many problems with Riley and Stephen," Jacob began. "Riley's as laid back as they come and makes friends with almost everyone he meets. Stephen is probably the most mature of the bunch. He has a degree in business, so he's my go-to guy when they're between managers. If you have any questions about the operations of the band, or if you have any problems with the club and venue managers, Stephen's the one you should go to."

Kerrigan swallowed her doubts. "Why hasn't he been able to keep the band solvent?"

Jacob shrugged his shoulders. "He does his best but says it's gotten harder to keep Sebastian and his spending in check. He's the one who notified me when he noticed how bad the problem was. And then there's Jack." Jacob sighed heavily.

She waited for him to explain but he remained silent.

"What's wrong with Jack?"

Jacob pressed his lips together and she could tell he was considering what, or possibly how much, he wanted to tell her. "Over the past few years, it seems he's been on a downward spiral. When I first met the band three years ago, he was moody and a bit of a playboy, but as time has gone on, he's become more detached from everything but the music. He can be as kind as Riley and as mature as Stephen if he wants to be."

"And if he doesn't?" Kerrigan's brow furrowed.

"Well, if he doesn't, he acts like a spoiled brat." Jacob shook his head. "Worse than Sebastian sometimes. And if he's in the mood to take Sebastian's side, sparks really start to fly between the four of them." He regarded her squarely. "Now that you know what you're walking in to, are you sure you still want to do this?"

Kerrigan held his startling clear gaze and narrowed her eyes. She wished she'd had more time to research the band. She had asked her brother what he knew about them, but Charlie had said he hadn't heard of them. He had suggested that she shouldn't take the job, but she had figured it was because he'd wanted her to stay home after being gone for so long. And his tone hadn't seemed that serious, so Kerrigan had ignored him.

"I won't cater to them," she began slowly. "Any of them. If one of them deserves to be punished, whether it's arrested, fired, or simply fined, I won't hesitate to have it done. Things won't improve if they continue as they have been."

Jacob nodded his agreement.

Kerrigan released a long, slow breath. "Sounds like I have my work cut out for me, but I'm ready for this challenge," she assured him with a nod of her head.

"Great." His smile widened, showing his perfectly straight teeth, and she wished she could feel some sort of interest in him. At the very least, it would reassure her that she was over Jackson.

Nothing else did.

"Good morning, Jacob," came a voice from the door. As Jacob turned around, Kerrigan looked up and saw two men entering the room.

The first was tall with light brown hair, thinning in the front but pulled into a short ponytail in the back. He was wearing a pair of jeans with holes in the knees and a T-shirt covered by a flannel shirt, buttoned up to the middle of his chest. From across the room, Kerrigan could tell his eyes were dark.

The other was an inch shorter and two inches broader across the chest with a head of short, spiky red hair, shaved on the side and longer on the top. His jeans had even more holes and his T-shirt was gray, whether by design or from dirt she didn't know. He caught Kerrigan's eye as they approached and gave her a wide smile that showed off his crooked teeth. Kerrigan tilted her head and studied him, wary of his friendly grin.

"Ah, Stephen. Riley. Good to see you this morning," Jacob said as he stepped forward to shake their hands. "Guys, I have a surprise for you."

"Oh, really?" asked the redhead in a thick Scottish brogue. He took a long look at Kerrigan. "Would it be this lovely lady behind ye?" His lips pursed as he gave Kerrigan a cheeky wink and her tension eased a bit.

"It is." Jacob motioned toward Kerrigan.

Without waiting for an introduction, Riley stepped around Jacob and bowed deeply with a flourish of his arm. "Riley Kincaid," he said as he rose. "Drummer extraordinaire. And who might ye be, m'dear?" He reached out his hand.

As she shook it, Kerrigan kept her arm stiff and straight. "I'm Kerrigan Dodd. It's a pleasure to meet you." She gave him a tight smile.

Jacob stepped farther away and gestured toward Stephen. "This is Stephen Jennings. He plays keyboard."

Kerrigan shook Stephen's hand in the same manner. "I've heard a lot about you. I believe you and I have some things to talk about."

"Oh really?" Stephen's eyes widened as he looked at Jacob. "Is she our new manager?"

"Yes, she is," Jacob answered. "I hope that's not a problem."

"Not for me." Stephen's shoulders relaxed, but a worried look came over his face. "But we both know Sebastian won't like it."

"No, he won't." Jacob raised an eyebrow. "But, I'm not sure I care about what Sebastian will or won't like right now."

"Ye've at least warned her, right? Ye aren't just throwing her to the wolves." Riley crossed his arms and leaned against the large table. His face wore a serious expression and concern filled his soft, brown eyes. "I'll do ma' best to keep her safe, but I can't promise they'll go easy on her."

"They?" Kerrigan asked. "So you don't think Jack will be happy about me either?"

Riley shook his head in response and Stephen shrugged, but it was Jacob's nod that gave her a chill of apprehension. She looked at her watch and her brows came together. Jacob had called this meeting to introduce her to the band and it was time to get started, but they were still missing two band members.

When she looked up, Jacob met her eyes. "They're late. That's normal."

"If you want a meeting to start on time, you should probably tell them it's ten to fifteen minutes earlier," Stephen offered. "At least."

Kerrigan rolled her eyes at the childish behavior.

They didn't need a manager. They needed a nanny.

"I hope they change their own diapers," she muttered.

Riley chuckled. "I think I like her."

Kerrigan looked up, surprised she'd spoken out loud. Luckily Jacob and Stephen looked as amused as Riley.

"That wasn't nice of me." She shook her head. "But Jacob, you didn't tell me I'd be working with children." She folded her arms across her chest. "And what's worse is it sounds like these two hold the rest of you captive, making you do things they want to do when they want to do them, and they don't seem to care about, or respect, anything outside of themselves. I'm thinking you should have advertised for a babysitter instead of a band manager." She raised an eyebrow and the men laughed again. "If you'll excuse me, it looks like I have time to get a cup of coffee."

She smiled and walked to the refreshment table in the small room across the hall. She poured a cup of coffee and added a packet of sweetener and a splash of milk. This job wasn't going to be as simple as she'd expected. She'd known the band had financial problems and had suspected there was a little strife amongst the members. With the numbers she'd seen, she didn't see how there couldn't be. But she had a feeling there was more to it than even Jacob realized, which may not bode well for her success. She shook her head as she stirred her coffee.

There had once been a time she could manage immature males. She'd had plenty of practice with her older brother and his friends. They hadn't exactly been difficult; they'd just always been around. And they'd loved to tease her, especially Jackson. She'd learned early how to respond with sarcasm and a sharp tongue.

When that didn't work, she could throw a mean right hook.

But she hadn't used any of those skills in several years. Now she preferred to avoid putting herself in situations that might require her to be defensive. Especially with men.

It was safer that way.

A rumble of voices began to grow from the conference room. Kerrigan stirred her coffee as she leaned against the doorframe, peering across the hallway into the room.

A man had entered through another door and was scowling at Jacob. His untamed black hair came to his shoulders like a lion's mane. His angular chin sported an anchor-shaped goatee under a set of thin lips. His sharp, straight nose flared slightly at the nostrils and even from across the room, Kerrigan could see the mischief and trouble in his dark eyes.

"Hello, Sebastian. So glad you could join us." Jacob's greeting was tense.

"You mean I had a choice?" Sebastian scoffed. "And here I thought all meetings with you were required affairs, no matter how boring and mundane."

Kerrigan frowned. She could already tell she and Sebastian were going to have problems. She stepped into the hallway and leaned against the wall beside the door. She couldn't see the men in the room, but she could still hear what was being said.

"I'm hurt you got this party started without me."

"Well, if you'd show up on time . . ." Jacob started.

"I am on time," Sebastian growled. "Those two jokers are just early. They make me look bad."

"No, Sebastian," Jacob corrected him. "You manage that pretty well on your own."

"Aw, Jacob. Are you still upset I ran Roger off?"

Kerrigan's brow furrowed at the proud tone and she inched sideways until she could see the malevolent sneer on Sebastian's face.

"And Kevin," Stephen muttered.

"And Josh," Riley added.

Sebastian nonchalantly shrugged his shoulders. "It's not my fault they were all incompetent bastards."

"They weren't incompetent," Jacob argued. "You're just an asshole who thinks he knows everything."

"I know what's important when it comes to my band," Sebastian roared as he took two angry steps towards Jacob. "I'm not twelve. I don't need curfews and allowances," he continued. "And I'll be damned if someone's gonna tell me what I can eat, how much I can drink, who I can fuck, and when I can take a piss."

Kerrigan shuddered and swallowed the large lump in her throat. If Sebastian had such a problem with structure and schedules, she really was in trouble.

"Such language in front of the ladies," an amused voice drawled.

Kerrigan froze and took a hesitant step toward the room. She knew that voice.

"I thought I'd asked the two of you to play nice," the voice continued as she drew closer.

Her eyes widened as the speaker came into view and her heart sank to her stomach.

Two

Standing just inside the doorway, a beautiful blonde on each arm, was Jackson. The man who'd given her the silent treatment for two years, then reappeared again at the worst moment of her life. She still remembered that day in Paris, when she could only look at him through the glass, like it was yesterday.

It was two days after the incident and she'd been called in to the police station to identify a man who had been lingering outside her apartment, looking for her. Jackson had been sitting at the lone table in the room, both hands in his chestnut hair that spiked through his fingers, a tattoo on the inside of his left wrist that she'd never seen before. His jaw was shadowed with stubble and his eyes were closed as she studied him through the window. When he'd looked up, despite knowing he couldn't see her, she'd stepped back into the shadows and watched him get up and slowly pace the room like a caged animal.

She'd had no explanation why he was there. If Charlie had known Jackson was coming, he'd given her no warning. She'd been battered and bruised, inside and out, and had been emotionally torn. The moment she saw him, she'd wanted him to hold her, the way he had when her parents had died. But she'd felt so ashamed, she couldn't face him. She'd told the officer that Jackson wasn't to blame for what had happened to her, but that she didn't want to see him. Then she'd walked away.

It was one of the hardest things she'd ever done.

In the four years since, she'd thought of him every day, but he hadn't tried to contact her again, so any ridiculous hope he'd been in Paris out of any true desire to see her had died a long time ago. Now he stood in the doorway, as tall and handsome as he'd ever been with his grassy green eyes, so full of laughter and life, and his blond, almost white, hair standing up all over the top of his head like he'd just rolled out of bed, and her pulse quickened.

The last time she had seen his hair, it had been brown. And not so short.

This wasn't right. Kerrigan took another step forward and frustratingly glared at her binder on the table in the conference room. She'd always spent at least a week researching everything about every client she'd ever taken on in Zurich. Yet she'd come into this job completely unprepared. She'd been so interested in the financial situation of the band that she'd only glanced at the personal information in the papers Jacob had sent her. Figuring she'd meet them face-to-face soon enough, she'd only taken the time to learn their names.

She fervently cursed herself under her breath for being so careless.

Mentally she went through the names she'd seen on the list of band members: Riley Kincaid, Stephen Jennings, Sebastian Bates and . . . Jack Hart.

"What are you arguing about this morning? Whose fault it is we keep running out of managers?" Jack was saying in his slow, Southern drawl.

Jack Hart? That was Jackson Harris.

Kerrigan's chest felt heavy as she braved another glimpse.

Those were most definitely Jackson's full lips, the ones she'd dreamt about kissing since she was a teenager. Those were his high cheekbones and scruffy, square jaw, his straight nose, his cute little dimples. Those were Jackson's strong arms, the ones that had held her the morning of her parents' funeral, now wrapped around two busty, tall blondes. Kerrigan stood frozen, staring unfocused into the room, suddenly wishing she'd listened to her brother's advice.

"Jack. Thanks for showing up," Jacob said tersely.

"Sorry," Jack said, not really sounding apologetic. "I was otherwise occupied." The blonde twins tittered.

Kerrigan felt tears sting her eyes and furiously blinked them away as she slowly stumbled backward until she felt the solid wall at her back. She blew out a shaky breath and forced herself to focus on the truth.

She needed to remember that he'd never known she loved him. She'd never worked up the courage to tell him before he'd walked out of her life. And he was a rock star now, so of course he could have any woman he wanted.

And probably did. She'd just have to get used to it, put her feelings aside, and learn to look the other way.

"Can we get started?" Stephen asked.

"Of course," Jack replied sweetly. "Ladies, it's been a pleasure."

As Kerrigan pushed away from the wall and stepped to the center of the hallway, she heard the women giggle.

"Twins?" she heard Sebastian's gruff voice ask.

Kerrigan turned her head toward the high-pitched chatter as the twins came around the corner.

Jack chuckled. "Yes, but not quite identical."

"They looked it," Riley said.

The women made eye contact with Kerrigan and their smiles grew more feline as their gazes wandered the length of her body.

"When they're clothed," Jack responded and Sebastian guffawed.

The two blondes seemed pleased with their assessment and laughed in a way that made Kerrigan feel inadequate. She pulled her shoulders back and looked away to hide the warmth in her cheeks from the women as they passed.

She raised an eyebrow and tightly pressed her lips together as she stared at their backs.

So these were the type of women Jack was interested in? She hated to admit it, but she'd always thought Jackson had better taste. The girls he'd followed around the campground at the beach had always seemed to be a little less . . . air-headed?

Someone in the conference room cleared his throat, drawing Kerrigan's focus from the door the women had just walked through and she shook her thoughts away.

"Okay, you guys can talk about that later."

"Spoilsport," Sebastian mumbled.

"We have business to discuss, I have a flight to catch, and you guys need to get on the road to Huntsville," Jacob continued.

Kerrigan's feet began to inch toward the lobby. She was no longer sure she could do this job. Managing the band was one thing. But she couldn't face Jackson or this new persona he had adopted. Not after what she'd just seen.

With an ocean between them, it was one thing to consider that he was involved with another woman. It had been an uncomfortable thought, but she couldn't deny it. To see the evidence with her own eyes wasn't something she'd been prepared for. It was why she'd felt the need to leave Rocky Creek again only three months after she'd returned. The thought of seeing him with other women around town had turned her stomach inside out.

"Fine, but can we make this fast?" Jack said, all humor gone from his voice. "I'm tired and would like to get some sleep."

"They keep you up?" Sebastian asked in a sardonic tone Kerrigan didn't like.

"God, yes," Jack answered. "And when I was no longer up, they giggled and talked all night long."

"If their mouths are full, they can't talk and giggle," Sebastian stated matter-of-factly.

"Tried that."

Jack's careless answer had Kerrigan's cheeks aflame and her stomach quivering.

"Enough!" Jacob snapped.

Kerrigan turned her attention to the cup of coffee in her trembling hand.

"Now," Jacob started, "it's been a week and a half since you ran your last manager off."

"He was an incompetent bastard," Jack muttered.

"Thank you," Sebastian said.

"He was not," Jacob snapped. "The two of you are just spoiled brats."

"Jacob, he thought we could save money by having room inspections every time we checked in or out of a hotel," Sebastian stated.

"And it appears he did," Jacob snapped. "In the ten days you've been without a manager, the hotel bills have skyrocketed. Between room service fees and the destruction of property, Sebastian, your bills alone have more than doubled. Stephen and Riley's shared room costs have been holding steady at about a quarter of yours."

"He treated us like we were in the army!" Sebastian ranted. "Room inspections, curfews, early breakfast, and then we had to be on the road at the same time every morning we had to travel, only after he'd done another room inspection."

Kerrigan eased closer to the room but tried to stay out of sight.

"You need that sort of discipline," Jacob said.

"He made me pay for any damage he found!" Sebastian yelled.

Jack chuckled. "Sebastian couldn't afford condoms for a week, Jacob."

Jacob groaned. "Great."

Riley stepped backward, into Kerrigan's line of sight. He turned his head and briefly met her stare with a wink, then looked at Jacob. "Oh, dinna worry. He had plenty of alone time."

"I'm gonna come across this table and smack that bloody grin off your face," Sebastian growled at Riley, who shrugged innocently as Jack and Stephen chuckled.

Kerrigan stopped at the edge of the door and frowned. This meeting was obviously out of hand, and if Jacob couldn't get them under control, what chance did she have?

"All right." Jacob's stern voice broke through the laughter. "Like it or not, Roger was on the right track. You guys have spent more money than you've made on this tour and it has to stop."

"I disagree," Sebastian muttered.

"I don't care," Jacob said shortly. "Sadly, your high hotel room bills are only the tip of the iceberg."

"Then Roger should have done something about that," Sebastian retorted.

Kerrigan rolled her eyes. After only fifteen minutes, she was already tired of Sebastian.

"You didn't give him time, Sebastian. Now shut up and listen."

Kerrigan was impressed with Jacob's authoritative tone and wondered if her predecessors had tried it. If so, had they had any luck with it? Sebastian clearly lacked any kind of respect for authority, something she'd never had to deal with. Every client she'd had in Switzerland had sought her company out for help and happily gone along with any plan she'd come up with. She had a feeling Sebastian wouldn't be so easygoing.

That left Jack as her only hope.

She closed her eyes and swallowed her groan.

She wasn't sure she could work closely with him. Not if she wanted to keep her secrets safe. Until she learned whether this 'Jack' persona was just an act or if it was the person he had become, she didn't want to risk exposing herself.

"Aside from your massive hotel bills, the food and drink costs have become outrageous. There is no reason for four people to eat eight hundred dollars' worth of food and two hundred dollars in alcohol after every performance. No, Jack. I don't want to hear excuses. Even if you each had one girl backstage with you after the concert, that's still too much food and drink. And can we talk about your rainy day funds?"

"What rainy day funds?" Sebastian asked.

"Those should still be untouched," Jack snapped.

Kerrigan's eyes popped open and she stared into the room at the wall behind Riley.

"Riley and Stephen's are. Yours and Sebastian's are nearly gone."

"Gone!" Jack squawked. "There's no way."

If she wasn't mistaken, that was panic in his voice.

"I'm sorry, but it's true." Jacob stated. "Since you started performing at small festivals eighteen months ago, we've gotten two dozen paternity claims against the two of you."

Kerrigan's knees weakened and her fingers grasped at the edge of the door as she leaned toward the opening. She had noticed the rainy day funds listed on the file she'd been sent and had meant to ask Jacob what they were and why they were so depleted. Now it appeared they were an insurance policy. Could Jackson have a child out there by some faceless woman?

She couldn't catch her breath.

Kerrigan realized now this was not the man she'd fallen in love with . . . and it nearly brought her to her knees.

She'd never forgiven herself for turning him away in Paris, and for the past four years—try as she might to forget him, to stop loving him—all she'd managed to do was build a shrine to him in her mind. She couldn't forget the sweet young man he'd been, the one who'd never had a cruel word to say to anyone. She'd never known him to treat women, young or old, with anything but courtesy and respect. She knew how much his last conversation with his father haunted him.

While they were growing up, he'd spent hours, almost every afternoon, at her house with Charlie, and while her brother could make her feel like a spoiled brat, Jackson always had a kind word or a secret smile for her. He'd always known how to make her feel better.

Jackson was supposed to be her hero, and her hero didn't treat women so carelessly.

She glanced at Jack's wrist and remembered the glimpse of a tattoo she'd seen at the police station in Paris. She felt certain he hadn't had it when she'd last seen him, when she was eighteen. It had niggled at her mind for the last four years and she'd wondered what other changes he'd made during their separation. Regardless of how unworthy she'd felt after Paris, she'd never considered he could change so much that he would be almost unrecognizable, or that those changes would make her question her love for him. Then again, she hadn't really wanted to stop.

But now, nothing about him was familiar. His appearance was different. His behavior was nothing she would have expected. On the surface, he seemed like a stereotypical rock star, and the idea that she'd lost that man she'd known made her want to cry for all the years they'd been apart.

"Who has more?" Sebastian said, drawing her focus back to the conversation.

"This isn't a game, Sebastian," Jacob said. "We put that money aside just in case you had a paternity claim or two filed against you. We can't keep covering your ass like this."

"How many?" Jack asked hoarsely.

"I told you this wasn't a game," Jacob replied sharply.

"I'm asking how many claims there are against me," Jack roared, "and how many are actually true."

Kerrigan laid her forehead against the cool wood, holding her breath, curiosity keeping her still when the rest of her wanted to bolt.

"Eight against you, Jack. Sixteen for Sebastian," Jacob answered and she heard the squeak of a chair, as if Jack had collapsed into it.

"Woo hoo, I win!" Sebastian cheered.

"Shut it," Jack growled.

"We're still waiting on all the results for Sebastian, but none were actually yours, Jack," Jacob said. "But we had to treat them as if they were until we knew for sure. Some of the money we paid out for tests will be returned to your account."

As she wrestled with the facts being laid out before her, Kerrigan heard a loud thud on the table and lifted her head from the door to peek into the room. Jack's forehead was flat against the table and she was almost moved to see if he was okay.

If it were any other member of any other band, she wouldn't care. She couldn't care less if every single one of the claims against Sebastian were true. That was his problem and he'd have to handle it. But the thought that there had even been a remote chance that Jackson had fathered children with multiple women left her reeling from a totally unjustifiable feeling of betrayal.

If she hadn't already shaken Jacob's hand and met with two of the band members, she'd have been out the door of the hotel the moment Jack had walked into the room. After seeing the files and hearing the facts from Jacob, Stephen, and Riley, she'd formed a mental list of the steps she would take to help the band out of their financial hole. Even after Sebastian made his appearance, she knew it would be difficult, but she'd felt she could handle his childishness.

Her plans were all scattered as soon as Jack had walked in and they'd taken her nerves with them.

She had no idea why he'd come to Paris to see her, or why he'd stopped talking to her before that, so she didn't know how he'd react to seeing her for the first time in six years. She was having a hard time reconciling her memories with the person he seemed to be now. She wasn't sure she wanted to. Right now, all she wanted to do was run away.

But Jacob had hired her with expectations that she could succeed in turning this band around.

And she hated to fail.

"But that's not why I'm here," Jacob continued. "I've hired a new manager for you."

Kerrigan pulled her shoulders back. After witnessing Jack's behavior, she wasn't sure he really was the Jackson she'd grown up with. But just in case, whether she liked it or not, she couldn't let him fail.

"Shit," Sebastian groaned.

"She's highly—"

"She!" Jack and Sebastian both exclaimed.

Kerrigan inhaled and exhaled a deep, cleansing breath. She would do this. She would make this band profitable—no matter what.

"—highly qualified to get you out of this mess," Jacob continued as if there hadn't been an outburst. "She majored in accounting and financial planning, so she'll be able to help you get out of debt and budget wisely, as well as marketing, so she'll be able to put a positive spin on all your bad behavior. Let's hope she doesn't have to use that skill too much."

Kerrigan silently blew the air past her lips. She would just make sure that she and Jack kept their relationship professional and formal. She would show none of the familiarity they had once shared.

"She's been working in Switzerland for the past three years and comes highly recommended by several of her past employers." Jacob continued singing her praises as Kerrigan steeled herself and stepped into the doorway.

"If she's so good, they can have her back," Sebastian grumbled.

"We don't need another manager," Jack agreed. "We can manage ourselves."

"I've noticed," Jacob said with more than a hint of sarcasm. "I've hired her already and you will have to deal with it."

"No, we won't," Sebastian snapped.

"You don't have a choice, Sebastian! You have one last chance and she's it. If you run her off, I won't have a choice." Jacob picked up a stack of papers and shook them. "This contract will be shredded and my production company will no longer make your music." Jacob slapped the contract on the table and glared at Sebastian.

Kerrigan nodded, reassuring herself. She could do this. She had to do this.

The first step was surviving this meeting. The second was figuring out how to get as far away from Jack as possible for as long as she possibly could.

"Now, as I was saying," Jacob said and looked up at her in the doorway. "Gentlemen, I'd like to introduce you to Kerrigan Dodd." He pointed to her with an outstretched arm.

She heard a sharp intake of breath as she squared her shoulders and walked into the room.

"Your band's new manager."

Three

Jack's mouth fell open and he stared at Kerri as she glided into the room. His feet were glued to the floor and he couldn't take his eyes off of her. He started to speak to her as she walked past, but the look she gave him was so glacial, the words froze in his throat.

Then he remembered Sebastian beside him and decided it was probably for the best.

She smiled at Jacob as she stopped beside him. "Thank you." She gave fleeting smiles to Riley and Stephen as well. They each gave her a sly grin in return and Jack's eyes widened as his mouth snapped closed.

They'd known she was there.

He swiveled his head toward the door she'd just entered from. How long had she been out there? What had she heard? Besides that . . . what had she seen?

Oh God . . . the twins. If she'd seen them, what would she think of him?

Swallowing the bile that rose, he turned his attention back to her.

"Good morning, gentlemen." Her voice, a voice that still haunted his dreams, caressed him from across the room. "As Jacob told you, my name is Kerrigan—"

When did she start going by her full name? And why is she wearing glasses again? She stopped that in ninth grade. Her wide, blue-gray eyes were so captivating. Why is her black hair pulled back into such a tight, uncomfortable-looking bun? How long is it now?

She was wearing a short, deep blue jacket over a collared, white dress shirt. Her long legs were covered by a knee-length, loose-fitting pencil skirt that tastefully showed off her small waist and narrow hips. It was too professional and uptight for Jack's liking, but it seemed to fit this persona she was now presenting. She seemed thinner than he remembered and she'd always been thin.

God, she's still beautiful.

"And you're our new manager," Sebastian interrupted as he elbowed Jack. "Yeah, sweetie, we got that."

Jack shook his head, pushing his thoughts away. Had Sebastian just called her "sweetie"? Never mind his condescending tone, he couldn't call her that. Jack fought the impulse to tell him off.

Kerrigan's eyes narrowed. "And you also got that your band is in trouble and I'm your last hope for salvation, right?" She dropped her purse onto the table next to Riley. "You got that you're spending too much on food and drinks and room service? You *got* that you're causing problems, both to your budget and your image, every time you destroy a hotel room?"

"Smart-ass bitch," Sebastian murmured and Kerri cocked her head to one side.

Jack's hand formed a fist. He could let "sweetie" slip, but "bitch" was unacceptable. Sebastian couldn't get away with that. He saw the mischievous grin on Sebastian's lips as he held her glare. Jack looked at Kerri again. She nodded to herself and, to his surprise, a cynical smile formed on her lips as well.

"I'm sorry you feel that way, Sebastian," she said sweetly as she picked up the contract Jacob had tossed down on the table earlier. "I had hoped we'd be able to work together, but if you're not even willing to try . . . " She stacked the contract on top of her binder, then placed her purse on top of them both. "Then what are we doing here?"

"*We* are having a meeting with our producer," Sebastian retorted. "We don't need a manager, so you must be here for our entertainment." The mischievous glint in his eye deepened. "You're really a stripper, aren't you?"

Jack saw her inhale sharply as her eyes widened.

"Go ahead and take something off," Sebastian continued. "That would be quite entertaining."

"What the hell?" Jack growled as he turned to Sebastian. There was no way he'd let Sebastian near Kerri.

He looked at her again and she finally met his gaze, but only for an instant. In that brief moment, he watched the icy glare give way to hurt. She turned her attention back to Sebastian, wiping all emotion from her face.

Why won't she look at me? Why won't she even acknowledge me? Had she seen the twins? The urge to have her look at him the way she used to ached in his chest.

But he couldn't forget Paris. He'd flown halfway around the world to see her, to tell her he was in love with her. Instead, he'd ended up in an interrogation room in a police station, with no idea why he was there or where she was. The police had reassured him she was safe and that she would join him shortly.

But she'd never shown up. Instead she'd sent word through the officer that he was the last person she wanted to see. He'd never felt that depth of hurt and anger before and hadn't allowed himself to care about anything enough since to experience it again. He'd spent the past four years trying to forget her.

Obviously to no avail. One look at her now and he knew he was gone. He'd follow her to Paris again. Hell, he'd follow her to the moon. Suddenly, the reason she'd refused to see him in Paris didn't matter as much as the fact that she was there now. Maybe this was his second chance.

All he had to do was make her forget about the two women he'd walked into the meeting with. She was never supposed to know that side of him. He'd created 'Jack Hart' out of a need to separate himself from the man who was desperately in love with Kerri Dodd. Being Jackson all the time was too painful, he hurt too much for the woman he couldn't have. But Jack could be as bad as he wanted to be, guilt free. And as ridiculous as it sounded, hiding behind his stage persona made him feel like he could return home without feeling like a disappointment to his father.

He'd never meant for Jack and Kerri to meet. To be honest, he'd never expected to see her again. Now that she was here, he'd do whatever it took to keep her around. But in order to do that, he had to make sure Sebastian didn't run her off before he got the chance.

"Well?" Sebastian practically laughed. "I'm willing to keep you around if you make it worth my time."

This is not going to be easy. "Just shut up and listen," Jack snapped. "You heard what Jacob said. She's our last chance, so you may as well cooperate."

Kerri's pert nose rose into the air a fraction and her eyes widened as her dark, angled eyebrows lifted dramatically. Jack studied her face and was amazed by how little she'd changed. Her cheekbones were high and looked sharper than they had the last time he'd seen her six years ago. Her full lips, lips he'd once wanted to kiss more than anything, pursed slightly.

Jack frowned. *What was she thinking?* She'd always hated confrontation. Sure, he and her brother had picked on her when they were younger, but they'd known her boundaries. Sebastian didn't. And when he found them, he'd push her to her limit and beyond. Jack wasn't entirely sure she'd be able to handle that.

"I'm afraid I didn't bring sock puppets and bedtime stories with me." Her voice held no emotion as she folded her arms across her chest.

From the corner of his eye, Jack saw Sebastian's lip twitch.

"Maybe we can find him some Legos and coloring books," Riley chimed in from his seat to Kerri's left.

"I'm sure that's possible," Kerri continued and Sebastian's smirk faded completely. "Jacob hired me to do a job, Sebastian, and that job is to undo your mess. You now have a choice. You can either work with me or you will find yourself without a band."

"You can't do that!" Sebastian roared. "This is my band and I'll be damned if some little Swedish bitch is going to take it away from me!"

She narrowed her eyes and released a long breath. "First, I'm American and I've been living and working in Switzerland, not Sweden. And second," she moved her purse and picked up the contract, "this contract says differently. This band belongs to Mattern, Nelson, and Goldberg Records, and they've hired me to get it out of the muck you've put it in. So as I said before, you will either cooperate or you will find yourself out of a job."

Jack could see the fire shooting from Sebastian's eyes and could almost feel the ice emanating from Kerri. He tugged on Sebastian's sleeve. "Sit down."

If she heard his support, she gave no indication. He hated to admit how much that stung.

"Fine, but don't expect me to like it," Sebastian grumbled.

"I don't care if you like it." Kerri glanced at Jacob, who nodded as the corners of his lips slowly turned up. Kerri opened the binder on the table in front of her and ran her finger down the page. "I've reviewed the numbers and after hearing what Roger was doing before me, I have to agree, he was on the right track. Room inspections will continue. It's the best way to ensure any problem is promptly addressed and the responsible party pays for the damage. The band can no longer afford to pay for damages to hotel rooms."

Sebastian's forehead hit the table and he groaned.

"On top of that, the budget for your pre- and post-concert food and drinks will be significantly lowered." She turned to Stephen, who smiled at her. "Stephen, I'll talk to you about that on the road so we can come up with a workable number." He nodded and she looked down at the figures in her binder again. "You'll each be given an allowance for room service. After reviewing the numbers, I think three hundred a night is fair."

Sebastian quickly lifted his head and glared at her. "I was holding steady at four hundred when Roger was here."

"And you've doubled that since then, which ate into what little the band had saved as well as what was earned," Kerri continued, unfazed by Sebastian's outrage. Jack was impressed with her calm demeanor.

But she still refused to look at him, and that left him with an ache in his chest that he hadn't felt since leaving Paris.

"I will call my father about this," Sebastian snarled, his stare directed at Jacob.

Kerri's brow furrowed in confusion and she looked over her shoulder at Jacob as well.

Jack noticed how Jacob's jaw was clenched with a slight curl to his upper lip, his narrow-eyed gaze directed at Sebastian. Jack couldn't say he was surprised. The tension between the half-brothers had been there before the ink on the contract was dry and had gotten worse over the past year and a half. Jack had always thought having these two in a working partnership was a bad idea, but Mr. Bates had wanted his sons to build a better relationship.

"Your father?" Kerri asked, confusion replaced by a hint of condescension as she turned to face Sebastian. "I'm sorry, I thought you were all grown men. I wasn't aware I needed your father's permission for anything I do with your band." She glanced at her watch. "As we go on, I'll make cuts to the budget and other changes as necessary. We need to get on the road soon, so you should all go pack your things now so I can have the inspections done."

Sebastian glared at her and his nostrils flared as they all stood.

"Please be in the lobby in forty-five minutes. I am leaving in one hour, with or without you." She narrowed her eyes at Sebastian.

He flipped her the bird before he turned and left the room.

Jack watched as Riley and Stephen spoke to Kerri and strained to hear their whispered words. As he stalked around the table to get closer, Riley and Stephen both nodded to her and turned to leave. She was closing her binder, but her hand slowed and her shoulders stiffened as Jacob walked up to her. Jack stopped to watch them interact.

He noticed that her posture remained tense. She nodded as she spoke, but her hand stayed frozen on the binder, as if she was holding herself as still as possible.

"You will keep me updated on the progress?" Jacob asked.

"Of course," Kerri replied. "I'll email you the numbers every week and call to discuss any ideas I come up with."

The thought of her emailing another man, for any reason, caused Jack's chest to tighten uncomfortably. He missed getting emails from her.

When he'd been in college and she was still in high school, they'd communicated almost daily through emails. They'd chatted mostly about the going-ons in Rocky Creek. She'd occasionally asked about his life at college but he'd always been hesitant to answer. Soon after he and Sebastian had formed the band their sophomore year in college, Jack had realized that women loved rock stars and he loved the attention. It was almost a given that he would be approached by multiple women after every show, each more willing than the last to show him a good time. As a red-blooded male, he'd be crazy to turn down the attention.

But Kerri hadn't needed to know about that. Even before he'd realized he loved her, just before his senior year, he'd tried to shield her from his womanizing behavior. Her messages had never failed to be full of life and cheer, a perfect representation of their sender, and he'd always looked forward to getting them. They'd been a bright spot in his otherwise tedious days.

Jack shook his head. As much as he liked to blame the events in Paris for ripping them apart, he knew the real damage had been done two years before Paris. After Jack had made his feelings for Kerri known to Charlie and had asked if he could date her, her brother had put a stop to everything. Because of the stories Charlie had heard regarding Jack's behavior at college, he hadn't thought Jack was good enough for her. Instead, Charlie had given Jack two years to clean up his act. The only stipulation had been that Jack could have no contact with Kerri in those two long years—no emails, no texts, no phone calls.

Charlie was the reason Jack and Kerri were practically strangers now. The remorse for all the time he'd missed with her stabbed Jack in the chest.

"That sounds great." Jacob looked at his watch then at her with a smile. "I have a plane to catch, but if you need anything, let me know. I'm looking forward to seeing how this plays out."

Kerri nodded and shook his outstretched hand. Jacob walked away and she stood there, stock still. Her head turned a fraction in Jack's direction before she picked up her purse and put the strap over her shoulder. After she'd gathered her binder and the contract, she finally turned to face him. He held her gaze for a moment before she tried to edge around him.

"Hi, Kerri," he murmured.

She froze, her shoulder almost touching his. Her eyes widened momentarily as she pulled back.

"It's Kerrigan," she said as she angled her head enough to throw a cutting glare at him, "*Jack.*"

Her offensive emphasis on his name took him aback.

"Are you the only band member who uses a stage name?" she asked tartly.

He sensed the anger in her tone, but as far as he was concerned, she had no right to be angry at him. She'd rejected him, not the other way around. Not like she would have cared if he had. She'd been living it up in Paris, probably not even thinking about him. His presence had most likely been an inconvenience to her.

He swallowed his irritation and barked a laugh. "Why should that matter?"

She narrowed her eyes.

"No. Sebastian uses his middle name, not his first," he answered. "But you should already know that." He'd talked to her about James, now Sebastian, and their band, plenty of times before their separation.

Kerri exhaled slowly then glanced at him again and shook her head. She turned to leave and he reached for her. As his hand approached her arm, she sidestepped away from him, avoiding his touch.

Her reaction drained all humor from him. "Didn't you know this was my band?"

She shook her head.

He gritted his teeth. "I would have expected you to do better research."

"I didn't have time," she snapped. "Jacob gave me a list of band members, but you're listed as 'Jack Hart' not 'Jackson Harris'. How was I supposed to know?"

"Didn't Charlie or anyone else at home talk about me or my band?" he growled.

Her lip curled. "I've been living in Zurich. I have only been home for a few months. Were you too tired to pay attention?" She cocked her head in feigned innocence. "Might I suggest you try just one girl at a time? You may find it a little less exhausting."

She quickly turned, but not before he saw the flush creep into her cheeks. She took two steps toward the door before he reached for her. Again, she jerked away from him.

Anger gripped his chest. "You didn't answer my question." He stepped in front of her and she looked up at him and swallowed.

"Charlie doesn't talk about you."

Of course not. Charlie had caused their separation, why would he talk to Kerri about Jack?

"I came home just before Pete's wedding." She lifted a brow and he looked away sheepishly. They were both aware he should have been at that wedding. Pete had been one of his closest friends his whole life. Pete had also been, and still was, friends with Charlie. Jack had pushed hard for the band's tour to start before the wedding so he'd had an excuse not to go.

He hadn't been certain Kerri would be there, but he hadn't wanted to take that chance.

"And if anyone talked about you, I didn't hear," she continued pertly.

"Of course. Why would you? I'm the last person you want to see, right?" he repeated the hurtful message that he'd received at the Parisian police station.

She gasped and drew back.

Good.

"You can hardly blame me." She shifted the binder in her arms and placed it on her hip. "Why were you even in Paris? You hadn't spoken to me for two years. Did you expect to just show up there and have us pick up like I was eighteen again and you hadn't left the beach house without saying good-bye?"

"No, I expected to have a conversation with you," he snapped. "Imagine my surprise when I show up to a swarm of officers in and around your apartment building and you're nowhere to be seen. Why did they take me in, Kerri?"

She quickly looked away, glancing first at her watch, then at the door five steps to her right. "I have to meet with Stephen."

"We're not done," Jack hissed.

"What is there to discuss, exactly? You tried to come back into my life after two years of complete silence. Two years, Jack." Her voice was taut but he thought he heard it shake a little. "First of all, the police told me you were there asking about me, not that you were demanding to speak to me, and they certainly didn't tell me why."

"I wasn't aware I had to give them my reasons," he snarled.

Her eyes rounded as her jaw clenched and she took a sharp breath. "Secondly, you hadn't said one word, hadn't replied to one email or text or returned even one of my phone calls for so long I hardly thought anything you might want to say could be that important," she continued angrily. She looked away and shrugged. "I figured you were simply passing through and had heard I was there." Slowly, she met his gaze again.

His eyes narrowed on hers. She always broke eye contact whenever she fibbed. He remembered that from their shared childhood. He knew she wasn't being completely honest with him.

The question was . . . why? What was she hiding?

"So, as much as neither of us wants this, we are stuck working together now—"

He held up a hand to stop her. "Kerri."

She stopped and her jaw tightened. "Kerrigan."

The corner of his mouth lifted in a teasing grin, one he hoped would remind her of their youth together. "Even for me? I've known you your whole life."

"Especially for you," she replied, then quietly added, "and no you haven't."

She looked briefly at the binder in her arms then back at him. "I use my full name for work and I would like to maintain a professional relationship between us. So please don't forget it."

"Fine," he agreed reluctantly. If she wanted to have a professional relationship, he'd do it. At least it was better than nothing. "But I didn't say I don't want to work with you."

She swallowed and inched toward the door.

"Are you saying if you'd known this was my band you wouldn't have taken the job?"

She continued to slide away from him.

"Kerrigan?"

Her jaw clenched and she took a few deep breaths. "Yes." She hesitantly met his stare. "If I'd known this was your band, I wouldn't have taken this job."

The air rushed from his lungs and she took advantage of his shock by hurrying to the door, pausing long enough to let him know that they were leaving in thirty minutes.

Four

It didn't take long for problems to arise. When Kerrigan asked Jack and Sebastian to pay for the damage done to their hotel rooms, a twenty-minute argument ensued.

Jack had apparently thought it was a good idea to tie sheets from the curtain rod to the headboard and create a makeshift hammock for himself and his playmates. As a result, they'd ended up pulling the curtain rod down, screws and all, and cracking the headboard. Sebastian's room hadn't fared much better with a side table smashed into the A/C unit and the desk reduced to firewood.

The battle ended when Jack, who had remained fairly quiet until that point, spoke up and willingly agreed to pay for the damage to his room, at which time Sebastian reluctantly pulled out his personal credit card. Kerrigan had taken pride in her small victory, but she couldn't prevent her thoughts from wandering to how, exactly, Jack's hammock was supposed to have worked.

She briefly pictured herself in it with him, but quickly shook the thought away.

The next fifteen minutes were spent arguing over riding arrangements and she'd had to choke down panic. She hadn't willingly put herself alone in the company of men, let alone strangers, in over four years. But in her hurry to get out of Rocky Creek, she hadn't really thought through what travelling with a rock band would entail. To make matters worse, her mind was still scattered from the surprise of seeing Jackson.

While the room inspections were being completed, she'd taken the time to look over the vehicles. The larger of the band's two vans carried all of the equipment and personal instruments. It was packed so full, the jump seat behind the passenger seat wasn't usable. That was the van Riley and Stephen traveled in. The other van was smaller, but only carried the luggage and had more empty space. It was Sebastian's preferred vehicle and Jack usually drove.

She hated the idea of being in a cramped space with strangers but resigned herself to the fact that she would have to squeeze herself and her bags into the van with Stephen and Riley. The ride might be extremely uncomfortable, but compared to riding with Jack, she decided it was the lesser of two evils.

Before she could say anything about her preference, Stephen tried to argue that if Kerrigan was going to ride with him, the three of them would be better off in the smaller, more spacious van. Sebastian refused to switch vans or have Riley ride with them. Kerrigan could have pushed the issue, but decided to save her breath for a more important battle.

She was sure there would be a few of those.

Stephen and Riley rearranged the equipment in their van and helped Kerrigan fit her two suitcases in. Then she'd ordered them all into their respective vehicles and they were off.

For the first thirty minutes of their drive, she sat in her seat behind Riley in silence. She let their conversation flow over her as she remembered the last time she'd seen Jack, when she'd still known him as Jackson . . .

Kerri had hobbled out of the police station in Paris as fast as she could on crutches, choking on the tears that had formed a lump in her throat. As she waited at the bottom of the steps for her best friend, Olivia Stump, to catch up to her, she put her sunglasses on and adjusted the scarf around her neck and face to cover her injuries. They proceeded to the nearest brasserie and grabbed a table near the window. Kerri stared out at the sparsely populated street as Olivia went to the counter and ordered. She returned with a cup of coffee and a pastry for each of them. Kerri pushed hers away, only to have Olivia push it back.

"You've barely eaten for two days," Olivia stated firmly.

Kerri shrugged as she drew the coffee closer and put a spoonful of sugar and a splash of milk in it.

"Why do you think Jackson's here?" Olivia asked.

Kerri ignored her. She didn't want to think about why Jackson was there, or what he might want. He hadn't spoken to her in two years.

No, that was putting it mildly.

First, he'd left her family's beach house without saying good-bye. Then he wouldn't answer her calls and texts. And because ignoring her emails hadn't been enough, he'd actually blocked her address completely. After six months of reaching out to him without a response, she'd started to feel like a stalker, so she'd stopped. It wasn't just her, either. He was pretending Charlie didn't exist as well.

After all this time, why he was there was less puzzling than how he'd managed to find out she was in Paris.

"Kerri, he's here for a reason," Olivia said as she took a bite of her chocolate croissant. "He wouldn't come to Paris on a lark."

"Then you talk to him," Kerri muttered softly. "I can't."

"He's not here to see me," Olivia continued in her sweet, Mary Poppins-esque tone.

Kerri looked at her friend's innocent, calm expression and raised an eyebrow. "What?" Her voice was surprisingly hoarse.

"Jackson. He didn't come here, to Paris, to talk to me." Olivia sipped her coffee then slowly lowered her cup. "It's been two years, Kerri. I know you still care for him. And here he is, when you could use him most. He's always known what to say to make you feel better. Go to him."

"No," Kerri answered with a shake of her head.

Secretly, she was thrilled to see him again. But there was no way she could see him. Not now. Maybe not ever again. She'd loved him since she was sixteen, had imagined telling him before he'd walked out of her life. But she could never deserve him now. She had no idea how Jackson would react if he found out what had happened to her two days before. She was afraid he'd be thoroughly disgusted and would never want to speak to her again. And she wouldn't blame him.

"Aren't you the least bit curious as to why he's here? Did you know he showed up almost immediately after . . ." Olivia's voice faltered and her eyes dropped to her croissant.

"How do you know when he showed up?" Kerri asked, taking a sip of her coffee.

"I spoke to Officer DuMar after you left. She said he showed up a few hours after we left for the embassy and stayed for the rest of the day, hovering right outside our apartment building." Olivia looked out the window and her shoulders dropped as she sighed. "Oh, there he is, poor thing. He looks like someone just ran over his puppy."

Kerri followed her stare and her eyes settled on Jackson as he stood on the corner waiting to cross the street. She pouted as she silently cursed her bad luck. They weren't far from the police station, so she should have known they might see him again.

Her frown deepened and tears sprang to her eyes as she studied his hangdog expression. His hands deep in the pockets of his leather coat, he looked one way, then the other before crossing the street. His full lips were pulled down at the corners, his shoulders stooped, and his stride slow as he focused on the road under his feet. Kerri felt an almost overwhelming urge to go to him and wrap her arms around him.

She shook it off and turned her attention back to her coffee. "Or like someone just scratched his Camaro," she added, trying to sound like she cared less than she did.

He'd started restoring his father's old car the summer he was twenty and Kerri was seventeen. Kerri had loved watching him work on it and had spent many afternoons sitting in the garage at his house, avoiding her own chores to help him when she could. He'd always gotten so excited when he found a part he needed and had been giddy when he'd gotten it running again. He'd even asked her what color she thought he should paint it and when she'd said "blue," the smile he'd given her had been so beautiful her heart had skipped joyously. Especially when he'd had it painted a color that matched the shade of her eyes almost exactly.

She'd been looking forward to riding in it with him when he finished it, but she never got the chance. He was out of her life two months later.

"C'mon, Kerri." Olivia sighed deeply. "Fine, maybe so, but do you even wonder why he's here? Why do you think he looks so dejected? Do you think, just maybe, he's disappointed you wouldn't see him?"

Kerri reluctantly shrugged her shoulders. She couldn't admit to Olivia that she was more than curious. Why was he there? It did seem peculiar that he would show up so suddenly in Paris, asking her neighbors and the police about her. But the hope she'd once had that he felt anything more than friendship for her had died when he'd walked out of her life. To spark that flame again now was simply something she couldn't do. If he rejected her now, it would be salt in her open wounds.

"Why do you think he's here?" Kerri asked.

"To be your knight. Your hero. You need help to get through this and here he is." Olivia's lips pursed and, as usual, her eyes danced with romance. "Just like he was the glue that held you together when your parents died, he's here to be your glue now."

"In case you hadn't noticed, my pieces are pretty shattered now. I'm not sure there's any putting them back together." Kerri's voice sounded dreadfully monotonous to her own ears. "And even if your theory was correct, I'm not sure I want him to help."

"Why? You still love him," Olivia stated.

Kerri sighed and looked at him again. "I probably always will."

He'd stopped on the sidewalk outside of the brasserie they were sitting in. Tears welled in her eyes at the lost expression on his face as he stared vacantly at the building in front of him.

"The difference is, when Mom and Dad died, he was my friend. He'd always been a part of my life; he was almost like family. But," she looked down as a tear rolled down her cheek, "he hasn't wanted to be in my life for the past two years and I'm not sure I want his pity now."

He looked around him at the restaurant's outdoor seating area and moved toward a table.

Great, Kerri thought as he sat down at a table next to the wall, still in her line of sight, facing the door of the building. She was glad for the scarves and sunglasses she was wearing and that the windows of the restaurant were tinted. She could look out, but he couldn't see in.

His shoulders seemed broader than they had been two years ago and narrowed only a little to his waist. His light brown hair was a little shorter, the sides barely gracing the top of his ears, the back ending just above his collar. His long legs were covered in a nice pair of dark wash jeans, his arms in his familiar, dark brown leather jacket.

She'd memorized the feel of that coat her senior year of high school when he'd lent it to her on more than one chilly night in the garage. Her fingers itched to touch the soft leather again and the memory of his cinnamon scent that had lingered in the leather teased her nostrils, even from this distance.

He lifted his left hand to flag a waiter down and the wrist of his jacket fell to the middle of his forearm. For the second time that day, she noticed the tattoo on his wrist and she narrowed her eyes as she studied it. She couldn't tell what it was, but she knew he hadn't had it two years ago.

Kerri felt a squeeze on her forearm and looked at Olivia.

"Go to him." Olivia nodded toward the window.

Kerri shook her head. "No."

Olivia pressed her thin lips together. "He's here to see you."

Kerri turned her attention back to Jack. She could tell by the wave of his hands he was having a heated discussion with the waiter standing over him. The server held his palms to Jackson and shrugged his shoulders, then walked away from the table and Jackson placed his fists on the table and focused on them.

A panic started to set in. He'd ordered something. Which meant he was going to be there for a while. What if the light changed and he could see inside? What if he had to come into the restaurant for something? What if he saw her?

She needed to leave.

Heart racing, palms sweating, she pushed her coffee and untouched pastry to the center of the table and stood. She placed her weight on her good foot as she turned to pick up her crutches from where they leaned against the window. With the crutches under her arms, she looked up and saw the waiter place a bottle of brandy and a glass on Jackson's table. An irrational sense of disappointment settled over her.

"He's just here to get drunk," she muttered, turning away. "Let's go."

Kerri aimed for the door in the corner. It was farther away, but it would take them outside, behind Jackson. He'd never see them. He'd never know she'd been so close. She exhaled and ignored Olivia's pleas for her to reconsider as she limped toward the exit.

"I'll bet ye're sorry ye took this job, huh?" Riley's Scottish brogue broke into her thoughts.

"You have no idea," Kerrigan mumbled without thinking as she watched the scenery pass by her window.

"What?" Stephen asked.

Kerrigan heard the concern in his voice and shook herself completely of her daydream.

Riley laughed at his reaction. "Can ye blame her? Sebastian certainly didn't show his pleasant side this morning."

"He doesn't have one," Stephen grumbled.

Kerrigan's lips twitched upward at their easy banter. "Don't worry. He won't get rid of me that easily." Kerrigan placed her purse in her lap. "I wouldn't want to disappoint the two of you."

"I don't think I'd be too disappointed." Stephen peeked over his shoulder at her then looked back at the road in front of them.

Kerrigan sat silently for a moment analyzing his tone of voice and decided it was probably better to ask. "You don't want to do this anymore?"

Stephen concentrated on the road and his eyes narrowed as he took a deep breath. "Sometimes, I think it would be best if I just walked away. I'm tired of being Sebastian's babysitter and always trying to keep his behavior and spending in check. I hate always being the responsible one."

"What keeps you here then?" Kerrigan asked.

"The music." The corners of his mouth turned up a little. "I love playing. I love the reaction we get from the crowds. It's exhilarating and addictive. I don't always love the songs, but seeing other people get so much pleasure from them makes up for it."

"You don't love your own songs?" Kerrigan's mind was spinning. She rubbed her temples. Their personal issues sounded deeper than perhaps Jacob even knew. "Okay, can we start at the beginning? How did the two of you get involved with the two of them to form a band that plays music you don't even like?"

Riley laughed and shook his head. "When ye put it that way, I wonder the same thing."

Stephen cleared his throat. "When we were all in college, Jack and Sebastian put flyers out, looking for band members. It was during my junior year; they were both sophomores. I had heard them play a couple of times. They weren't bad. But their keyboardist dropped out of school and left town and their drummer had seen that as his opportunity to leave as well."

"That should have been a warning to everyone else." Riley turned in his seat, putting his back against the door so he could look at both her and Stephen. "I auditioned wi' them too, but I was the third drummer they hired."

"What happened to the first two?" Kerrigan asked.

"Sebastian ran roughshod o'er both of them, insulted their abilities, and pretty much made their lives miserable. Neither o' them wanted to be in a band bad enough to put up wi' that," Riley said with a chuckle.

"And you did?" Kerrigan's brow rose with her question.

Riley shook his head.

Kerrigan's mouth fell open. "Didn't he try the same thing with you?"

"O'course. That's what he does." Riley gave her a toothy grin. "I just gave it right back." He winked at her. "He didn't like it, but Jack found it amusing and asked me to stick around."

At the mere mention of his name, Kerrigan's heart skipped a beat. She quickly regained her composure and nodded. At least she knew Riley could stand up to Sebastian. That was at least one of them on her side. She turned to Stephen, determined to keep the conversation going so she wouldn't dwell on Jack.

"What about you? Were you the first new keyboardist, or did they go through a string before you, too?"

"No, I was the only one, and I was lucky to get the job. Sebastian decided the band didn't need another keyboard player. He thought they cramped his style." Stephen's tone sounded slightly regretful.

"So what happened?" she asked cautiously.

"Jack convinced Sebastian a keyboard would only improve the music, that it would provide a more rounded sound than guitars alone." Stephen shook his head as he continued, "Jack and I actually hit it off pretty well. We both like writing music and our styles are very similar."

"But country pop-slash-Southern rock isn't Sebastian's style," Riley added.

Kerrigan looked at him as she considered what she was hearing. "And Sebastian's style is?"

"Hard rock, heavy metal," Stephen answered.

"So I guess you only play hard rock and heavy metal, then?" Kerrigan already knew the answer, but their nods confirmed it. "Who writes the songs?"

"Sebastian does," Riley answered, "and they're bloody awful."

Kerrigan pursed her lips. "How is that possible?"

"He's a bad songwriter," Riley replied matter-of-factly and Stephen chuckled.

Kerrigan rolled her eyes and bit back her grin.

"Jack and I usually sit down and rework them," Stephen answered, amusement still lacing his words. "It's not always to our taste, but Sebastian barely even notices the changes."

Kerrigan's jaw clenched and any sympathy she may have had for the band's plight slipped away. It was beginning to sound to her like the problems were equally Sebastian's fault and self-inflicted by the rest of the band. She considered this in silence for a few minutes.

"You do realize that doesn't help your cause, don't you?" she asked quietly.

Another minute or two passed before Stephen finally broke the silence. "What do you mean?"

"I mean, you're feeding his ego by re-writing his songs. If he doesn't even notice the difference then he doesn't realize he's not that good at it," she stated.

"I told ye that two years ago," Riley said with a chuckle.

Stephen raised his shoulders in a shrug. "His ego can't get much bigger."

"What do you mean by that?" Kerrigan asked.

Stephen frowned. "You know who he is, don't you? Or at least who his father is?"

She searched her memory. Sebastian had mentioned his father earlier, but she didn't understand what he had to do with anything. She shook her head. "No, I'm afraid I don't."

"He's one o' the biggest real estate developers in Chicago," Riley explained, not looking particularly impressed. "Rich as Croesus."

Kerrigan's mouth fell open and quickly snapped shut as her brow furrowed. "How did Sebastian end up at a small town university in Virginia?"

"His mother's family lives in northern Virginia," Stephen answered. "She moved back with Sebastian after she divorced his father."

"So . . ." Kerrigan wasn't sure she understood the correlation between Sebastian's parents' divorce and his enlarged ego.

"So, Daddy never told him no," Riley answered her.

"Neither does Mommy for that matter," Stephen added. "Sebastian has never wanted for anything in his life. He's never had any limitations and has pretty much gotten away with everything." Stephen briefly met her gaze in the rearview mirror. "He asks, and his dad gives it to him, regardless of what his mother thinks."

"'Tis how we got signed with Jacob's company."

Kerrigan's eyes widened. "Not because of talent?"

"Not Sebastian's talent," Stephen scoffed and Riley laughed.

"Jacob was interested in Stephen and Jack, but dinna want to sign us because of Sebastian," Riley answered through his chuckles.

Kerrigan could sympathize with Jacob's hesitation. If she'd been in his position, she wouldn't have wanted to be burdened with Sebastian either.

"So, Sebastian had Daddy step in and promise to pay some extravagant amount of money to the record label." Stephen nodded as he kept his focus on the road. "And then his lawyers looked over the contract to make sure Jacob couldn't get out of it on a whim."

"Wait." She held up a palm and shook her head, trying to organize the facts in her head. "Is it normal for bands to pay money for a contract?"

Stephen shook his head and his ponytail dusted his shoulders. "Not to my knowledge. The money was an insurance policy. He paid half up front and the rest is divided over a five year period."

Kerrigan looked from Stephen to Riley. "Why five years?"

"That's how long he has to keep us around," Riley answered. "Jacob's company gets money every year our contract is valid. But, if we haven't proven profitable in five years, Jacob is free to cut us loose."

"However, if he does decide to re-sign us," Stephen took over, "there's no more money from Mr. Bates."

Kerrigan heard the resignation in his voice and saw the look of calm acceptance on Riley's face. Their days were numbered and they knew it. Based on what she'd seen in the files, there would be no renewing their contract unless Sebastian's father stepped in again, but she got the impression that, at the very least, Stephen and Riley weren't thrilled by the current arrangement.

"How long have you been under contract?" She stared out of her window as she waited for an answer.

"Three years," Riley answered as he turned toward the front of the vehicle.

Kerrigan nodded and sank deeper into her seat. A lot could happen in two years. If she could turn the band around before the end of the tour, it was possible Jacob would re-sign them. The real question was, did her two travel companions want him to?

And what did Jack think of their situation?

Was his attitude more like Sebastian's or did he feel more like Stephen? She'd have to find out for herself. She stared out the window, not really seeing anything, as a frown pulled at her lips.

As much as it needed to happen, Kerrigan wasn't sure she was ready for such a personal conversation with Jack.

Five

Sebastian laughed from the passenger's seat. "I love this part."

Jack rolled his eyes and kept his focus on the road in front of them.

Jack wasn't sure which episode of VH1's *Behind the Music* Sebastian was watching. He wasn't sure he cared. Sebastian watched reruns of the show religiously. Every time they were in the van. Whenever he was alone in his hotel room. Between setting up for the show and showtime. Any free moment Sebastian had, he was watching some heavy metal episode, hoping to pick up behaviors or ideas he could imitate.

Jack used to watch them, too, but had grown bored after seeing most of the episodes a second time.

Usually, Sebastian's absorption in YouTube bothered Jack, but this morning he was thankful to have his travel companion distracted. It would give him time to think. Since seeing Kerri—she'd always be Kerri to him—he'd felt off balance. After Paris, he'd never wanted to see her again. He'd crawled into the bottle for a month, trying to forget her.

Over the years, he'd purposefully lost track of where she was and what she was doing, staying busy with the band so he'd have a reason to avoid Rocky Creek. He could have probably asked Charlie, but Charlie was the reason he and Kerri hadn't spoken for those two years before Paris. Jack would never forget that fateful mistake.

Jackson had finally been on the two-week beach vacation he'd been looking forward to for months. He was staying with Charlie and Kerri in the beach house they'd inherited from their parents. It had been an annual trip for them since the summer he and Charlie were thirteen, but in the last two years, he'd been more excited to spend the time with Kerri. Not that he would admit that to Charlie.

It was the second night of vacation, in the middle of a game of Monopoly, when his feelings for Kerri finally came crashing down. Since her parents' funeral, he'd noticed a shift in the way he responded to her, but he'd spent the last two years trying to deny his feelings were anything more than brotherly. He'd convinced himself that the tug on his heart when he saw her was still sympathy for her situation, even though she'd seemed to have accepted it and was, more often than not, smiling again. But as he sat there, staring at her beautiful face with her laughing eyes and her perfect smile, he realized he'd been lying to himself.

Kerri had been dominating the game, drawing it out as she was prone to do instead of buying hotels and bankrupting everyone, and an argument had broken out between her and Charlie, as usual. In the middle of the argument, her friend, Olivia, had interrupted and asked Charlie if they could indulge in a beer. Kerri and Olivia were only eighteen and Charlie wasn't going to allow them that luxury.

Jackson had enjoyed watching the banter back and forth between Olivia and Charlie, but everything changed when Olivia brought up college. More specifically, the college boys that she and Kerri would be meeting in just over a month. Olivia teased Charlie about how little control he would have over Kerri's life when she went away for school, how handsome and fun the college boys would be, and how they would probably buy beers for the two of them.

Jackson had started to see green at that point. And then red. He knew college guys better than Olivia. He was one, after all. But he couldn't get past the idea of college men talking to—let alone hitting on and flirting with—Kerri. Something in him came very close to snapping. He looked across the table at Kerri and watched her try to contain her amusement with the discussion her brother and best friend were having. When she met his gaze, her smile shifted from enjoyment to something softer and kinder. It was a look that reflected the gentleness in her soul and that was when the tidal wave of feeling crashed over him.

He loved her.

There was no more denying it. There was no escaping it. And what surprised him most was that he didn't want to.

The next morning, he waited for Kerri and Olivia to head out before approaching Charlie. He wouldn't typically go to a girl's father, or in this case older-brother-slash-guardian, to ask permission to date her. But this was different.

When they were fourteen, he, Charlie, and Olivia's older brother Pete had made a pact not to date each other's sisters. It had been inspired by some movie or television show they'd watched, and, like the impressionable teenage boys they were, they'd thought it was a great idea. They created this "bro code" pact with each other because the last thing they wanted was for some girl to interfere with their friendship. And while most guys would make that pact regarding ex-girlfriends, they recognized—even then—their tastes were different enough it wouldn't cause trouble for them. But sisters might, even if Kerri and Olivia had been eleven at the time and Jackson had felt certain he would never be interested in either of them.

For seven years, it had kept them out of trouble. Their friendship had remained strong, even though they eventually had all gone to different universities in different parts of the state. But now, as he and Charlie held their staring contest in the living room, Jackson wasn't so certain that pact had been a good idea.

Charlie took a deep breath and looked away. "No."

Jackson jumped to his feet. "What do you mean, no?"

"I mean, no, you can't date my sister," Charlie answered with a shrug. "I'm sorry."

Jackson scowled at his friend then turned his back on him and walked toward the window. He leaned his back against the wall beside it and folded his arms across his chest. This was not how he'd pictured this conversation going. "May I ask why?"

Charlie held up a hand and raised his index finger. "I know what you're like around campus. You party every weekend, especially when you have a gig with that band of yours." Another finger went up as he continued, "You drink excessively before, during, and after your shows." He raised a third finger. "You occasionally do pot and a few other drugs."

"Who doesn't in college?" Jackson shrugged, still meeting Charlie's eye.

"And I know about the women."

Jackson swallowed the sudden lump in his throat and lowered his gaze.

"I know you've cheated on at least two girlfriends and I know that you have at least one woman in your bed every weekend." Charlie rose and walked towards Jackson.

"How would you know something like that?" Jackson turned to his friend—his soon-to-be-former-friend if Charlie continued to be so stubborn.

Even though Charlie had dropped out of college to take care of Kerri after their parents had died, Jackson thought Charlie was being a bit too overprotective. Hadn't Olivia pointed out the night before that, with Kerri away at school, Charlie wouldn't have so much control over her? With or without Charlie's permission, perhaps Jackson should just tell Kerri what he felt for her anyway.

"You're not the only person we went to high school with that goes to your university. I hear stories." Charlie tilted his head to the side.

Jackson turned away from the uncomfortable scrutiny.

Charlie folded his arms across his chest. "You're not denying it."

Jackson continued to stare out the window.

"You really think I'm going to let someone who plays with women the way you do date my sister?" Charlie hissed lowly. "It's disgusting and I won't let you break her heart."

"It's not like you were a monk in college," Jackson snapped. "I'm sure you had your fair share of bed buddies."

Charlie's eyes narrowed menacingly. "Not a different woman, or two, every weekend, if I understand things correctly."

Jackson frowned. "Does Kerri know?"

"Not to my knowledge, but do you really think I'd talk to her about it? Do I look like an idiot?"

Jackson opened his mouth to answer, but Charlie continued.

"You say your feelings for her started the morning of the funeral, two years ago, yet in those two years, you've been with how many women? Do you even know? That's not the way someone in love should behave. More importantly, that's not how I would expect someone who claims to love my sister to behave."

"Charlie, I understand—"

"No!" Charlie's voice boomed through the room. "I don't think you do." He took a deep breath, dropped his arms to his sides and took a few steps backwards. "You know what our parents' death did to her. She wouldn't even come out of her room for the funeral, remember?"

Jackson nodded. He remembered her grief very well.

Charlie continued, "She became mine to look after, mine to protect, and I'll be damned if I'm going to let you hurt her. I don't care that you've known her all her life. I don't care that you are like a brother to her. I care about who you are, and what you are doing, now. You're on a downward spiral, and I'll be damned if you think I'm going to let you take her down with you." Charlie sat down heavily in his chair and rubbed his face with his hand. "I'm sorry to have to say this, but no. As much as I appreciate you asking, you can't date my sister."

Jackson studied his friend in silence and contemplated his next step. He did understand Charlie's point, and looking at the facts in such a cold light, Charlie was right. Jackson drank too much, experimented with drugs too often, and had had more than his fair share of women in his bed. If he were in Charlie's shoes, Jackson wasn't sure he'd let someone like him date his sister either. Kerri deserved better. But could he be man enough to change?

"How long will you give me to change? I didn't become this way overnight and it will take me some time to . . . improve myself." Excitement rushed through Jackson's body. He had no doubt he could do this. "Six months? A year?"

Charlie appeared deep in consideration. "Two," he said. "Two years."

Jackson's chin dropped. "Why?"

"She's eighteen. She's just graduated high school and will be starting college in the fall. Give her time to experience a little bit of life on her own. If you're clean, sober, and woman-free in two years you can ask me again."

"No," Jackson stated defiantly. "When I'm clean, sober, and woman-free in two years, I'm going directly to her."

Charlie narrowed his eyes on Jackson for a moment then nodded once. "Fine. But not until then." Charlie held out his hand. "One more thing," he said before Jackson grasped it to shake on their agreement.

"What?" Jackson hesitated, keeping his hand out of Charlie's reach.

"Don't tell her any of this. Don't let her know what you're doing. Or why. You have to do this on your own, not because she's cheering you on. I know you've been texting and emailing her and I'd like you to stop. You both need to be free of the other's influence for a while. I want you to do this for yourself as much as for her." Charlie looked at his open hand then into Jackson's eyes.

Jackson's lip curled in disgust. No emails, no texts, no phone calls? He always looked forward to receiving her messages. They were always so witty and full of life and joy. Two years without them might drive him completely insane.

But he knew Charlie would not agree to this any other way. As much as Jackson hated to admit it, the death of his parents and the added responsibility of raising his sister had matured Charlie well beyond his twenty-one years. There was probably a good reason for his request, even if Jackson wasn't happy about it.

Jackson gripped Charlie's hand and pumped it up and down. "Fine. But I will be back for her in two years."

He immediately packed his things, hopped into his newly restored 1968 Chevrolet Camaro, and left the beach house before Kerri could return home and cause him to break his promise to her brother.

The next two years were going to be the longest in his life.

"I want her gone," Sebastian growled.

Jack shook his head of the memories and frowned at his travel companion.

"Like, now." Sebastian hit Jack on the arm. "I have a plan."

Jack reluctantly pulled his gaze away from the back of the van in front of them. "You do?"

"I do." Sebastian's smile grew even more impish.

Jack felt a chill of foreboding. Whatever his plan was, Jack knew it wasn't good for Kerrigan.

"Shouldn't take me more than a week to make her leave. Depends on how stubborn she decides to be, but my charm should overcome that pretty easily."

Jack turned his focus to the road. She could be quite stubborn when she wanted to. "What are you thinking about doing?" He didn't really want to hear what Sebastian had planned, but if he didn't know, he couldn't stop it.

"Fucking with her," Sebastian said flatly.

He had Jack's full attention.

"She strikes me as the kind of woman in need of a good man," Sebastian began.

"And you're that man?" Jack scoffed, trying to sound less interested than he was. "I think you need a new plan."

"No, I'm not the man for her, but I can make her think I am." Sebastian looked up at the van in front of them and studied it for a moment. "She seems like the kind of girl who would fall for a guy just because he showed her some attention, and I intend to use that to my advantage."

Jack rolled his eyes. She most definitely wasn't the type to fall so quickly. He could vividly remember all the boys who followed her around at the beach, trying to get her attention. The summer she was fourteen, he would happen across Kerri and her entourage of boys clamoring to do every little thing for her—whether it was carrying her towel or the groceries from the camp store, or trying to give her a ride in their golf carts so she wouldn't tire from her walk. She had such a musical laugh when she'd tell them all, "no, thank you" and continue on her way.

Remembering their earlier conversation, though, he wondered if it was possible she may have changed in the last six years. For all his faults, Sebastian's intuition regarding women was usually pretty sharp. And that worried Jack a little.

"And once she falls, I can easily break her. First, I'll take her to bed a few times," Sebastian casually stated.

Jack's eyes sharpened on the road in front of him.

"Then I'll let her find me in bed with another bitch. She'll be so embarrassed she'll slip away in the night and we'll never hear from her again."

Jack swallowed his bile and rage. There was no way in hell he'd let Sebastian touch her. "And she'll take our contract and careers with her," he managed tightly as his fingers itched to wrap around his bandmate's throat. Not only was he being careless with regard to Kerrigan's feelings, but Sebastian was willing to throw the rest of the band away too, all to make a point.

"Someone else will be more than happy to pick us up." Sebastian leaned his head back on the headrest, a smug look of triumph on his face. "And if not, I'm sure my father can find another record label in need of a steady cash flow." Sebastian looked away, but Jack still heard him mumble, "Not like Jacob, the little bastard, deserves another penny of my father's money anyway."

Once he had a plan in mind, Sebastian was quick and ruthless in acting on it. Usually, Jack sat back and simply watched things happen. It was a whole lot easier than trying to stop him and helped Jack maintain more of a good guy image. And while Kerrigan may have handled Sebastian better than Jack would have expected during the meeting, there was no way she'd be able to stand up to him if he decided to go through with this plan. More importantly, Jack didn't want her to have to.

Images of Sebastian intimately touching Kerrigan came unbidden to his mind.

"What if I do it instead?" he blurted. Then he wouldn't have to watch Sebastian do all the things he wanted to do himself. After the words were out, he felt a weight lift.

Sebastian blew out a breath. "Thank God. I really didn't like the idea of having to fuck that icy bitch."

Jack's fist tightened around the steering wheel.

"But why would you want to? You usually like to keep your hands clean of these things."

Jack could feel Sebastian's scrutiny and schooled his features into a mask of calm indifference. "I can't let you have all the fun. What you say about her may be true, but she's not your type and I can assure you she already knows that. Anything you do to try to make it seem differently will only put her on her guard. I could almost guarantee, if she's guarded, it'll take a lot longer than a week to get rid of her."

He thought about the way she'd pulled away from him, the chill in her tone when she spoke to him, and the deadness in her eyes when she looked at him.

"Hell, it may even take me longer," he muttered.

"Not too much longer, I hope," Sebastian grumbled.

Jack's smirk slowly grew as he began to develop an agenda of his own.

One that would ensure he'd finally get what he wanted, what he'd been waiting six long years for. No, he'd take as long as he needed. And once he had her, he had no intention of letting her get away from him. He wasn't letting her out of his life again.

"Just leave it to me."

Six

After almost four hours on the road, followed by another two getting themselves acquainted with the modest bar they'd be performing in later, Jack found Kerrigan sitting at a small table in a dark corner, as far from the stage and the front door as she could possibly get. She had one palm on her forehead, her fingers splayed in her hair, and the forefinger of her other hand running down a list of items on the open page of the binder in front of her. He approached her slowly, never taking his eyes off of her face as she stared at the papers. When he was five steps away her finger froze.

"Did you have a good trip?" Jack asked. *Really?* Was that the best line he could come up with?

"Uneventful." She didn't even look at him. Her brows came together as she flipped back and forth between two of the pages.

"Well, that's a plus."

"Mm-hm."

She hadn't invited him to sit, but since she hadn't even acknowledged his presence he took it as a mere oversight on her part. He pulled out the seat across from her and sat down. She didn't seem to notice.

"What did you guys talk about? Anything I can help with?"

What was wrong with him? He sounded like such a dork, even to his own ears. This was Kerri he was talking to. He'd known her since she was two, loved her since she was eighteen. They should have been past the awkward teenage crush phase, but that's exactly how he was acting now.

Only, it wasn't really Kerri. She was now Kerrigan and had made it clear they were no longer friends. He wanted to blame her for that, but knew at least half of the burden was his.

"No." She finally looked up at him, pushed her glasses higher up the bridge of her nose, and tilted her head. "I just learned some things about the band. And its members."

He gave her a half smile. "There's at least one member you should already know fairly well."

She pursed her lips as she studied him. "I would argue I don't really know him at all."

His heart pounded in his chest as she looked back down at the book. She began to steadily drum her fingers on the table while he tried to ignore the sting of her words.

It shouldn't surprise him she would feel this way. Wasn't he just thinking the same thing about her?

"What happened to you?" Her serious tone took him by surprise.

"What do you mean?" he asked cautiously. If she was about to ask why he was in Paris, or why he'd left two years before that, he wasn't sure he could answer either of those questions yet.

She folded both hands on the binder and her bluish-gray gaze pierced him. "Based on what Riley and Stephen told me this morning, they're both here because of you. If you hadn't pushed Sebastian, he wouldn't have kept them in the band. You re-write Sebastian's 'bloody awful' songs yet don't push to have your own played."

Great. She was talking business. He should have figured.

This was not the conversation he'd been hoping to have with her.

Her jaw clenched for a moment before she continued. "I get the impression you, and probably you alone, could keep Sebastian in check if you chose to, but Stephen and Riley both think you don't care enough to do it. If that's the case, then you do realize you are just as much to blame for the problems your band is facing as Sebastian is?"

"Wait just a minute." Jack leaned forward and Kerrigan sat up straighter. What kind of lies were those two jokers feeding her?

"Did you know Stephen has one foot out the door?"

What did she just say? Jack began to shake his head. She simply nodded hers in response then took a deep breath. She folded her arms across her chest as her gaze softened on him in a condescending, pitying stare.

He wasn't sure he liked that.

"I know a little about the deal with Sebastian's father, so I know your band only has this contract for two more years." She paused to take a deep breath. "If we can't turn things around during this tour, Jacob may not re-sign you guys, and I'm not at all certain Stephen would mind that too much. He's ready to walk away. He loves the music, but he's fed up with babysitting Sebastian and cleaning up his messes. Riley is enjoying himself, but I get the impression he would follow Stephen out the door. Sebastian is clearly under the delusion you are the next Rolling Stones or Aerosmith and will be selling out crowds well into your seventies."

Jack couldn't say he was surprised that Stephen and Riley had been so forthcoming with information. Facts were facts, and so far everything she'd said was true. Except Jack hadn't been aware that Stephen was ready to pack it all in. He'd have to have a talk with the keyboardist. He put his elbow on the table and rested his chin in the palm of his hand as he held her steely regard.

"You've seen the numbers and heard the stories, so what do *you* think?"

Her gaze fell just past the right edge of the table as she spoke. "I think, regardless of whether I stay or not, your band won't make it to the end of the year." She looked at him again, her face emotionless and cold. "You're not functioning the way you should to be successful. There are far too many underlying problems for me to fix without help."

"What do you want me to do?"

Her mouth opened a fraction and he heard the quick intake of air. She was obviously taken aback by his question but recovered quickly.

"Be engaged." She made it sound so simple as she waved her hand in front of her. "This is just as much your band as it is Sebastian's. You formed it together, right?"

Jack nodded slowly.

"So why don't you care about it as much as he seems to? Why aren't you as passionate about its success?" She sat up and closed the binder. "When was the last time you actually sat down and talked about the band with Stephen or Riley? When was the last time you looked at the budget? When Sebastian ran managers off, did you try to stop him? Did you give any assistance to Stephen in managing the band's business?"

Jack's mouth opened and closed as he tried to answer each of her questions, but realized he couldn't.

"You don't even play your music, Jack."

Wow. They'd been extremely thorough in ratting out his rotten behavior.

Only, it hadn't seemed rotten when he was doing it. Kerrigan made it sound horrible. He felt like he was standing in the living room of her beach house, hearing all of his faults spelled out by her brother.

Actually . . . this was worse.

"I'm still looking into it, but it seems that if you had shown as much interest in recent months as you did in the beginning, Jacob may not have needed to hire me to clean up this mess." She looked him squarely in the eyes as she delivered those words.

Ah, the truth was out.

"So that's what it comes down to. You not wanting to be here?" Jack shook his head in disbelief. She must really be angry at him to be trying so hard to get out of this job. He stood so abruptly his chair fell backward. "The tour ends in just over two months, if you think you can manage to be near me for that long."

"This isn't about me and you," she murmured. She picked the binder up and held it to her chest as she leaned away from him. "I'm here to do a job. I take pride in my work and I won't leave until the job is done. I want to know if you can be part of the solution or if you're going to continue to be part of the problem. I'm trying to figure out if you have the desire to see this band succeed."

He placed his palms on the table and leaned closer to her. "You have no idea what my desires are," he said in a low, slow voice.

Her eyes widened and she rose slowly. "You think I don't want to be here? My question to you is . . . do *you* want to be here? Maybe you should think long and hard about your answer."

She snatched her purse off of the back of the chair, watching him as she did, then eased her way around him. Only after she was gone from the room did he exhale slowly and wonder what in the hell had just happened.

As Kerrigan reached into her purse for the envelope containing the band's money, she wondered if this day could possibly get any worse. In the eight hours since joining the band, she'd already had two confrontations with Jack.

Even though the second one had been over an hour ago, her nerves were still on edge. And now, she'd been in the middle of going over the budget with Stephen when they'd been interrupted by a woman claiming Sebastian had hired her for a five-hundred-dollar massage.

Kerrigan pulled out five twenty-dollar bills and held them out to the masseuse.

The woman stared at the money, looked at Kerrigan, and then back at the money. "Fine," she spat as she yanked the money from Kerrigan's hand. "But don't think I won't spread the word about this and what a bitch you are. I'll make sure no one in this town deals with you or your band again." She turned on her heels and stormed toward the front of the bar.

As much as Kerrigan hated doing it, she let her go with the last word. It was better to be rid of her before Sebastian came in to add his voice to the argument. At least the hundred dollars Kerrigan had just parted with was less than the money Sebastian had promised the woman. And Kerrigan now had more of an idea why the band was in such dire straits.

A slow clap started from the wall and she looked over to see Jack smiling at her as he applauded and strolled closer. Panic began to settle when she looked around and saw Stephen had disappeared and she and Jack were alone. She took a deep breath then looked directly into his green eyes, her heart thudding against the wall in her chest.

After all this time, why did he still affect her this way?

"Bravo," he stated. "Reminded me of a girl I used to know. She could hold her own with the best of them. However, her temper was a little less under control."

She tried not to smile. They were both aware he'd been on the receiving end of her temper on more than one occasion. "Perhaps she grew up and learned to control it."

"Pity." Jack stopped clapping when he reached the empty chair beside her.

Kerrigan was at a loss as his words fully sank in. Was he really sorry she'd changed from the girl she used to be? What had he expected? She'd been an innocent eighteen-year-old when he'd left her behind, and then he'd ignored her for six years.

She was probably just imagining his wistful tone.

"Where did Stephen go? I had more questions for him," Kerrigan said, deciding against pursuing his comment.

Jack frowned and looked to his left. "He decided you were handling things pretty well without him, so he opted to go find food for everyone."

"I've already taken care of that." Kerrigan eased into her chair and pulled her binder closer.

"I guess he didn't know." Jack sat down in Stephen's vacated seat.

Kerrigan picked up her pen and stared at the page in front of her, but the numbers wouldn't come into focus. Her heart was still fluttering and her mind, despite her attempt to dismiss them, was still searching his words for any double meanings. She knew it was wishful thinking but couldn't help herself.

"Is there something I can help you with?"

She looked up and met his clear, wide gaze. "I'm not sure. Jacob suggested I ask Stephen about any financial questions."

He grabbed the binder with his left hand and slid it toward himself. "He's not the only one who has answers."

She noticed a brown, leather cuff around his wrist and stared at it, trying to remember if she'd ever seen him with it before. The last time she'd seen him, in Paris, he'd had a new-to-her tattoo on that wrist.

"You like it?" he asked as he lifted his wrist toward her and tilted it side to side, giving her a complete view of the cuff. The walnut colored leather was about two inches wide and had smaller, slightly darker leather straps crisscrossing the length.

Kerrigan's fingers itched to touch it, to feel the softness of the leather and the warmth of him under her fingertips.

"It's nice," she said, folding her hands on the table and directing her gaze to his face. "Fashion statement?" She'd never known him to be conscious of the fashion trends. He'd always worn whatever he felt comfortable in. But to her, that cuff didn't look very comfortable.

Jack stared at the cuff, a sardonic smile forming on his lips. "I wear it to hide my secrets."

Kerrigan snorted, then covered her mouth and nose when Jack's laughing eyes met hers. "Guess your secrets aren't very big."

The humor drained from his face, leaving a look Kerrigan, in her limited experience, could only describe as seductive.

"You have no idea." His voice was a low purr that sent a shiver down her spine.

How had she not remembered the soothing timbre of his voice? She shook her head and broke eye contact. This was beyond ridiculous. She had to put these feelings back in their locked box before they ruined her.

Clearing her throat, she reached for the binder in front of him and turned it so they could both look at it. "Let's see if you can answer my questions before I hunt Stephen down again."

"Sure." Jack leaned closer and she could feel the heat emanating from his body.

"Sure," Kerrigan repeated. Was she really breathless? She inhaled and gave him a small nod. "Okay, Jacob hired me yesterday and immediately emailed me all of these files. I had time to print them off, but not to look at them before I had to leave for my flight. And you know I can't read and ride without getting sick."

Jack nodded. "Even flying?"

"Afraid so." Kerrigan shrugged. "So, I hadn't studied the books as thoroughly as I should have and didn't have these questions ready for Jacob when he met me in the lobby this morning."

"Kerri . . . gan," Jack said and pulled a face that told her he hadn't meant the slip of the tongue, "don't be so hard on yourself. You're obviously making up for that now. So what's your question?"

"Well, thanks to that masseuse, I've pretty much figured out all of the expense columns but I can't figure out the income. There's some sort of code beside each of the venues and I don't know what it is or why they vary so much." Kerrigan pointed to the columns in question and Jack nodded.

"Oh, that's simple." He grinned at her and her stomach did a flip. "There are three different ways we get paid." He looked at the book and pointed to the codes. "'G' is for guarantee, 'SPL' is for a split and 'TKT' is ticket sales."

As he went on to explain the differences and how the band used them to their advantage, her thoughts began to drift as she watched his lips move. The familiarity of his voice and the fact she was hearing it again, even if he was only talking about band business, filled her with longing and regret. She regretted all the time they'd spent apart and longed very much to rekindle their friendship. Anything else, if there could be anything else, would have to come after that. He'd always been her rock; he'd almost always been there when she'd needed him.

Until he wasn't.

That's what she should remember. He'd walked out of her life without any explanation, hadn't bothered to talk to her at all until he'd just shown up in Paris, and then not again after that. If he'd only tried to communicate with her after Paris, she may have responded.

Maybe.

The moment her foot hit the sidewalk, she'd regretted walking out of that brasserie without talking to him. But in the four years since, he'd never tried to contact her again. And while she liked to think that she would have picked up the phone on the first ring if she'd known it was him, the events that had led to her refusal to see him in Paris were never far from her mind. She didn't want to face his rejection again if he learned the truth.

"Kerrigan, are you listening?" Jack asked.

She looked up and found his brow furrowed as he stared at her.

"Yeah, of course," she replied with an uncomfortable laugh. She repeated everything he'd said back to him, almost verbatim, and he nodded with a faint grin as he listened. When she finished, Jack's smile widened and Kerrigan tried to ignore the bubble of giddiness.

"Impressive." Jack leaned closer. "I thought for sure you were a million miles away."

Kerrigan's mouth went dry. What would he say if she told him she had been?

"Thinking of something in particular?" he asked, his hand snaking closer to hers.

She pulled her hand off the table and leaned away. "No. I'm not thinking of anyone . . . thing. Anything," she stuttered as she clasped her hands in her lap and felt the burn in her cheeks. "So, that explains the main income, but what about supplemental? Do you guys have merchandise to sell?" She glanced at him and he sat up straighter, his arms across his chest as he studied her.

Slowly, he nodded. "We have CDs of our album, T-shirts with the album cover on it, and eight-by-tens of the band and each member. We usually set up after the show to sell them."

"Where are they now?" She pulled the binder closer to her and studied the merchandise column. The numbers were lower than she'd expected.

"They're in the back of the van you rode in." When Kerrigan opened her mouth to ask why they weren't already out, he held up his hand and stopped her before the question passed her lips. "We don't have anyone to man the sales table during the shows. Afterwards, Riley, Stephen, and I take turns."

He leaned his elbows on the table, his gaze never leaving hers. She suddenly felt off-balance. He'd predicted her question before she'd asked, like he used to predict her behavior when they were teenagers. When she was fifteen, she'd tried to sneak out to a party her parents had forbidden her from going to. As she'd thrown her leg over the branch of the tree outside her room, she'd heard Jackson's voice from below and she'd looked down to see him staring up at her with his arms crossed, shaking his head with a knowing smile on his lips. She hadn't even told Olivia she was going to sneak out, so she wasn't sure how he'd figured it out. He'd remained there, sitting on the patio, for at least two more hours, until she'd completely given up and gone to bed.

It scared her that he still knew her well enough to know her thoughts. Being this close to him again, would she be able to hide her darkest secret from him?

"Where the hell is she?" The roar came from the door and Kerrigan jumped and turned to see Sebastian storming into the room. "Where is my masseuse?"

"Gone." Kerrigan stood as he stopped inches from her.

"What do you mean, *gone*?" Sebastian asked, mimicking her tone. "I need a massage before I can go on stage."

"I'm sure you don't," Kerrigan stated, pulling her shoulders up as tension infused them.

"That just proves you don't know a fucking thing." Sebastian took a step closer. "Are you going to take her place then? Give me a good rubdown?"

"Hardly," she scoffed.

"Sebastian, you know the band can't afford that luxury for you, right?"

Jack asked. He'd risen and taken a step around the table, placing himself directly between her and Sebastian.

"It's hardly a luxury." Sebastian lifted his arrogant nose in the air as Kerrigan raised a skeptical brow. "I was told that if you want to make it big, you have to act like you're already there."

She met Jack's gaze and he looked just as unconvinced as she was. He turned to Sebastian again. "Who told you that?"

"Never mind." Sebastian glared at Kerrigan again and she tried not to cringe. "I need that damn massage. It helps me relax so I can perform better. And trust me, this has been a stressful enough day without adding this to it. You get her back. Now!"

Kerrigan lifted her chin. "No."

Sebastian's eyes widened and he took a step toward her. As she inched backward, Jack moved himself into Sebastian's path.

"No, I will not," she snapped. "Five hundred dollars for a forty-five minute massage? Really? Do you know how outrageous that is? And where is that money supposed to come from? You're only guaranteed five hundred tonight and you want to spend it all on a massage? That's the most arrogant and selfish thing I've ever heard. It's bad enough I had to pay her a hundred just to get her to leave. And you will reimburse the band for that, by the way."

Sebastian's mouth opened and closed like a fish out of water. He took another step forward but Jack held his ground.

"And another FYI, I will tell Jacob about this and make sure any future invoice that comes to him with your signature on it comes directly out of your personal account." Kerrigan closed her binder and picked it up. When she looked at Sebastian again, the calculating look in his eyes sent a chill down her spine.

"Have it your way." He turned and walked out of the room.

Kerrigan met Jack's wide-eyed glance—a mirror of her own—for a second before he turned and quickly followed Sebastian.

Seven

Jack paced his hotel room, trying to focus on the song he'd been writing for two days without much luck. After all these years away from Kerri, writing songs inspired by her, he would have thought it would be easier with her sleeping across the hall. But no, instead he was too concerned about what Sebastian had in store for her to be able to focus on the feelings he still had for her.

When he'd caught up to Sebastian after his argument with Kerrigan the day before, Sebastian had been furious that Jack had taken her side. Jack hadn't uttered a word before the anger turned to speculation and just as quickly to acceptance. Sebastian had assumed Jack was just trying to get on her good side, as part of the plan he'd agreed to. Jack had stared dumbfounded at him for a moment before slowly nodding.

It couldn't hurt to let Sebastian think that.

But what Sebastian said next still chilled Jack.

"That icy bitch will get exactly what she deserves. I don't know who she thinks she is, but she'll pay for interfering with my massage," he'd growled.

Jack swallowed his irritation and calmly asked, "What are you going to do about it?"

Sebastian simply smirked. "You'll know when it happens." He chuckled as he walked away.

The fact it hadn't happened yet, over twenty-four hours later, worried Jack more than it probably should.

He tried to shake his fears away. He really wanted to get this song finished. Even if they'd never record it, he'd always found songwriting calming.

Writing songs with Kerrigan so close by hadn't always been this difficult. He used to write them all the time at the beach house.

Jackson had tilted his ear toward the door of his room at the beach house when he'd thought he'd heard a knock. Everyone else was supposed to be asleep.

The two-story house had a master bedroom downstairs and four bedrooms, one in each corner of the second floor. He, Charlie, and Pete each had their own rooms while Kerri and Olivia shared the one across the hall from him. Since they all kept the same rooms every summer, Mr. and Mrs. Dodd had allowed him to decorate his room to his liking. He'd kept the furnishings sparse: a wood-framed, twin bed in front of the window over the porch, a matching, small, light maple desk in front of the other window, and a four-drawered dresser beside the door.

He heard the light tap again and turned toward his door. "Come in."

The door slowly opened and Kerri peeked her head in. "Hey," she whispered as she entered the room. "Whatcha doin'?"

He glanced at the words on the page of the notebook in front of him as the corner of his lips lifted. He'd been working on a song, inspired by one of the girls he'd seen around the campground that day. His stare shifted to Kerri as she sat beside his guitar at the foot of the bed.

"I didn't wake you, did I?" he asked. She and Olivia had gone to bed before he had. He, Charlie, and Pete had been the last ones to turn in, over an hour ago.

She shook her head as she plucked a string. "Olivia was talking in her sleep and rolling around too much. I couldn't get to sleep." Her gaze drifted around the room, coming to rest on the open page in his notebook. Her smile widened and became mischievous. "You didn't answer my question."

"I didn't?" He laid his hand across his work-in-progress.

"No, you didn't." She rose to her feet and took a step toward him. "Are you keeping a diary?" she taunted.

Jackson rolled his eyes. "Seventeen-year-old guys don't keep diaries."

Her hand snaked around him toward the song.

"Then what are you writing?"

He stood and grabbed the notebook off the desk, putting it behind his back as he kept her at an arm's distance.

"It's nothing," he said as she struggled to reach around him.

His arms were longer than hers, but she was sneaky. She faked movement in one direction then quickly reached for the other side as soon as he'd adjusted. Her giggles were hushed but infectious. He struggled not to laugh along with her.

"You shouldn't be in here." Jackson tried to sound stern as they semi-danced around the room. "Your parents will kill you if they catch you."

He stumbled when his calves hit the bed and Kerri jumped onto the mattress, snatched the notebook out of his hand, and scurried to the window before he could recover.

"Then I can't let them catch me, can I?" She laughed quietly as she pushed the window screen up and scrambled out onto the wide, gently sloping porch roof.

He hurried after her, hoping it would be too dark outside for her to see the words he'd penned earlier. As he stuck his head out, he cursed under his breath.

The moon was full.

And if that weren't enough light, the street lamp, two houses down, made up for it.

It wasn't as bright as day, but it was close.

He climbed onto the roof and eased his way to her side, watching her face as she read the lyrics. The crash of the waves in the distance provided the beat for his words. Her lips were pursed and her brow furrowed, and as her eyes made their way over the page, both puckers deepened.

"You don't like it?" He placed his feet flat on the roof and laid his forearms over his bent knees.

She tilted her head from side to side as she lowered the paper. "I don't know," she answered with a shrug. "It just seems so superficial."

Jackson raised an eyebrow. "How so?"

"Well . . ." She pointed to the words. "You talk about the length of her legs and her bright blonde hair, but that's it. Everything else is . . ." She waved her hand as if searching for the right word but let it fall to her lap without adding anything. "You've told me nothing about the girl herself or how she makes you feel."

Jackson laughed out loud. "What would you know about it?" It may have been a first draft, but he'd thought it was pretty good. And everything that had interested him about her was in the song. "It's not like I'm in love with her."

"Then why write a song about her?"

Her wide eyes were so full of innocence he suddenly felt dirtied by the thoughts that had gone into his song. "Why not?" he mumbled as he averted his gaze and focused on the roofline of the house across the small, dirt road. "Songs are just poetry put to music. And poets write whatever they feel like writing."

Kerri remained silent but out of the corner of his eye he saw her picking leaves off of the roof and tossing them over the edge. He heard her breath deepen and turned to look at her.

"True, I guess. I always considered songs to be more like little stories put to music." She turned toward him and the impish twinkle in her eyes returned. "And good stories are about more than the subject's looks," she finished with sass. "It should have more depth. If it were a song about me, I'd be severely disappointed."

"Severely?" he teased.

She nodded once.

"So if I were to write a song about you, it should be deeper?"

"Absolutely."

Jackson chuckled under his breath. "I could probably do that. I could write about your stubbornness."

Her mouth fell open.

"And about how mischievous you can be. That could be an entire song by itself," he added flippantly. "I have plenty of examples to choose from."

"Hey," she protested as she faced him again.

He stroked his chin. "I could probably write about your wit and sarcasm. Those are always fun to deal with." He rolled his eyes for emphasis.

Her mouth closed and he could tell she was fighting a smile. "Exactly," she said. "You've just made my point for me. If you're going to write a song about someone, you should probably know a little more about them." She looked at her lap. "And you should probably feel something a little stronger than lust for them."

Jackson's cheeks felt suddenly warm. She was clearly more perceptive than he'd expected a fourteen-year-old girl to be.

He'd have to add that to the song about her but for now, he had to change the subject.

"So what did you do today?"

That night on the roof under the moonlight had been the first of many conversations they'd shared at the beach house as everyone else slept. Those chats gave him the opportunity to see her as her own person, and not just Charlie's little sister, and as they'd gotten older, their late night talks had become a nightly occurrence.

And he'd never forgotten her words about that song.

Over the past six years, he'd penned numerous songs about Kerri, with depth that would make her proud. He'd always felt closer to her when he was writing about her, the girl he'd fallen in love with. It made the differences he now saw in her that much more difficult for him to deal with.

Jack walked back to the desk and reached for his notebook. His hand froze as a low rumble reached his ears. He listened closely and realized they were male voices, and more than he could count. A pounding sound against a nearby door had him on his feet, sprinting toward the door.

He opened the door to his room and was shocked to see a line of men stretching down either side of Kerrigan's door. "Oh no," he muttered, a sinking feeling in his stomach.

The short, balding man standing in front of Kerrigan's door reached up and pounded on it with the palm of his hand. "Ma'am, I'm the hotel manager. You need to open up please."

"Yeah, open up so you can open up." This crude statement was followed by a round of guffaws and high-fives.

"What is this about?" asked a soft voice from the other side of the door.

Jack turned the swing bolt on his door and stepped into the fray. "What's going on here?"

"Sir, this is none of your concern," the manager said, followed by a male chorus calling "go away" and "back of the line."

Back of the line? What the hell? Jack looked up and down the hall filled with men, then at Kerrigan's door and saw her widened eye peeking through the opening in her door. She'd had the same idea he'd had with the bolt, only she'd chosen to stay on the inside of the room. Jack stepped between her door and the hotel manager and tried to smile at him despite the protests of the other men.

"She's my band's manager so she kinda is my concern." Jack spoke calmly, though his blood was boiling. This had to be Sebastian's doing, but he had yet to determine what the asshole had actually done.

"Did you know she is illegally running a business out of her hotel room?"

Jack tilted his head. "What kind of business?"

"A massage parlor," the manager stated, making air quotes around the words. "She was handing out flyers at your concert earlier."

"I was personally invited."

"Yeah, me too!"

Jack's jaw tightened as he listened to the men around him shout and agree.

"Jack," came her whispered voice behind him as she opened the door a mere inch. "I have no idea what he's talking about."

Was there a quiver in her voice? He turned and through the small open space, he could see the haunted look in her eyes.

"I know," he murmured and gave her a reassuring smile. "I'll take care of it." She nodded and he turned around. "I'm sorry, but I think you're mistaken. She wouldn't do that."

"Wouldn't hand out flyers?" The manager turned and held his hand out. At least five of the men around him shoved a piece of paper at him.

"No, she wouldn't run a massage parlor," Jack replied between clenched teeth.

"I hope not. I was hoping for a rubdown of a different sort."

Several men chuckled as Jack scanned the crowd for the heckler who was about to become toothless. The manager held up a flyer and Jack took it and read.

FREE! Tonight only! In the mood for a good 'massage'? Starting at one o'clock, first come, first served! Open until the sun comes up. Get some while you can! Kerrigan's room number was written at the bottom.

Suddenly, assault wasn't the worst crime Jack wanted to commit that night.

He was ready to kill Sebastian.

"You see? There's the proof." The manager pulled his shoulders back and still the top of his head barely reached Jack's eyes. "This is illegal. She can't do this in our hotel."

Jack laughed. It was better than screaming at them all to leave her alone. "Are you kidding me? You accuse her of running a business and this is your proof? There are so many things wrong with that assumption."

"Like what?" the manager asked as he folded his arms across his chest. The male voices chorused in agreement and the group seemed to close in on Jack.

"First of all, if this were true, which I assure you it's not, she's not charging anything for this service so it's hardly a business transaction." He heard Kerrigan's gasp from behind him and cringed. "Secondly, I know for a fact this is a practical joke, pulled by one of our band members with a terrible sense of humor."

"So, no massages?" one of the men ventured.

"Of any sort?" another added.

"No." Jack looked over the hotel manager's head, not hard given the man's stature, and eyed several of the men directly as he continued. "You'll all have to find your entertainment elsewhere tonight fellas." There was a rumble of discontentment from the crowd. "And if I catch any of you hovering around here, I will escort you out of the hotel myself."

Slowly the group turned and made their way toward the elevators and stairwells. As the final few wandered off, Jack glared down at the manager eyeing Kerrigan's door.

"That goes for you, too," Jack snapped. "What kind of manager would try to put a stop to something illegal with a horde of willing participants trailing behind him?"

The hotel manager's face turned a pale shade of pink and his mouth fell open. "I'll have you know, this crowd was gathered before I arrived."

"Funny," Jack scoffed. "I didn't hear them until you started pounding on her door."

The manager avoided eye contact.

"So unless you're lingering to apologize to the lady, I suggest you leave as well. My temper is on a very short leash right now." Jack's jaw clenched as he scowled. The manager took a few steps backward before turning and speed-walking to the nearest exit.

Jack released a breath and turned to look at Kerrigan, only to find her door closed. He pressed his forehead against the cool wood then raised his knuckles to rap on the door. After a few moments without a response, he tapped again.

"Kerrigan," he called quietly. "It's just me."

"Are you alone?" she asked. Her voice sounded like it was just on the other side of the door.

He laid his palm to the door, imagining it was touching hers.

"Yes, all alone." He stood against the door for a few more minutes without hearing anything. "Are you going to let me in, or should I find a window to climb in?"

The door opened a crack and her eyes peered at him through the slight opening. "That's not funny."

"You're right. I'm sorry." He stood up and took his hand off the door. "Can I come in?"

She warily peeked around him as best she could. Gradually, she opened the door, stepping behind it as she did. When he was inside she quickly shut it, threw the swing bolt, then undid it again. She turned around, backed into the corner behind the door and folded her arms across her chest. She looked directly into his eyes and his breath caught in his throat.

Her hair was loose around her shoulders, longer than he'd ever remembered seeing it, and had a delicate wave—probably because of those tight buns she'd worn for the last two days. Her blue-gray eyes looked silver in the dull light of her room and were wide and cautious. She was wearing a loose tank top and shorts. After seeing her in stuffy business attire, her casual appearance had his eyes wandering over the exposed skin of her shoulder and legs and his mind wandering into even more relaxed territory.

He turned away before she noticed the affect she had on him in his loose, gray lounge pants, and looked into her sparse hotel room. She had the same, standard furniture he did—a bed, dresser with a television on top, and a desk—but her suitcase was tucked away in the corner and closed. Nothing else in the room would indicate someone was even staying there.

"I think you should stay in my room tonight." Jack took another step into the room. He turned and found that she was squatting in the corner, gently rocking back and forth as she stared at the floor. "Kerrigan?" She lifted her gaze to his as he took a step toward her and fought the urge to run to her, to put his arms around her and comfort her. "Are you okay?"

"Yeah," she quickly stated as she looked away and nodded. "Yeah, I'm fine. Why? Why do you ask?"

"Oh, I don't know. It could be because you just had a swarm of men outside your door and you're currently sporting a 'deer in headlights' look on your face."

He knelt in front of her as he gave her a crooked smile. She lifted a shaking hand to her forehead. As she lowered her hand, he reached for it and she jerked away and pressed herself into the corner again. He placed his other knee on the floor and inched closer.

"I'm not going to hurt you." He frowned at the fact he had to assure her of that. "Kerri, you're safe with me," he whispered and laid his wrists, palms up and open, on his thighs.

Her throat bobbed as her gaze fell to his hands then lifted to his face. The breath she took was shaky. "Thank you," she murmured. "For what you did out there." She motioned toward the hallway with her head and met his eyes.

"You're welcome." He shuffled closer. "I think you should sleep in my room."

Her eyes widened and she pressed herself tighter into the corner of the wall. He didn't understand her reaction. He'd known her for over twenty years. They'd been a lot closer, physically, than they were right now and she'd never reacted like this to him.

As he stared into her silvery gaze, he realized there was something else wrong with this picture. In the past two days he'd watched her stand up to Sebastian a number of times, seen her hold her own against the venue managers, and send an irate masseuse packing without even batting an eyelash. As a matter of fact, in all the time he'd known her, he'd never known her to back down from a fight, verbal or otherwise. He'd seen her punch her brother and been on the receiving end of her right hook on more than one occasion.

At the moment she was wedged into the corner, her arms wrapped around her body like she was physically holding herself together, her eyes rounded and full of fear. Something had happened to her and his desire to do bodily harm to someone grew stronger. He only needed to know who and what they'd done.

"I don't think that's necessary." She shook her head. "You've sent them all away, the manager knows better now, and I think it'll be fine. I don't need to sleep with you."

Wait. What?

He blinked slowly as his blood heated and began its slow journey below his waist. Images of her splayed in his bed, her black hair haloed around her on the pillow, popped into his mind and he closed his eyes and turned his head away from her.

"No, Kerri . . . gan, it won't be fine. And I know you weren't responsible for these flyers." He held out the flyer he'd dropped beside him and, with an unsteady grasp, she took it. He peeked at her again as she stared at the piece of paper.

Her face paled even more. "Sebastian," she murmured as she closed her eyes and let the flyer fall to the floor. "I guess I had hoped they were mistaken."

He took a deep breath and kept his gaze averted from the temptation she presented. "Sadly, they weren't, and some of them won't be turned away so easily. I'll wager some of them will be back. You'll be safer in my room."

"Where will you be?" she asked hesitantly.

He wanted to say he'd be lying next to her in bed but knew that wouldn't be happening. Not anytime soon anyway.

"I'll stay in here. That way if any of them come looking for you, they'll find me instead." He smirked at the thought of taking out his frustrations on one of those creeps.

"You look like you'd enjoy that." Her voice was closer and he turned toward it. She had relaxed away from the corner but was still well out of arm's reach.

"Could be fun." He shrugged.

She gave him a small smile before looking down again. This was definitely not the same person he'd grown up with. She wasn't even the same woman he'd seen for the past two days. This version of her seemed less comfortable in her own skin, shy and somewhat fragile.

"Should I take my suitcase?"

Jack rose to his feet as he shook his head, shaking away his own questions as he answered hers. "Just take what you'll need first thing in the morning. I'll come over and get you after I wake up and we can trade rooms again."

He held his hand down to help her up. One of her hands lifted toward his, then she paused and lowered it to the floor and pushed herself up to her feet. Avoiding his gaze, she scurried off to the bathroom, just as quickly returning with a small bag.

"I'm ready." She handed him her room key and walked to the door.

Eight

Once Kerrigan was settled in his room, Jack left her with instructions to bolt the door behind him. As if he had to tell her that.

When she'd been cowering in the bathroom to escape the noise of the mob in the hall, Jack had come to her aid. His behavior, an echo of the boy she used to know, had left her aching for the familiarity they'd once had with each other. Now with one hand on the bolt and the other against the door, she stood still, hoping to regain her equilibrium.

Once she felt stable again, she turned to look at his room, hugging her arms to her body to fight the chill that hadn't left her body. The bed was still made and she wondered if he'd even been trying to sleep before the debacle in the hallway. On top of the desk was an open notebook with a pencil lying beside it. Some of his clothes were stacked in a pile on top of the dresser, his suitcase sat open and neatly packed on the floor beside it.

Her eyes landed on the leather coat folded and lying on top of the clothes in the suitcase. That would warm her up.

She scurried across the room and gently lifted the coat from its resting place. With shaky hands she brought it closer to her nose and inhaled deeply.

It smelled exactly as she remembered it. The faint, earthy smell of leather was accompanied by the sharp, spicy cinnamon and smooth, woodsy sandalwood aromas that were, and always would be, Jackson. She slid her arms into the jacket's sleeves then pulled the collar to her face and closed her eyes.

"I'd like my sweater back, please," Kerri had hissed through gritted teeth.

These boys had been harassing her and Olivia all day. She'd hoped to be rid of them after refusing their invitation to watch the evening's fireworks together, but they were relentless and, apparently, couldn't take no for an answer. To make matters worse, the breeze off the water was chilly, and if they continued to be difficult, she would have to go back to the beach house, where her parents would try to rope her and Olivia into another board game.

As much as she enjoyed a good game of Monopoly, her parents had given Charlie and his friends permission to hang out on the beach every night and Kerri wanted to see what all the fuss was about. She was fifteen years old and it was time her parents let her stretch her wings a little. She'd promised to stay out of trouble, and she didn't want these jerks to make her break that promise.

"If you're chilly, I can warm you up," said the blond ringleader as he inched closer. "It would be my pleasure." He waggled his eyebrows up and down as his three friends guffawed behind him.

"C'mon, Kerri. Let's go," Olivia said and tugged on Kerri's upper arm.

Kerri gently shook her off and clenched her jaw tighter as she reached for her sweater. He swished it behind his back and she stumbled into his scrawny chest.

He took the opportunity to put his arm around her. "I knew you'd come around."

"Let. Me. Go." She lifted her leg and brought her heel down squarely on his toes.

In the soft sand, it wasn't the hard landing she'd hoped for, but it still had the desired effect. He groaned in pain and shoved her away from him. She landed on her butt in the sand and stared up at the mass of masculine immaturity headed toward her. Placing her hands behind her on the sand, she crab-walked backward, trying to squash the fear and frustrated anger in her chest.

Two large hands slipped under her arms and lifted her out of the sand.

"Let me help."

Kerri closed her eyes with relief when she recognized the warm baritone.

Once she was firmly on her feet, Jackson stepped between her and the four boys. She could see the scowl on his face and was glad that she wasn't on the receiving end of it for a change.

"Is there a problem here?" Jackson inched forward and all of the boys except Kerri's tormenter backed up.

"She said she was cold. I was just offering to keep her warm," the boy said with bravado.

Kerri rolled her eyes as she dusted off the back of her shorts.

"Is that true?"

She looked up to see Jackson's green eyes focused on her. Her mouth suddenly went dry and she nodded, then realized what she was doing and shook her head.

"He took my sweater," she muttered.

Jackson chuckled as he took his leather coat off and draped it over her shoulders. He turned his attention back to the boy and Kerri slipped her arms into the sleeves. The jacket was still warm and Jackson's scent rose from it like burning incense.

"You've been following her around all day," Jackson said, striding toward the boy.

"Yeah, and?"

"I believe I heard her ask you several times to leave her alone." Jackson's voice had become a low growl and the boy fell back a step. "I also heard her tell you she didn't want to watch the fireworks with you."

"So," the boy said, his voice quaking a little in spite of his effort to keep up the show of courage. "What's your point?"

Jackson folded his arms across his chest and towered over the younger boy. "My point is, if a girl tells you to leave her alone, you leave her alone. If she tells you she doesn't want to go somewhere with you, you don't follow her around and force her to pay attention to you."

Kerri moved to stand beside Jackson, feeling emboldened by his presence. "It means you don't take her sweater so she'll have to talk to you, asshole." She held her hand out to the boy.

He looked down at his hand and gave a start, like he was surprised to see her belongings in his grasp.

"Give it back," Jackson ordered and the sweater was tossed into Kerri's hand. "Now . . . apologize."

The boy's mouth fell open and his eyes moved from Jackson's face to Kerri's.

She tilted her head to the side and stared at him with a raised eyebrow. "You heard him."

"I'm sorry," he bit out and turned to join his friends, now standing several yards away.

"Don't bother me again," Kerri called after him.

If he heard her, he didn't acknowledge her words.

Kerri didn't care.

She looked up at Jackson as he stared after the boy for another few seconds. He met Kerri's gaze, concern in the emerald depths of his eyes.

She pressed her lips together. "I was handling things well enough."

He raised a thick eyebrow. "I noticed."

She ignored the flutter in her stomach. Jackson was her brother's best friend and three years older than her. It probably wasn't a good idea to allow herself to develop a crush on him.

"You should probably thank me for stepping in when I did," she continued, teasing as she held his stare.

"I should thank you?" His serious tone was contradicted by the twitching lip. "Why should I thank you?"

"Because, you're eighteen and a head taller than most of those boys," she replied as she turned to walk away. "It would have hardly been fair to them if I had allowed you to teach them a lesson in manners with your fists."

She heard his chuckle close behind her.

"And then you would have had to deal with irate parents."

His hand snaked around her upper arm and she froze.

"And I'm not sure I could have gotten you out of that kind of trouble."

She turned to face him and saw the amusement in his eyes.

"You getting *me* out of trouble?" He pursed his lips. "Now that's funny."

Kerri beamed at him and he laughed loudly.

When he finally stopped laughing, she looked away. "Thank you for your help. I didn't mean to bother you."

His fingers gripped her chin and he looked deeply into her eyes. "If you need my help, just ask. You're never a bother."

Even in the darkness, she could feel the sincerity of his words. She inhaled a deep, salty, breath of air and nodded.

Kerrigan heard a knock—a pounding really—across the hall and tiptoed to the door. Looking through the peephole, she could see a man standing outside of her room, talking to Jack.

Listening to Jack, anyway, who looked rather furious as he pointed down the hallway toward the elevator. She heard the rumble of his voice, and the few words she could hear made it clear she wouldn't want to be standing in that stranger's place.

She watched as the man finally turned and left, leaving Jack clearly in her line of vision. Freely, she studied him and her breath stopped in her throat. For the second time that night, he appeared like the boy who had crawled through her window when she'd refused to come out of her room for her parents' funeral. Like the boy who'd stood up to the boys who'd teased and followed her and Olivia around the campground when she was fifteen. Like the boy who, despite being her brother's best friend, had never made her feel like a nuisance.

Before he turned to go back into the room, he stared at the door she was standing behind and she felt like he was actually seeing her. The look in his eyes shifted and her heart stopped. She recognized the depth of concern and the kindness he'd always shown her in their youth—two of the things she'd grown to love about Jackson.

And just as suddenly the look was gone as he entered her former room. She turned and pressed her back to the door and pulled his coat tighter around her. Was it possible that he could still be the boy she'd fallen in love with?

Nine

"Psst, Jack."

Jack halted on his way to the van when he heard the sweet, hushed voice. Kerrigan was standing on the other side of the van she would be riding in. As he approached her, she looked around. When he was also hidden from the lobby of the hotel, she gave him a tentative grin and held up a cup.

"Here. You looked tired in the meeting and I thought you could use this."

He took the cup and held it up to his nose.

Coffee.

As he studied her face, full of anticipation, he took a sip. It was just the way he liked it, a hint of sugar and even less milk. Even after six years, she hadn't forgotten. He tried to hide his smile.

"Did you get any sleep last night?" she asked, her voice low and secretive.

"Not much. You?"

She shook her head as she looked at the ground between their feet. "A little bit."

He took another sip as he tried to figure her out. She'd been very gracious when he'd taken her back to her room that morning and had seemed more relaxed in his presence, even if she still wouldn't let him touch her. But now, she was acting shy and nervous and he wondered if they'd moved forward as much as he'd thought.

"Thank you," he said, holding his coffee cup up in salute.

She beamed for a moment, then just as quickly it was gone. "You're welcome." She turned to walk toward the front of the van.

He didn't want the moment to end. "Kerrigan."

She stopped and faced him.

"Why didn't you say anything to Sebastian about last night?" Jack had been itching for an argument. He'd been ready to come to her defense, but she hadn't given him the chance.

She chuckled as she shook her head and her eyes brightened a little. "What good would it have done?"

Jack opened his mouth to speak, but closed it again. She was probably right. If she'd shown that she had been bothered by it, the likelihood of Sebastian repeating such a stunt would increase. Hopefully, ignoring it the way she had this morning meant Sebastian would lose interest and not attempt to do anything like that again.

"Exactly," she said with a laugh. "Have a safe trip," she added as she waved and walked away from him.

He sauntered around the other side of the van, toward the one he'd be driving. As he took a sip of coffee, he looked up to see the rest of the band come out of the hotel. They all climbed in their respective vehicles and were soon on the road to Birmingham.

Half an hour later, Jack's coffee was gone but he was still savoring the memory of receiving it. Sebastian was engrossed in another episode of *Behind the Music* and Jack was enjoying the quiet while it lasted.

"Fifty fucking dollars," Sebastian grumbled. "How the hell am I supposed to eat on that?"

Jack rolled his eyes and stared at the road ahead of him. Kerrigan had informed them all that morning that their new per diem amount for food would be decreased to fifty dollars. "I'm sure you'll manage." He was still not in the mood to talk to Sebastian. During the night he'd spent in Kerrigan's room, he'd had to send away at least ten men, none of whom went quietly. They'd all thought he was the current "client" and were perfectly content to wait their turn in the hallway.

He would love nothing more than to curse Sebastian until his ears bled for the prank he'd pulled on Kerrigan. Jack hadn't found it funny at all. But because Kerrigan had chosen not to confront him, Jack couldn't say anything either.

If he showed too much interest in Sebastian's shenanigans or tried to defend Kerrigan in any way, Sebastian would get suspicious. And if Sebastian found out that he and Kerrigan had grown up together, or that she was the only woman he'd ever loved, then things would only get worse. Sebastian had already proven that by running Stephen's fiancée, Debra, off of the tour.

Debra had enjoyed touring with the band, and almost all of them had enjoyed having her with them. She was always a help, making food runs, helping backstage, even manning the merchandise table. She'd also been one of the few people to stand up to Sebastian. And that had been her downfall.

Jack couldn't let the same thing happen with Kerrigan. Now that she was back in his life, he'd be damned if he'd let Sebastian run her off. But he was stuck, not able to say anything to prevent that from happening. Unless Sebastian brought it up first.

"I got good and even with her last night. I hope the bitch didn't get any sleep." There was no mistaking the smugness in Sebastian's voice as he told Jack everything he'd done the night before. "I was hoping she'd try to call me out for it this morning, I was itching for a fight."

Jack couldn't believe his luck as he glanced at Sebastian, but he had to be careful not to appear to know too much. "Why would she say something to you? What would it have accomplished?"

Sebastian remained silent for a few minutes then shrugged. "Nothing."

"Exactly." Jack looked out the front windshield. "Did you consider that you could have gotten her arrested with your little stunt?"

"Why should I care if she gets arrested? Any good manager should know how to talk their way out of jail," Sebastian said with a laugh.

"Damn it, *you* can't even talk yourself out of jail. You always call your father to bail you out." Jack took a deep, calming breath and chose to focus on Sebastian's question. "You should care because, one, she had nothing to do with those flyers being handed out. Two, if they'd been traced back to you, and I'm sure they would have been, then you'd have been arrested. And three, if you're in jail and we can't perform, we no longer have a contract. Is that what you want?"

"Okay, one," Sebastian began mockingly, "no one would have connected me with that flyer. Her info was all over it."

"Right, and the people who handed it out for you? If they were asked, would they lie for you?" Jack tightened his grip on the steering wheel. "One guy with a flyer can turn in the person who handed it to him who can then lead the cops to you. It doesn't take much."

"B, it's not like those guys would have remembered who handed them what at that concert. And I'm sure the people handing out the flyers weren't giving out their names either." Sebastian looked out of the corner of his eye at Jack. "And three, I've been thinking."

That's never good. "Don't hurt yourself," Jack muttered.

"We run her off and Jacob tears up the contract, and what then?" Sebastian continued as if he hadn't heard. "His company won't get the money my father promised them and if Mr. Perfect can't succeed without my father's money he deserves to flop anyway."

Jack raised an eyebrow as he resisted the urge to scoff openly. From everything he'd heard about the brothers, it had always been Sebastian getting the bailouts from their father. Jacob's successes had come mostly without any help from Mr. Bates.

In the eight years since Sebastian was first introduced to Jacob, Jack had slowly learned more details about their family, even though Riley and Stephen remained in the dark. It wasn't something Sebastian wanted made public knowledge.

Mr. Bates and Jacob's mother had been high school sweethearts, but things had become tense after he'd gone off to college at the same time she'd found out she was pregnant. They broke up soon after Jacob's birth and Jacob's mother had eventually married a man who had adopted Jacob and treated him like his own son.

Mr. Bates' first wife, Sebastian's mother, hadn't liked the idea of her husband having another child and had prevented him from having a relationship with Jacob during their marriage. Even after their divorce, when Mr. Bates had begun to rebuild his relationship with Jacob, his ex-wife had made sure to keep Sebastian in the dark about his half-brother. Sebastian was a sophomore in college when his father finally introduced the half-brothers to each other.

After that introduction, Sebastian complained for a week, and after all this time, things hadn't improved.

"I hate that my father forced us to sign with Jacob's company. I hate working with that bastard," Sebastian snarled.

Jack shook his head and took a deep breath. "Your father didn't force us to sign with Jacob's company," Jack replied steadily. "He forced Jacob to sign us."

The band had shopped around for a record label for two years and no one had been interested in signing them. If it hadn't been for Mr. Bates's involvement, they'd still be playing college towns and spending more than they were making in a trip.

"Whatever," Sebastian mumbled. "The point is, we should rid ourselves of them and break off on our own." Sebastian kept ranting. "Stephen's a waste of space. I told you that when he joined us and I'll say it again: we don't need a keyboard player and he's too goody-goody for our image. And Riley's cool with the Irish accent and all, but he's almost as boring as Stephen. Sure he's fun to drink with, and he's a pretty good drummer, but we can find better."

"Riley is Scottish, not Irish," Jack corrected and rolled his eyes. Riley had been with them for almost eight years—Sebastian should know where he was from.

"Whatever." Sebastian waved his hand dismissively. "My point is, we can do better without them. If Jacob tears up the contract—and let's face it, we're going to get rid of her so he will—we'll move on, find another drummer, find another label, and be better than ever."

Jack considered Sebastian's words. "How long have you been thinking about this?"

"A few weeks probably. Let's be honest, the problem isn't really with the managers leaving. The problem is that the two of them," he pointed to the back of the van in front of them, "are dragging us down. Stephen never thinks my songs are good enough, even after you've made copies and we've played through them. And Riley should have picked a side years ago, but he never gives an opinion one way or the other."

"That's just how he is." Jack looked at the taillights of the van in front of them. "You seriously don't get it, do you?"

"What?" Sebastian snapped.

"The managers leave because you drive them away and you drive them away because you don't like what they're telling you."

"I've tried their way. It doesn't work," Sebastian grumbled.

"That's almost laughable. You don't try things their way unless it suits your wants, and even then not for very long. The problem isn't them, it's you." Jack paused to take a few deep, calming breaths.

"I told you the other night that if we want to be big, we have to act big." Sebastian looked at Jack with a slight smirk.

"Who told you that and how much did you pay them?" Jack already had a pretty good idea.

"Madame something-or-other," Sebastian shrugged.

Probably one of his kook psychics and another former drain on their budget. Jack had figured as much.

"Wow, such important knowledge and you can't even remember the name of the woman who gave it to you. I'm sure she'd be crushed," Jack replied monotonously. "Did it even occur to you that when the past managers told you that we, as a band, couldn't afford something like a massage or a personal chef just for you, they actually meant that we, as a band, couldn't afford it? They weren't trying to be difficult, they had a job to do—one you constantly made harder by acting like an ass."

"You've never cared about that before. Are you taking her side over mine?" Sebastian growled.

"No," Jack groaned in frustration. "This isn't her versus you. This is about what's best for the band. I finally looked at the numbers. I saw how little money we're bringing in compared to how much you're singlehandedly spending," Jack spat as he turned to glare at Sebastian. "So, until things improve, you'll have to survive on your damn fifty dollars a day."

Sebastian scowled at the road in front of them and Jack glowered at the side of his face for another second. When he finally turned his attention back to the road, he released a long breath and thought about everything he'd said. Satisfied it hadn't sounded too much like a defense of Kerrigan, he finally relaxed into his seat and they rode in silence.

After a few more mile markers passed, Sebastian finally spoke again. "I think I know what I'm going to do to her next."

Jack raised an incredulous eyebrow and gave Sebastian a side-eyed glance. "Do I want to know?"

Sebastian laughed. "Probably not."

"I said leave it to me."

Sebastian smiled widely. "Just trying to help you out."

Jack's palms suddenly itched to wring Sebastian's selfish neck.

Three hours later, Jack sat on the stage tuning his guitar as he watched Kerrigan talk to the venue director just off the side of the stage. She held her black binder like a shield against her chest. When she wasn't pointing and waving to different areas of the auditorium, she wrapped both arms around the binder. Jack noticed her feet were squared with her body, but if the man moved, Kerrigan did as well, maintaining the same distance between them. The man didn't really seem to notice it, and Jack wondered if Kerrigan was even aware she was doing it.

The movement was so subtle, Jack had almost missed it. But coupled with her reaction to the mob of men outside her room the night before, there was something about her behavior that bothered him. Something wasn't right, but he had no idea what it could possibly be.

"I'm not sure I like the way you're watching her," Stephen said as he sat down on the edge of the stage next to Jack.

Jack shrugged and focused on his guitar.

"Is there something I should know about?" Stephen asked carefully.

Jack looked at him. "What do you mean?"

"I saw your little conversation this morning. Or . . . let me clarify. I saw you go behind the van and then after a while I saw you both come out from behind the van in different directions, both of you with smiles on your faces." Stephen leaned back on one hand. "So, is there something going on between the two of you?"

Jack shook his head. "No, she was just giving me coffee and we had a brief chat." Now he had an idea why she'd been so wary.

"Coffee, huh?" Stephen nodded and looked toward Kerrigan. "Why?"

"Why not?"

"There was coffee in the lobby of the hotel. If you'd wanted some, you could have gotten it there." Stephen's stare focused on Jack's face, boring into him.

Jack weighed his options. Their conversation had been innocent enough, but his feelings for her weren't. If he told his friend the truth, he'd have to be careful not to say too much.

However, unlike Sebastian, Stephen would probably approach the situation with more sympathy and understanding.

Jack blew out a breath. "It was a 'thank you' of sorts. For last night."

Stephen's eyes widened and filled with anger. "Last night? What the hell, Jack? She's not one of our groupies, she's our manager and deserves more respect than that."

"I respect her more than you could ever know," Jack snapped, not appreciating the conclusion Stephen had jumped to. He quickly explained Sebastian's prank from the night before and the actions he'd taken to defend and protect Kerrigan from the horde of men.

Stephen's mouth fell open as his head shook from side to side. "Sorry, man, I didn't realize."

"No problem," Jack muttered, knowing that Stephen and Riley's room had been on the floor above his and Kerrigan's. As he watched Stephen now, he realized it was the first time they'd had a chance to talk in private since Kerrigan had joined them. "Why didn't you tell me you want to call it quits?"

Stephen looked at the floor. "She told you that, huh?"

"Yeah," Jack answered. "She did. You should have."

"I know," Stephen said as he lifted his face to Jack's again. "Truth is, I've wanted to go since Sebastian ran Debra off. She didn't let me choose. If she had, I would have chosen her."

Jack nodded and looked toward Kerrigan, who was still talking to the director. If she asked him to choose the band or her, what would he choose? Three days ago, he would have easily said the band.

Now? He wasn't so sure.

"So why do you stay?" Jack questioned, turning his attention back to his friend.

Stephen's lips lifted and he chuckled to himself. "To keep you out of trouble."

"Hmm." Jack tilted his head. "You haven't been doing a very good job of it."

"No, I haven't, have I?" Stephen agreed. "It would help if you would cooperate with my efforts."

They both laughed quietly and Jack noticed Kerrigan briefly glance at them. As his laughter faded, he turned to Stephen again. "What's she doing?"

Stephen blew out a long, slow breath. "She's trying to find out where she can set up to sell merchandise during the show."

Jack looked at Kerrigan again then at Stephen. "Who's going to man the table?"

"She is."

Jack's brow furrowed. "By herself?"

Stephen nodded and Jack's jaw dropped. Kerrigan would be alone in the middle of the rowdy concert crowd. She'd spent the last two concerts hovering at the side of the stage, her back to the wall, avoiding interaction with everyone but the club managers. And after what he'd witnessed the night before and the way she was behaving now with the director, he wondered if she would truly be comfortable selling to the crowd by herself.

"Is Debra in town?" Jack asked.

Even though she'd had problems with Sebastian, if she wasn't working, Stephen's fiancée still joined him, in a separate hotel of course, when the band stayed multiple nights in one location. It was Friday night and they'd be in Birmingham all weekend so Jack hoped she'd be there.

"Yeah," Stephen answered. "She's just waiting to check in to her hotel."

"Do you think she'd mind lending Kerrigan a hand tonight?" Jack asked.

Debra would be familiar with the merchandise and she'd always done well selling it. And more importantly, Kerrigan wouldn't be alone.

"Probably not, but you know Sebastian won't like that." Stephen gave a small chuckle. "I think the more important question is, why are you so concerned?"

Jack watched Kerrigan shake the director's hand, literally keeping him at arm's length. "Just because," he muttered as Kerrigan started walking toward them.

He turned his attention to his guitar and was looking down when her feet stopped in front of him. Not surprisingly, there was a distance between them similar to the one she'd kept between herself and the venue director. He looked up, hoping to see her smiling face. Instead, she held her binder tightly in front of her and was looking at Stephen.

"He thinks the best place to set up will be beside that staircase right there." Kerrigan pointed as she spoke. "That is the main entrance. Most people will be coming in that door so we'll be directly in their line of sight. He's going to lend us a table."

"We have one of those," Stephen said.

"True, but his will be larger. More space equals more merch on the table." Kerrigan gave Stephen a bright smile.

When she turned that grin on him and met his stare, Jack's heart skipped a beat.

"Now," she said, slowly pulling her gaze away from his and focusing on Stephen again, "do we have a tablecloth?"

"No." Stephen shook his head. "The ones we use are disposable and we throw them away every few shows."

Kerrigan quickly typed something into her iPhone. "That won't do. We need something sturdier and longer lasting. I'll pick up one of those today. Do we have a cash box?"

Stephen nodded.

"Does it have cash in it?" Kerrigan continued her questions.

"I think so," Stephen answered.

"I'll check before I go out. If I need to run by the bank, I've already found a branch close by."

"You're going out?" Jack asked as he set his guitar back onto its stand behind him.

"Of course," Kerrigan nodded. "I have things I need to do before the show tonight and I have a meeting at tomorrow night's venue. Also, I can see about getting our hotel rooms ready while you guys are here setting up."

Jack tried to think of a way to offer to go with her. He wanted a chance to find out why she'd been so frightened the night before, if for no other reason than to make sure it didn't happen again.

"I'll come with you," Stephen offered as he rose to his feet.

"Don't you need to stay here and help set up?" Kerrigan asked as she stepped backward.

Stephen thumbed over his shoulder. "Jack can handle that."

Kerrigan raised an eyebrow as she looked at Jack. "Really?"

Jack frowned. Did she have to sound so doubtful?

Stephen laughed. "Yes, really. Besides, there's someone I'd like to introduce you to," he said as he headed toward the door.

"Who?" Kerrigan asked as she turned to follow him.

Jack noticed Kerrigan was careful to keep a safe distance from Stephen as well.

"My fiancée." Stephen smiled widely at her.

Kerrigan looked puzzled. "You have a fiancée?"

Jack couldn't tell by her tone if she was disappointed or just surprised, but his relief was palpable when Stephen nodded his head and Kerrigan grinned.

"She's in town?"

Stephen's head bobbed again and they continued to walk toward the door. Jack watched them until they disappeared from his sight, then went backstage to see what he could do to occupy his time.

Ten

Kerrigan took an immediate liking to Stephen's fiancée, Debra Scott. She was a few inches shorter than Kerrigan with shoulder length hair the color of rich mahogany. Her bright green eyes sparkled with intelligence and more than a little mischief.

As they set up the table for the merchandise, Debra told her stories of how she and Stephen had met and gave Kerrigan a few peeks into the band's early days. Debra talked about a time when all the members of the band got along, before they got their contract with Jacob's record label.

"What happened?" Kerrigan couldn't help but ask as she folded the T-shirts and laid them out on the table.

Debra sighed. "I don't know. Sebastian's always acted like a spoiled brat. With a rich father who never said no to him and a mother who wouldn't discipline her son because she didn't want him to dislike her, how could he not be? Even though Stephen and Jack wrote all of the songs, Sebastian sang them and people always told him how wonderful he sounded. He started believing all the hype and got it in his head that the band's success was all his doing and started acting outlandishly.

"At first, it was a little amusing," Debra continued with a shrug. "His behavior wasn't much more outrageous than he'd done before, so it worked for a while and the other three sort of let him be. When it started to become problematic, it was too late for them to step in and stop it."

Kerrigan picked up another plastic tub and set it on the table. "So, how long has it been a problem then?"

"A year and a half. Maybe longer."

"What ha—" Kerrigan took the lid off the tub, expecting to find more tees. Instead, the tub was filled with colorful scarves. She picked a couple of them up and studied them, looking for a band logo, or something to identify them as merchandise. Finding nothing, she held them up to Debra. "What are these?"

Debra's lips turned up. "Those are Sebastian's." She pointed toward the stage. "The ones he ties to his mic stand."

Kerrigan glanced at the stage and saw five or six colorful scarves draped from Sebastian's mic stand. "Why does he need so many?" Kerrigan asked as she placed the scarves back in the tub.

"They're his invitations." Debra answered and Kerrigan's confusion must have still shown on her face. "Don't tell me you haven't seen him hand them to fans. Usually younger blonde women." Debra bent down and picked up a small box as Kerrigan tried to remember.

"Oh, yeah. I have seen that," Kerrigan answered.

"Well, didn't you see the women backstage after the concert? Or at the hotel?" Debra asked as she opened the box.

Kerrigan nodded. "Ah, I get it. No, actually, I didn't see the women backstage, but then I don't linger after the concerts either." She peered into the box Debra had opened and saw it was filled with guitar picks. "Those would be good to sell. Do they have the band logo?" She picked several up and examined the front and backs. The only thing she saw was a "U" on one side and an "I" on the other.

Debra laughed. "No, those are Jack's calling cards. 'I' pick 'U'. Get it?"

Kerrigan dropped them back into the box as if she'd been burned. Yeah, she got it. She tried to remember if she'd seen him hand any out at the last two concerts.

"How delightfully chauvinistic," she muttered.

She should have expected it. That was part of the reputation of any rock band. But the idea that the Jackson she knew would do such a thing left her with a sour taste in her mouth. It just drove home her impression that he was no longer the man she'd once known. She couldn't decide if she was more saddened or repulsed as she pushed the box away.

"Do I even want to know what Riley does?" Kerrigan put the lid back on the tub full of scarves.

"Probably not. His is probably the most superficial and medieval, but being behind the band and unable to see the crowd, he doesn't have much choice. He tells Jack and Stephen what he's looking for that night, you know, blonde and busty or brunette and rail-thin, and they scan the crowd for him." Debra shook her head. "I'm really not sure who to feel sorrier for, him or the girls."

Kerrigan remained silent as her mind began to work. She decided not to focus on how sexist the practice was and instead tried to figure out if she could turn it to their advantage.

"Hi Jack," Debra said and Kerrigan looked up to see him standing directly in front of her.

"Hi Debra," he responded in his slow drawl as he smiled at her. "How have you been?"

Debra walked around the table and wrapped her arms around Jack's neck and Kerrigan quickly squashed the feelings of jealousy that surfaced. Despite his chivalrous actions the night before, he had changed over the years from the Jackson she'd fallen in love with. The discovery of his picks just reinforced what she'd realized at her first meeting with the band. She needed to remember they were both different people now.

Debra released him. "I've been good, how about you?" she replied as a smirk started to form on her lips. "Did you come for these?" With a giggle, she opened the box of picks and slid them toward Jack.

He glanced at the box and his cheeks turned a light shade of red. He looked back up at Kerrigan and she quickly averted her gaze and began to busy herself with the CDs on the table. How would he answer that question?

More importantly, why should she care?

"Uh, no, I'm good."

Kerrigan's hand stilled as she closed her eyes for a moment, relief washing over her. At least she wouldn't have to think about him with another woman for one more night.

"So what brings you over here?" Debra asked and Kerrigan allowed herself a brief glance at Jack.

She wished she hadn't. He was staring at her, and as soon as their eyes met her heart skipped a beat and butterflies began fluttering in her stomach. His eyes darkened slightly and she suddenly felt warm all over.

Without taking his eyes off of her, he answered Debra's question, "Just came to see if you need any help."

Kerrigan shook her head. "No, I think we've got it. Are you all ready for the show then?"

"Yeah, everything's done." Jack nodded then glanced at Debra and looked startled, almost as if he'd forgotten she was there. He inched backward.

"You okay?" Debra asked and Kerrigan looked at her. Debra's brow was furrowed as she stared at Jack. "You seem a bit distracted."

"Nah, I'm good. Just looking for something to do," Jack answered as he looked down at the table and straightened one of the CDs. "I guess I'll go double check things on stage." He turned and walked away from the two of them.

With a faint smile, Debra shook her head as she watched him go. "Poor thing," she murmured as she moved behind the table and picked up the tub of scarves.

Kerrigan patiently waited for her to elaborate. She wanted to know why Debra sounded so sympathetic toward Jack, who had seemed fine to her, and, as ridiculous as it sounded, what she could do to help him feel better. In silence, Debra placed the tub under the table and slid the box of guitar picks toward herself.

Tired of waiting, Kerrigan asked, "What do you mean?"

"What?" Debra looked up and met her stare and Kerrigan waved in Jack's direction. "Oh, it's nothing." Debra laid her hands on the top of the box and glanced toward the stage. "I just worry about him. He used to hand these things out like candy." She patted the box of picks.

Kerrigan's nose wrinkled at the thought.

"But now, more often than not, he just doesn't seem interested."

"Really?" Kerrigan breathed her relief. "Why?"

"I wish I knew." She frowned. "Stephen worries that Jack's on a downward spiral. He says that since the tour started, he's seeing Jack act more and more like Sebastian. Sometimes worse. Stephen's tried talking to him, but Jack doesn't listen." Debra shrugged and looked at the table. "Until he wants help, there's nothing we can do."

Kerrigan felt light-headed and pressed her palm into the table. "Alcohol?" she offered, remembering the bottle he'd ordered at the brasserie in Paris. It was the only thing she could think of.

Debra shook her head. "Sorry to say, it's not. If anything, Stephen tells me he's drinking less now than in the seven years they've known each other." She drummed her fingers on the box. "They once did a four-month tour of college towns, before they got picked up by Jacob's label. Jack handed these picks out like he was giving candy to children. And he was drinking like a fish. I'd never seen anyone go through so much beer in such a short amount of time as Jack did on that tour. But recently, he's been off the booze."

Kerrigan could check alcoholism off her list of concerns then.

Debra's hands stilled and she stared at the stage. "Back then, it almost seemed like he was trying to forget something. Or someone. After that tour they got picked up by Jacob's company and he's been better." Her head bobbed from side to side. "Until recently, anyway." Debra pointed to the box again. "He went through a box half this size in that first tour."

Kerrigan eyed the box carefully. It was just slightly smaller than a toaster. That was a lot of picks. A lot of women. Her stomach began to roll and she leaned against the rail behind her.

"I guess the good news is, he's had this box for a year and a half and it looks like it's still half full." Debra turned to Kerrigan and her smile quickly faded. "Are you okay? You look a little pale."

Kerrigan swallowed. "Yeah, I'm fine. I just haven't eaten much today."

"Why don't we remedy that?" Stephen said as he approached. "I'm starving."

Debra walked around the table and put her arm around Stephen's waist as he kissed her forehead.

Kerrigan looked away from the tender act as tears formed in her eyes. She'd long ago accepted that she'd probably never marry. Her pending old-maid status was even a running joke between herself and Charlie. She'd gotten used to seeing her brother and friends share sweet moments like this one between Debra and Stephen. But being so close to Jackson again and realizing that he was really not the Jackson she knew, made her realize she still wanted someone to share those moments with.

To make matters worse, she realized she still wanted that someone to be Jackson. She was just no longer sure *that* Jackson still existed.

"Kerrigan, you coming?" Stephen asked and motioned toward the exit with his head.

Kerrigan looked at her watch.

"Of course she is, she looks like she's about to pass out." Debra gave her a large smile.

"Great," Riley said as he stopped on Stephen's other side. "Party of five. Let's go, I'm starving."

Jack slowly approached them, his focus on Kerrigan.

How was she going to get out of this? She had half a mind to "accidentally" clear the table of all the merchandise so she would have to stay and set it up again, but quickly crossed that off the list. They'd probably all volunteer to stay and help. Her eyes landed on the box of picks, then lifted to Riley. Ah, yes. Work.

"I can't, I have some things I need to take care of before the concert."

"Like what?" Jack asked.

Kerrigan hated the way his voice still had a way of soothing her.

"Kerrigan, it can wait. You need to eat," Debra said as she held her hand up and waved Kerrigan closer. "C'mon. Whatever it is, I can help after dinner."

Kerrigan was frozen to the spot but her eyes were drawn to Jack again. He was still staring at her and as she met his gaze, his lips turned up slightly. He nodded with his head toward the door and she shook hers. His smile flat-lined.

"You guys go on ahead. We'll be right behind you," he said and the others turned and walked out the side exit.

She listened as their footsteps faded. Jack stepped around the table. He stopped just before he reached her and her heart began to race. He hadn't touched her; she didn't know what she'd do if he did. Her flight response was on high alert and ready to take her away, but underneath that, a very small part of her knew she was safe with him. She hadn't felt truly safe with any man since Paris.

"It's dinner, Kerrigan," he stated smoothly. "You need to eat."

"I know," she replied petulantly. "I just have work to do."

"You always have work to do. I've watched you work through seven meals now. I've also watched you eat next to nothing since you joined us." He stepped directly in front of her and leaned his hips against the table as he folded his arms across his chest. "If I weren't going, would you have gone with them?"

Kerrigan looked at the floor. "Probably not."

He chuckled. "That's what I thought."

She looked up at him, her brow furrowed in confusion.

"You're lying."

Her jaw dropped. "How dare you."

"What? Call you on it?" Jack lifted an eyebrow and she felt some of her tension drain away. "You forget I've seen you lie to your brother? And Olivia?"

She pressed her lips together until the urge to smile passed. "Yes, I guess I forgot." She crossed her arms as she stared at him. "Can you blame me?" It was his turn to look confused so she pointed to the box behind him. "I certainly wouldn't have expected the guy I knew to use guitar picks to invite women to his bed. And a whole box in four months?" She clucked her tongue at him as she shook her head.

He reached around and picked up the box, a self-deprecating smile on his face. "I really wish you hadn't found these."

"Why?"

"Because that guy isn't someone I wanted you to know." He looked at her and the look in his emerald eyes took her breath away. "He isn't someone I'm proud of."

She could see the honesty in his eyes, along with turmoil and a hint of sadness. She wanted to wrap her arms around him to try to soothe him, at least a little, the way he used to comfort her. But Kerrigan hadn't hugged any man but her brother in years. She wasn't sure she could start with Jack. Not yet anyway. Not until she was over him.

She pulled her arms closer to her body. "You don't have to be a person you're not proud of."

Jack stood and took a step toward her. Kerrigan waited for her heart to race and her feet to itch to get away, her automatic response when any man got close.

"You make it sound so easy." He shook his head. "If you only knew how much I've tried." He turned and put the box on the table and opened it. "What else did Debra tell you?" he asked over his shoulder.

Kerrigan watched mesmerized as Jack dipped his hand into the box and lifted it out as the picks ran through his fingers like sand. "Nothing."

"You're sure?" He turned around to face her.

"I'm just hungry," Kerrigan said as she looked away from him again. She felt him lean closer and her heart finally sped up, but she was surprised to realize it wasn't because she wanted to run from him. His cheek was nearly touching hers.

"You're lying," he whispered, his words caressing her ear.

She could feel his heat and her breathing became shallow and fast. She closed her eyes and tried to relax her heartrate and breathing back to normal.

She'd already accepted that Jack may have the same packaging as Jackson, but they were not the same person. The sooner her heart recognized what her head already knew, the sooner she could stop reacting like she had when it had just been a schoolgirl crush. She was older and wiser now; it was time she acted like it.

"Hey," came Riley's Scottish brogue from across the room and her eyes popped open. "Ye coming to dinner?"

Jack pushed away from the table and stared deeply into her eyes. She felt like he was seeing into her soul even as he stepped back and motioned for her to lead the way. When she looked ahead, she saw that one of Riley's eyebrows had nearly disappeared into his hairline. She avoided meeting his gaze as she walked past him and out of the auditorium.

Eleven

From beside the stage, Jack watched Kerrigan as she and Debra chatted behind the merchandise table. Debra was pointing at Kerrigan's hair and touching her own shoulders.

"She's quite smart, don't ye think?" Riley said, twirling a drumstick between his fingers as he leaned against the wall behind the stage. "And witty as well."

"Mm-hm." Jack couldn't take his eyes off the two women as he tried to figure out what they were saying.

"I love the way she handles Sebastian," Riley continued. "Do you think she'd go out wi' me?"

That last statement caused an alarm to go off in Jack's head. He turned his attention to Riley and narrowed his eyes. "Who are you talking about?"

"Kerrigan, o' course." Riley rolled his eyes upward as he chuckled. "Did you know she'd lived in London? We talked about it during dinner. Made me a little homesick."

"You're not from England," Jack replied testily.

"No, but talking to her about the city, the sights, the sounds, the tastes . . . It brought me closer to home than I've been in a long time." The drumstick stopped spinning and Riley got a glazed look in his eyes.

Jack nodded and turned toward the merch table again. His eyes widened when he saw that Kerrigan's hair had been released from its tight bun and was falling in waves over her shoulders. His mouth was suddenly dry when she turned slightly and he caught a glimpse of the side of her face, her pale skin surrounded by a halo of ebony hair.

"I thought she was living in Switzerland." Jack turned to Riley, determined to focus on the conversation before his attention to Kerrigan was noticed.

"She did, but she was in London before that," Riley answered. "And before that, Paris."

Jack nodded as he tried to plot her path in his mind, filling in all the years he'd missed.

Riley began twirling his drumstick again. "So, d'ye think I could ask her out?"

Jack pressed his lips together as he scrambled for an answer for Riley. An answer that, God willing, wouldn't make him look like a total hypocrite later. He simply shook his head.

"No?" Riley tilted his head and looked toward the ladies behind the table. "Probably not her type, right?"

"How the hell should I know?" Jack scoffed as he pretended to look at the growing crowd. "She doesn't seem to be the type who would be into rock-star drummers though."

"Aye," Riley slowly dragged out the word. "But maybe she could be into rock-star guitarists, right?"

Jack stiffened and shifted his eyes to see Riley in his peripheral. "Doubt that, too," he answered and his chest tightened like a vice.

He'd been trying not to consider those words or that sentiment since she'd walked into that meeting room two days ago. While he still blamed Charlie for denying him a relationship with Kerri in the first place, over the past few years he'd been doing everything in his power to avoid seeing her, or even hearing about her. He realized now it had been fear that she'd find out about his behavior. And now that she knew, he'd seen the disappointment in her eyes.

And he hated it more than he'd expected.

"Well then, won't know until we try." Riley's voice was suddenly a bit brighter.

Jack glared at him. "No," he practically growled.

"No?" Riley raised a thick, red eyebrow. "Are ye agreeing wi' me?"

"No, I'm telling you not to try it. She's off limits," Jack answered tightly.

"To everyone?" Riley tucked his drumstick into the back pocket of his jeans with the other one. "Or just me?" There was a brief pause as Riley rose to his feet and took a step closer to Jack. "I've seen the way ye watch her. I can tell ye're interested."

Jack's jaw clenched as he folded his arms across his chest. That made two of his bandmates that had noticed his attentions. Had Kerrigan noticed them too? Until he could figure out how solid his footing was, he'd have to be more careful. She'd always had a tendency of running from situations she wasn't comfortable with, and the last thing he wanted her to do was run from him.

"We should go get ready for the show." Jack walked past Riley, farther backstage, deciding it was best to ignore Riley's questioning tone.

Kerrigan ran her hand down the length of her hair again and tried not to frown as she took money from a customer. Except for special occasions, she'd worn her hair up for four years. Her hair had always been long and dark, something that garnered compliments and unwanted attention from strangers. Or from people she'd once considered friends. Because of that, she felt vulnerable with it down.

She hated feeling vulnerable and she hated the reminder of why she felt that way.

But Debra had convinced her that letting out her hair might make her more approachable. Kerrigan had tried to argue that assumption until Debra pointed out it could boost sales. Reluctantly she'd pulled out the elastic band and finger-combed the loose waves.

"Stop it, you look fine."

Kerrigan looked up and met Debra's smiling gaze, then realized her fingers were threaded in her hair again. She eased her hand down as she stepped toward the table and began straightening the CDs.

"You're not used to having it down, are you?" Debra asked as she moved to Kerrigan's side.

"No, not really," Kerrigan admitted softly as she shifted the last CD half a millimeter so it was flush against the one next to it. She dropped her hands to the edge of the table and turned to face Debra.

Debra set her hip against the table and smiled. "Did I hear you tell Riley you grew up in Virginia?"

"Yes, I did," Kerrigan replied.

"Did you know that Jack and Stephen both grew up in Virginia, too?"

Debra beamed as she cast a quick glance at the stage over the standing crowd.

The band had been playing for about half an hour and what had started as a small crowd of dancers between their table and the stage had steadily grown as the crowd had slowly trickled out of the seats behind them and onto the floor in front. There was no more room to dance, so the sea of heads were all bobbing in unison, with an occasional bounce of excitement when a new song started. Kerrigan hated crowds, so she was glad she had the space of the table between her and the audience and thankful Debra was beside her. Otherwise, this could have possibly been her worst idea yet.

"It hasn't come up," Kerrigan said honestly as a knot formed in her stomach. She hoped Debra didn't ask more about her childhood or talk too much about Jack's. Kerrigan wasn't sure she wanted Debra to know she and Jack had grown up together. It just felt wrong to admit it since the man he was now wasn't even a shadow of the man he used to be.

At least to her.

"Yeah," Debra continued, facing Kerrigan again. "Stephen grew up at the beach. Jack grew up in a little town called Rocky Creek."

Kerrigan nodded slowly. "Is that so?" She reached for her water bottle under the table and lifted it to her lips.

"We live there now, actually," Debra announced.

Kerrigan's eyes widened slightly before she took a long, slow gulp of water. She lowered the bottle and took her time twisting the top back onto it.

"Have you ever heard of it?" Debra's eyes sharpened on the water bottle in Kerrigan's hand.

"I'm not sure." Kerrigan bent over and set her bottle back under the table. "Where did you grow up?" she asked as she rose and turned toward Debra.

"A little town just outside of Raleigh. What about you?" Debra smiled.

Kerrigan cursed under her breath. She should have known that would be the next question asked. "A small community in the foothills." At least it was truthful. "Did you meet Stephen in college then?"

Debra frowned for a moment then just as quickly it disappeared. "Yes, we were both at Tech. I was with him before he joined the band. What about you, where did you go?"

"James Madison," Kerrigan answered.

Debra nodded and opened her mouth to speak again but was beaten by a masculine voice from the other side of the table.

"I'd like to buy some CDs and a T-shirt," the man said, beaming widely at Kerrigan.

She smiled in return and took a step toward the edge of the table and gave him a once over. She supposed he wasn't bad looking: his blond hair was short and combed neatly to one side, his square jaw bore a hint of shadow, and he was about a head taller than her. She looked at the items in his large, strong hands and felt panic rise in her chest. He was the perfect example of a man she would normally avoid at all costs. He looked kind enough, but she knew how much danger could lie behind a kind facade.

Her smile tightened and she wished there was more than a table-width between them as she reached for the items he was holding out. He gave her a lascivious smile and held tight to his merchandise. She let go, refusing to play tug-of-war, and reached under the table for a plastic bag, keeping her focus on him the whole time.

"They have you chained to that table?" he asked as his eyes traveled the length of her body.

"I'm sorry?" she asked, keeping her voice as steady as she could. She managed to stop her hands from shaking as she reached for the items again. He let her have them and she slid them into the bag.

He held his cash to her. "I was just wondering if you could get away," he purred. "Maybe let me show you a little bit of fun." He winked as she took his money.

Kerrigan stared at the cash in the box and focused on making change for him. This was why she always wore her hair up. It helped prevent this sort of attention.

"Who do I need to talk to?" he continued.

Kerrigan looked up to give him his change, surprised to find him within inches of her face. She fell back a step. "Talk to?"

"To get you out of work." He gave her a lopsided grin that made her stomach turn. "What about after the show?"

Her body stiffened as she held his change out to him. "I'm sorry, sir," she said tightly, fighting the urge to run. "But there's a roomful of women here who would probably be more than happy to consider your offer."

His grin widened. "But most of them are hoping to have some fun with the band after the show." He took his change and wrapped his hand around hers. "You don't look as interested in the band, so I thought I could interest you in some fun of your own."

Fear shook her entire body as she tugged on her hand, trying to ease it out of his grip. "I'm the band's manager," she stated, trying to sound as composed as possible.

His eyes widened in surprise and he released her.

"And I assure you, I have better things to do with my time." She gave him his bag.

"Well, if you change your mind—"

She held up her hand, the steady one, to stop him. "I won't."

He gave her another once over, shrugged, and turned. She blew out a shaky breath and looked around the crowd, waiting for the tension to recede. She looked toward the stage and saw Jack's gaze fixated on her. Even from this distance, she could recognize the concern in his eyes. She gave him a single nod and the tension drained from her body.

When she turned to Debra, she was surprised to see the other woman staring at her with a raised eyebrow.

"What?" Kerrigan asked.

"First of all, good job. That guy was a jerk and you were much kinder than I would have been," Debra said with a small laugh that quickly faded. "Don't ever worry about that. If I'm here, I've got your back."

"And if you're not here?" Kerrigan scoffed.

"Then you will most likely have help from the stage."

Kerrigan looked toward the band again and saw Jack's eyes still full of concern and focused on her.

"Where did you say you were from again?" Debra repeated even though they both knew Kerrigan hadn't told her.

"Just a tiny little place," Kerrigan said as she looked at the table. "Why?"

Debra remained silent until Kerrigan met her stare again. "It's just the way Jack stares at you. So intently, so often. Almost like he knows you." Her lips lifted and she waggled her eyebrows. "Or he'd like to anyway."

The heat began in Kerrigan's chest and slowly crept to her cheeks. "He does not."

She cast a quick glance toward the stage and saw Jack was now focused on the fret board of his guitar. Kerrigan noticed his leather cuff as his fingers slid along the fret's length.

Her eyes narrowed as she remembered his words. Debra seemed to know almost everything about the band. Would she know Jack's secrets?

"Is Jack hoping to start a new trend with that cuff?" Kerrigan laughed, hoping to divert Debra's attention. She looked at the other woman.

Debra smiled. "I know, right? I once asked him why he wore it and he said ''cause I want to'." She shrugged then chuckled as she greeted the next customer.

Kerrigan frowned but remained silent. So Debra didn't know everything. Jack must have a reason for keeping that secret to himself.

He wore the cuff on the same wrist as the tattoo. She couldn't help but wonder why, or how she could find out, without asking him about it.

Twelve

Uncooperative and disrespectful. Exhibits self-destructive behaviors. Concern for his mental stability.

Kerrigan frowned and read the words again.

It had taken a few days to get through all the files Jacob had emailed her, but she was finally getting to the documentation of her predecessors' experiences with Malhypnus. She was currently reading through a final email correspondence between Jacob and one of the band's former managers.

Those words had been typed about Jack.

"Jackson is not self-destructive," she muttered out loud. She looked at her reflection in the hotel room mirror and her frown deepened.

She had to stop thinking of him as Jackson.

The Jackson she knew wouldn't hand out guitar picks to random women as a sign he wanted to sleep with them. It was beyond disrespectful. She still remembered what Jackson had told her about his last conversation with his father. Police Lieutenant John Harris raised his sons to treat women with respect, and this kind of behavior would have appalled him.

And then there were the twins. Kerrigan couldn't forget the image of him walking into that first meeting. She couldn't stomach the idea that that was a regular occurrence for him.

She turned away from the mirror and exhaled a breath of frustration.

On the other hand, Jack's behavior really hadn't been all bad since she'd joined the band. He had come to her aid after Sebastian's massage stunt the other night and she hadn't had an ounce of trouble out of him. He had also been contrite regarding the picks. These were things she would have expected from Jackson, so maybe he wasn't really as different as she wanted to think.

She plopped onto the bed.

There were so many reasons she should stop thinking of him as Jackson and start seeing him as Jack, the man he wanted to be now. It was better for her that way. If she thought of him as a stranger, it would be easier to keep a safe distance between them, the way she did with all strangers. She would never tell a stranger about the darkest moments in her life, and the last thing she wanted to do was tell Jack what really happened in Paris. It was safer for her heart, which would ultimately break if she let herself believe he was the same person and he proved her wrong.

She almost wished he would do something dramatic to make it easier for her to separate his past persona from his present. But she was afraid that no matter how outrageous it was, she would never be able to completely forget her feelings for him.

A soft knock sounded on her door and she moved to answer it. Without looking in the peephole, she threw the door open.

Her eyes widened and she swallowed the lump in her throat. "Jack. What are you doing here?"

Jack smiled lazily at her as his eyes wandered the length of her body. She was wearing form-hugging workout clothes that showed off her feminine curves. For the first time, he could clearly see what he'd noticed the first day. She was much thinner than she used to be, and the fact that he hadn't seen her eat much since joining them added to his concern.

"Looking for you." He leaned his shoulders against the door frame.

"Why?"

He heard her hesitate and tried not to frown. Did she have to make his company sound like such a chore?

"Because you snuck away last night—"

"I didn't sneak away," she interrupted, looking him squarely in the eyes, and he raised an eyebrow. "Well, I didn't." She averted her gaze, focusing on the door frame beside him. "I just finished up before the rest of you and Debra was kind enough to give me a ride back to the hotel."

"But she had to come back for Stephen," Jack stated and Kerrigan shrugged one shoulder. "You could have waited for the rest of us."

"I didn't know how long your after-party would last." Her cheeks turned slightly more pink as she looked at the floor between them.

So she wasn't telling the entire truth. He could almost guess what she hadn't wanted to stick around for. The after-after-party. When the band members usually left with their female companions for the evening. What piqued his curiosity was, why did she seem so embarrassed by it? Or was he just imagining things?

Sebastian had been the only one with female companionship the night before. And Stephen, of course.

"Whatever." Jack waved her comments, and his thoughts, away. "Can I come in or should we continue this conversation in the hallway?"

"Depends," she answered with another shrug. "What conversation did you come here to have?" Her eyes met his, defiant and challenging.

He'd seen that look before and tried not to smile at the memory of her as a teenager.

"Does it matter?" He folded his arms across his chest as he continued to lean against the doorframe. "After the way you snuck me a cup of coffee yesterday, I got the impression you didn't want to be seen with me."

Her mouth fell open as she gasped. "That's not—"

He held up his palm to stop her as he laughed at her discomfort. "That's not how I meant it either. I actually think you were on to something. You never know what conclusions Sebastian might jump to if he saw us together."

Like that Jack was trying to carry out Sebastian's plan. And then Sebastian would expect updates and ideas as to when Jack might complete it.

Kerrigan's mouth snapped closed and she looked both ways down the hallway. Without looking at him, she stepped back so he could enter.

"What have you been up to this morning?" he asked as he walked past her into her room.

"I went to the gym after I got up." She moved past him and toward the desk where she closed her laptop. "And I've been doing some work."

"I didn't think you liked to exercise," he said, remembering the girl who had faked illness to get out of PE in high school and had never joined in any type of sports activity outside of school if she could help it.

Her eyes were dull as she avoided his gaze. "People change," she murmured. "What is it you came here for?"

"I came to find out how the sales went last night." Jack folded his arms across his chest and watched with delight as her face slowly transformed.

Her eyes widened as she stared at him in disbelief. It was clear she hadn't been expecting his question. Her steely blue gaze held his as her lips lifted in a slight smile.

"It went well," she answered with a nod. "Debra said it's the best sales she's seen in a long time. Hopefully we can continue the trend and start to see movement in the right direction."

"Good," Jack said. "Congratulations on thinking outside of the box."

Her grin widened. "Thank you. I can't believe none of the other managers thought of it first."

"They didn't want to man the table themselves." Jack shrugged.

While he didn't really think their previous managers had all been incompetent, they certainly had lacked the desire to get their hands dirty with actual work. Something, it seemed, that didn't bother Kerrigan in the least. Even Sebastian had sounded surprised when Jack mentioned Kerrigan's willingness to sell the merchandise herself.

They fell silent and Kerrigan diverted her eyes again, looking anywhere in the room but at him. Jack waited for her to meet his gaze. He'd come to her room to ask her several things, the least important being about the sales, but now that he was with her, none of the questions would form on his tongue. Her hair was in a loose ponytail at her neck, but a few tendrils had escaped and hung freely, curling around her face.

What would those tendrils feel like wrapped around his finger?

He cleared his throat. "Why didn't you tell me you'd lived in London?"

She glanced at him for a moment. "I didn't realize you needed to know."

"You told Riley," Jack stated.

"Riley asked."

Was it really that simple? Had Riley shown an interest in her that Jack had taken for granted? Jack had simply expected her to talk to him the way she used to, freely and openly. He realized then that in the past three days, not once had she reacted to him the way she once did.

"I didn't realize I had to," Jack mumbled.

Kerrigan's brow furrowed. "Why wouldn't you have to?"

"You used to tell me everything." Jack took a step toward her and she backed up, warily watching his movements. "I guess I thought you would now too."

She froze and her head jerked up. "Of all the arrogant things."

"Arrogant?"

"Yes. Arrogant." She pressed her lips tightly together and took a few deep breaths as her stormy eyes held his. "First, I didn't always tell you everything. Second, when I did, I was sixteen and thought we were friends."

"We were friends," he snapped.

She shrugged a delicate shoulder and turned away.

"You knew I considered you a friend," Jack growled.

"I knew you considered me to be Charlie's little sister."

"You know that's not—"

She held up her hand and shook her head. "I'm sure any other questions you have can wait until our meeting. I really should take a shower and get back to work." She took a step toward the desk and laid her hands on the back of the chair.

Jack's heart rate sped up and his entire body warmed with a mixture of anger at her attempt to dismiss him, and lust. After all, she *had* mentioned a shower.

He stood his ground and crossed his arms. He'd been about to tell her she'd meant more to him than just Charlie's little sister. He most likely wouldn't have stopped until he'd told her that he'd been in love with her.

However, given their interactions over the past few days, that probably would have been a bad idea. It was no doubt a good thing she'd stopped him.

Why had she stopped him?

Had she known what he was about to say and she didn't want to hear it? Had Charlie told her about the argument they'd had? Is that why she had refused to see him in Paris? Part of him didn't want to know the answers to those questions. Another part of him wanted to clear the air between them, for better or worse. He couldn't stand the tension.

"Have you had breakfast?" he asked. That should be harmless. Stephen and Riley wouldn't think anything was out of the ordinary if they saw them eating together and, since they weren't travelling that day, Sebastian would probably sleep until noon so he'd miss them too.

Her eyes narrowed and she shook her head. "I have oatmeal." She pointed.

He moved in the direction of her finger and found several packs of instant oatmeal sitting next to the coffee maker. She appeared to be stocked for the next few days. She wouldn't have a reason to eat breakfast with anyone.

He frowned at how lonely that sounded.

"Fine." He looked at her and smiled. "Bring it with you and have your oatmeal with me."

The crease in her brow grew and her lips pursed. "I'll have it in here, thank you. I'm not eating with you."

"Weren't you just complaining that I wasn't asking you enough questions?" Jack smiled.

Kerrigan's eyes shifted side to side as she thought. "No, I was simply pointing out that Riley had asked and I had answered."

"Well, have breakfast with me. I have some questions you can answer." Jack folded his arms across his chest. "You wouldn't want me to eat alone, would you?"

"That's your business," Kerrigan said. "I do it all the time. It doesn't hurt."

Jack flexed his fingers in frustration. "I'm not taking no for an answer."

She shook her head and blew out a breath. "You're so damn stubborn," she mumbled.

"Hi Pot, I'm Kettle."

Her response was a look no doubt intended to render him dead on the spot. Instead, he simply smiled and leaned back against the wall. They were both silent for a little while, but he could tell by the glint in her eyes that she was considering a comeback.

Finally, she nodded. "Fine, if I have breakfast with you, all of your questions had better be band related. I'm not answering any personal questions from you."

Jack scoffed and stood up. "That's hardly fair. You answered Riley's last night."

"Yes, but Riley was trying to get to know me better," she said with a shrug as she moved toward the coffee maker. "You don't need to get to know me." She picked up a packet of oatmeal and waved him toward the door.

"Deal," he said as he turned to leave. Once they were eating, he would ask whatever he wanted.

He just hoped she would answer.

He opened the door and stepped out into the hallway, then turned to wait for her to join him. She was stepping through the door when he heard the thud of footsteps behind him.

"Jack, there you are," Sebastian called out. "Oh. And you." His lips curled as he glared dismissively at Kerrigan's face. "Breakfast, Jack?"

Jack cursed under his breath and glanced briefly at Kerrigan. She eyed Sebastian with her head tilted and her lips curved upward.

"Looks like your problems are solved." She turned to Jack with a full smile. "Now you don't have to eat alone." She stepped back into her room and met Jack's gaze, her eyes twinkling with mischief. As the door closed between them, she held her hand up and waggled her fingers at him.

He nearly growled out loud.

"Seriously, you wanted to have breakfast with her?" Sebastian clapped Jack on the back and steered him toward the elevator. "Oh, that's right, I nearly forgot our plan. How's that going, by the way?"

"It would go better if you didn't interfere," Jack ground out through clenched teeth.

"I haven't even begun to interfere," Sebastian stated. "Yet."

That's what Jack was afraid of.

Thirteen

"I don't care what they want, I won't do it!" Sebastian yelled across the table at Kerrigan.

It was three mornings later and they were in a hotel conference room near Tuscaloosa. They'd traveled from Birmingham the day before, and Kerrigan had found time before the previous night's show to secure another venue for a bonus performance that evening. The catch was the club required every act to perform one particular song at some point in their show. Kerrigan had agreed to have Malhypnus do it without checking with the band.

"Sebastian, please, it's not an unreasonable request. They ask all the bands to do it," Kerrigan said calmly as she rubbed circles into her temple.

"We're not a cover band—we don't sing other people's songs. Especially stupid, twangy Southern rock." Sebastian slammed his palms on the table and stood up. "Tonight was supposed to be my night off."

The door to the conference room swung open and Jack walked in . . . finally. The meeting had started five minutes ago. Kerrigan had told them all about it the night before and when he hadn't arrived on time, she'd decided to go ahead and start. It had been better than waiting and wondering where he was. At least she could credit him with the fact she'd been with the band for almost a week and this was the first time he'd been late to a meeting.

"You don't need to shout," Jack snapped. "What the hell are you yelling about anyway? I could hear you all the way down the hall." He met Kerrigan's stare. "Sorry I'm late, my alarm didn't go off."

She raised an eyebrow. As far as she knew, he hadn't handed out any picks the night before, so she guessed she could believe him.

She hoped.

"Kerrigan booked a show for us tonight," Stephen answered Jack's question. "The manager of the club has asked us to sing a particular song."

"What song?" Jack asked as he walked around the table and sat in the chair next to Kerrigan.

"If you'd been here on time, you'd know," Kerrigan muttered without looking at him.

"I told you, my alarm didn't go off," Jack repeated his excuse.

She shrugged a shoulder and kept her eyes fixed on the table.

"It doesn't matter what the song is, we're not doing it. And if that means we don't do the show, then so be it. You should have asked me before you made this arrangement." Sebastian glared at her across the table.

"The last time I checked, I was the manager of this band." Kerrigan rose to her feet. "That means I get to make the decisions regarding your performance schedule and you'll do as you're told."

"If you hadn't wasted all the band's money on frivolous crap at the beginning of the tour, she wouldn't have to add shows to our schedule," Stephen snapped at Sebastian.

"Don't you *dare* take her side over mine!" Sebastian roared as he took two steps toward Stephen. Riley stood and stepped between them.

"Why not? O' the two o' ye, she's the one wi' the entire band's best interests in mind." Riley folded his arms as he stared Sebastian down. "I say we're doin' the song and I don't give a damn what ye think."

"What song?" Jack asked again, rising to stand behind Kerrigan's shoulder. She sensed his proximity and had to suppress the shiver that ran through her.

"We can't say no, Sebastian." Stephen stepped around Riley. "What they're offering is too good to pass up."

"Enough!" Jack bellowed and Kerrigan jumped as the room fell silent.

She turned and looked at him for the first time, surprised by the dark circles under his eyes and the flaring anger in the emerald depths. He clenched his jaw as he stared at the other three band members in turn. When he looked at her, the fire faded from his green eyes, but only slightly.

"I have apologized for being late, I truly didn't mean to be, but I would like to know what is going on here," he said calmly. "Now, what song are you talking about and what is the deal they've struck with us to perform it?"

Kerrigan took a deep breath and turned her body toward his. "The club asks all bands that perform there to sing 'Sweet Home Alabama' at some point during their show. Do you know it?" She already knew the answer.

The narrow-eyed look he gave her told her he was not amused by her feigned ignorance. It was one of her favorite songs and he'd always played it for her when she had watched him and Charlie practice in her parents' garage. She'd even occasionally brushed off her homework or chores to interrupt their practice, pretending she hadn't known they were there, just to hear him sing it. She swallowed the memory and tried to shake off the warmth that had crept into her cheeks.

"Yeah, I think I can manage it," he replied drily.

"Good," Kerrigan croaked. "The manager of the club has promised half of the beverage sales during the song and for fifteen minutes afterwards. He says the bands that sing it later in the set usually see the most money."

"And what kind of payment system do they have without the drink money?" Jack asked.

"A guarantee of five hundred." Kerrigan had thought that for a last-minute booking on a Tuesday night, it had been too good of a deal to pass up. Especially knowing she could probably make almost that much in merchandise sales for the night. The band could potentially clear a thousand dollars with this last minute addition, and that could only move them in the right direction.

She watched as Jack nodded his head then looked across the table at the others, settling his gaze on Sebastian. Kerrigan couldn't take her eyes off of the lines of Jack's face, especially the dark stubble lining his jaw. Her fingers tingled to touch it. Was it soft or coarse? She shook the thought away and focused on the wall directly across from her.

"We're doing the show and we're doing the song," Jack said simply and Kerrigan's eyes jumped to his. "We won't pass this up."

"I won't sing it," Sebastian argued.

"You don't have to," Jack replied. "I'll take the lead. You can just play."

"No."

Jack blew out a long breath. "Have it your way then. The rest of us will perform the song and you can stand on the stage and look like an ass. I really don't care."

Kerrigan's mouth fell open and she snapped it shut again as she turned to face Sebastian. His nose flared in anger and his eyes shot daggers at Jack. Without another word, he turned and walked out of the room, slamming the door as he went.

Appearing unfazed, Jack turned to Stephen and Riley. "We'll need to rehearse. Could you get the instruments out of the van and take them up to my room? I need to talk to Kerrigan for a moment but I'll be right behind you."

Kerrigan's heart skipped a beat and she felt almost giddy at his display of command and control. When he finally looked at her, her heart began to race for an entirely different reason. He stared at her like he could see every secret she kept hidden from the world and she felt exposed—but surprisingly not afraid.

"Thank you," she managed after she'd moistened her tongue enough to speak. "For backing me up."

"Not a problem." He shrugged as he took a step toward her. "I am sorry I was late. I set the alarm clock in the room and didn't hear it when it went off."

She turned her focus to the papers on the table. "Whatever, Jack. Who . . ." she cringed at her slip, "what you do in your spare time is none of my business."

"Kerri," he said smoothly.

Hearing him say her nickname took her back to a time long ago. A time when having him near was calming and exhilarating at the same time. A time when she could trust him with her secrets and her heart.

Now, his closeness only reminded her of what she'd learned about him over the past week. She couldn't trust him not to use her the way he did other women. She needed to get over her schoolgirl crush and the sooner the better.

"Kerrigan," she muttered half-heartedly.

She felt his hand on her chin and froze at his touch. Gently, he turned her face to his.

"If you insist." The corner of his mouth lifted as he released her chin. "I swear to you I wasn't with anyone."

"You look so tired." She frowned and reached her hand toward his face, as if she could wipe the dark circles away. She realized what she was doing and let her arm fall to her side. "I just assumed you didn't sleep much last night."

"I didn't," he answered as he released her. "But it wasn't because of a woman in my bed."

Kerrigan nodded, but stopped herself from asking what had kept him up late.

"Kerrigan, I'd like to talk to you."

"Isn't that what we're doing?" She picked up her stack of papers and slid them into her binder.

"I mean a nice, long conversation," he said. "About us."

The binder slipped out of her hands and onto the floor. "There is no 'us'," she blurted as she knelt to pick everything up.

He knelt beside her. "There used to be. We used to be friends and I'd like to talk about what happened."

She could tell him exactly what had happened. He'd walked out of her life and she'd started questioning if they'd ever had a true friendship or if he'd just been nice to her because she was his best friend's sister.

Kerrigan gathered her binder in her arms and rose to her feet. "I should think it's obvious what happened, Jack. You had a fight with my brother and decided neither of us was good enough to be around anymore."

"That's not true." Jack shook his head as color rose to his cheeks. "That's what I'd like to explain."

"I don't need an explanation." Kerrigan closed her eyes and tilted her head up, forcing her dreams back into their locked box before she said too much. With a shaky breath, she met his stare. "What's done is done. It can't be changed, so we should just leave it alone."

Jack pursed his lips, sharpening the distinction between his cheekbones and cheeks. He looked like he wanted to continue to argue with her, but instead nodded his head and looked away. "Would you like to watch us rehearse?"

Like you used to? She could almost hear the question in her mind.

"No, I've got—"

"Work," Jack finished her sentence. "Always." He took a step back and turned to leave. "You know where we are if you change your mind."

Kerrigan watched him leave, silently cursing herself for forcing him to walk away. Every conversation they had made the ball of tension in her stomach grow larger. She wanted more than anything for them to find the easy companionship they used to have but feared that it would end again when he found out what happened to her in Paris. She should've been comforted by the fact he was reaching out to her. Instead, it just broke her heart a little more each day.

Kerrigan smiled as the customer walked away from the table then looked nervously at her watch. The band's shows were typically around ninety minutes long and they'd been going for over an hour. They hadn't done the song yet. She'd thought the manager of the club was a nice guy, but the look he gave her across the room was mutinous. If not murderous.

And she was stuck behind the merchandise table and couldn't communicate with the band to find out what they were up to.

For the most part, the crowd was into the show, screaming loudly and singing along. However, Kerrigan could sense the anticipation building. She guessed most of these people were local, or at least knew of the tradition, and were expecting to hear Malhypnus's take on their favorite Lynyrd Skynyrd song.

The current song was winding down and Kerrigan's attention was drawn completely to the stage. Sebastian finished with a long, drawn out, slightly off-key chord and a wide grin to the crowd who went wild. When the song was over, Sebastian set his guitar on its rack behind him and walked up to the microphone.

"I understand you all have a certain song you like to hear," he began and a knot formed in Kerrigan's stomach.

Knowing his disdain for the idea, she could only pray he didn't say anything rude, but her attention was drawn to Jack as he sauntered toward the amplifier that controlled the mics. She watched Jack as Sebastian continued his rant.

"I, for one, don't think—"

In an instant, Sebastian was silent and Jack was ambling away from the amp, stepping up to his own microphone.

"My understanding is that it's tradition for every band who comes here to perform a certain song about your great state," Jack began, his Southern twang more pronounced than usual.

She couldn't help the smile on her face.

"Well, who are we to go against tradition?" Jack's voice boomed through the club as the crowd went crazy and Kerrigan heard the first few chords of the song. Sebastian stormed off the stage, but no one else seemed to notice as Jack's low baritone voice sang the words to "Sweet Home Alabama."

Kerrigan met Jack's gaze and he stared at her as if she were the only person in the room. As his voice caressed her from across the room, she was taken back to a time when they'd actually enjoyed each other's company.

Kerri tapped the ball of her foot against the metal leg of the barstool as her gaze bounced around the game room at the back of Finnigan's Pub. The pub had been around for several decades but the game room was a recent addition and had quickly become the favorite hangout spot for local teens. Mr. Finnigan had five children and the oldest had just turned fourteen, and Kerri figured that was a major reason behind the addition of the game room. It was a place where she could get away from her brother, and had on more than one occasion. Sadly, this was not one of those times. She frowned as she looked from Charlie, who was playing a game of pool with his friend Pete, to the door of the game room.

She was there to see Jackson.

He'd come home from college the night before and had promised to meet her there. She last saw him during his spring break, but in the eight months since the death of her parents, not a day had gone by that she hadn't thought of him. She'd started to develop a crush on him when she was fifteen, but over the past several months, that had grown into a deeper affection. She had no idea how he felt about her, so she was afraid to call it love. But she was certain it was close.

So certain, in fact, that she had taken extra time to get ready that afternoon. It was a delicate balance, putting on enough makeup to impress a boy but not enough to draw the attention of your older-brother-slash-guardian. Who also happened to be Jackson's best friend. But she'd managed to pull it off. If Charlie had noticed, he hadn't said anything.

Now she just had to wait to see if Jackson saw the difference.

She looked at her watch and frowned.

"He'll be here soon," said Olivia as she squeezed Kerri's arm.

"I know." Kerri looked toward the door. "But he's late."

Olivia laughed, a light musical tone that always made Kerri smile. "Pete slept until noon the day after he got home from college. And then he gave Mom a month's worth of laundry to do and spent the next two hours raiding the fridge and pantry." Olivia looked toward her older brother, playing pool with Charlie, and grinned. "I'm sure Jackson's going through a similar ritual."

Olivia sat in the chair next to Kerri and reached for the nut and chocolate mix that sat in a bowl in the center of the table. Kerri smacked her hand and pulled the snack mix toward her.

It was for Jackson. A mixture of his favorite, cashews, and her favorite, M&Ms. It was a combination created by them when she was fifteen. As she'd watched her brother play a round of pool against Jackson, she'd dumped a bag of candies on a napkin on the table. When the game ended, Jackson sat down at her table with his bag of nuts and dumped them onto her napkin.

She'd whined for him to get his own napkin, he'd told her to 'suck it up, buttercup', and she'd proceeded to try to pick her chocolate out of the nuts. They'd had a brief spat about her pickiness before he forced her to try the two together. It quickly became their favorite snack combination, and they always had some as they had talked late into the night at the beach house for the past two summers.

"Besides," Olivia continued with a slight pout as she rubbed the back of her hand. "He hasn't seen his mom in two months. I'm sure he wants to spend some time with her."

Kerri nodded. Olivia was probably right and she was just overly anxious.

The door opened from the outside, momentarily flooding the doorway with bright sunlight. Kerri breathed a sigh of relief when she recognized the silhouette of the man she'd been waiting to see walk into the room.

As the door closed, his forward momentum was abruptly halted by a group of girls by the door. Kerri had seen them sitting there but hadn't thought anything of it. Now, as she watched the high school's biggest flirt throw her arms around Jackson's neck, she wished she'd thought to strike up a conversation with them so she could have been in their group when he entered.

"Relax," Olivia murmured.

"I am relaxed."

Olivia laughed her tinkling laugh. "You look like you want to claw somebody's eyes out."

Kerri's scowl deepened as she narrowed her gaze on the girl currently draped over Jackson and considered the possibility.

"I know what you're thinking and I'm not sure that would impress him that much." Olivia draped an arm over Kerri's shoulder. "Do you think he'd really want to visit you in jail?"

"He might," Kerri answered with a shrug.

"I'm not sure she's his type anyway. Lord knows Tori throws herself at everything with two legs." Olivia leaned closer to Kerri's ear. "And if she is his type, sweetie, you can do better."

Kerri's mouth fell open and she turned her face to Olivia's innocent expression. They both laughed and Kerri felt a weight lift. Olivia had made another good point, and as usual had helped lighten the mood.

Olivia straightened and smiled. "He's not here to see me, so I'm gonna wander on over there," she said with a wink as she separated herself from Kerri and wandered toward the pool table.

"What's so funny?" Jackson stopped inches from her chair.

She gave him a small grin as she rose from her seat. "Nothing," Kerri answered as she walked into Jackson's open arms.

It was just like any other hug he'd ever given her, warm and friendly, and smelling like cinnamon, but her heart fluttered wildly in her chest anyway. She was doubly pleased when she realized that he hadn't hugged any of the girls in the group by the door this way. Sure, Tori had nearly tackled him, but he hadn't returned the favor. This hug was just for her.

"Welcome home."

As they sat down, he chuckled. "You make it sound like I've been gone for years instead of two months."

"Do I?" she asked, pushing the snack mix toward him. Her smile widened as he took a handful and popped it into his mouth.

Charlie, Olivia, and Pete came over to greet their friend but returned to their game of pool and Kerri was left with Jackson all to herself. They made small talk for a while. She asked about his life at college. Then he asked about their mutual friends, and she filled him in on the local gossip. It occurred to her that she'd probably told him half of the stories in their almost daily emails back and forth, but he didn't seem to mind hearing them again.

After the nuts and chocolates were gone, he grinned as he rose from his chair. "Wait right here."

Before she could respond, he was on the other side of the room, flipping through the jukebox selections. She wanted to go look over his shoulder to make sure he played some of her favorites. After pushing a few buttons, he turned and walked back toward her, a playful smile on his lips.

He was halfway across the room when the first notes to one of her favorite songs, "Sweet Home Alabama," played over the speakers. Jackson had selected that song for her. By the time he reached the table, he was singing along with the words. Kerri adored the baritone of his voice.

She was now absolutely positive that she was in love with him.

Kerrigan sighed and shook free from the memory. As Jack continued to sing, occasionally meeting her eyes, she suddenly missed him so much she was nauseous, and the weight of his absence over the last six years was like a boulder around her neck.

Maybe he was right and they should talk about their past. As much as she'd tried to convince herself otherwise to ease the pain of their separation, they had been friends. She needed to remove that weight and find a way to make the last six years up to him, because as much as she wanted to lay it all at his feet, the separation wasn't entirely his fault.

His cuffed wrist flashed suddenly into her line of sight and she had to look away. He'd said that cuff hid his secrets, and the truth of the situation added to the already heavy boulder. They each had secrets. After six years apart, how could they not? Obviously she had no idea what his were, but she feared that hers would always stand between them.

She swallowed her disappointment and tried to smile at a young woman approaching her table. The past she and Jack shared was probably best left alone.

Fourteen

Kerrigan held the phone against her ear with her shoulder as she took her bag of laundry from the housekeeper. "Thank you," she mouthed as she handed the woman a tip and closed the door.

"I'm pleased that last night's show went so well," Jacob said on the other end of the line. They'd been talking for the last twenty minutes about the progress Kerrigan had made in the past week. "Do you think you'll be able to add more shows?"

"I'm going to try," Kerrigan replied. She'd been pleased with the previous night's addition; they'd managed to bring in over two thousand dollars in total. A lot more than she'd been expecting. But it had also taken hours of research for her to find a location that would let them perform at the last minute.

"Is there anything else?" Jacob asked.

"Just one question." Kerrigan dropped her laundry on the bed and walked to the desk where the file with the band's contract sat open on her computer. She scrolled through, looking for the paragraph she'd highlighted. "I was looking through the contract and came across the paragraph regarding the production company's payment and the band's salaries."

"Okay, what about it?"

"I see your company is expecting twenty percent of the profits from the tour or fifty thousand, whichever is greater. Is that correct?" Kerrigan asked, re-reading the sentence just to be certain.

"That's right," Jacob answered.

An uneasiness settled in the pit of her stomach. "So, what happens if the band doesn't meet these requirements?"

"Then the band doesn't make a second album." Jacob's tone was distinct and matter-of-fact. There would be no arguing. "And we would be within our rights to cut our losses and let them go."

Kerrigan's brow furrowed. "Immediately?"

"Yes."

She skimmed the document for any clauses that might save them. She couldn't find any.

"Is there a problem?" Jacob asked.

Her apprehension grew. *Yes, there was a problem. A big one.*

"No. No problem at all," she replied. "Just wanted to make sure I was reading it correctly."

"Of course," Jacob said blandly. "Anything else?"

"Would the money you receive from Sebastian's father factor into this contract in any way?" she asked, knowing it was probably a shot in the dark. She hadn't seen any documentation, but felt certain the promised money from Mr. Bates was to help the record label, not the band.

There was a heavy exhale on the other end. "How do you know about that?" His tone was suddenly clipped and irritable.

She pulled the phone away from her ear and glanced at the earpiece as if that could explain the sudden change she'd heard in Jacob's voice.

"After Sebastian mentioned his father at the first meeting, I asked Stephen about him," she answered matter-of-factly. "He told me what he knew about the agreement you made with Mr. Bates."

"It's nothing you need to worry about," Jacob said. "If there's nothing else, I need to go. I will talk to you next week."

"Yes, I'll keep you updated." Kerrigan closed her eyes and let her head fall back. "Thanks for your time, Jacob. Good-bye."

"Of course." Jacob's end of the line went silent.

Kerrigan laid her phone on the desk beside her laptop and walked to the bed. Sitting down on the end of it, she pulled the laundry bag onto her lap and opened it. As she mulled over the conversation she'd just had with Jacob, she began pulling out her clothes.

Jacob had just confirmed what she'd suspected, and it didn't bode well for the band. The previous managers' unwillingness, or inability, to stick to the original budget now had the band in dire straits. They were dangerously close to not being able to reach that fifty-thousand dollar minimum the production company wanted. Their contract could be nullified, regardless of whether she left before the end of the tour or stayed for its duration.

Pulling them out of debt wasn't impossible, but it would take some creative thinking. She had to make cuts to the expenses, but where? What could she do to bring in more income?

Why were all her clothes lime green?

She looked at the stack of clean clothes in front of her and frowned. It wasn't just a touch of lime green—they were all completely dyed. Her jeans, her underwear, her T-shirts, everything. She held up one of her formerly pale blue tees and let out a long breath.

Her ears perked up to the sound of voices in the hall. Shirt in hand, she rose and walked toward the door. The closer she got, the more recognizable one of the deep voices became. She put her hand on the doorknob.

"You did what?" Jack snapped at Sebastian.

He'd come to Kerrigan's room to find out what she was doing on their night off that evening and found Sebastian hovering by her door. That had been a bad sign, and when he'd asked Sebastian why he was there, the answer had raised Jack's hackles.

"I told you," Sebastian whispered. "I emptied a bottle of dye into the washing machine with her laundry."

"Why would you do that?" Jack shook his head, trying not to let his anger show.

Compared to his previous stunt, this one was childish and stupid, but it seemed Sebastian was determined to run her off any way he could. And he was, apparently, not content to let Jack do his part.

Her door opened and Kerrigan briefly met his eyes in surprise before she turned to Sebastian with a frown.

"This is funny to you?" she asked calmly, holding up a lime green shirt and waving it slightly.

"I thought you said lime was your favorite color," Sebastian replied with an impish smile.

"You know I never said that." Kerrigan lowered the shirt and raised an eyebrow.

"Oops." Sebastian laughed.

She stood in the doorway, her arms folded across her chest. Jack saw the distress in her face as she glared at Sebastian. Was she that upset about her clothes? How much of her wardrobe had he ruined? Upon closer look, he realized it was stress, not anger, in the silvery depths. And if he had to guess, the tension probably wasn't caused by Sebastian. What else was going on?

"Sebastian," Kerrigan began in a motherly tone, "this is rather childish, don't you think? How old are you?"

"A gentleman never tells," Sebastian retorted.

"You're hardly a gentleman." Kerrigan replied drily, then held up her hand as if waving her comment away. "Anyway, the point is, I think you're a little old for these stunts. Just try to stay out of trouble today, okay?"

She stepped back into her room and let the door close on its own. Jack carefully slid closer to the door and stuck his fingers into the opening to prevent it from closing entirely. He put his back against the door and looked at Sebastian.

"What the hell was that?" Sebastian grumbled. "She didn't get angry. She acted like she didn't even care."

"Did you want her to get mad?" Jack asked, feeling fairly certain of the answer.

"Yes, damn it," Sebastian snapped. "Guess I'll have to try harder." Sebastian turned to walk away and Jack grabbed his upper arm.

"I said leave it to me," Jack hissed.

"Fine, but you have one more week." Sebastian looked over his shoulder. "Then it's my turn." He violently shook his arm out of Jack's loose grip and stomped off down the hallway toward his room.

Jack turned and knocked on the door before easing it open and slipping his head in the crack. "Kerrigan, can I come in?"

"It's open?" Her faint voice made him smile and he poked his head in.

"Yeah, sorry. I didn't want to disturb you," he answered sheepishly as he met her stare.

She was standing in front of the window with her arms across her chest and she nodded once before turning back around.

"Are you okay?" Jack asked as he entered the room and closed the door behind him.

She remained silent, staring out the window, hugging her arms to her chest, as he approached.

"Hmm? What?" She glanced at him when he reached the desk.

"Are you okay?" Jack repeated, leaning his shoulder against the wall beside the window.

Instead of answering she turned back to the window. He saw the slow rise and fall of her chest as she blew out a breath. "I just got off the phone with Jacob."

Jack wasn't sure how to take that. Was it band related? Or something more personal? Jacob was a single man and as far as Jack knew, Kerrigan was single, too. He recalled the way Jacob had smiled at her that first morning, and how Jacob was the only man she hadn't kept completely at arms-length when they'd shaken hands. Jack wasn't sure he could handle a more personal discussion.

"Okay," he said slowly.

She stood stiffly in front of the window then gradually turned. Her blue-gray eyes were sad and her brow furrowed as she looked at him. "I'm not sure I can save your band."

Jack popped away from the wall and closed the distance between them. "You're leaving?" Panic tightened his chest. She couldn't leave. He couldn't lose her. "If it's the clothes, I'll buy you a new wardrobe."

Her head tilted and she leaned back slightly, studying his face. "No, it's not about the clothes. I don't care about that. Clothes can be replaced."

"You don't care?" he asked. "Why?"

"Because, if Sebastian is focused on pranking me and ruining *my* things," she began as she stepped away from him slightly, "then he's not focused on destroying his hotel room."

Jack absorbed her words then slowly nodded his agreement. "Good point." He noticed the distance she put between them and decided not to push his luck. He stepped back and resumed his position against the wall. "Then why are you leaving?"

Her lips turned up slightly and she shook her head. "I'm not leaving."

"Thank God," Jack muttered under his breath. "So then, what's the problem?"

Kerrigan's gaze dropped to the floor as she lowered herself into a chair.

Jack rolled the desk chair toward her so he could sit and face her. Once seated, he leaned forward with his forearms on his thighs and studied her dark hair gathered in a ponytail that hung over her shoulder. Her bangs touched just below her arched eyebrows, just above the rim of her glasses. With his eyes, he followed the line of her sharp jaw from the base of her ear to the rounded tip of her chin and imagined laying kisses along that jaw.

He shook the thought away. Now was not the time to entertain thoughts like that. He'd find out what was wrong with the band, he'd fix it, and then they'd talk . . . about them.

She lifted her face to his. "You know about the paragraph in the contract regarding the money the record company gets, right?"

Jack searched his memory for details about the contract. "I think it says something about how much they'll take from the profits. Is it twenty-five percent?"

Kerrigan frowned, clearly disappointed that he didn't know. "No, it's twenty percent," she said calmly. "Or fifty thousand, whichever is greater."

"Whichever is greater?" Jack repeated. *That couldn't be right.* "So which is it?"

"At this point, it would be fifty thousand," Kerrigan answered. "But you're about sixty thousand away from that goal."

Jack's eyebrows disappeared into his hairline. "What?"

Kerrigan nodded. "The budget has been completely disregarded and now the hole is so deep . . ." She pressed her lips together and looked at her lap. "I'm not sure I can get you out of it."

Jack sat straight up and closed his eyes. This couldn't be happening. Her words from her first day on the job came back to haunt him. If he'd been more involved, if he'd paid more attention to what was going on around him from the beginning, then maybe they wouldn't be in this mess. He pinched the bridge of his nose and considered their options.

"Jack, I'm so sorry," she said softly.

Jack dropped his hand and opened his eyes. The disappointed look that she gave him stabbed him in the chest. "Sorry for what?"

"I thought I could pull this off, but I didn't realize how bad it was," she said, her voice wavering. She looked at the floor beside her. "It's just so frustrating."

He knew how much she hated failure. She'd always been so meticulous and detail oriented in everything she did, every school project, every chore, all because she didn't want to disappoint anyone. Which she rarely did.

He inched toward her. Cautiously, he took her hands in his and shifted so he could see her face.

"This isn't your fault," he whispered.

"I know," she muttered with a pout as she nodded. "I'm just not sure what to do. I've been poring over the numbers all week and I know there's a solution, I just don't know if it's enough."

"Show me."

He slowly rose to his feet, then pulled her up beside him and led her to the desk. He rolled the chair behind them, positioned it in front of her laptop, and she sat down. She showed him the original budget, then pulled up the Excel file of the band's actual budget to date, and the floor dropped from under him. He laid one palm on the desk beside her laptop to hold himself steady.

She wasn't overreacting—it was pretty bad. No wonder last night's additional show had been so important. They'd have to fill every empty night and then some to make up this difference.

"So what are your ideas?" Jack croaked, still stunned by the evidence in front of him. *How could things have gotten this bad?*

"We have to cut expenses," Kerrigan said, straightforward and without hesitation.

Jack nodded his agreement. That much was obvious, but how? He studied the numbers again to see if he could come up with any answers.

"Per diem has to be lowered even more," she began cautiously.

He felt her eyes on his face, but couldn't look at her yet.

"It should have been fifty a day from the beginning, but I'm assuming that wasn't the case?" she asked and he finally looked at her.

"No, you were the first to implement that. The other managers let us have however much we asked for," he answered with a frown. *Why had she been the first?*

Kerrigan's head bobbed once. "And I think cheaper lodging. Seventy-five a night, per room, should still be fairly nice."

They'd been spending twice that.

"Can we go lower?" Jack asked and was rewarded with a brief smile on her perfect lips.

"We can try," she said, finally sounding hopeful. "Also . . ." her voice trailed off as she rose and walked toward the window again.

"What is it?" Jack followed her, stopping short when he remembered the distance she liked to keep between them.

"You won't like it." She shook her head as she turned to him.

"I don't like being in this hole either," he snapped and she jerked backward. "I'm sorry," he murmured. He wasn't upset with her, he was angry at the situation and the fact that the weight of it rested, at least partially, on his shoulders. "What's your idea?"

"Cut your salaries," Kerrigan blurted and then recoiled further.

Jack put his hands on his hips and stared over her shoulder as he considered her suggestions. They didn't need to get paid while they were on tour; everything was pretty much taken care of for them. He'd have to convince Sebastian it was a good idea. Better to cut their income now so they could continue to have it after the tour was over.

"To what?" Jack asked.

"The contract insures your minimum monthly payment is twelve hundred. I suggest we take it down to that," Kerrigan answered.

That was half of what they were being paid now. He walked back to the computer and studied the numbers on the screen.

"That's fine," Jack agreed then pointed to the van rental number and looked over his shoulder at her. "I think we can cut back to one vehicle as well."

Her mouth fell open. "Really?" She sounded unconvinced. "Which one?"

"Neither."

He turned completely and grinned, already warming up to the idea of finally traveling with her. It wouldn't be completely without problems, not with Sebastian in the same van. But he focused on Kerrigan's beautiful face and decided he could continue to suffer Sebastian's company if he could sit with her.

"Neither van we have is large enough," he answered thoughtfully as another idea came to him. "What if we bought a trailer? Then we could rent a mini-van or an SUV that could tow it."

She shook her head. "Jack, we can't afford to *buy* anything."

He bobbed his head as the idea solidified. "No, the band can't," he agreed as he walked toward her. "But I would be willing to put forward my own money to purchase one, and Stephen and Riley might be willing to contribute. I imagine that will help save money for the rental and should definitely save on gas."

Kerrigan slowly nodded. "I hadn't thought of that, but you're probably right. We should see if we can find one locally as soon as possible." She walked past him and sat back down in front of the laptop. Her fingers flew over the keyboard; he assumed she was making adjustments to the budget. "That would help," she muttered. Her fingers stilled and she looked at the screen. "I think if we can add at least eight more shows and pull in seventeen fifty a night, we might be able to pull this off."

She turned and gave him a wide smile and his heart rate tripled. It was the smile he'd been waiting for since she'd joined them the week before. It was the smile he'd missed for the last six years. She popped out of her seat and hurried toward him. He expected her to stop before she reached him, but instead she threw her arms around his neck.

"Thank you for your help," she said, her voice a breath across his ear as he put his own arms around her waist and pulled her to him.

"My pleasure," Jack replied, his voice thick as his desire for her took hold.

It only took a second for her to stiffen in his arms. Slowly her hands slid to his shoulders and down his chest as she pushed herself away. He didn't want to let her go, but when he noticed the surprise and discomfort in her wide eyes he reluctantly loosened his grip. The space between them widened, but she remained in his arms.

Her lips were right there—all he needed to do was lower his head an inch and he'd be kissing her. He knew she was going to bolt. Any second now she'd push away and be on the other side of the room before he could blink. He should take this opportunity while he had it. Her eyes dropped to his mouth as her tongue brushed her lower lip.

"Don't," she said, almost pleading, on an exhale.

"Why?" he asked.

The color in her cheeks had risen and her breath was shallow. He could tell she wanted this almost as much as he did. What was holding her back?

"You don't really want to do this," she said as she gently pushed away and turned.

Wanna bet? He raised an eyebrow at her back.

"We shouldn't," Kerrigan stated and he couldn't tell who she was trying to convince.

Because it wasn't working on him.

"Why shouldn't I kiss you?" Jack asked.

"I'm your manager," she answered, turning to face him.

"Try again," he said through clenched teeth. She had five seconds to give him a good reason before she found herself in his arms again. He took a step toward her.

Kerrigan struggled to come up with something, anything, to stop him. His arms were circling her, his mouth was slowly lowering toward hers.

Say something!

"Are you suicidal?"

Jack froze, his lips inches from hers, and confusion filled his eyes.

"What?" he scoffed.

She wriggled out of his loose hold but couldn't bring herself to step any farther away.

He shook his head. "You've known me for how long and you ask me that?"

She hadn't meant to bring up what she'd read, but her curiosity, combined with her concern for his well-being, had tumbled out of her mouth in that moment of panic. Now she'd have to figure a way through this topic.

She'd better do it fast, before that look in his eyes returned. The one that said he might eat her up.

She was only a little terrified to realize she'd probably let him.

"I've been reading the correspondences between your former managers and Jacob," she answered simply.

Jack's brow furrowed. "And they think I'm suicidal?" His voice was cautious and probing at the same time.

"Not exactly," Kerrigan answered. "But they do think you're wasting your talent and have self-destructive tendencies."

Jack looked at her and cocked his head to the side. "Self-destructive is hardly suicidal."

"I know," Kerrigan stammered as she stepped backward.

Jack looked like he would pounce at any minute and she was almost excited by the idea. Since Paris, if any man had looked at her the way he was looking at her at that moment, she would have fled fast and far away. She certainly wouldn't be entertaining the idea of encouraging him.

What is wrong with me?

Except this was Jack. And he'd been acting more like the Jackson she remembered. She was feeling off balance and that just wouldn't do.

"Kerrigan." Jack's commanding voice reached her and slithered down her spine. "What did those emails say?" He took another step toward her.

"Just that . . ." she began, but found it hard to continue with the way he was looking at her. She turned her back to him and took a steadying breath. "Riley has talent and they would hate to see that go to waste. Jacob wants to see if he can be groomed for another band. They all agree that Stephen is an amazing songwriter and keyboard player. The record label definitely wants to keep him around. Sebastian isn't as great as he likes to think he is. Most managers agreed that he's the least talented of all of you." She paused for breath and couldn't help but smile. "But we already knew that."

His hands lightly came to rest on her upper arms and his breath brushed past her ear. "And me?"

Kerrigan closed her eyes and tried to focus on something other than his gentle touch and soothing voice to control her shaking.

"You're more talented than the rest of them and write better songs than Stephen. Most of the managers felt that you would make a better lead singer and would have liked for you to have taken on a stronger leadership role." She spat out the words, hoping it would help calm her. "At one point, there were discussions between the manager at the time and Jacob about getting rid of Sebastian and asking you to take over for him. But by the time each manager left, they all felt you were too distracted and uncooperative."

He stepped closer, squeezing her arms and pressing his chest to her back. "And self-destructive?"

His grip held her frozen. She couldn't even take air into her lungs. All she could do was nod.

"I'm not suicidal," he whispered into her ear. "And I'm not really feeling that self-destructive anymore. I think you've cured me."

She blew out a shaky breath and closed her eyes, relieved of that worry and giddy that she may have, in some way, helped. "Good," she muttered.

"Very." Laughter rumbled in his chest and vibrated through her body.

She gently shook free of his grasp and turned to face him. "Why?"

He raised an eyebrow. "Why what?"

"Why did you behave that way?" Never, in all the time she'd known him, had he acted out in the way the previous managers had described. She'd wanted to ask him about it for days. "What happened to you?"

He gave her a lopsided grin. "That's my secret," he teased. "Would you like to know it?"

Yes. Maybe? She wasn't entirely sure. She wanted to know what had been going on in his life for the past six years. But at the same time, if he shared his secret, would he expect her to share hers? It would only be fair.

His hand was on the snaps of his cuff but she laid hers over it.

"I'll let you keep it," she said steadily then took a deep breath and let her hand fall to her side. Pulling her shoulders back, she tried to sound more decisive than she felt. "I'm sure you have other plans for the day, so—"

"No." Jack took a step back.

"No?" Kerrigan frowned. Had she asked a question?

"No, I don't have other plans. I thought I might spend some time with you," he replied.

Kerrigan felt suddenly dizzy and sunk onto the corner of the bed. "Why?" she asked, surprised by the breathless quality of her own voice.

"Why not?" Jack squatted in front of her and took her hands in his. "We used to spend a lot of time together."

"But then we stopped," Kerrigan said, trying to ignore the warmth emanating from their joined fingers and creeping up her arms.

"True," Jack agreed. "But I think we should start again."

She focused on their hands. "Why?" she repeated and watched as one of his hands left hers and reached for her chin.

He lifted her face to his. "Because I've missed you."

Her eyes widened on his and her mouth felt like a desert. What was she supposed to say? She'd missed him terribly in the last six years? She was sorry she'd turned him away in Paris four years ago? She'd been in love with him since she was sixteen and would happily follow him anywhere now?

Except she couldn't forget the rejection she'd felt by his abandonment. And she couldn't forget how unworthy she felt of any man, especially him, after Paris.

"I have work to do," she whispered.

A smile slowly formed on his full lips and she wondered what they'd feel like against hers. She leaned away, pulling her chin free of his loose hold. He rose from his squat and held his hand out to her.

"Then let's get to work," he said as he lifted her to her feet. "What would you like me to do?"

A knock on her door drew their attention and she turned toward it. Before she could move, Jack had brushed past her and opened the door.

"Hey, Jack," Riley's Scottish brogue reached her ears as the man himself pushed the door open further. "How interesting to find ye here." Riley gave Jack an unusually sardonic smile before turning and grinning widely at Kerrigan.

Stephen stepped into the doorway. "What's going on?"

Jack met her gaze and Kerrigan nodded her approval.

"Funny you should ask," Jack answered. "Come in and we'll tell you."

Fifteen

Jack tossed his leather cuff onto the side table as he threw himself onto the middle of the bed. He rubbed at the damp skin and stared at the initials tattooed on the inside of his wrist. In bold calligraphy, the letters KRD had been inked there over six years ago as a reminder of what he'd wanted.

Kerrigan Renee Dodd.

After all these years of silence, he'd almost told her earlier that day what she'd meant to him then. What she still meant to him.

He'd wanted to show her the tattoo; his fingers had been itching to remove the cuff right then and there. Every day that passed in her company, the urge to confess his feelings to her grew stronger. He wanted no more secrets separating them and he was tired of the distance she kept between them. He had to tell her, and the sooner the better.

Why had she balked at the idea of seeing his tattoo? It was almost like she was afraid to see it. Had Charlie told her what their argument had been about and why he'd left? Maybe she suspected that his love for her was his biggest secret. Had she refused to see him in Paris because she didn't reciprocate the feelings? If that were the case, the continued silence between them probably hadn't changed that to his benefit.

That can't be it.

He'd been with enough women to know when they were aroused, when they wanted to be kissed, and more. Kerrigan was certainly showing the signs this afternoon. So why had she shied away from what they'd both wanted?

He had to tell her why he'd disappeared from her life six years ago. He had no idea how she might react to that information, whether it would be to his benefit or not. He had to learn more about the last six years of her life, maybe then he would have some idea. But getting her to even talk to him in the past week had proven far more difficult than he had expected.

Jack leaned his head against the headboard. He'd spent the last four years telling himself he was over her, that he didn't care if he ever saw her again. Now that she was back in his life, he realized he'd been lying to himself. Having her as his band's manager was not a role he wanted her to be in, but she was here and that would have to do. For now. He'd find a way to talk to her and ultimately tell her how he felt about her. After that, it was up to her.

"Like hell!" Sebastian yelled across the table in the conference room the next morning.

Kerrigan blew out a breath as she bowed her head. Her fingers made small circles on her temples as she tried to steady her temper by slowly counting backward from ten.

"I'm not sleeping in a flea-bag of a motel and I'm not sharing a room," Sebastian continued to rant.

Kerrigan stopped at five and started over again. *Maybe I should start at twenty instead.*

"Yes, you are," Jack said calmly from the seat on her right. "You no longer have a choice, Sebastian."

"You've almost single-handedly racked up so much debt we had to spend all day yesterday figuring out how to get us back on track," Stephen stated furiously.

Kerrigan finished her countdown and opened her eyes.

"It's hardly my fault that she can't manage our money," Sebastian spat as he jumped to his feet.

Jack popped out of his seat and placed both palms on the table. "*She* didn't do this."

"You *would* defend her," Sebastian scoffed.

Kerrigan glanced at Jack's face. His cheeks were flushed and his jaw clenched. Kerrigan looked at Sebastian and saw the impish glint in his eyes. Was she missing something?

"These problems started long before she arrived," Stephen said as he stood as well.

"Then you should have kept a closer eye on things." Sebastian glared at Stephen, his brown eyes shooting daggers across the table.

Kerrigan inhaled as she slowly rose to her feet between Jack and Stephen.

"Enough," she said calmly as she stared at Sebastian. "This isn't entirely your fault, Sebastian. It seems like your previous managers had no interest in even trying to stick to the budget. While most of the contingency budget went to cover your mischief, that's about all we can lay at your feet." Kerrigan looked at Jack for a moment, then turned to Stephen and Riley. "Unless you want to tell me Sebastian threw a tantrum about the type of hotel from the beginning of the tour, or that he refused to accept his per diem limit, then this isn't entirely his fault. I told you all that yesterday."

Kerrigan focused on Sebastian again, who was now looking at her with a slack-jawed shock on his face.

"But you know it wasn't Stephen's job to fix things. He only stepped in to manage the money when you didn't have a manager. You also know," she continued speaking to Sebastian, "that if he had tried to curb your spending, you would have made it difficult." She held her palm up to him when he opened his mouth to argue. "I'm not here to place the blame on anyone, so don't take my head off."

Sebastian's mouth snapped closed.

"We can only go forward from here, and I'm afraid your only option is to share a room in flea-bag motels with Jack until the end of the tour," Kerrigan continued in her steady, soothing voice. "As for our mode of transportation, we have no choice but to cut back to one vehicle."

"No," Sebastian snapped.

Kerrigan pressed her lips together and released a long breath. "Yes."

"We've found a trailer that Stephen and I are going to purchase outright and tow behind another van we've rented to accommodate it. The van is slightly smaller than the ones we have now, but it will save us in the long run," Jack added, inching closer to Kerrigan.

"I'm not riding in a van full of people," Sebastian argued.

"Fine," Kerrigan snapped. Her irritation with his childish attitude was beginning to bubble again, but she maintained her outwardly calm façade.

"Fine?" Jack squawked as he turned to look at her.

Kerrigan kept her eyes focused on Sebastian. "Yes, fine," she answered Jack, then said sharply to Sebastian, "You are perfectly welcome to find your own vehicle and your own room in a better hotel."

Sebastian's lips turned up slightly and he folded his arms across his chest triumphantly.

"But," Kerrigan continued and Sebastian's smile started to fade. "*You* will be responsible for the expenses. The band's reservations are made and those are the only expenses the band will have. Anything additional will come out of the individual member's pocket."

Sebastian's muddy eyes bore into hers with a steady determination. She could tell he was trying to formulate some sort of argument and she prepared to counter it. When his arms fell to his side and he looked away, she nearly fell backward.

"Fine," Sebastian quietly agreed. "Are we done?"

"Not yet," Kerrigan answered.

"What else are you going to take away? You've already lowered my pay and now I have to share a room with him," pointing to Jack, "and ride in a van with you." He finished with a curl of his upper lip.

"I'm not taking anything," Kerrigan said. "We need to increase our merchandise sales. We're going to have the band's logo screen-printed on bandanas and I'd like to know what color you would prefer."

Sebastian tilted his head. "Black. Why?"

"That will be your color then," she replied.

"I don't wear bandanas." Sebastian put his hands on his hips.

"You'll start," Kerrigan said.

"But—"

"Shut up and listen," Jack growled.

"I don't care if you wear them on your head, around your neck, tied around your arm, thigh, wrist, whatever." Kerrigan ignored both interruptions. "You'll each have a signature color, you'll all wear them on stage, and you'll promote their sales. Think of it as a way for fans to have a piece of their favorite band member."

Sebastian's scowl lightened. "So, I can wear them anywhere?" he asked as a mischievous spark crept into his eyes.

"Anywhere," Kerrigan answered slowly.

"It has to be tasteful and visible," Jack added. "You can't wrap it around your cock."

Kerrigan's eyes widened as she looked at Jack. *He wouldn't.*

Jack glanced over his shoulder and shrugged.

Apparently he would.

"Fine," Sebastian grumbled. "Can I go now?"

"Go." Kerrigan waved toward the door and he turned toward it. "Just stay out of trouble today, please," she called at his retreating figure.

"Whatever," he replied as he reached the door.

"We can't afford it, Sebastian," Stephen added loudly as Sebastian left the room.

As the door closed behind him, Kerrigan released a slow breath and her shoulders dropped slightly. She hadn't realized how tense she was until she had fully exhaled.

"Would you like me to call Debra then?" Stephen asked.

Debra was an artist as well as a teacher, and she was currently working on a design for the bandanas. She was also going to see what other creative additions she could make to the merchandise.

"I can call her about those. Orange, green, and blue?" Kerrigan pointed to Riley, Stephen, and Jack, verifying their color choices. After they each nodded, she smiled at Stephen. "I'll handle it. You're going to take care of the vans and trailer, right?"

"Riley and I were going to do that now," Stephen replied. "Is there anything else we need to do?"

Kerrigan shook her head. "No, I think that's it. Thank you so much for all your help."

"It has to be done," Stephen answered. "We'll find you when we get back."

He and Riley quickly left the room. Kerrigan looked around to make sure there was no trash left lying around then stepped around her chair. She pushed hers under the table then began doing the same with the others, fully aware of the gaze following her every move.

"I want to thank you, too," she said quietly. She looked up and finally met Jack's intense stare across the table. Her heart fluttered and she suddenly felt warm.

Jack picked up her binder and strolled around the table toward her. "Of course. If we don't all do our part, we all find ourselves without a job at the end of this tour." He stopped beside her. "None of us really want that, do we?"

Kerrigan shook her head and shrugged. "No, I wouldn't want you guys to lose your label."

"What about you?" Jack's brows came together. "You're not sticking around after the tour, are you?"

"I was only hired to help you complete this tour," Kerrigan replied. "I'm only a short-term solution to your long-term problem." His face darkened at her answer and she frowned. "Wasn't it the same with the others?"

Jack shook his head. "Not to my knowledge." His eyes dropped to the binder in his arms and he held it out to her. "Is the band's contract in there?"

Her hand brushed his as she took the binder and she nearly dropped it from the shock of his touch. His eyes sparkled when they met hers and she felt a pull toward him. She pressed the binder to her chest and folded her arms across it to prevent herself from doing something stupid.

"No," Kerrigan squawked and paused to clear her throat. "It's in my room. Why?"

"Last night, I was thinking it might not be a bad idea for Mason to have a look at it," Jack answered. Mason was Jack's older brother and a corporate lawyer.

Kerrigan tilted her head. "Why would we do that?"

Jack laid his hand on the back of the chair beside him and leaned into it. "It couldn't hurt to have a lawyer look at our contract. I want to know if there's an out for us, just in case we can't make the money we need to give Jacob. It's hardly fair that we should be punished when our previous managers didn't even try to stick to the budget."

Kerrigan thought over his argument. She had not even considered the possibility there could be a loophole just in case they didn't make the fifty thousand dollars. "That's probably not a bad idea. Mason would be more familiar with the legal wording." And knowing his brother's career could be on the line, Mason would probably be very thorough in his study. "Why don't you call him and explain everything first. If he's willing to look at it, then we can send him a copy."

"Sounds like a plan." Jack smiled widely and Kerrigan went weak in the knees.

She was reminded of the young man she fell in love with. Always coming at problems from angles no one else would have thought of. When he smiled at her like that, she could almost forget the six years of silence.

And everything that had happened to her since.

If he found out what happened to me in Paris, would he still smile at me like that?

"Right," she agreed, gathering her strength. "Let's get to work." She turned on her heels and led him out of the room.

Two mornings later, Kerrigan pushed open the door to the coffee shop in Montgomery, Alabama, with her hip, juggling her wallet, coffee, and pastry in one hand as she held her phone to her ear with the other. Since cutting back on the rooming expenses, she'd started to venture out of her motel room for breakfast. The coffee cups in the room just weren't large enough for her morning consumption.

Her brother had called while she was waiting in line to pick up her order. They'd made small talk, but she enjoyed hearing his voice and wasn't ready for their conversation to end.

And she had a question for him that she really needed an answer to.

She stepped off the sidewalk between two parked cars and looked both ways.

"So, do you think you could do me a favor?" Kerrigan asked.

"Sure," Charlie replied. "What do you need?"

"Clothes." Kerrigan was out of the way of moving cars and slowed her pace toward the motel.

"Didn't you pack enough?"

She could almost hear the laughter he was holding back and rolled her eyes.

"Yes, I packed enough," she grumbled. "But there's been a little mishap with most of what I packed."

Charlie was no longer hiding his amusement. "What kind of mishap? Scissors? Shrink in the wash?"

She blew out a breath. "I have a prankster to deal with. He thought it would be funny to dye my clothes."

His laughter slowly died. "Really?"

Kerrigan didn't think he deserved an answer and remained quiet.

"So, how am I supposed to get these clothes to you?"

"I've invited Olivia to spend an evening with me in Tallahassee next week. You could send them with her." Kerrigan took a sip of her coffee and took in her surroundings as she approached the motel parking lot.

"She didn't tell me that," he said.

"You're not married yet—she doesn't have to tell you everything," she quipped. "Besides, it was an open invitation when I left and I haven't exactly given her all the details yet."

Charlie rumbled his response. "I see."

As she strolled across the parking lot, she waited for him to speak again. "Well?" she asked as she reached the van and trailer. She set her cup of coffee on the bumper of the trailer and her wallet beside it.

"Fine," he answered. "If I can find them."

"Shouldn't be that hard. All my clothes are in suitcases or boxes. Just look through them until you find what I need." She realized she hadn't told him what she needed yet. "I'll text you a list this afternoon."

"I'll ask Olivia to find your stuff. She'll know what to look for better than I will."

Kerrigan agreed and lifted her shoulder to hold her phone against her ear. She pulled a piece from her chocolate croissant and popped it into her mouth.

"You don't have to do that, you know," Charlie said.

Her brow furrowed. "Do what?"

"Have all your stuff packed. You don't have to move out."

The seriousness of his tone made her chew slowly, stalling before she had to respond. It was the same thing he'd told her, consistently, since she'd come home three months ago.

"Yes, I do," she replied after swallowing. Charlie and Olivia had been engaged for nearly a year and their wedding date was fast approaching. "You're getting married. You don't need me as a third wheel living in your house."

"It's your house too. We both inherited it," Charlie retorted.

"Charlie." She half laughed. "Are we supposed to live in it together forever? You, with your wife and kids. Me, the single auntie who will spoil them rotten. What fun would that be?"

"You've been gone for four years, Kerri," he stated. "Maybe I just want to spend some time with you. I miss having you home."

"I know." She leaned her shoulder against the trailer and looked toward the motel.

"Besides. You may find a husband who can live with us, too. Then we can raise our kids together," he joked. "Won't that be fun?"

Kerrigan's appetite disappeared. She still hated to admit, even to herself, that she'd only ever pictured herself married to one man.

Jackson.

She was no longer sure that man even existed anymore, but the mere idea of marrying someone else didn't sit right with her. Perhaps, after this tour was over and she was away from him again, she could try harder to move on. But until then, she'd have to suffer his presence and keep her feelings, and secrets, to herself.

"Charlie," she asked soberly. "Did you know this was Jackson's band?"

With his exhalation, she had her answer.

"Why didn't you tell me?"

"Would you have taken the job?" he deflected her question.

Probably not. "I didn't think you wanted me to take the job," she answered.

"When was the last time you actually did anything I suggested?"

Kerrigan frowned. "What do you mean by that?"

"Kerri, if I had told you it was Jackson's band, you would have stayed home," Charlie answered. "And probably fretted for the next few months about what you would do when he finally came home."

Kerrigan tilted her head and nodded. He did have a point.

"And as you worried, you probably would have found another job that would take you as far away from Rocky Creek as possible."

She pushed away from the trailer and picked up her things. "So by telling me not to take the job as the band's manager, you were actually hoping I would take it?"

"Yes," Charlie answered. "You're so damn stubborn that you automatically do the opposite of what I tell you."

"That's not—" She was going to say "true" but she realized that he was right. Especially since he'd become her guardian. "Why would you want me to take this job?"

"I honestly didn't," Charlie replied. "But it's what you needed to do, Kerri. Even if you didn't want to."

"Charlie—"

"Sorry, sis, I gotta go. I have to drive Olivia to work because we have wedding stuff to do when she gets off this afternoon," he said. "Call me later. I love you."

"Love you, too." Kerrigan hung up and pushed her phone into her pocket. She deposited her pastry in a trashcan as she turned the corner toward her room.

What did he mean it was what she needed to do? She'd needed to see Jackson again like she'd needed a hole in her head. Avoiding him was the primary reason she'd taken this job, and Charlie should have given her a heads up, regardless of what he thought she needed.

She should have never told her brother how she felt about Jackson. But she'd been so angry at him when Jackson had left the beach house that her feelings had spilled out before she'd been able to control them. Charlie had tried to convince her that she should forget about Jackson. He'd told her that she would meet plenty of other men in college and Jackson wasn't good enough for her. As if Charlie knew what was good for her.

She'd yelled and screamed at him until her throat had hurt, and she'd threatened to go after Jackson. The whole time, Charlie had sat in their father's chair, listening to her and looking resigned and unsurprised by her rage. When her tantrum had waned, she'd run upstairs to Jackson's room, collapsing on the bed in tears. Olivia had sat on the floor beside her, silently offering her support until Kerri had fallen asleep.

It had been six years, but apparently Charlie hadn't forgotten.

And he was still wrong.

The rumble of male voices around the corner slowed her down.

"After I went through all that trouble for you, too."

Kerrigan rolled her eyes when she recognized Sebastian's voice. She wondered how much trouble he'd gone to, and how much it would cost the band. She took a step forward but froze when the next man spoke.

"I didn't ask you to," Jack stated.

"But, Jack, you saw them. They were hot and ready for you," Sebastian stated. "The least you could have done was stick around long enough to sample their wares. You would not have been disappointed."

Sebastian chuckled and Kerrigan could almost picture the leer on his face. The image made her shudder with disgust. She hated that chauvinistic sneer.

"I've told you not to pick women out for me. I'll do it myself." Jack's voice was sharp with irritation.

Kerrigan perked up.

"But you've never turned them down before," Sebastian replied.

Kerrigan pressed her back to the wall. Jack had turned down a woman? She couldn't be hearing this right.

"There's a first time for everything, I guess," Jack answered slowly. "And I'm sure you benefitted from my absence, so I'm not sure why you're complaining."

"I'm not complaining," Sebastian snapped. "I just thought you could use a good romp. You've been in a pissy mood ever since Her Highness started working with us. I was trying to help you out."

Kerrigan's lip curled.

Her Highness indeed.

And Jack had been in a fine mood since she'd joined them. Sebastian must be imagining things. Or trying to get a reaction from Jack for some reason.

"I have not." Jack's response was cool and collected. "I just had no interest in either of the women in our room last night and opted to room with Riley for the night. And as for Kerrigan, she's doing a damn fine job fixing everything you've screwed up in the last four months so you should be grateful she's here. Otherwise we'd all find ourselves without a label at the end of this tour and you'd have no one to blame but yourself."

"You're taking her side?" Sebastian scoffed.

"I'm taking the band's side, Sebastian," Jack's voice boomed. "And it wouldn't hurt you to do the same."

"Whatever," Sebastian muttered.

Kerrigan's heart raced with excitement as she listened to Jack stand up for her. Did he know she was there? She glanced at the floor to check for a shadow. She could see theirs, but not hers. She was momentarily tempted to step out and thank him, but that would be a bad idea with Sebastian standing there.

They were silent for the longest time and Kerrigan watched their shadows to make sure they weren't moving toward her. They were still stationary.

"I'm going to get breakfast," Jack said.

"I'll join you," Sebastian grumbled and the shadows began to move away.

Kerrigan slowly continued toward her room, replaying what she'd just heard. If nothing else, that little conversation gave her more to consider about Jack and made her ridiculously giddy.

And it *was* ridiculous.

She was trying to get over him but he was making it exceedingly difficult. Ten days ago he'd come into the meeting with a woman on each arm and she'd determined he was no longer the man she'd fallen in love with. She'd sworn to herself to get over him, to move on, that he wasn't worth the heartache.

And every day since he'd done his best to prove her wrong.

Sixteen

Kerrigan gave a wan smile to the customer as she took their money, then turned to the next person in line. The music seemed louder than usual and the songs longer. The merchandise sales were on track to meet their goal for the night, and she knew how important that was, but Kerrigan only wanted to be in the silent solitude of her motel room.

She had thought staying busy would help her forget it was the anniversary of her parents' death, and for most of the day, she'd been right. Then the concert had started and she began to feel completely alone.

"Ma'am, this isn't right."

Kerrigan looked at the man who had spoken as he held up the CD, T-shirt, two bandanas, and the change she'd given him.

"I'm so sorry, I owe you another dollar, don't I?" she asked and reached into the cash box. "Here you go. Enjoy the show." She smiled weakly as she handed him the rest of his money and he nodded and walked away.

Kerrigan forced herself to focus on the next person in line. And the next, until she was down to only two people waiting to make purchases and she heard the first chords of the next to last song in the show. As her last customer walked away, she began to pack up the items on the table, keeping an eye out for anyone else who might want to buy any band merchandise. By this point in the show, that was unusual, but she stayed alert just in case.

As the final note played, the crowd began to scream and jump up and down and call out for more. She fervently hoped tonight would not be the night Sebastian broke his 'no encore' policy. The noise became a dull roar as the lights on stage dimmed. Kerrigan closed the lid on the last tub and slid it under the table, pulled off the tablecloth, and began to fold it as she cast a quick glimpse toward the stage.

Jack and Sebastian had their backs to her, putting their guitars and leads away. Stephen was taking the cords out of the back of his keyboard and looked up as he began to wind them. She caught his eye and motioned him over to her. He nodded and she finished folding the tablecloth then tipped the table onto its side as she waited.

"How'd it go tonight?" Stephen asked when he finally joined her. He'd had to fight through the crowd to get to her, but he was smiling warmly.

"I'm not sure," Kerrigan replied with a careless shrug. "I'll figure it out tomorrow morning. I was wondering if you could take me back to the motel now."

Stephen frowned. "But we're still packing up." He waved toward the stage.

"I know, and you can come back for them. I've got everything here ready to go and I'd really like to go back to the motel," Kerrigan stated. She was beginning to feel closed in by the crowd and just wanted to be alone.

"Yeah, I guess." Stephen sighed as he looked at her. "Is everything okay? You look a little . . . frazzled."

"Yeah, yeah." She waved off his concerns as she picked up the merchandise tubs with the tablecloth and cash box stacked on top of it. "Just leave the table and grab that tub."

She turned and led Stephen to the van parked behind the building. Kerrigan waited as patiently as she could for him to get the trailer doors open and push his tub in before turning to take hers. She snatched the cash box off of the top and walked around to the passenger side of the van, opened the door, and slid into the seat.

Stephen opened his door and looked at her, the frown still puckering his brow as he sat down in the driver's seat and turned on the engine. "Are you sure you're okay? If you want to wait here, I'm sure I can speed the others up."

"No," Kerrigan blurted, then pressed her lips together and shook her head. "I'm fine and there's no need to rush the others. Let them enjoy their fans. I'll leave the merchandise in the trailer, just in case."

Stephen nodded his agreement as they pulled out of the parking lot. Kerrigan was relieved he didn't ask any more questions during the ten-minute drive. He parked the van in front of her room and she opened her door as soon as the vehicle had stopped.

"Thanks." Kerrigan turned and smiled. "And I'm serious. Take your time, enjoy the crowd. I'll see you all in the morning."

"Good night," he replied slowly as she closed her door.

She turned her back on the van and looked up at the door to her room on the second floor. She hated that they were now staying in rooms that opened to the outside instead of into a hallway, but they'd had to sacrifice some comforts because of the budget. This was their second night in Mobile, but she still wasn't sure of her surroundings.

With her head down and the cash box clutched to her chest, she made a beeline for the stairwell. When she made it onto the second floor landing, she pulled her key out of her jeans pocket and had it ready when she reached her room. Once inside, she quickly threw the swing bolt and pressed her back to the door as she blew out a long breath.

She stood and walked into the room, set the cash box on the desk and took the elastic band out of her hair. Kerrigan hadn't been able to heed Debra's advice and keep her hair loose, but she usually wore it in a low ponytail, a happy medium and one she was comfortable with. And she hadn't noticed a decline in sales because of it.

After dropping the hair tie next to the cash box, she moved toward the fridge. She opened the door and pulled out the ice bucket she'd placed in there earlier, happy to see most of the ice was still there. She grabbed the bottle of apple juice from the door and set the two items on the tray on top of the fridge. Bending over, she grabbed one last thing from the bottom shelf of the fridge and smiled at the cool, clear liquid in the Mason jar in her hand.

By the time Jack reached Kerrigan's door, he was fuming. After noticing Kerrigan had disappeared after the show, Jack had looked at his watch and realized what day it was. He'd cursed himself for not paying attention sooner and his concern for Kerrigan's well-being had only grown when Stephen had reappeared at the club without her. He'd been all but pushing the band out the door for the last hour, all the time worrying about what he might find when he finally reached her.

He vividly remembered the days after Mr. and Mrs. Dodd's deaths and how despondent Kerrigan had been. She was an orphan at sixteen, and the loss had hit her hard. He thought about her every year on the anniversary but had never been able to be with her.

Charlie had told him she'd spent the first anniversary in bed, claiming she had a headache. She hadn't eaten anything that day and very little for the following few days. When Jack had called Charlie a few days later, Charlie told him of his concern for his sister and Jack had asked to speak with her. She'd come to the phone and had been fairly quiet for the first few minutes of the call, but by the end he'd been able to make her laugh. He'd called again a few days later to check on her and she'd sounded better.

The following year hadn't been much better for her, even though he'd called her on the anniversary day. He had no idea how she'd dealt with it over the last six years. Would she be curled up in her bed? Would her face be red and tear streaked? He couldn't remember if she'd even eaten that day. Would she even open the door for him? He wouldn't know until he knocked.

He counted slowly to ten before he knocked. He waited and counted to ten again. When he reached five, the door opened and she greeted him with wide eyes and a lift in her lips.

"Jackson," she said with a slight slur. Her cheeks and nose were flushed and her breath smelled fruity. "What are you doing here?" She propped her shoulder against the frame of the door as she stared at him.

"I thought you could use a friend," he answered and watched the tears fill her eyes.

"You remembered." Her voice quivered and was almost inaudible.

He stepped toward her and took her in his arms, cradling her head on his shoulder. "Of course I remembered."

Jackson and Charlie had seen their homes as interchangeable in middle school, but when they reached high school, Jackson had preferred the Dodd home. His father was dead, his oldest brother tried too hard to be a substitute, and Jackson enjoyed the warm, cozy environment of his friend's house. He was there so often, his mother had stopped calling him home for dinner. Mrs. Dodd had never once complained about the extra mouth she had to feed. And Mr. Dodd's interest in Jackson's day had been equal to his interest in Charlie's and Kerri's.

He'd loved his mother and father—that had never been questioned. But he'd loved Mr. and Mrs. Dodd almost as much.

"They were second parents to me."

She sniffled into his chest. "They were first parents to me."

He walked forward, backing her into her room until he could close the door behind them. She lifted her head and turned to lead him further into the room. She plopped down in the armchair and picked up her glass. He looked around, quickly spotting the half-full bottle of juice and the quart jar of clear liquid, just under three quarters full, beside it. He watched as she shakily poured two fingers of the fluid from the jar, then twice as much of the juice, into her glass. She took a long sip, draining most of the concoction, before setting the glass down on the table.

"Every year," she began, her slur thicker, "I think about all the things they've missed. I think about the things they're gonna miss." She put her hand to her chest and her face scrunched and she looked up at him, tears flowing freely. "And it hurts so much." She balled her hand into a fist and lightly tapped her chest. "It hurts, and I miss them. I miss them every day and I can't bring them back."

Jack grabbed the desk chair and rolled it toward her. He sat down and took her empty hand.

"They didn't get to see my graduations," Kerrigan continued. "Either of them." She sniffed loudly. "And poor Charlie had to give up college to stay home with me." She looked at Jack and frowned. "They're going to miss his wedding, too."

He lifted her hand and pressed his lips to her knuckles, looking down to hide his frown. He hadn't known Charlie was engaged. That would be both of his childhood best friends married before him.

She picked up her glass, drained it in one swallow then set it back down. "Do you know what I miss?" She dropped her gaze to their hands and a lock of hair fell in front of her eye. "One of the many things I miss, I guess."

Jack shook his head as he tucked the loose strand behind her ear. His fingers tingled where they touched her. She drew back slightly and focused on his face with a dazed look.

"What do you miss?" he asked softly.

She relaxed and took a shallow breath. "Mom's singing. She always sang. Do you remember?"

"I remember," Jack said with a small smile. "She had a beautiful voice. If I remember correctly, you inherited it."

"I'm not nearly as good." She shook her head and looked toward her glass. "I used to sit at the counter and watch her dance around the kitchen and sing as she fixed dinner. Then Dad would come in from the garage and catch her in mid-swing and dance with her. Oh, and he'd laugh." Kerrigan laughed once. "He had such a hearty laugh."

She was suddenly sobbing again and Jack knelt in front of her. She looked at him and his heart wrenched in two. He rose on his knees and opened his arms to her. She eyed his outstretched arms and slowly lowered herself into them. He folded her to his chest as she shook with tears.

"Charlie got that," she said between sobs.

He closed his eyes and laid his head on the crown of hers. He'd let her down. He'd promised himself he would never allow her to feel that pain of loss again. That he would be there when she needed him. For the last six years he'd thought of her on this day but had hoped her pain had eased.

She laid her hands to his chest and he loosened his hold on her. She sat up and pushed herself back into her seat. Pressed into the corner, her eyes glazed over as she looked toward the side table. After wiping the tears from her cheeks she was quiet as Jack looked around the room. His eyes landed on the Mason jar and he looked at her.

"Is that moonshine?" he asked.

She slowly looked at him and he pointed to the jar. Her eyes followed the direction of his finger and one corner of her mouth turned up slightly.

"Yeah," she said with a giggle.

He raised an eyebrow. "Where did you get it?"

Her head fell back and both sides of her lips lifted. "It was Dad's. I rescued it from the renovation." She lifted her index finger to her lips and made an exaggerated *shush* sound. "I don't think Charlie knows."

Jack couldn't help but grin at the mischievous twinkle in her eye. Despite her sorrow and drunkenness, she still had that glimmer of humor he'd always loved. That humor slowly faded and her gaze became distant again.

"What renovation?" he asked as her breathing became slower.

"The one Charlie did to the house," she answered slowly, her focus across the room.

Her hair was loose around her shoulders and his eyes were drawn to the black waves as he waited for her to continue. She remained silent.

"When did he do that?" he murmured and inched closer until his elbow was propped on the cushion of the chair, beside her thigh.

Her brow crinkled as her eyes looked upward. "Three . . . no, four years ago."

"When you were in Paris?" Jack couldn't believe her brother would have done something as major as a remodel while she was gone, but she nodded her head.

"It was why I went to Paris. We didn't see eye to eye on the remodeling." Her eyes shifted to his face and she took a deep breath. "He was determined to do it and I was tired of arguing with him. So I left."

Jack's blood warmed in his veins. A fight with her brother was what had driven her to Paris? He wasn't surprised; flight had always been her first response. He could remember the way she'd hide in her closet from her mother when she'd done something wrong. Or how she'd run into the woods to climb a tree to get away from Charlie's, and sometimes his, teasing. She'd always tried to avoid confrontation.

And he couldn't help but think Charlie had known what her reaction would be. That he'd picked this fight so Kerrigan wouldn't be there when Jack came back to confess his feelings for her. The question now was, had Kerrigan known he was coming back, or had Charlie kept that from her too?

"You were still in school; you didn't have to go to Paris," he stated. *You could have stayed home and waited for me.*

"You sound just like Livie," she answered with a smile, but as it faded, sadness crept into her eyes. "Charlie wasn't the only reason I left. The opportunity to study abroad came when I needed it. I convinced Olivia to apply with me so I wouldn't have to go alone. We were accepted, and off we went."

Jack started to lift his hand to touch her upper arm but froze midway. He lowered it to her forearm and rested it just above her wrist. The far off look in her eyes remained so he wasn't sure she'd noticed.

"Kerri, what happened in Paris?" he asked hesitantly. She'd never brought it up but he had a feeling that something significant had happened to her there. The problem was, he couldn't begin to guess what it was or how much it had affected her.

She blinked sluggishly and he couldn't be sure if it was because of the liquor or whether she was considering his question. Slowly she turned to look at him and gave him a wan smile.

"You don't really want to know," she reassured him.

He perked up. "Kerrigan," he said and waited until she looked directly at him. When she finally met his gaze, he added, "I wouldn't have asked."

Her eyes filled with tears and she looked away. "You won't like it," she croaked. "You won't like me."

"Kerri." He took her hands and squeezed them. "Nothing you tell me could change what I think of you."

She sat silently for a moment, then looked away as her tongue slid across her bottom lip.

"I met a man," she began and he immediately felt sick.

She was probably right. He knew he wasn't going to like whatever followed.

"He stole your heart?" Jack tried to joke but the pain in his chest put an edge to his voice.

"No," she replied, seeming not to notice as she laid her head against the seat. "That was already gone."

She said it so airily yet so matter-of-factly that he felt certain her heart was still gone. He just wished he knew who had it.

"He stole much more than that," Kerrigan continued.

Jack fought the urge to ask and a rock formed in the pit of his stomach. It would be better to let her tell her story in her own time.

"His name was Raoul, and we met him about two weeks after we arrived in Paris," she whispered, her drunken slur suddenly gone as she began to talk softly. "He was French—he said he was Parisian—and he became our guide to the city." She sounded detached. "He showed us all the best places to eat, the places the locals went, not the tourists. We considered him a friend, but we were always careful."

"You didn't trust him?" Jack asked as the rock grew larger.

"It wasn't that," she answered, her head turning side to side. "Neither of us wanted to date, and we didn't want to risk giving him the wrong idea, so we never went alone with him." She paused and took a few breaths then sighed. "About six weeks after we met him, he came by the apartment and asked if I wanted to go to dinner with him. Olivia was still at the campus library so I called her. She said she'd be late and would pick up something on the way home and that I should go out with him. We felt like we'd known him long enough so we didn't think there would be a problem."

She shifted in her seat, pulling her feet up to the cushion and turning so her knees rested against one arm, her back against the other. One of her hands moved to her lap while the other remained in his.

"We walked to dinner, ate, paid separately, then walked back to my apartment." Kerrigan turned her head toward him but didn't look at his face. "I told him good-bye on the sidewalk then watched him walk away before I turned and went up the steps. I didn't think anything of it when he reappeared and held the door for me and picked up our conversation like it had never stopped. We talked all the way up to the third floor and I stopped before unlocking my apartment door." Her eyes shifted to her lap. "I started to feel uneasy but tried to laugh it off as I told him good-bye again. He smiled like it was nothing and walked away."

Kerrigan grew silent and Jack sat motionless. Not sure what to say, not sure he wanted to hear what came next, he waited for her to continue. After a while, she nodded.

"I waited until I heard him reach the second floor landing, then unlocked my door and went into my apartment. Before I could close the door again, he was there, with his foot blocking the door and his hand just above the doorknob. I had barely registered that before he pushed the door open, knocking me backward, and before I could recover, the door was closed and his mouth was on mine." A single tear trickled down her cheek.

Jack had no voice. This explained the way she reacted to men now and he wondered if it had anything to do with her rejection of him in Paris. He was numb to think this was what had kept them apart.

"I tried to fight him," she continued in an even smaller voice. "I pushed him, I hit him, I tried to run. But the more I fought, the more excited he became. He liked the challenge and eventually I realized that." She gently rocked herself from side to side and Jack had to look away. "He wrestled me to the floor and I kneed him in the groin. When he rolled off of me I tried to crawl away but he grabbed my ankle and twisted it until I felt it pop. I gave up after that. He cut my pants off." Her eyes closed and the lump in her throat bobbed up and down. "When he finally . . . you know," she stuttered, "I bit my lip against the pain and let my mind wander. I thought of home, and . . ." Her lips came together and quivered.

Jack waited for her to elaborate further, but instead the tremor sped up. He hated that he'd caused her to remember such a horrible experience. Anger seared through his veins. He wanted to hurt the man who'd done this to her. If given the chance he'd probably commit murder. Gently, he laid his hand on her shoulder and began to rub in small circles.

She shook quietly for a few moments then regained her composure. "The next thing I remember was Olivia screaming like a banshee as she pulled him off of me. Her screaming brought the neighbors running and he took off. The woman who lived across the hall came in and covered me up, then tried to comfort us both as she called the police. Our neighbors chased after him but they never caught him."

"What . . ." Jack cleared his throat. "What happened next?"

Kerrigan turned her head to look at him, held his gaze for a moment, then glanced at her drinking glass on the side table. She released his hand and reached for the empty glass.

"Let me," Jack said and she put her hand down on the seat of the chair and watched him. He poured a little moonshine into the glass and added more apple juice. He handed the glass to her and she took a small sip. He refrained from repeating his question, allowing her to regain her strength from the drink.

After another sip, she cradled the glass in her lap and stared at it. "The police came. Olivia told them what she'd walked in on, I gave my side of the story, and the female officer escorted us to the hospital. They examined me and stitched me up."

Good God. Jack was nauseous. How rough had he been with her?

"Stitched you up?"

"He sliced my hip when he cut my pants off, so they had to stitch that up." She rubbed a spot on her jeans, just above the pocket, then slid the same hand up to her jaw. "He cut me here when I kept fighting."

When her hand moved away he noticed a pale scar along her jawline. It was thin and about two inches long. He ran the tip of his finger along the length of the white line, lingering when it reached her chin as his gaze rose to meet hers. Her breathing was shallow and her eyes had widened slightly.

"They gave me a pill to prevent pregnancy," she whispered as his finger skimmed down her neck and across her collarbone.

His brows came together as his finger froze. "You weren't using birth control?"

She shook her head. "I was a virgin. I hadn't needed it."

He lowered his hand to the seat beside her as she turned her face away. She took another sip of her drink and he swallowed the lump in his throat.

"Olivia had to talk me into it. I hadn't wanted to at first; I'd wanted to wait until I knew for sure if I needed it," she muttered, almost to herself. "We were pretty sure he hadn't finished completely, but Olivia convinced me it was better to be safe. She said it would be easier to take the pill than to have to consider my options later." She inhaled deeply through her nose and blew the air past her lips as she looked down. "She figured I would want to be done with it in case I met the right man for me, the one I could have a future with. Then I thought about you and took the pill."

Jack's heart stopped then began racing. His mouth was so dry his tongue stuck to the roof of his mouth. Had he heard her correctly? It was almost too good to be true. If she'd felt that way when he'd come to Paris, why hadn't she seen him? She'd needed him, almost as much as he'd needed to see her. She had to know he would have comforted her.

If he asked, would she answer?

He moistened his mouth. "What did you just say?"

It was almost slow motion, the way her eyes rounded to the point they looked like they would pop out of her head. Her chin lifted and she turned away and laid her forehead against the back of the chair. She was not going to make this easy. He pushed himself back into the desk chair and wheeled closer, until his knees were pressed against the seat of her chair.

"Kerrigan," he softly said as he placed his hand on the arm of her chair, behind her back. His palm itched to touch her, to pull her into his arms and comfort her the way he hadn't been able to in Paris.

She remained stiff in her seat as she lifted her glass to her lips and drained what was left. He saw the tremor in her hand as she lowered it to her lap. He heard the rasp of her throat as she cleared it. Sluggishly, she turned and gave him a wan smile.

"I'm tired. I think I'd like to go to bed now."

He choked back the frustration and lifted the corner of his mouth. "Of course," he said and wheeled his chair backward.

As he stood, she lowered her own feet to the floor and unsteadily rose from her seat. She stumbled as she took a step and Jack grabbed her elbow to keep her from falling. He wrapped his other arm around her as her forehead fell against his chest. She softened into his embrace and he rested his chin on the crown of her head, deeply inhaling her honeysuckle and lemon scent and closing his eyes.

He was supposed to be comforting her, but the calmness that came over him, simply from having her in his arms, was astonishing. This was where he'd wanted her for eight long years. This was where she belonged. He would do whatever he had to do to make sure she knew that.

She laid her hand on his chest and gently lifted her head. She tilted her face toward his and blinked slowly.

"Can you help me get ready for bed?" she slurred as he lost himself in her silver eyes.

Jack nodded then helped her across the room, closed the bathroom door behind her, and waited outside. When she opened the door, her face was still damp, her glasses slightly askew, and her breath smelled minty. He straightened her glasses as she looped her arm through his and they walked back toward the bed. He pulled back the sheet and comforter and eased her onto the mattress. She pulled her feet up and stretched out and he covered her as she rolled onto her side.

"All set?" He put his hands behind him and stepped back. He had a sudden, strong urge to kiss her, to hug her, to crawl into the bed beside her and just hold her.

When she nodded, he said, "I'll see you in the morning then," and took a step toward the door.

"Jackson."

The sound of his full name in her sweet voice slithered down his spine like the tickle of a feather and his breath hitched. He turned to look at her, his gaze slowly travelling up the outline of her body under the blanket, settling on the soft curve of her cheek. Her eyes slowly opened and met his.

"Yes?" he asked just as softly.

"Can you sit with me?" she asked. "Just until I fall asleep," she added and a tear slid down her cheek. "I don't want to be alone."

Her final statement was barely audible and filled with sadness . . . how could he refuse her? In an instant, he was kneeling beside the bed, her hand in his.

"Whatever you need."

She gave a watery smile. "Thank you."

He kissed her knuckles as she closed her eyes. He remained immobile, mesmerized by the stillness of her features and the sound of her steady breathing. She slipped her hand out of his.

"You might want to sit in the chair—it would be more comfortable." She pointed at the armchair before opening an eye. "I don't think you'll be there long," she teased and her lips lifted slightly.

He tried not to grin as he sat in the chair she'd formerly occupied. "Kerri," he said softly after he was settled, surprised to see her eye closed again.

"Hmm?" she responded.

"Was he ever caught?" Jack had to know if the son of a bitch who had violated her was still at large. His brother was a police officer; there had to be something he could do for her.

Both of Kerrigan's eyes opened this time and her brow furrowed as she lifted her head. "Who?"

"Raoul?" Jack thought that was the name she'd given.

"Oh," she breathed and lowered her head back to her pillow. "Yeah, he was. About six months later, after I'd moved to London, I got a call from the French police. He was in custody and awaiting trial. They asked if I would be willing to testify against him."

Jack's lip curled. They would ask her to do that after what that man had put her through? "What did you say?"

"I said I'd think about it. They had other women who would do it, other victims. The evidence they already had against him, and the fact he'd been caught in the act, was enough that they didn't really need me," she answered, her blinks getting longer until her eyes remained closed.

"Caught in the act?" Jack asked, his nausea bubbling into a rage.

"Mm-hm." Kerrigan nodded and rolled slightly, her entire face now visible to him. "By the fiancé of a woman he attacked. He nearly killed Raoul, but she stopped him so he wouldn't be charged with murder."

Jack wanted to shake the man's hand. Given the chance, he would have done the same thing.

"They called me a few weeks later and told me Raoul was dead and my testimony wouldn't be needed." She inhaled deeply and Jack watched the rise and fall of her chest.

"How did he die?" Jack hoped it was slow and painful.

Kerrigan's eyes opened a sliver. "Beaten up in jail." Her eyelids fell, her lashes long across her pale cheeks. "Died of his injuries a few days later."

Good, Jack thought as he watched her. He only regretted he hadn't been able to stand up for Kerrigan himself. How long had it been between the rape and his arrival at her apartment in Paris? Had he missed it by minutes? Hours? Days?

He'd gone to see Charlie as soon as he could that summer. Kerri had been out of school for at least a month and Jack had expected to find her at home. When he'd walked into their house, he'd noticed the remodeling but hadn't realized the significance of it. When Charlie told him Kerri wasn't there, that she'd gone to Paris, Jack had been furious. He'd left the house as soon as the words had been out of Charlie's mouth, assuming Charlie had encouraged her to go.

He understood now that Charlie hadn't encouraged her; however, Jack couldn't help but wonder if he'd tried to stop her. Jack had spent the next few weeks debating whether or not he wanted to go after her or wait for her to come home. It seems he should have been a little faster in his deciding, but how much time would have changed things?

"Kerri," Jack whispered.

She didn't stir. Her breathing remained steady and her eyes didn't move. He got out of his seat and knelt beside the bed.

"Kerrigan," he tried again, softly.

Still nothing. He gently took her glasses off her face. She sighed and rolled onto her side, her hands coming up to rest under her cheek.

He thought his heart would burst from his chest. She was so beautiful and so courageous to have suffered like she had and still been willing to testify, to relive everything. If he'd only known, he would have done anything to carry that burden for her.

And after her earlier slip, he felt like all he had to do was reach out to her and they could finally have what it seemed they both wanted. He still wanted her, more now than he ever had. She was tough and fragile at the same time. Over the past two weeks, she'd shown on more than one occasion how she could stand up to Sebastian, or a tough club manager, and not back down. He now understood better what it had cost her, and how much she still needed someone to stand beside her, to stand up for her if she needed them to.

Would she let him do that for her?

He folded her glasses and set them on the side table, then rose to his feet. He picked up the juice and moonshine and took them to the refrigerator. While he was there, he grabbed a clean glass and dunked it into the ice bucket, filling it with more water than ice. He walked back to her bedside and set the glass on the table. She would need the water when she woke up in the morning.

She frowned as she rolled to her other side, her back now to him as he hovered beside her. He'd done what she'd asked and stayed with her until she fell asleep and he knew he should leave. But he just couldn't. He'd known how difficult this night, the anniversary of her parents' deaths, would be for her. He was sorry to have caused the other memories to resurface.

Did she relive the rape every year too?

Kerrigan moaned and Jack glanced down at her. Her frown had deepened, and her brow was wrinkled with distress. She groaned again and her arms came up and pushed away something he couldn't see. Her head began to shake side to side. She mumbled something and her flailing arm motions became more frantic.

She was clearly having a nightmare.

"Kerri," Jack said as he walked around the foot of the bed, watching her face distort with anguish. He stopped on the other side and sat on the bed, facing the head and her. "Kerrigan," he repeated her name more firmly.

She mumbled incoherently and continued to push her demons away, starting to shake more intensely. “No,” she stated, pushing him away as he reached for her hand. “No.”

He gently gripped her forearms as he lowered himself to the mattress beside her. “Kerri.”

Her body calmed and her arms slowly lowered to her side, but her head was still moving from side to side. “No.”

Jack slowly slid his hands up her arms until he was holding her against his chest. He slipped one arm between her and the mattress and used it to cradle her body. With his other hand he stilled her head. He made a *shhh* sound softly into her ear and felt the tension slowly leave her body.

“Jackson,” she cried and he looked down at her face. Her body had relaxed, but her eyes remained closed and a tear slid down her cheek. “I’m so sorry. I tried to stop him.”

“Shh,” Jack soothed, wondering why she was apologizing. “I know you did.”

“I tried,” she slurred and went still in his arms.

Jack laid his head on the pillow beside her, cradling her body to his. He couldn’t leave her now. What if she had another nightmare? He wouldn’t be able to sleep thinking she might be restless. There was only one thing he could do to ensure they both had a good night’s sleep.

Seventeen

As she woke up, Kerrigan noticed an unfamiliar weight draped across her waist and a solid wall of warmth against her back. Lying still, eyes closed, she tried to remember what had happened the night before, but her memory was foggy. The last thing she remembered was opening her door and finding Jack standing outside. He'd remembered it was the anniversary of her parents' deaths and had thought she might not want to be alone.

He'd been right.

She'd been so relieved to see him, she'd led him into the room and fixed another drink. The last few years she'd been alone in Europe on the anniversary and had allowed herself to indulge in her self-pity with alcohol. Otherwise, she rarely drank and certainly almost never got drunk. She was fortunate not to be feeling hung over from the night before.

Her memory, however, had not escaped the effects of the alcohol and she struggled to remember what had gone on after that.

The pressure on her waist shifted to her hip and a warm breath ruffled the hair on the back of her head. Kerrigan stiffened as her eyes popped open. She looked down to where she felt the pressure against her hip and saw a masculine arm lying over her body. Unless she'd let someone else into her room the night before, she had a feeling she knew who the arm belonged to. But she couldn't remember anything clearly, so she couldn't be positive.

Her heart sped up and her lungs felt tight as her gaze followed the length of the arm until she saw the body it was attached to. When her eyes finally came to rest on Jack's face, she relaxed and released a slow, silent breath. Her panic subsided as she took in his features as he slept.

She could almost see the boy she knew in the man who lay there beside her. His cheek was smooth but his jaw was peppered with dark stubble. His closed eyes were softened and she could see the faintest laugh lines stretching from the corners.

What was he doing asleep in her bed?

As she turned her head, she noticed he was sleeping on top of the flat sheet, and she was under it. It made it easier for her to slide out of the bed without disturbing him, but as her feet hit the floor, she turned around to make sure he was still asleep. She looked down at her clothes, surprised to see she was still in the jeans and shirt she'd worn to the concert the night before. Her glasses were on the bedside table, next to a full glass. She picked it up and took a sip. Happy to discover it was water, she drank it all as she put her glasses on.

Tiptoeing across the room, she set the empty glass down on top of the fridge and continued to her suitcase. She grabbed a pair of loose workout pants and a T-shirt then walked to the bathroom to change.

When she was dressed, she crept back into the room, grabbed her room key and phone off of the desk, slipped her shoes on, then glided back toward the door. She really needed to clear her head. Hopefully a large cup of coffee would help.

She cast a quick glance at Jack, still asleep in her bed, and her heart skipped a beat. What had she said to him last night and why was he still there?

She'd have to figure that out before she would be ready to talk to him. She left the room, making sure the door closed quietly behind her. As she walked toward the motel lobby, where she knew she would find a pot of coffee, she wracked her brain to remember the night before. He'd come in, they'd talked about her parents for a little bit, and then about Charlie . . . and then . . .

She froze and lifted her gaze straight ahead.

And then she'd brought up Paris.

She blew out a breath as she slowly began to move forward. Why had she done that? Clearly she hadn't been thinking at all. She'd only ever talked about the rape with her therapist in Paris, and never again since. She'd only told Charlie because Olivia had insisted he needed to know, and she'd never wanted anyone else in Rocky Creek to find out about it. Especially Jackson.

She didn't want people judging her and their pity was an even less palatable idea. But worst of all was the idea of Jackson looking at her differently.

Now she wondered how much she had told Jack the night before. How many things she didn't want him to know had she blurted out in her drunken state?

Kerrigan stopped in front of the door of the reception area, looked through the window at the coffee maker and the small cups beside it, and decided that just wouldn't be enough. She turned and scanned the parking lot. Just across a side street stood a donut shop and she began moving toward it.

She couldn't do anything about whatever she'd told Jack the night before, so the question now was what should she do next? She could probably blame the alcohol and feign ignorance, pretending she couldn't remember what she'd said and denying anything he brought up. Given that she actually couldn't currently remember everything she'd told him, that wouldn't be far from the truth.

She looked both ways as she crossed the small street then hopped over the curb into the parking lot.

The image of him, sound asleep in her bed, gave her pause, in step and thought. She vaguely remembered having a nightmare during the night. She'd been back in that Parisian apartment, fighting for her life and her innocence, when suddenly a comforting arm and the soothing smell of cinnamon surrounded her. She hadn't woken up, but the dream had shifted to her childhood bedroom, to the morning of her parents' funeral, and she'd been in Jackson's arms again.

Had Jack stayed with her simply to be there if she needed his comforting touch? If so, then lying to him, or denying the truth, would be the wrong way to go. Whatever horrors she'd told him last night, if he asked more about them, she should be honest. She'd wanted to keep the truth from him because she didn't think he'd want to be with her if he knew. But she had a feeling she'd already told him everything anyway, so she really had nothing else to lose.

Olivia had always said she was crazy for thinking Jackson would look down on her for the rape. But Kerrigan's therapist had said her reaction was completely normal. Since she'd stopped seeing the therapist after six months, she wasn't sure how long that feeling was supposed to last. She still felt that way, but she was starting to suspect it was more of a shield than anything else.

She walked into the donut shop, ordered a large hazelnut coffee for herself, a black coffee for him, and two chocolate chip scones, then walked out with her head high.

She quickly made her way back to her motel room, sipping her coffee as she built her confidence. She may as well get it over with.

When she reached the top of the stairs, she heard male voices and slowed her pace.

"You promised me two weeks, Jack," Sebastian grumbled. "You said you could seduce her and make her leave in two weeks. Your time is up."

Kerrigan stopped dead and turned her ear toward the conversation just around the corner. Her heart leapt to her throat. What had they been up to?

"I need a little more time," Jack stated.

"Why? You fucked her last night, didn't you?" Sebastian was almost yelling and Kerrigan's cheeks felt suddenly warm. "Get another woman in your bed, have her find you there, and make her leave."

Kerrigan's eyes widened. That had been their plan? Did Jack think she would be that easy to manipulate? She wasn't that desperate.

"Damn it, Sebastian, lower your voice," Jack growled. "I said I would get it done and I will, in my own time. This isn't as easy as I thought it would be."

As easy as he thought it would be? Tears stung Kerrigan's eyes. He'd been using their childhood friendship against her. And she'd believed in his sincerity. She may not be desperate, but she was obviously foolish.

She looked at the second cup of coffee in her hands and tossed it in the nearest trashcan.

"She's half in love with you already, with the way you stand up for her and stuff," Sebastian stated.

Kerrigan pulled her shoulders back and started moving in their direction, pushing her tears, and her heart, back down. She'd make Jack regret this.

"What did you say?" Jack asked.

"Doesn't matter." Sebastian shrugged. "Just that your job shouldn't be that hard. Deal her the final blow so we can be free of her shackles."

Kerrigan stopped two feet behind Sebastian. "Did you come up with that plan all on your own?"

Jack heard the steeliness in her voice and his heart rate sped up as he looked over Sebastian's shoulder. Her face was a thundercloud. How much had she heard?

"I must admit, Sebastian," she began coolly and a chill ran down Jack's spine, "I hadn't thought you capable of such an elaborate plan. It's just too bad it wouldn't have worked. And it certainly won't work now that I know."

Sebastian turned and Kerrigan's eyes narrowed on his face.

"What do you mean, elaborate? It was pretty straightforward," Sebastian snapped.

"Maybe. But in your expectation to get your own way, as you usually do, you failed to take one thing into consideration," she said with a slight curl of her lips.

Jack swallowed the lump in his throat. He'd seen that look on her face before and she was getting ready to unleash hell.

"Oh yeah?" Sebastian's arms folded across his chest. "Like what?"

"Like me." She pursed her lips and let the silence draw out for a moment. "You failed to consider how I might feel about *him*. I can assure you, Jack's not my type."

The sting of her words hit Jack square in the chest. As angry as she was, that had probably been her point. She was lashing out, and rightfully so, but he needed her to know things weren't exactly how they seemed at the moment. He slid away from her door so he would have a more direct line of sight to her.

"But he spent the night in your room." Sebastian pointed to her door.

"Why would you think that?" Kerrigan scoffed.

"He was just coming out of there." Sebastian's volume rose slightly and Jack noticed the color in his cheeks.

"I'm not sure why." Kerrigan held up a coffee cup in one hand and a paper bag in the other. "I was getting breakfast. Clearly only for myself. Don't you think if he'd been in there when I left, I'd have brought one for him too?" She shook her head as she walked past Sebastian. "It would be bad manners not to."

Jack frowned as his stomach growled in protest. Maybe she hadn't expected him to be there when she got back. He needed to come up with an excuse as to why he was there but had no idea what it would be. She seemed to have it under control, so anything he said might do more harm than good.

She stepped past Sebastian and turned her back to Jack. He couldn't see her face, but saw the way she held her shoulders, tight and erect. He'd seen her angry plenty of times, but this was different.

"It's too bad though," she continued, still focusing on Sebastian. "I'm curious as to how you think the drama should have played out. Regardless, I won't be going anywhere. I have a job to do. But you're free to plot against me if you'd like. You and Jack should have plenty of time to come up with something good before the end of the tour."

Jack avoided giving Sebastian the furious glare he deserved. He had no intention of participating in any more of Sebastian's schemes, and he was sorry he'd agreed to this one. Not that he'd liked the alternative, but she wasn't happy and he was to blame. He glanced at her, hoping to see her face, to see if he could gauge her anger and hurt, but she was staring at her doorknob, fiddling with the key in her shaking hand.

"Next time, though, may I suggest you not discuss your nefarious schemes in front of my door?" She pushed the door open and turned to look at Sebastian again. "You have forty-five minutes to have your stuff out of your room and into the van. We're leaving in an hour and a half."

With that she walked into her room and closed the door.

Damn it. Now what was he going to do?

When he'd woken up, he'd been surprised to find her gone but anxious for the conversation they would have when she returned. Before falling asleep, with her in his arms, he'd come up with a list of questions he wanted to ask her. About what happened in Paris and why she'd refused to see him, but more importantly, what had she meant by her apology or why she'd thought of him in the Parisian hospital. He'd been optimistic she'd had feelings for him then and was hoping she still had them.

"Let's go," Sebastian grumbled.

Jack looked at him and shook his head. "No, I want to see how we did last night with sales. You go on, I'll be there in a few minutes."

"Whatever." Sebastian started walking in the direction of their shared room.

Once Sebastian had turned the corner, Jack knocked on Kerrigan's door. After a minute with no answer, he knocked again. Silence. She wasn't going to make this easy for him.

He hammered again and stepped closer to the door, putting his mouth close to the edge that opened into the room. "Kerri," he called and waited. After counting to one hundred, he called her name again and counted again, one hundred more. "Kerrigan, can we talk?"

He'd just reached fifty again when he heard the swing bolt move inside the room and the door opened. He held back a groan when he saw she'd bolted the door against him. She pushed a folded paper through the opening.

"That's last night's numbers," Kerrigan stated as he took the paper from her. Her focus was on something over his shoulder as she continued, "along with a request for more bandanas for Debra. If you want to look at it, fine. Otherwise, could you give that to Stephen for me? Thanks."

She closed the door.

He stared at the space that had just been open to him, his mouth slightly agape. He rapped his knuckles on the red wood again. "Kerrigan, I'd like to talk to you please."

The door remained closed.

"Fine," he snapped, his frustration bubbling into anger. "Then I'll stand out here and yell what I want to say. Would you prefer that?"

The door flew open, but only as far as the bolt would allow. He was greeted with steely slits above rosy cheeks.

"I have nothing to say to you," she hissed. "Nor do I think you have anything to say that I want to hear." She inhaled quickly. "How dare you use me so carelessly? How dare you use the friendship we used to have against me in such a ruthless way? Did you honestly think I wouldn't find out? Or that I wouldn't care? I trusted you and you abused that trust."

She abruptly closed the door again as he processed her words. Just as suddenly it opened again but her face didn't appear.

"Unless you have business to discuss with me, I have nothing more to say to you. Ever. Don't bother trying for a casual conversation—it won't happen. Are we clear?"

"Kerrigan, I'm sorry," Jack said, stepping closer to the void. "Please let me in so I can explain."

"No," she snapped. "I don't want to hear your explanations or excuses. Are we clear?" she repeated.

"No," Jack answered. He was not about to agree to not talk to her. Not until this was cleared up and he could explain what she'd overheard.

"Have it your way. You now have thirty minutes to pack."

The door closed again.

Jack was torn. He could stand there and continue to try talking to her, or he could leave, regroup, and try again later.

He opted for the latter.

True to her threat, Kerrigan refused to speak to Jack unless it dealt with band business. While she remained cordial toward him when other band members were around, she avoided being with him one-on-one. And when he caught her alone and approached her, she'd get up and move to a more crowded place.

Two cities and two mornings later, he was fed up. As he, Stephen, and Riley loaded their luggage into the van, Jack kept an eye on Kerrigan, standing a few feet away on the sidewalk and studying something on her phone, and silently rehearsed the conversation he would have with her as soon as they were alone. He needed to explain that she had misunderstood the conversation she'd overheard. He wanted to tell her he would never use her and would rather die than hurt her.

He watched Riley and Stephen wander off and waited until they were out of earshot to approach her. Her head turned slightly in his direction and her lips tightened but she remained silent.

When he was beside her, he spoke gently. "It's my turn to drive this morning."

She lowered her phone and narrowed her eyes as she turned her face toward him. "I know."

"Well, I need a cup of coffee and thought you might want one, too." He gave her his kindest, least threatening smile, hoping to show her he was interested in a truce.

She studied his expression for a moment then looked away. "I'm good, thanks."

So much for subtlety. "Kerrigan, can we talk?"

She tilted her head back and her gaze drifted somewhere over his head. "Is this something you could have brought up with the rest of the band?"

While her tone was weary, there was an edge to her voice that Jack couldn't place. He wasn't sure he liked it.

"No," Jack answered. "I want to talk about what you heard."

Her eyes lowered to his and one eyebrow shot up. "I don't think we need to talk about that."

"Kerrigan," Riley called as he trotted up beside her. "Hazelnut coffee, just like ye asked for."

She held Jack's gaze for another beat, then turned to Riley with a large, warm smile. Jack's heart sank. He'd wanted that smile for himself.

"Thank you, Riley," she said as she took the coffee from his outstretched hand.

"I brought ye breakfast, too. Would ye like to go o'er there to sit and eat it?"

"As long as we're within sight of the hotel."

Riley assured her they would be and they strolled across the parking lot to sit on the curb and enjoy their breakfast.

Jack's disappointment turned to anger as he watched the two of them laugh. That should be him sitting beside her. She should be smiling serenely at his stories. Instead, he suddenly felt like more of an outsider in her life than he'd ever felt before.

Even in Paris.

"I'm beginning to think there's something I'm missing."

Jack jumped at the sound of Stephen's voice so close to him.

"Maybe they'll find it during the room inspection," Jack replied without taking his eyes off of Kerrigan's face.

"That's not what I mean." Stephen stepped between Jack and his view of Kerrigan.

Jack took a step back. "What do you mean then?"

"I mean, there's something almost obsessive in the way you watch her," Stephen answered. "I've never seen you like this before and, I hate to admit, it worries me. A lot."

"Well, don't," Jack scoffed as he stepped to the side so he could focus on Kerrigan again.

"I've also seen the way she interacts with you, Jack," Stephen continued.

Jack turned his head toward Stephen and glanced at him for a moment.

"I've noticed a change in the last few days." Stephen placed himself in Jack's line of sight again. "What happened?"

Sebastian happened.

Jack swallowed the bile and rage in his throat and wiped the frustration off his face before he focused on Stephen. He lifted his shoulders casually. "It's just a misunderstanding." One that he fully intended to clear up as soon as she decided to stay in his company for longer than two seconds.

Stephen pressed his lips together and held Jack's stare. After a moment of silent consideration, he nodded and shrugged. "Fine. Don't tell me. I just hope it's not something that will cost us the best, most organized, most disciplined manager we've ever had. We can't get any better than her, Jack. Don't run her off with your misguided flirtations."

"My flirtations?" Jack snapped and pointed in Kerrigan's direction. "What about Riley?"

"Riley acts that way with every woman he meets." Stephen shook his head. "Even Debra. He's never serious."

Jack wasn't so sure of that. He hadn't forgotten the conversation he'd had with the drummer.

"Jack." Kerrigan's voice was sharp and close.

Jack looked up and saw her in the middle of the parking lot, moving toward the motel with the motel manager by her side.

"Find Sebastian and meet me in your room."

Given the scowl on her face and the determination in her stride, Jack didn't hesitate. Because he'd known that there was work to be done, Sebastian was nowhere near the van, but Jack had discovered his hiding spot as he'd come down the steps from his room on the second floor. Sure enough, he quickly found Sebastian tucked away under the stairs and already absorbed in an episode of *Behind the Music*. Jack yanked out his earbuds, grabbed Sebastian by the arm, and dragged him to the room they had shared during their overnight stay before Sebastian could utter a single word of argument.

When Jack walked into the room, he thought he might have stepped into a war zone, only on a smaller scale and confined to this one room. This couldn't possibly be the room he'd left less than an hour ago.

Both of the mattresses were overturned, sliced open with springs sticking out like coiled porcupine needles. The headboards had been ripped away from the walls and splintered in the process. It appeared Sebastian had used one of the larger splinters to gouge the surface of the desk and dresser and to rip the holes in the mattresses. The lampshades and desk chairs had broken frames and had been tossed into the space left empty by the displaced mattresses.

From where he stood, Jack could see the mirror was streaked in black, most likely Sebastian's eyeliner, but mercifully couldn't see any damage to the marble countertop or sink. He had no idea what the bathroom might look like. Wide-eyed with disgust and amazement, he turned to Sebastian, who simply returned his stare with a smirk.

"Why did you do this?" Kerrigan snapped and Jack turned his attention to her. Her cheeks were red, her jaw tight, and her eyes narrowed on Sebastian.

Jack breathed a sigh of relief. Even though they had shared the room, she didn't appear to be blaming him for any of the damage.

"I was bored."

"Bored?" she spat through clenched teeth. Her shoulders slowly lifted and fell and she lifted her chin. "Well, I hope you've satisfied your boredom. It's going to cost you." She took a piece of paper from the manager. "Twelve hundred dollars."

Jack's chin dropped and he quickly covered his mouth with his palm. Sebastian laughed and Jack's free hand twitched to punch him.

"You also have a six hundred dollar food bill from the motel restaurant last night," she added.

"Oh well." Sebastian shrugged. "I don't have the money."

"You just got paid."

Jack heard the tremor in her voice and now realized her entire body was shaking, most likely with the anger she was suppressing. He needed to step in.

"Sebastian," Jack said, his focus on Kerrigan's face. "Pay it. We need to go."

"I can't," Sebastian replied smugly. "Perhaps I can be motivated to find the money if she agrees to leave the band."

Kerrigan moved toward Sebastian. "I'm not going anywhere. Get that through your thick skull."

"Then I'm not paying a penny." Sebastian took a large stride toward her and Jack stepped between them.

With his back to Kerrigan, he put his hands on Sebastian's chest. "Give me a minute, Kerrigan," he said and pushed Sebastian out the door before she could argue. Once they were outside, Jack gave into his urge to punch Sebastian and landed his fist on his friend's bicep. "What the hell, Sebastian?"

"What?" Sebastian rubbed his arm.

"That room did not look like that when I left it this morning." Jack kept his voice even and reigned his temper back in. Arguing with Sebastian never did any good. "Did you stay up all night planning this?"

"Maybe." Sebastian chuckled. "My finest work, don't you think?"

Jack *thought* he might want to strangle Sebastian. Or at the very least beat some sense into him.

"You will pay what you owe. And you will never do this again." Jack stepped backward and motioned toward the room.

Sebastian's shoulders fell and he looked into the distance over Jack's shoulder. "I can't."

"What do you mean you can't? We got paid two days ago. You can't possibly have spent it all already," Jack snapped, knowing it was absolutely possible for Sebastian to have done just that.

He'd done it before, on women, booze, tattoos, whatever had struck his fancy. When payday came around, Sebastian's money was usually burning a hole in his pocket before it was in his hand. His silence was evidence that he was most likely telling the truth.

Jack threw his arms out to his side. "Call your father then," he said. "He's bailed you out before."

"Not this time," Sebastian grumbled.

The air slowly escaped Jack's lungs as he waited for Sebastian to continue. "What do you mean?" he finally had to ask.

"I mean . . ." Sebastian pressed his shoulders against the wall and stuck his hands in his pockets, "I called him last week to see if he would call Jacob and get this bitch off our tour, but he refused."

Jack bristled at the word 'bitch' but quickly calmed down upon hearing Mr. Bates wouldn't do Sebastian's bidding.

"He said it's time I start doing as I was told and making an effort to succeed rather than just goof off with this band." Sebastian's lip curled as he looked at the sidewalk. "He's probably spending his money on one of his other brats."

Jack was struck dumb. In the weeks since Kerrigan had joined them, Jack had been thinking exactly the same as Mr. Bates: Sebastian needed to make an effort to help the band fix the problems he'd caused. But if Jack had said anything, he doubted it would have had the same effect on Sebastian as his father's words apparently had. Even if Sebastian would rather blame it on his younger half-siblings, Jack could tell that his father's refusal to help had struck Sebastian deeply.

Jack almost felt sorry for him.

"Okay," Kerrigan said, sounding chipper, as she came out of the room. "It's taken care of. We can go."

Jack met her gaze and, for the first time in two days, she didn't look away. The fortitude he saw in her eyes filled him equally with pride and curiosity, and more than a little desire. He could almost forget she was his band's manager and was currently not on speaking terms with him.

"We can?" Sebastian asked, pulling Jack back to the reality of their situation. "What did you offer him?"

Kerrigan's lip lifted at the corner and she turned her focus to Sebastian. "Money," she answered. "I paid him out of the band's account and your pay will be docked until it's replaced. I think nine hundred out of each of the next two checks."

Sebastian's mouth fell open. "That only leaves me with three hundred. That's not fair!"

Her eyes became steely as they narrowed on him. "No, Sebastian, what's not fair is the rest of the band being delayed and losing money because of your immaturity. That's not fair. And if you pull a stunt like this again, I'll keep all of your pay until the expenses are paid."

"Sounds fair to me," Jack felt the need to add. If Kerrigan heard his supportive words, she ignored him as she continued staring down Sebastian. "We should go."

She glanced at him, then back at Sebastian with a smile. "Yes, we should." She turned and walked in the direction of the van and under his breath, Jack cursed the missed opportunity to clear his name.

Eighteen

"I cannot tell you how happy I am to have a night out."

Kerrigan smiled at Olivia. "We went out before I left. It's only been two and a half weeks," she laughed.

"Feels like forever." Olivia's eyes widened dramatically as she dragged out the last word. "You're so lucky."

Kerrigan raised an eyebrow. *Lucky?* Yeah, right.

When Kerrigan had invited Olivia to join her in Tallahassee for a night out, she hadn't considered Jack. At the time, Jack had started to remind her of the Jackson she'd grown up with, so Olivia finding out that Kerrigan was managing his band wouldn't have presented a problem. But Kerrigan had spent the past week avoiding Jack like the plague and it was starting to take a toll on her. She was barely sleeping, had little appetite, and was tired of coming up with excuses to leave a room every time he walked into it. She was exhausted and more than tempted to return to Rocky Creek with Olivia when she left in the morning.

The last thing Kerrigan wanted was for Olivia to find out she was in daily contact with the man she'd avoided for four years. That's why Kerrigan had immediately rushed Olivia away from the motel and to a bar where they were now privileged enough to be listening to some of their favorite songs being butchered by some more-drunk-than-talented bar patrons. But Olivia loved karaoke—watching, not singing—and it got them away from the motel, so Kerrigan was happy to suffer.

"Lucky?" Kerrigan asked. "How so?"

"Well," Olivia said after a sip of water. "Look at all the places you get to go. Do you get to do any sightseeing? Or is it all work? How many nights off have you had?"

"We've only had four nights off," Kerrigan answered after quickly adding them up in her head. "I haven't done any sightseeing and have spent most of my free time in my room trying to book more shows for the band." *And avoiding Jack.*

Olivia's lip curled and her excitement faded. "You still don't know how to have any fun."

Kerrigan chuckled and shook her head. "I wasn't hired to have fun. I was hired to do a job. And it's turning out to be harder than expected."

Olivia's green eyes filled with curiosity. "Is it hard? Managing a band?"

"No harder than babysitting." Kerrigan laughed lightly.

"That bad, huh?"

Kerrigan shook her head. "No, not really. It's just busy. It's a lot of travel and a lot of late nights." She shrugged. "But then I get an occasional night off to spend with my best friend and future sister and it's all good."

Olivia grinned. "Thank you for flying me down. I needed the night away. This wedding planning is driving me crazy. And Charlie's not being very helpful."

"I've heard most men aren't," Kerrigan retorted as she leaned back into her chair and tried not to frown at the thought that she may never know firsthand.

"That's what my mother says." Olivia sat up taller and pasted a matronly grin on her face. "Oh, honey, just tell the boy where he needs to be and when. That's all he needs to worry about," she mimicked her mother perfectly.

Kerrigan chuckled even as she felt the pang of absence in her chest. Olivia's mother had become a surrogate to her after her own mother's death. Between Mrs. Stump and Mrs. Harris, Jack's mother, she and Charlie had managed not to starve in those first six months while Kerrigan was learning to cook for the two of them.

"Is it really too much to ask that the groom show at least a little interest in selecting the location of the reception or the cake flavors? I mean, really, he's gotta eat the cake too," Olivia grumbled as she folded her arms across her chest. "I may have to tell him that if he doesn't help me pick it out, he'll find himself wearing more than just a bite at the reception."

Kerrigan chuckled at the image in her mind of her brother wearing a black tuxedo with icing and cake crumb accessories. "You know his favorite flavors," Kerrigan said with a smile. "Chocolate with a bit more chocolate, covered in chocolate. How hard could that be to pick out?"

Olivia's eyes rolled upward as she inhaled deeply. "I know," she agreed, her voice thick with reluctance. "Besides, he has been really busy lately. He's taken on three new clients since you left. I think he's just trying to avoid your house."

All humor drained from Kerrigan. "Olivia, don't."

"Why not, Kerri? One of the reasons you came home was to pack so you could move out." Olivia leaned forward and held her palm up. "Not that I'm saying I want you to or anything—you know I would love to have you stay with us for as long as you want. Especially since we haven't seen much of you for the last four years." She shook her head quickly. "But anyway, you came home to pack and then you left again before you'd barely gotten started. And he misses you so much."

"I know he does, Livie." Kerrigan sat straighter in her seat. "He was spending every evening trying to convince me to stay and come work with him. He wants to make his contracting business a family affair. I just don't know if I want to stay in Rocky Creek for the rest of my life."

"Because of Jackson?" Olivia's tone was direct, even if her eyes did fill with sadness.

Kerrigan looked at the salt shaker in the center of the table. She'd have to get Olivia to change the subject if she didn't want to end up in tears. Which she didn't. But the sting of his betrayal was still raw and angry in her chest.

"You know, it's a shame the two of you never got together," Olivia continued. "I thought for sure when he came to Paris that he was your Romeo."

Kerrigan snorted. "How tragic."

"True," Olivia muttered thoughtfully. "Fine, your Prince Charming then."

"I always preferred Aladdin," Kerrigan stated off-handedly.

"You would." Olivia waved the comment away. "Whatever, you know what I mean. I just can't believe he never tried to contact you after that."

They sat quietly as Kerrigan slowly blinked the tears away and tried to school her features before she could look at her friend.

"Do you know what you need?" Olivia asked abruptly.

Kerrigan's eyes shifted to Olivia's face, her head slowly followed the direction of her gaze. "What?"

"A date to my wedding." Olivia's grin stretched from ear to ear.

"No, I don't. I'll be standing beside you during the ceremony and Pete will walk me back down the aisle," Kerrigan replied. Pete, Olivia's brother, would be Charlie's best man. It saddened Kerrigan slightly to think the other member of their trio, Jackson, would most likely not be at the wedding. She wasn't sure he and Charlie had ever settled their differences. Jack probably wouldn't even be invited, which, right now, suited her just fine.

"You'll need one for the reception," Olivia continued, undeterred. "To dance with."

"Nope." Kerrigan shook her head. "I'll dance with Charlie and Pete. I don't need to dance with anyone else."

"I have the perfect person in mind." Olivia's eyes took on an impish sparkle.

"Are you even listening to me?" Kerrigan felt the need to ask even though she already knew the answer.

"He's one of Charlie's new sub-contractors. I think he does kitchens and bathrooms." Olivia's focus drifted to the side. "His name is Quinn Taylor, he went to our high school, but I don't remember him. He was two grades behind us."

"I don't date younger men," Kerrigan blurted.

Olivia rolled her eyes and scoffed. "Sweetie, you don't date anyone. I think it's time you start. You have dreamed about that boy long enough. It's time you got over Jackson and found a man who will love you the way you loved him."

Kerrigan's heart sank. She wished it was 'loved' in the past tense. She knew his most recent betrayal had hurt so much because a part of her, a very small part, was still in love with him.

Olivia did have a point though. She should at least make the effort to move on.

"I don't want a blind date to your wedding," Kerrigan said firmly. "I'll work on dating as soon as I get home, but don't you dare set me up with anyone."

Olivia's sad grin turned mischievous. "I'll make a deal with you."

Uh oh. "What?"

"You sing a song, right now, and I won't find a date for you," she started. "But if you don't, your date for my wedding is my choice."

Kerrigan frowned. She hated singing in front of an audience. She still had nightmares from having to do it in the church Christmas programs when she was a child. She could refuse to sing and hope that Olivia would be so distracted by her wedding plans that she would forget to find her a date. Given that Olivia already had someone in mind, though, didn't bode well for Kerrigan.

She looked around the packed bar, at some of the faces of the people who had already performed that evening. They'd survived, and no matter how poorly they'd sung their song, they'd all received loud applause. Her chances of surviving one song, no matter how much she butchered it, were pretty good.

Suddenly, Jack's words about her mother's singing voice came back to her. *If I remember correctly, you inherited it.* Apparently she hadn't been quite drunk enough to forget that compliment.

The ache in her chest made her wish she had been.

So he'd proven to be a callous jerk. That didn't mean she wanted to date someone else to make up for it. In the six years since he'd walked out of her life, she hadn't managed to get over Jack. She wasn't sure she'd accomplish that in the next few months. However, he had succeeded in showing her that even a man you grew up with, and once thought of as a brother, could not be trusted. She wasn't sure she wanted to give a complete stranger the chance to let her down.

"I want it in writing," Kerrigan said, pulling a beverage napkin toward her.

Olivia laughed. "Don't you trust me?"

"Not with this." Kerrigan raised an eyebrow. Olivia had been encouraging her to try dating since they'd started college. Living abroad for the last four years had probably been the only thing to save her from Olivia's matchmaking.

"You'd actually sing to get out of a blind date? Wow, I'm impressed." She pulled a pen from her purse and held it out.

Kerrigan took the pen from Olivia and tapped the end against the table as she thought of the correct wording for their agreement. Olivia sat back in her seat, trying not to smile as she watched Kerrigan. Finally, Kerrigan put pen to napkin and drafted their "contract."

On this date, Kerrigan wrote on the napkin, *Ms. Kerrigan Dodd agreed to and complied with a request from Ms. Olivia Stump/Mrs. Olivia Dodd to perform a karaoke song. As a result of this agreement, Ms. Stump/Mrs. Dodd is hereby prohibited from arranging a wedding date, or any other date, blind or otherwise, for the aforementioned Ms. Dodd. This contract is legally binding and any breach of terms will result in a VERY painful punishment, possibly death, for Ms. Stump/Mrs. Dodd.*

Kerrigan drew a line across the bottom of the napkin and slid it toward Olivia. "Sign there." Kerrigan tapped the line with the point of the pen.

"Not until I've read it." Olivia sat straight in her seat and skimmed the words on the napkin. "You put my married name on here, too." She frowned at Kerrigan.

"I have to cover all my bases. I don't want you to think you can get away with matchmaking once you've married my brother." Kerrigan pressed her lips together as the pout on Olivia's face became more of a scowl. She knew her best friend well.

Olivia read through the napkin contract and picked up the pen. "You take all the fun out of it," she grumbled as she signed her name on the line. She slid the napkin toward Kerrigan again and dropped the pen into her open purse.

Kerrigan shook her head, trying not to laugh, and waved a server over.

"Can I get you ladies anything?" the petite brunette asked with a smile.

"I'll have a whiskey sour," Olivia answered.

"I'll just have more water," Kerrigan said, tapping her glass. "Do you have the karaoke playlist available?"

"Sure thing." The server pulled a paper list out of her apron and handed it to Kerrigan. "I'll be right back with your drinks."

Kerrigan thanked her as she walked away then looked down at the list in her hands.

"I wish Finnigan's would have a karaoke night," Olivia said as she peeked at the list over Kerrigan's shoulder.

The women discussed some of the songs on the list. Kerrigan's choices leaned toward slow and meaningful while Olivia pointed out songs that were more upbeat and fun. Kerrigan found a good compromise and, without telling Olivia which song it was, slowly approached the stage.

When she stepped up to the microphone, she briefly introduced herself and announced her song of choice, Katy Perry's "The One That Got Away." There were a few groans, but Kerrigan ignored them and started the song. By the chorus, the repulsed looks had turned into smiles and she saw a few heads bobbing with the music. As she stared out at the grinning faces, the tapping feet, and the swaying shoulders, Kerrigan relaxed and began to enjoy herself. She wondered, for the briefest moment, if this was the thrill Jack got every time he got up on stage, but quickly pushed that thought away.

Could she just not think about him constantly?

As she reached the third verse, Kerrigan scanned the room and, as if her thoughts could conjure him, her gaze came to rest on Jack, leaning against the wall near the door. His arms were folded across his chest and when their eyes met, he grinned as her smile faded. The next heartfelt verse had her eyes widening as her cheeks tingled and warmed. She'd picked this song because it related to her feelings about Jack. Not that he would know that. But she did, and that was bad enough. She completed the verse and moved right into the chorus.

Her eyes swept side to side, looking for another way to her table. Jack was in her direct path, she'd have to do a lot of bobbing and weaving through the crowd if she wanted to avoid him. Even then, there was no guarantee he wouldn't follow her to her table. By the time the song ended, she'd accepted the fact she would have to confront him directly and prayed she could make him leave before Olivia discovered he was there. Kerrigan had no idea how she would explain this to Olivia.

She put the microphone back in its stand and took a small bow, smiling tightly to the crowd as they applauded her performance, a knot forming in the pit of her stomach as she prepared to deal with Jack. Pulling her shoulders back, she walked down the three steps that led off the stage. She made her way toward her table, avoiding Jack's stare even as she felt it like the sun on her face, warming her to her toes. When she reached him, his hand shot out and she stopped before they made contact.

She looked up and their eyes met. His lips held a secretive smile and his eyes were filled with . . . pride? Kerrigan's confusion at his apparent approval, combined with a strange desire to step into his outstretched arm, made her stomach flutter and a lump form in her throat. Even though her back was exposed to the crowd, with his arm still up, she felt trapped and couldn't move.

"I believe your talent surpasses your mother's." Jack's soft drawl caressed her and drew her closer.

Kerrigan stopped herself mid-lean and straightened up, her cheeks flaming, her heart racing. She closed her eyes and slowly blew out a breath. "What are you doing here?" she hissed as her lids lifted.

His smile fell until small wrinkles appeared in the corners of his lips. "It's my night off," he replied coolly, "and it's a free country. I can go where I please."

"Then please *go* somewhere else." Kerrigan rolled her eyes as she folded her arms across her chest.

His chestnut brows came together and his eyes narrowed slightly. "No."

She pressed her lips together as frustration tightened her chest. Why did he have to suddenly be so difficult? His plan had been exposed—couldn't he just leave her alone?

"Besides, if you didn't want to be followed, you probably shouldn't have told him," he gestured with his thumb over his shoulder to Riley who was chatting with a woman on the other side of the door frame, "where you were going."

"I didn't think he'd follow me," she whispered loudly as Riley's conversation came to an end and he looked at her.

Jack shrugged nonchalantly and Riley joined them, grinning widely.

"That was lovely!" Riley pointed toward the stage behind her. "Ye have a bonnie voice. Maybe ye should replace Sebastian as our lead singer."

Kerrigan shook her head. "No, sorry. I don't really like to perform."

"That's a pity," Riley said as he stepped closer. "Can we join ye at yer table? Is yer friend here?"

Kerrigan focused her attention on Riley and her stomach dropped to her knees. He'd met Olivia briefly at the motel when he had caught Kerrigan leaving for the bar. She'd quickly made the introductions so they could be off, not because she was trying to be short with Riley but because she'd wanted to escape before they saw Jack. She was certain if Olivia knew Kerrigan was managing Jack's band, she would have insisted on finding him.

And after she'd found him and they were alone again, Olivia would have spent the remainder of the visit talking about him. And grilling Kerrigan on whether she'd confessed her feelings yet. Kerrigan had been hoping to avoid that.

That would be impossible now.

She turned back to Jack who raised an eyebrow. "Great," Kerrigan mumbled. She inhaled deeply and blew it slowly past her lips. She turned and began to lead them toward her table and felt a steely grip on her arm. Her whole body tensed as her pace slowed.

"Relax," Jack's voice brushed her ear and a shiver went down her spine. "It's just crowded in here. I wouldn't want to lose you."

She walked a little faster. "Too late," Kerrigan muttered under her breath and the fingers on her arm tightened.

"What did you say?" he asked as they approached her table.

Kerrigan ignored the question as she looked up and saw Olivia standing beside their table. Kerrigan closed the distance until they were a few steps from her seat.

"Oh my goodness," Olivia skipped toward Kerrigan. "That was amazing!" Her arms flew around Kerrigan's neck and pulled her into a hug. "Who were you talking . . ."

Olivia slowly pushed away from Kerrigan, her eyes focused on the man standing at Kerrigan's shoulder.

"Oh. My. God," Olivia breathed as tears formed in her eyes. "Jackson?"

"Hi, Livie," Jack said softly.

He gave Olivia a hug and Kerrigan felt a twinge of jealousy. She shook it off as Jack broke the hug and smiled at Olivia.

"Oh wow," Olivia said. "How have you been? It's been so long."

Out of the corner of her eye, Kerrigan saw Jack's head tip to the side as his eyes shifted to her face.

"I can't believe you're here!" Olivia turned to Kerrigan. "Can you believe it?" she asked with a wide grin, a tear sliding down her cheek. She looked back at Jack. "What are you doing here?"

"Kerrigan didn't tell you?" Jack asked with a surprised chuckle.

Riley's eyes bounced shrewdly between Olivia, Jack, and Kerrigan.

"It's your band?" Olivia's mouth fell open as her wide eyes shifted to Kerrigan's face. "You manage Jackson's band? And you didn't tell me?"

"Surprise," Kerrigan muttered unenthusiastically with a shrug as she dropped into her seat. The others followed suit, Olivia sat in a chair to Kerrigan's left, and, much to her chagrin, Jack took the seat to her right. Kerrigan turned her body away from him to look at Riley as he sat across from her.

"Jackson?" Riley asked, his sharp focus on Olivia, his lips upturned in an impish smile. "So ye ken him, then?"

"Of course," Olivia replied.

"And ye ken Kerrigan?" Riley continued his interrogation.

Kerrigan looked toward the crowd, trying to ignore the conversation. She and Jack had never mutually agreed not to tell the other band members they had grown up together, but they'd also never brought it up. She hadn't known whether he'd mentioned it when they were apart, but it was clear now that Riley hadn't known. She could only wonder why.

Olivia laughed. "Obviously."

"How?" Riley asked.

Out of the corner of her eye, Kerrigan caught Olivia's glance. "You don't know?"

Kerrigan turned her attention back to the others at the table. Riley shook his head and glanced at her. Ignoring Jack, he focused all of his attention on Olivia.

"We all grew up together," Olivia stated. "Kerri and I are best friends and our older brothers were best friends with Jackson."

"It's Jack," Kerrigan muttered.

"Jack?" Olivia chuckled. "You used to hate it when I called you that."

"That's because you usually whined it like only a little sister could," Jack quipped fondly.

Kerrigan cast a quick glance at him and saw the amused look in his eyes as he stared at Olivia and felt another pang of possessiveness. She mentally pushed that ridiculous feeling away. Why shouldn't he look warmly at Olivia? They'd all grown up together. Olivia had been just as much a part of his life as Kerrigan had.

Apparently, though, whatever had come between them didn't extend to Olivia. Not yet anyway. Kerrigan wondered how Jack would react when he found out Olivia was engaged to Charlie.

"So, the two of ye ken one another?" Riley's question brought Kerrigan back to the present. He was staring directly at her.

"No," she answered as Jack responded, "Yes."

Riley raised a brow.

"No," Kerrigan stated again.

"Yes," Jack repeated.

"No," Kerrigan said firmly, turning her head toward Jack, "we don't."

"Yes." Jack's voice was just as decisive as he met her glare. "We do."

"What in the world?" Olivia exclaimed, amused. "We grew up together, of course you know each other. Why are you denying it?"

"Thank you," Jack retorted.

Kerrigan focused on Riley. "Yes, Riley, Jackson and I grew up together. But we haven't spoken in six years and I would wager to say, in that time, we've both changed enough to not know the other person anymore."

"It's semantics, Kerri," Jack snapped.

"It's the truth, Jack," she countered and looked over her shoulder at him.

"Whatever." Jack rolled his eyes. "We haven't changed that much."

"Oh really?" Kerrigan turned her body toward him as the betrayal, frustration, and hurt made her vision blur. "The guy I knew wouldn't have volunteered to seduce a woman and abuse a friendship simply to meet his own selfish goals."

Jack's upper lip curled and tension lines crept outward from the corners of his eyes. "I have tried to explain that but you won't give me the chance."

"I don't want to hear your excuses," Kerrigan scoffed. "Why should I believe you anyway?"

"What is going on with the two of you?" Olivia asked. "This is not what I was expecting from a reunion between you."

"What did ye do now, Jack?" Riley drawled slowly.

"You mean he doesn't know?" Kerrigan asked innocently.

Jack's face tightened more. "No," he bit off.

"Well then," she turned her attention to Riley. "Let me enlighten you."

A low growl emanated from her right.

"Sebastian decided the best way to get rid of me would be for Jack to seduce me and make me think he cared. Apparently, they thought I would fall head-over-heels," she tilted her face in Jack's direction and harrumphed before turning back to Riley, "and then he would let me find him with another woman. I guess I was supposed to run away either out of shame or embarrassment."

"That was not what happened," Jack snarled.

"Jackson, how could you?" Olivia cried simultaneously.

"I didn't." His voice grew louder as he looked at Olivia. "That's not what I agreed to do and if Kerri would just listen, I would explain that."

Kerrigan snorted in disbelief.

"Damn it, Kerri." Jack's palm hit the table and she jumped. "Stop being so stubborn and let me tell you what happened."

Kerrigan folded her arms across her chest and inched away from him as she looked over Olivia's shoulder.

"I'm sorry," he muttered, close to her ear.

She moved farther away and pressed her lips together, hoping to keep the tears away. Out of the corner of her eye, she saw Olivia staring at her, a pleading and curious look on her face, then felt a kick against her shin. Kerrigan glared at Olivia and shook her head. She refused to delve into this conversation when she was alone with Jack; she certainly didn't want to do it with an audience.

"Charlie always said you were too stubborn for your own good," Olivia stated and Kerrigan heard a rumbled agreement from Jack.

Kerrigan's chin dropped. "My own good?" she scoffed. "How is this for my own good?"

"I don't know." Olivia shrugged. "But neither do you until you listen to what he has to say."

"Thank you," Jack muttered.

"You're seriously taking his side?" Kerrigan couldn't believe the betrayal. Olivia was her best friend, was about to become her sister-in-law, and she was siding with Jack.

Olivia rolled her eyes and took a sip of her drink. "I'm not taking either side until I hear both of them."

"I always knew you were the reasonable one," Jack stated, his words like ice through Kerrigan's veins.

"Okay, buddy." Olivia smirked. "You're not off the hook yet. I just want all the facts, in case Charlie asks about his sister's well-being when I get home." Olivia shrugged. "I'm not sure he'd like to hear you were using her."

"Why would you have to tell Charlie anything when you got home?" Jack snapped.

Kerrigan shifted in her seat and saw the tautness in Jack's face. His brow was furrowed as he stared at Olivia, his lips turned downward in a deep frown.

"I tell him everything. What would you expect?" Olivia held up her left hand, wiggling her ring finger. "We are engaged after all."

Jack's eyes widened in surprise.

"Kerri didn't tell you?" Olivia asked.

Jack turned his attention to Kerrigan's face. "No."

"Surprise," Kerrigan whispered as she looked at the wooden table top.

"You know, Olivia. I think I'd like to tell you my side of the story now," Jack said and Kerrigan heard his chair slide against the tiled floor.

Olivia rose to her feet as well. Suddenly, there was a warm body hovering over Kerrigan's shoulder.

"Don't go anywhere," Jack hissed across her ear, sending a shiver down her spine.

Kerrigan watched as he and Olivia walked toward a less crowded part of the room.

"Were ye all close?" Riley asked, his thick accent helping pull her back to his presence.

Kerrigan focused on him and shrugged. "Olivia and I were like his little sisters."

One corner of Riley's mouth turned upward. "I doubt that."

She frowned. "What?"

"I doubt ye were both like sisters to him," Riley said and glanced over his shoulder at the conversing pair. "One o' ye, maybe." He turned and looked at Kerrigan again. "But I dinna think he sees ye both the same way."

Kerrigan's eyes narrowed. "What do you mean?"

Riley remained silent and leaned across the table as a smile formed on his lips. Kerrigan wasn't sure how to interpret that.

"The two o' them may act like brother and sister," Riley finally began and Kerrigan leaned forward as well. "But the two o' ye?" His grin widened. "Ye act like an old married couple."

She leaned back into her seat, her eyes rounded on Riley as he turned to watch Jack and Olivia. Had he been hitting the scotch before they'd come out? An old married couple? Her and Jack? That was absurd enough to make her want to laugh.

Riley had hardly seen them act like a married couple. They'd barely interacted at all around the band. Unless it was band business, all of their conversations had taken place in private.

Her tongue stuck to the roof of her mouth. Throughout their childhood, Olivia treated Jackson the same way she'd treated Pete. She had teased him the same way as she did her brother. Jackson had always returned the favor, joking with Olivia the way he had with Pete and Charlie.

But Jackson had always made her feel special. When he came home from college, he'd hug her last, and longer than anyone else in the group. During their beach vacations, if he was going somewhere, even if it was just to the concession stand for an ice cream, he'd ask her first if she wanted to walk with him or if she wanted anything. From evenings on the porch roof of the beach house, to their afternoons in his garage as he repaired his car, they'd shared a lot of private moments growing up. Moments that were seared in her memory. Moments she'd recalled during her darkest days after the rape and the loneliest nights in London and Zurich.

What if Olivia and her romantic notions had been right? What if he'd been in Paris because he'd cared for her?

Kerrigan's mouth fell open as she focused on Jack and Olivia, deep in conversation on the other side of the room. She shook her head as the walls seemed to be closing in.

But she and Jackson hadn't spoken for two years at that point, so that couldn't possibly be true. Could it? All these years they'd spent apart, he couldn't possibly be in love with her. He'd abandoned her. And now that he knew about the rape, there was no way he would want her.

But what if he did?

And what if he had come to Paris for her?

Her trembling fingers rose to cover her mouth and she couldn't catch her breath.

What have I done?

Kerrigan picked up Olivia's drink and swallowed it in one big gulp.

"Could you order another one for her?" Kerrigan asked Riley as she put the empty glass back on the table. "A whiskey sour." She pushed her chair back and stood.

"Where are ye going?" Riley asked.

"I need air," Kerrigan muttered as she turned and walked out of the bar.

Nineteen

Jack had told her to stay put. Given the depth of Kerrigan's stubborn streak, coupled with her tendency to run from tense situations, he should have known she wouldn't listen. But he had hoped. It was only too bad September evenings in Florida were not as cool as they were at home. As he stepped out of the bar, Jack could have used the crisp fall air he was familiar with to soothe his hot temper.

At least his conversation with Olivia had gone well. She had listened to him and, even though she'd thought he should have been up front with Kerrigan from the start, had eventually agreed that he'd probably done the right thing. Now, if only Kerrigan would be as cooperative.

He found her leaning against the side of the building, her attention turned away from the door. Jack paused a moment to study her figure in the soft glow of the street light. She was dressed more casually than he'd seen her in the past three weeks, in a pair of dark wash, boot cut jeans that hugged her hips but weren't too tight and a shirt that was part long black tank top that reached her hips and part gauzy, long-sleeve, see-through teal shirt that covered it. Her hair was down, and finally, after three long weeks, he was able to see her eyes without the frame of her glasses around them.

The vision she presented was enough to calm him, which was a good thing. If he approached her angrily, she would strike back hard and fast. He wouldn't be able to get a word in before she'd flee and they'd get nowhere. He let his gaze travel the length of her body and closed his eyes to enjoy the serenity overcoming him. He remembered how she'd looked on stage, relaxed and calm and almost like the girl he'd fallen in love with. It had given him hope the Kerri he knew was still there.

But when she'd seen him, a switch flipped and a chill went through the air.

He opened his eyes and blew out his breath as he started moving toward her. He wouldn't let that happen again. He would plead his case to her and make her listen. When he reached her, she straightened and he saw the tightening of her shoulders and neck.

"I thought I asked you not to go anywhere," he drawled as he stopped at her shoulder.

"That was a request?" she asked innocently, her focus remaining somewhere on the horizon. "It sounded more like a command." Her eyes shifted to his face, then straight ahead again. "And you, of all people, should know how well I respond to commands."

He was well aware of her tendency to bristle at her brother's orders and do the exact opposite of what he'd told her.

"How could I forget?" he murmured and thought he caught a flash of sadness in her eyes as she turned her head away.

How different she'd become since her teenage years. He felt a wave of sorrow at having missed those years. It didn't help knowing that because he'd abandoned her and given her the silent treatment for so long, and because he hadn't reached her in Paris soon enough, the cause of some of her changes lay partially at his feet.

"Kerrigan," he began, stepping in front of her.

"Why are you out here?" Her gaze lowered to the ground between them as her arms folded across her stomach. Her tone spoke of defeat. "You know I don't want to hear it, Jack. It's enough for me that you chose to go along with his plan—I'm not sure it matters why."

Jack frowned as he closed the distance between them and gently placed his hand to her chin. She allowed him to lift her face to his but wouldn't make eye contact.

"You've barely said two words to me in the last four days and now it doesn't matter?" He searched her face for some sort of emotion, some clue as to what she was thinking. "What changed your mind? Did Riley say something to you?"

She shifted her gaze to his as her brows came together. "What would Riley have to say? I didn't think he knew about your plan."

"He didn't know a lot of things until tonight," Jack mumbled as he released her chin.

Surprisingly, she didn't retreat. She remained motionless, frozen to the spot. "Was it because of Paris?"

He shook his head and narrowed his eyes. "What?"

Her lids closed as she pulled her head back and deeply inhaled. After opening and closing her mouth, twice, as if she wanted to speak, she finally opened her eyes but couldn't meet his gaze.

"Did you agree to this plan because I turned you away," she murmured, "in Paris?"

"No," he readily answered. "That had nothing to do with this."

She nodded and briefly met his stare, her eyes cloudy and full of sadness. He took another step closer.

"Was it because of Charlie? Because of your argument?"

He shook his head and laid his hands on her elbows. "No," he repeated and the crease in her forehead deepened. "I thought you said the reason didn't matter," he tried teasing, hoping to help her relax.

Kerrigan's head bobbed as her gaze fell to his shoulder. "You're right. I did."

"But you're close." He inhaled her lemony scent and let it envelop his senses.

"What do you mean I'm close?" Her breath brushed his cheek and sent a shiver of pleasure down his spine.

Jack looked down to find her staring up at him. Her lips were pursed with the last word she'd spoken and he felt the overwhelming urge to press his to them. What would she do? At this moment, he was no longer certain, but he was determined to find out before this conversation was over.

He swallowed the lump in his throat. "I mean that both of those events have something to do with why I volunteered to carry out Sebastian's plan."

Her shoulders fell and she began to pull away from his grasp. He tightened his hands around her arms.

"But it's not what you think," he quickly added and she stopped moving. "Sebastian's plan was for him to seduce you, but I couldn't stomach the idea of watching him flirt with you, let alone try to touch you." Jack reluctantly released her and took a step back.

"It never would have worked," she murmured in a matter-of-fact manner.

"I know that," Jack agreed.

She exhaled slowly. "If you know that—"

"It wouldn't have stopped him, Kerri." Jack shook his head at the deeper truth to that statement. He knew Sebastian well enough to know that he would have stopped at nothing, including assault, to get his way. "He is determined to make you leave. And I can't let him do that."

Kerrigan's brows came together and her head drew back somewhat.

"I can't let you out of my life again," Jack admitted.

She cocked her head and pursed her lips. "So this is where Charlie and Paris factor in?"

He nodded and held up his cuffed, left wrist. "And this."

"Your secret?" She sounded uncertain, but her gaze drifted to the cuff.

Her eyes were fixated on the leather as he unfastened the snaps and slowly stripped it from his wrist as he studied her face. Her eyes widened as the letters were revealed and he smiled when her mouth fell open slightly. Slowly, her trembling fingers reached for his arm and she traced the tattoo. The faint pressure sent tiny shocks coursing through his body and his heart began to race. He bit back a groan as her head lifted to meet his gaze.

"My initials?"

He nodded and her eyes fell back to the tattoo and she lightly traced the letters again.

"They don't stand for anything else?" she questioned him and he wondered if that was hope he heard in her voice.

"They stand for the only woman I've ever loved."

Her gaze flickered to his and her eyes widened even more.

"Loved," she breathed as her head moved slowly from side to side. "That's not possible," she whispered.

Not the response he'd been hoping for.

"Why?"

The corners of her mouth turned downward. "You left me." Her bottom lip quivered and she paused and blew out a breath. "You had a fight with Charlie and you left me. You wouldn't have done that if you loved me."

"I did it because I loved you," Jack said. "Charlie didn't think I was good enough for you and he asked me to make some changes."

"Charlie was your best friend," she snapped defensively. "He would never ask you to change."

"He did, Kerri," he replied, his calm voice a contradiction of the turmoil in his chest. "He was right to. I was using drugs, I drank all the time, and I used women horribly. He was right to ask me to give up those habits. You deserved better. You still do."

Her eyes scanned his face, but he couldn't read her expression.

"You should have told me," she said, looking away from him again.

"I couldn't." Jack closed the distance between them and lowered his head into her line of sight. "I needed to make the change for me more than I had to make it for you. I hated him for it, but Charlie knew what he was talking about."

Her head bobbed as she turned her back to the wall and her arms fell to her side. "How long did it take you?"

"Nine months," he answered as he repositioned himself to stand in front of her.

Her focus was on the horizon as her brows came together and she pressed her lips together to form a straight line. "How long did Charlie tell you to stay away from me?"

"Two years."

All expression and color drained from her face. "Paris," she muttered as her shoulders fell backward against the wall. To his surprise, tears filled her eyes and she quickly looked down.

He closed the distance between them and grasped her upper arms. He pulled the crown of her downturned head to his chest and offered what comfort he could.

"Yes," he replied.

She shook her head and her body began to tremble. "You made all those changes. For me. And I refused to even see you."

"Kerri," he started, but she began to shake her head.

Slowly, she lifted her face to his. "After everything you did for me. You should hate me."

He raised his palm and cupped her face. "I could never hate you."

"I would," she admitted with a pout.

Jack chuckled quietly as he lowered his face to hers. "Good thing I'm not you."

As he slipped his arms around her back, he pressed his lips to hers.

They were firm and her body tensed alongside his as he held his mouth against hers. As her tension dissipated, he eased her into the shelter of his body. Her lips slowly softened and moved against his, sending sparks of lust and hunger through him every time they met, reaching into his core and shaking everything up. She leaned into him, her hands around his waist, her fingertips branding him through his shirt.

She was responding in a way he never would have imagined. Her lips were sweeter than he'd dreamed, her touch more powerful than he ever could have thought. He wanted to press her against the wall, let her feel what she did to him, but the fact she hadn't expressed her own feelings, in words, stopped him. As much as he didn't want this kiss to end, he knew it needed to before he lost all control.

Reluctantly he pulled his mouth from hers and looked into her dazed eyes. Her breathing was as quick as his and he knew she was as affected as he was.

Her mouth fell open as she lifted her gaze to his. "Have you really changed?" she whispered. "Those twins. The box of picks. You still use women."

He looked at the wall over her head and let out a deep sigh. She'd probably never believe that since Paris, women had become more of a tool to help him forget her. At least for a little while. It never worked for long, but the times he needed a woman in his bed were becoming fewer and farther between. Not because he was getting over Kerri, but because sex with other women was never satisfying enough to suppress the guilt it brought on.

"Not as much as I did," Jack answered, "before."

"Oh." The disappointment was heavy in that breathed syllable. "Does that really make a difference?"

"It was a mutual agreement," he chuckled uncomfortably.

She raised an incredulous eyebrow and he felt the need to defend his actions, if that was possible.

"For four years I've thought I was the last person you wanted to see. What would you expect?"

She nodded and bowed her head. "Did you ever think about contacting me again?"

His eyes widened. Was she really going to blame this all on him? "Did you ever think to talk to me?" he snapped out of frustration more than anger. This wasn't the conversation he'd expected to have after their first kiss.

He had been hoping for something other than conversation.

She lifted her chin and met his stare, her eyes calm and rounded. "I didn't have all the facts. I didn't know why you'd stopped talking to me."

"I didn't know why you'd refused to see me in Paris," he retorted as he released her, his voice rising as he spoke.

She stepped backward and crossed her arms. "I didn't know why you were there," she said softly.

His anger died just as quickly as it had flared. He now knew what she'd been going through in Paris just before his arrival. What he didn't know is why that had stopped her from seeing him. He would have held her in his arms until she'd forgotten that bastard who had hurt her. Whatever she'd needed, he would have given it to her. She should have known that.

"You're right," he said and pressed his palm to the wall beside her head. "But I promise you, if I had known what had happened to you, I never would have left Paris without seeing you."

Her eyes filled with tears. "But you did."

Panic tightened his chest. "Kerri?" He had no idea what was happening, and he didn't like it. He'd imagined this conversation for years. It had never gone like this.

"I'm sorry," she stated.

"Sorry?" Bending his elbow closer to the wall he closed the distance between them. "For what?"

"Everything." Her gaze lowered and he reached for her chin. She gently pushed his hand away and shook her head. "I'm sorry for turning you away in Paris. I'm sorry I hurt you. And I'm sorry for the last four years."

Her soft-spoken words stabbed him through the heart.

"I forgive you." He tried again to lift her chin and she moved it out of his reach. He lowered his forehead to hers. "Give me a chance and nothing will ever come between us again."

She slowly lifted her head and straightened herself, keeping her gaze averted. Her shoulders and chest rose with her deep breath. Her lips pursed as she blew it out.

"I think I'd like to go inside and sit down." Without waiting for a response, she slowly turned and walked back toward the door of the club.

Jack pushed away from the wall and watched her walk away. With a loud groan, he fastened his cuff around his wrist and trudged along in her wake.

Twenty

Kerrigan stared at her reflection in the mirror, not really seeing herself as she ran the brush through her hair. Olivia was in the bedroom packing her suitcase. Kerrigan was thankful she wouldn't have to do that for a few more days. The idea of packing didn't really appeal to her at the moment. She felt dazed and was slogging through the simplest of activities as it was. Her hair had already taken an additional ten minutes to brush this morning. Her shower before that had been three times longer than usual.

"Are you finished yet? Too much longer and I'll miss my flight."

Kerrigan met Olivia's concerned gaze in the mirror. It was the same look Olivia had worn on her face every time she looked at Kerrigan since Jack had joined them at the club.

"Yeah," Kerrigan answered. "Sorry."

Her thoughts drifted back to the conversation she'd had with Jack outside of the bar the night before. And the kiss they'd shared. Kerrigan was still trying to figure out whether she could believe that Jackson was in love with her. Or even if she wanted to. The worst part about it was she couldn't seek advice from her best friend. She knew that even if she swore Olivia to secrecy, she'd still say something to Charlie about it when she returned home.

Since Charlie had caused the separation between her and Jackson, Kerrigan wanted to be sure she was the first one to say something to Charlie. However, given that she was fluctuating between understanding his behavior (her brother had simply been looking out for her) and feeling totally frustrated and angry (he had no right to make that kind of decision for her) she wasn't entirely sure he would want to hear what she had to say.

It didn't really matter anyway. Kerrigan knew where Olivia stood on the idea of Kerrigan dating Jackson. She'd been firmly in Jackson's corner since they were juniors in high school. Kerrigan just wasn't sure how she'd feel about being with Jack instead. They were still two different people in her mind, even if his actions lately, actions she'd thought were entirely Jack, were turning out to be more Jackson in nature.

She shook her head. *Did that even make sense?*

"Let's go," Olivia moaned. "I'm starving."

Kerrigan exhaled silently as she put the brush down on the counter before plastering a smile on her face and turning to her friend.

"Me too," she agreed as she grabbed the room key from the desk. "We should go. Charlie probably wouldn't forgive me if you accidentally got stuck with me instead of coming home to him."

"Well, I enjoy spending time with you," Olivia smirked, "but being with him does have its advantages."

Kerrigan's eyes widened and her mouth fell open in a laugh as she turned to Olivia. "I don't want to know."

"I wasn't going to tell," Olivia cackled as she picked up her suitcase and walked toward the door.

Kerrigan shook her head as she slipped her feet into her shoes and followed Olivia out to her rental car. Olivia moved in slow motion as she opened the back door and slid her suitcase onto the seat. Over the roof of the car, she met Kerrigan's glance and gave her a small smile.

"Have you told Jackson yet?" she asked and immediately looked away.

Kerrigan's eyes narrowed and her jaw clenched. "Told him what?"

"That you love him." Olivia turned and her wide eyes, innocent and serene, bore through Kerrigan.

Kerrigan knew that look. It was the look that Olivia gave her whenever Kerrigan needed to do something she didn't really want to do. It was the look that Olivia had given her in Paris, anytime they'd discussed Jackson and Kerrigan's refusal to see him.

Kerrigan rolled her eyes and yanked on her door handle. "I don't love him anymore."

She slid into the passenger's seat and waited for Olivia to get in. Once they were both settled, she reached for her seatbelt.

"I meant what I said last night," Kerrigan continued. "I don't know him anymore. I can hardly be in love with someone I don't know."

Olivia snorted as she buckled her seatbelt. "You do still love him. I saw that clearly last night. Because if you didn't, then what he did, or what you thought he was doing, wouldn't have bothered you as much as it did."

"That's not true," Kerrigan argued, then wondered if maybe there was a hint of truth to Olivia's words. Had she become so upset because she still loved him? Or was it simply because, of the four band members, her trust in him had been automatic because they'd once been friends? "It was because we were friends once, that's why it hurt. I trusted him, Livie. More than any of the others, I was most comfortable with him."

"Tell yourself whatever you want," Olivia said as she turned the key in the ignition. "But last night was the first time in a long time I've seen you allow a man to touch you. When Jackson had his hand on your arm, you may have felt the usual tension you feel when men approach you, but that's not what I saw. If you truly felt nothing for him, you would have shaken him off, or put up a fight as soon as he touched you."

Kerrigan stared through the windshield at the door to her motel room. Maybe Olivia was right. Kerrigan would think about that later.

As they slowly drove through the parking lot of the motel, Olivia continued. "Look, I don't know what Jackson has been like in the last three weeks. I don't know what he's been like for the last six years. But however this Jack persona he's adopted and has acted, it's been just that . . . an act. When he was explaining to me what he had agreed to do and why, that was Jackson to the core. Deep down, he's still Jackson. You can't ignore the fact that he's still the kind-hearted, fun-loving, sweet boy we grew up with and the protective, gentle, compassionate guy we once knew."

Kerrigan shook her head and folded her hands in her lap. He had come to her rescue more than once already. And despite her best efforts, she had enjoyed the time she'd spent with him before the revelation of Sebastian's plan.

And just the memory of that kiss made her heart race and her toes tingle.

Olivia laid her hand on Kerrigan's shoulder. "Kerri, I think you're grasping at straws to keep him away."

"I'm his band's manager, Livie. It wouldn't be appropriate," Kerrigan said as she looked out of her window. "Even if I felt anything for him, now would not be the right time for us to do anything about it."

"It couldn't hurt for you to at least tell him. You need to move on, one way or another. If he feels the same then you can discuss your options. If he doesn't then maybe you can let it go and try to find someone who can love you the way you deserve to be loved," Olivia said. "I just want you to be happy. And let's face it, you haven't been yourself in a long, long time." Olivia gave Kerrigan's shoulder a squeeze then placed her hand back on the steering wheel. "I love you and I'm always here for you."

"I know," Kerrigan murmured as she turned and gave Olivia a soft smile. "Do you know if Jack and Charlie have made up?"

Olivia shook her head. "No. And I'm not sure they ever will. I asked Jackson about the argument that separated them and he told me to ask Charlie myself."

Kerrigan's brows came together. Now that she knew what the topic of the fight had been, she couldn't understand why they hadn't made up in the last four years. She'd have to figure out which one of them was holding the bigger grudge and see if she could mediate a peace between them.

She pushed that thought away. They were grown men—why should she care if they weren't speaking to each other? Hadn't she just told Olivia she didn't still love Jack? So his friendship with her brother shouldn't mean anything to her. That was Charlie's business; he could deal with it.

Except, she suspected she was lying to her friend. She couldn't deny that she'd begun to doubt her success in getting over him the moment she'd seen him again. The days spent in his company had only strengthened that doubt. But after his confession, and that kiss, the night before, she realized she'd completely failed. She was fairly certain she was still in love with him. Having her brother make up with Jack would go a long way in smoothing the way for a relationship with Jack. If that was what she decided she wanted.

The car engine stopped and Kerrigan cleared her thoughts as she looked around. They were across the street from the motel.

"We could have walked," Kerrigan said as she and Olivia opened their doors and got out. "You didn't need to bring your car."

"I thought I would leave straight from here." Olivia held the door of the restaurant open for Kerrigan. "I can drop you off if you'd rather not walk."

Kerrigan moved toward the hostess station and held up two fingers. The hostess nodded and began making preparations.

"Wouldn't that defeat the purpose of you driving here in the first place?"

Kerrigan turned to face Olivia, but became distracted when the doors opened again and a male figure walked in. "Jack?" she breathed when she saw him and Olivia spun to face him, a smile already on her face.

"Jackson," Olivia squealed. "What are you doing here?"

Kerrigan's eyes narrowed on the back of her friend's head.

"Breakfast," Jack answered, as if it should be obvious.

Olivia grinned. "Of course." After a quick glance over her shoulder at Kerrigan, she turned back to Jack. "Why don't you join us?"

Kerrigan groaned as she closed her eyes and lifted a finger to her left temple. She'd known it was coming but had hoped Olivia wouldn't ask. It would probably have been rude not to and Kerrigan really didn't want to deny her friend time with Jack. They had been friends too, once upon a time.

"If that's okay with Kerri," Jack answered.

Kerrigan's finger froze in mid-circle as she opened her eyes to look at him.

"Please, Kerri," Olivia whined with a pout. "I would love to have breakfast with two of my best friends before I have to go home."

"When did I reach 'best friend' status?" Jack chuckled and Kerrigan turned to him.

"Okay, fine." Olivia blew out a breath and Kerrigan was beginning to feel like she was watching a tennis match as she shifted her gaze to Olivia. "My bestie and my brother's bestie. And I guess my fiancé's former bestie." Olivia's brows came together and she frowned. "Are you guys ever going to tell us why you fought?"

Kerrigan stepped away from the conversation, but not out of earshot, to the hostess station. "It will be three now, please."

The hostess nodded and Kerrigan felt a presence behind her. Jack maintained a distance between them, but she swore she'd just felt him inhale as if he wanted to say something.

"Actually, it's still just two," Olivia chirped and Kerrigan turned to face her. "I just looked at my watch and realized I have to go. My flight leaves in three hours and I really should be heading to the airport."

An angelic smile lit her face, but the impish twinkle in her eyes gave her away.

Olivia had set her up.

Despite the agreement she'd signed the night before, Olivia had just arranged a date, of sorts, between her and Jack. Olivia's twinkling gaze met Kerrigan's menacing glare and she lifted her perfectly arched brows higher, practically daring Kerrigan to call her out.

Kerrigan had a feeling she would enjoy plotting her revenge.

"Jackson." Olivia flung her arms around his neck. "It was so good to see you again. You have to promise to come to my wedding."

"I'll come to yours," Jack stated as he wrapped his arms around her and looked directly at Kerrigan. "But I'm not coming to Charlie's."

Kerrigan was about to snap at his comment, but he winked at her and the words died on her tongue.

Olivia pulled away from him and swatted him on the arm. "You're horrible. You're coming to our wedding and you're sitting on my side of the church." She tipped her head in Kerrigan's direction. "It'll give her at least one more person to dance with at the reception."

"At least one?" Kerrigan questioned Olivia incredulously.

"In addition to Charlie and Pete, of course," Olivia added smugly.

"Of course," Kerrigan mumbled her agreement, fairly certain that wasn't what Olivia had meant. "And that's it."

"Hmm," Olivia giggled and wrapped Kerrigan in a long, friendly hug. She turned and took a step toward the door, then stopped and turned to level her gaze on Jack again. "Jackson, be a dear and make sure she eats. A lot. I can't have her looking skinnier than me on my wedding day." Her musical laughter filled the waiting area as she caught Kerrigan's gaze. "Love you, darling. I'll text you when I get home." She waved her fingers and sauntered out of the restaurant, leaving Kerrigan staring at her back.

Olivia had just left her in the one place she did not want to be right now. Alone with Jack.

She had no idea what she should do next.

Twenty-One

Kerrigan slid into the booth, trying to avoid Jack's gaze which had been focused on her since Olivia was out the door. Just knowing his eyes were on her drove the butterflies in her stomach into a mad flutter.

As he settled into the booth across from her, Jack chuckled. "Livie hasn't changed much."

Kerrigan turned her face to him and gave him a weak smile. "She actually seems to have regressed quite a bit in the last twenty-four hours." She considered picking up the menu in front of her but settled for folding her hands on top of it instead.

Jack mimicked her pose. "I suppose you think that's my fault?"

Kerrigan saw the humor in his emerald eyes and tried not to smile. "It would be nice to blame you, yes." She shook her head. "But she was in a weird mood the moment she arrived, so I may just have to chalk it up to excitement."

"If you must," Jack said with a shrug. "I'm still trying to wrap my head around her and Charlie together. How did that happen?"

Kerrigan's amusement quickly drained when she recognized the teasing tone he'd used when he, Charlie, and Pete entertained themselves by exchanging insults with each other. Somehow, she wasn't certain any insult he was about to hurl toward Charlie would be meant in jest.

"The way it normally happens," she replied slowly. *For everyone but us, apparently.* "They fell in love."

Jack turned his attention to the window. "They just seem so different. She's so youthful and exuberant."

Her laugh escaped like the pop of a balloon and she covered her mouth. Jack's gaze returned to her face, his expression relaxed and amused.

"You mean childish," Kerrigan said with a smile.

He shrugged, a smirk still on his lips. "No, I mean youthful and exuberant. And completely opposite of your brother who's so . . ." his eyes rolled upward like he was searching for the right words, "serious and mature."

Kerrigan looked at her hands. "He's not so serious," she said softly as she opened the menu. "And he had reason to mature faster than you did." Without lifting her head, she shifted her eyes to his face. "He had to raise me."

The lightness drained from his expression and he opened his mouth to say something, but they were interrupted by the server placing napkins on the table in front of them. She took their drink order, lavishing attention on Jack, then left just as quickly as she'd arrived.

Jack's hand came to rest on top of Kerrigan's. "I'm sorry. I shouldn't be so harsh on him."

She looked down at their joined hands then up at his face. "It's fine." She turned her attention to the vinyl picket fence that surrounded the restaurant's parking lot. "I understand now."

A pair of small white ibises poked at the ground as they strolled along the bottom of the fence. Kerrigan watched them, contemplating what she wanted to say. And what she wanted to ask him. There were still things she wanted to know, but at the same time didn't.

The pressure on her hand gently increased. "I guess you didn't tell Olivia?"

Kerrigan looked down at their hands. The warmth from the connection seeped into her veins, making her feel light-headed and almost giddy. "Tell her what?" she managed steadily, even though she was shaking all over.

He slid his hand under hers, placing their palms together, and closed his fingers around hers. She nearly stopped breathing. He gently squeezed her hand until she looked up at him. His eyes were calm and focused on her face; his lips were together, but relaxed. He looked much more serene than she felt. At least one of them was.

"Tell her about the argument." His smooth, silky voice glided over her like a warm, comforting blanket.

She held his bright green gaze as she lifted a brow. "No, I didn't," she answered quietly.

His brow furrowed and he dropped his stare to their hands. "Did you tell her anything about last night?"

She inhaled deeply. "No."

His jaw clenched as his head bobbed. He released her hand as he sat back in his seat and turned his focus outside. Kerrigan studied his face, saw the slight narrowing of his eyes. The familiarity of that simple action, knowing it came from frustration, caused an ache in her chest. She wanted to comfort him, and she felt pretty sure she knew how, but what happened if she told him how she felt? The next step made her more nervous than the first.

Jack's lips tightened as he faced her and leaned forward, placing his forearms on the table. "Do you remember what you told me that night in your hotel room, on the anniversary?"

Kerrigan shook her head. "I'm afraid not."

"When you started your story about Paris, you said he'd stolen something from you." He took her hand in his again. "Selfish me thought your heart was the worst thing he could take, and for that I'm sorry."

Her cheeks burned as she tried to pull her hand out of his but he tightened his hold and leaned in closer.

"But you told me that was already gone," he murmured.

She closed her eyes and bowed her head. It had been so foolish of her to let him in to her room that night. Alcohol always loosened her tongue. It was one of the reasons she rarely drank.

"I said that?" she asked, hoping he'd misunderstood.

"Yes." He tightened his thumb on her fingertips and lightly pulled her hand toward him. "Who is he?"

She lifted her face to him and saw the determination in his eyes. Words escaped her. It was time to confess, but the words stuck in her throat.

"Here you go." The server returned and gently placed Jack's water and orange juice on the table in front of him.

She wasn't as careful with Kerrigan's coffee and Kerrigan slid her hand from Jack's, picking up her napkin, and immediately mopped up the mess.

"So, are you ready to order?"

Kerrigan dropped the sopping napkin on the edge of the table and looked up, unsurprised to see the server's attention completely on Jack. Under the table, Jack's toe slid up her calf and she jumped from the shock. Wide-eyed and breathless, she looked at him and he smiled.

"Trust me?" he mouthed as he pointed to the menu.

She didn't even pause before her head bobbed up and down.

"She'll have two eggs, fried medium, and an order of the country potatoes, no onions or peppers," Jack began.

Her giddiness turned to pleasant warmth all over.

Every morning during their summer stays at the beach house, either Kerrigan or her mother would fix breakfast for the bunch. The meals Kerrigan fixed were always eggs and potatoes of some sort. Maybe fruit, if it was in the house.

He had remembered.

Kerrigan tried not to smile as she watched Jack order his own breakfast. She watched the way his lips moved and remembered, again, how kissable and full they were. His high cheekbones were smooth and his rounded jaw looked freshly shaved. Her eyes traveled to his hair where his chestnut colored roots were beginning to show more prominently against the bleached blond spikes. She was glad it was growing out—she hated it so short and bright.

Maybe Olivia was right. Maybe he really was more familiar to her than she had allowed herself to believe over the past three weeks. As she gazed at his face, she recognized every angle, every freckle, every smooth plane of the face she hadn't seen for six years. She was suddenly sorry for all of the time they'd been apart from each other, needlessly it seemed, all because she'd been too afraid to see him in Paris.

Jack completed the order and the server left. He met Kerrigan's stare again and her heart ached with loss. They sat in silence for another moment and he slid his hands back under hers.

"So who is he?" he asked simply.

Her brow furrowed, her mind trying to recall the conversation before the interruption. She remembered and turned her attention to the window. "Why do you want to know?"

"Because I want to know my competition," Jack said, his voice all seriousness. "But I'll tell you right now, if the idiot doesn't know what a good thing you are, then you can do better."

Kerrigan smiled sadly and shook her head. "I'm not a good thing, Jack. I'm damaged beyond all repair and I have no idea why you think you love me."

"Really?" His fingers touched her chin and pulled her face to his again. "You're witty, you're fun to be around, you're easy to talk to and a good listener. I've always enjoyed your company and the way you didn't get upset when we teased you but gave it back better than you got it. You're compassionate and I don't know if I've ever heard a mean word pass those beautiful lips of yours, even now with Sebastian to deal with."

Her vision became watery.

"I have more, should I go on?" he asked, one corner of his lips turned up slightly.

She shook her head and gave him a wobbly grin.

"Any man who can't see that is not worth your time." Jack released her chin and lowered his hand.

Kerrigan closed her eyes as her head dropped. She took a deep breath, steeling her nerves for what she was about to do. She didn't know why she was so nervous. Last night he'd confessed his feelings when he'd shown her the tattoo. He'd given her reasons why he loved her, so she knew her words would be met with a positive reaction.

Except, for the past four years, she'd convinced herself she was no longer good enough for him. That she wasn't good enough for anyone, thanks to Raoul. What if his confession had been more of a release for himself, the way Olivia had suggested hers could be? Would his feelings remain when he found out the truth?

"There is no competition," Kerrigan answered softly, turning her head toward the window before she opened her eyes. She focused on one of the dips in the fence and stared at the spot as she continued.

"So you lied under the influence?" Jack's thumb made small circles on the back of her hand. "I'm impressed. That's quite a feat."

She laughed silently and shook her head. "I didn't lie." She shifted her eyes to his face.

The crease in his forehead deepened as he tilted his head to the side. "What are you saying?"

"It's you."

He pushed himself out of his seat and in a heartbeat he was beside her, his arm behind her waist and her hand in his again.

"I'm sorry I couldn't see you in Paris." She closed her eyes against the sudden rush of tears. "I felt so battered and broken. I didn't want you to see me that way." She opened her eyes again and focused on his fingers as they intertwined with hers. "And now you're almost unrecognizable. I have a hard time seeing the boy I fell in love with in the man you are now."

Jack pressed his lips to her head. "I'm not that different," he said against her skin. He lowered his gaze to hers and his eyes darkened as his brows came together. "Not anymore. I'd forgotten that boy until I saw you again. You remind me what's important to me. It's not the rock-and-roll lifestyle I've been living. It's not the carelessness toward other people. It's not the way Jack has been living."

Kerrigan tilted her head and he raised his hand to cup her cheek. "What do you mean?"

Jack took a deep breath and slowly released it. "I mean I don't want to live like that anymore. I want to be the right man for you. I made the change once; I'll do it again. Say the word, Kerri. Say you love me. I've wanted to hear those words from your lips for six years."

Her gaze softened as she frowned. "I don't know that I can."

He closed his eyes and laid his forehead against hers. "Can we try to make it work?"

Kerrigan took a breath then pulled her head away from his and looked at his closed eyes, saw the tension invading all of his features, and her heart lightened. There was something about the way he held her against himself in that cramped booth, something in the way he cradled her face in his hand that reminded her of the way they used to be. It reminded her of the man she'd pictured him becoming when she'd recognized she loved him.

She suddenly wanted to be with him more than she wanted air to breathe. Her heart had already accepted what her mind couldn't. This was Jackson holding her. Jackson loved her. If she said yes then it would be Jackson beside her. And then it wouldn't be long before she could say those words he wanted to hear.

She slipped her fingers between his and lowered his hand from her cheek. His frown deepened as she lifted her lips to his cheek and placed a gentle kiss on the smooth slope.

"Yes," she answered on a breath across his ear and his arms tightened around her.

Twenty-Two

She'd said yes and Jack's heart had nearly leapt out of his chest.

Yes.

He couldn't believe his luck.

But his battle was far from over. She'd said she'd loved him once but couldn't be sure she still did. He couldn't blame her; he understood why she thought he was different. Before she came back into his life, he was different.

Their breakfast had arrived almost immediately after her yes. As they ate, they reminisced about their teenage years and their time spent together. Jack could hardly believe it was less than ten years ago. It felt like another lifetime.

"So, you swear you had nothing to do with setting up that breakfast?" Kerri asked as they stepped into the parking lot of the restaurant.

He squeezed her hand, firmly grasped in his, as he looked at her. "No, I promise you, that was all Olivia. I had expected to eat with her and was hoping you would join us. I wasn't expecting her to bail."

Kerri laughed and shook her head. "I'm not surprised."

"Why?" Jack asked, stopping them on the sidewalk and turning her toward him.

Kerri grinned at him. "She's been your biggest cheerleader since we were sixteen."

"I wish I had known that." Jack closed the distance between them by a step. "I would have recruited her for the cause sooner." He slowly leaned toward her, eager to finally steal a kiss from her lips.

"She would've gladly helped," she replied softly. She glanced at his lips as they approached hers.

Just before they touched, she stepped backward.

"We shouldn't." She shook her head as she looked at the sidewalk between them.

"Why not?" Jack placed his fingers on her chin and lifted her face to his.

"We might be seen," Kerrigan answered and nodded toward the motel.

Jack looked at it and realized his and Sebastian's window was facing them. Riley and Stephen's room was three doors down. If any of his band members happened to look out, they would surely see him and Kerri together.

"You're right." He scowled in frustration. "Although Riley already has his suspicions about us after last night."

Kerri's lips lifted. "How could he not?"

Jack chuckled as he turned them toward the road again and looked in both directions. "Sebastian will think I'm simply carrying out his plan," he continued as they stepped onto the street and hurried across. "And Stephen's been concerned about my interest in you from day one."

They stepped onto the curb and Kerri slid her hand out of his. He tried not to let his disappointment show.

"Why? Would he be against us together?" Kerri's brow furrowed as she glanced at him.

Jack shrugged. "I'm just not sure he likes the idea of me dating our manager."

She looked at the motel and slowly nodded. "Well," she started. "You explained things to Riley, I'm sure you can explain them to Stephen, too." She sighed. "Until you do, we'll just have to be careful."

Jack inched closer to her, close enough to smell the faint honeysuckle scent he'd associated with her for at least a decade. The familiarity of it calmed him.

"I guess I'll just have to steal kisses from you whenever I can," he stated in a low voice as they walked across the small strip of grass that separated the sidewalk from the motel parking lot.

She glanced up at him through dark lashes and gave a sultry grin. "All you have to do is ask."

Blood rushed from his head to parts below his belt and he couldn't stop the possessive smile on his face. "In that case, I'm asking when we get back to your room."

"I'll see what I can do for you," she teased as she kept walking.

She led him up the stairs and around the corner to her room, on the opposite side of the building as the other two. He'd noticed she always asked for a room on the second floor and more often than not, had ended up farther away from the band's rooms. This could come in handy.

When she had the key in the door, Jack heard footsteps coming quickly toward them. He turned to look as Riley came around the corner at a jog. Jack inwardly groaned. He'd have to get rid of him before he could get that kiss.

"There ye are," Riley said, slightly out of breath.

"Hey," Kerri replied as she pushed open the door to her room. "What's up?"

"Have ye seen Sebastian this mornin'?" Riley asked.

"No," Jack answered tautly. "We just got back from breakfast."

"That's what I thought," Riley said. "I saw him fifteen minutes ago and he said he'd just paid Kerrigan a visit."

A chill went through Jack's veins. He glanced and Kerri who was standing stock still in the open doorway with her hand on her doorknob. Jack slowly lifted his gaze and his eyes widened as they fell on the room in front of him.

"Did you and Olivia have a huge party you failed to invite us to?" Jack asked casually as he took in the trashed motel room. Clothes were strewn everywhere, hanging from every surface. "Or a huge fight?"

"No," Kerri replied, still motionless.

"I didn't think so," Jack said as he continued to study the damage. The lampshades had been removed from the lamps; one now hung from the curtain rod, the other was stuffed into the drawer of the bedside table. The sink was turned on and overflowing, water running off the counter and onto the floor. He cursed under his breath as he quickly stepped into the room.

He turned off the water and removed the washcloth that was covering the drain, then grabbed a few towels and tossed them onto the floor, hoping to sop up a good portion of the water. His gaze traveled over the black and red streaks all over the walls. Probably lipstick and eyeliner. He glanced at Kerri who had ventured a little farther inside but still wore a look of shock on her face. Riley came in behind her, a calm expression on his always cool face, but his eyes told a different story. He was almost as unhappy about this as Jack.

Almost.

Jack was ready to kill Sebastian.

"I guess I'm just surprised it took him this long," Kerri muttered as she touched the mirror over the dresser. A crack in the glass ran from one corner to the other. "I wonder how much this is going to cost me."

"Cost *you*?" Riley spat, echoing Jack's feelings on the matter.

Kerri met Jack's stare and nodded as she turned to look at Riley. "This is my room and that's my rule."

"But ye dinna do this!" Riley exclaimed.

Jack approached Kerri and laid his hands on her waist. "If she doesn't pay for it, the band has to," Jack said calmly as he tried to figure out a way to make Sebastian reimburse her for this. "We can probably clean up most of it."

"Not the water damage." Kerri pointed to the mirror. "Or the broken glass."

Jack turned her around to face him. "Hey," he said and she looked up at him. "Pack up your stuff. I'll go see if I can get you moved to another room. Then I'll come back here and we'll clean up what we can."

"I'll help," Riley offered.

Kerri nodded slowly, giving Jack a wan smile.

He bent over and gave her a quick kiss on the cheek. She leaned into it and he wanted to linger. "I'll be right back," he said as he reluctantly let her go. Before he left the room, he gave Riley a look that let him know he would find Sebastian and make him regret his actions.

Jack's first stop was his own room, but it was empty and surprisingly neat. He turned and rushed toward the reception area, nearly running into Sebastian as he came around the corner of the building.

"There you are," Sebastian exclaimed, an enigmatic grin forming on his lips. "I've been looking for you for the last hour."

Was that before or after he'd trashed the room, Jack wondered. Despite the fury he was feeling toward his bandmate, he knew Sebastian well enough to know he simply needed to give him a little rope. He'd hang himself with it before the conversation was over, Jack just had to wait patiently.

"I went to breakfast," Jack said.

"That's what Riley said." Sebastian's head cocked slightly to one side and Jack looked away.

"Did you need something?" Jack asked, trying to keep him on topic.

"Not anymore." Sebastian chuckled lightly. "I took care of it myself."

"Took care of what?" Jack's temper was starting to get the best of him. His heart was racing and his entire body felt warm.

Sebastian leaned in conspiratorially. "I trashed her room," he whispered. "I know it probably won't run her off. Not yet. But maybe if I can keep it up, she'll go broke having to pay for the damages."

Jack's teeth clenched so tightly he thought they might chip. "How would that run her off?"

"Dude, really?" Sebastian leaned away and looked at Jack like he thought the answer was obvious. "She's gonna know it's me, and if she doesn't guess, I'll start leaving clues. But she won't be able to do anything. If she doesn't pay, the band has to. Her rule. And she won't let that happen. I figure that when the damages start to be more than her paycheck, she'll decide that it's not worth it to stay. She'll leave, we'll be free of her and our contract with Jacob and all our problems will be solved." He grinned widely.

Jack took slow breaths as he slowly counted to ten. "No," he finally said.

Sebastian's slimy grin began to fade. "What do you mean, no?"

"I didn't stutter." Jack's lip raised in a snarl and Sebastian took a step back. "I'm telling you this one more time, and only one more time. Leave her alone. She is the best manager we've had and we need her to keep our band alive."

"Best manager my ass," Sebastian snapped. "She knows nothing about the music industry."

"She knows money, how to manage it and how to earn it. We can teach her the rest," Jack growled. "I know you're still pissed about being under contract with your brother—"

"Half-brother," Sebastian hissed.

Jack's nostrils flared at the interruption, but he continued. "We are obligated to pay his company a certain amount after this tour and she's getting us there."

"So you're on her side then?" Sebastian hissed.

"I'm on the band's side!" Jack took a step toward Sebastian. "I'm on the side that will keep us out of legal trouble, which we will all be in if we don't meet Jacob's requirements."

"I don't care!" Sebastian yelled.

"I do!" Jack screamed back, now nose to nose with Sebastian. "She stays." Jack poked a finger in Sebastian's shoulder. "You *will* leave her alone, got it?"

Sebastian stepped back from the offending finger, his face now a thundercloud. Jack almost wished he'd say something else; he'd love to have a reason to take out his frustrations. He was beginning to wonder how he could have ever picked Sebastian as a friend. He was a bully and a spoiled brat. Riley, Stephen, Jacob, and every manager they'd had probably knew this well. How had he not seen it before?

"Fine," Sebastian snapped, turning on his heels and strolling away.

Jack took a deep breath of the fresh, morning air to calm himself as he watched Sebastian go. Once he had disappeared, Jack continued to the reception area. He walked straight to the desk and reached into his back pocket for his wallet.

"Can I help you, sir?" asked the dark-haired woman behind the desk.

"Yes," Jack began. "I'm with the band Malhypnus. One of my fellow band members has trashed our manager's room. I'd like to cover the costs of repairs for her and see if we can get her moved into another room for the remainder of our stay. Could you please bill it to my card?"

The woman's mouth had fallen open at the word "trashed," but she quickly regained her composure when Jack laid his credit card on the table.

"Certainly," she said as she moved her keyboard closer. "What room number?"

Twenty-Three

Kerrigan put her toothbrush down on the counter as she heard a knock on her door. Her heart skipped a beat as she momentarily froze, wide-eyed. She had a feeling she knew who was on the other side. The next knock was slightly faster, followed by the familiar baritone she'd been expecting. The corners of her lips turned up and she skipped to the door.

When she opened it, she was greeted by a beaming Jack as he came into the room and immediately pulled her into his arms. Her memory of Paris suddenly filled her mind and her entire body tensed as he leaned in to kiss her. When his eyes met hers, just before their lips touched, he stopped and his grin fell.

"Kerri, I'm so sorry," he said, relaxing his hold on her, but not letting her go. "I was so excited to see you, I didn't think about what I was doing."

Her tension lessened and she laid her head on his shoulder in his protective embrace. Clearly he remembered what she couldn't about her drunken night in her hotel room. He hadn't meant to surprise her, and she had overreacted. She slid her hands up his back and rested them just under his shoulder blades and deeply inhaled his sandalwood and cinnamon scent.

"I'm okay," she stated as she blew out. "Just surprised." Lifting her head, she smiled up at him. "What are you doing here?"

"I missed you." He gave her a gentle kiss on her cheek.

A shockwave traveled from where his lips touched her all the way to her toes, causing everything in her to tingle.

"Missed me?" Kerrigan laughed, slightly breathless, as she glanced at the clock. "It's only been thirty minutes."

Jack shook his head as he released her and turned to walk back to the door. "It felt like longer." He shut the door firmly, made sure it latched, then walked to the window and drew the curtains together. "How is it," he pivoted to look at her, "that we work together so closely, yet in three-and-a-half days, we have only managed two-minute conversations? I feel like I haven't had any time with you since Monday morning at breakfast." He raised an eyebrow.

"Perhaps because every time you got anywhere near me, Sebastian's eyes sharpened on us like a hawk and neither of us could behave the way we wanted to with him watching us so closely." Kerrigan folded her arms across her chest and saw a twinkle appear in Jack's eyes.

"How did you want to behave?" He took a few steps toward her, his eyebrows waggling suggestively and she tried not to laugh. She wasn't about to let him distract her from finding out what she really wanted to know.

"I think the more important question," she began as he continued to stalk closer, "is why is he being so attentive all of a sudden?"

Jack stopped inches from her and frowned, the mischievous sparkle dimmed a little.

"Did you say something to him?" Kerrigan asked, staring at him over the rim of her glasses.

He looked toward the floor beside her. "Maybe," he admitted quietly.

Her jaw dropped. "About us? I thought we had agreed—"

He put his fingers to her lips. "Not about us—we did agree to keep that from him." Jack lowered his hand from her face and took her hand. "But I may have said something to him about trashing your room."

"Jackson," Kerrigan whispered sharply. The idea that Sebastian might suspect anything between them sat like a rock in the pit of her stomach.

The smile she received in response was wide and boyish. "You used my full name," he stated and leaned over. His lips hovered just above her pout. "I love it when you call me Jackson."

Her pout waned and her heart tripped. "It is your name," she said, anxious to feel his mouth against hers. But they weren't finished with their conversation, and she was starting to lose focus. "Do you think he suspects something between us?"

Jack pressed his lips together and exhaled sharply as he straightened. He took a step around her and sat down onto the edge of the bed. "I don't know and I'm not sure I really care," he snapped. "Can we please not talk about him? He's run his mouth all night for the last three nights," Jack looked up at her, "which is why I wasn't with you like I wanted to be."

She had wondered if he would come to her room, but had chalked it up to wishful thinking on her part, or exhaustion on his. Kerrigan slowly closed the distance between them and sat on the bed beside him.

"How did you get away tonight?" she asked, turning her body toward his.

"He invited some women over and I told him I wasn't interested in partying with them." Jack shrugged. "Then I left. They'll probably spend the night."

Her heart skipped again. "Where are you planning on sleeping then?"

He glanced at her, the twinkle back and brighter than before. "I guess we'll have to wait and see."

Kerrigan's heart almost stopped completely. She was partly excited by the idea of having him spend the night, but partly terrified by the idea of what he might expect from her. "Jack," she began, shaking her head slowly as he leaned closer. "I don't think . . ."

He touched his forehead to hers as he cradled the back of her head. "Shh, sweetheart," he soothed and she closed her eyes. "I have no expectations tonight except to spend time with you, talking and catching up on the last six years. And then to sleep beside you when we're too tired to talk."

She smiled at the memory of the two of them at her family's beach house, staying up until dawn talking as everyone else slept. He'd tease her about the boys who had flirted with her; she'd pick on him about the girls who practically threw themselves at him. He'd give her tips on how to fend the boys off, while she would question him about what he'd liked about the girls.

She'd wanted so much to be more like those girls, because regardless of how he'd reassure her he hadn't noticed them, he had. How could he not? He was seventeen and they all wore teeny bikinis.

Their nightly conversations always started with teasing, but once that stopped, they would have lengthy, whispered discussions about practically everything. She could still remember the way his eyes looked more hunter green in the moonlight and the way the softer light played off the highlights in his hair. She sighed at the memories.

She'd missed those stolen moments. That had been the hardest part of the separation, not having someone to share inside jokes and secret looks with. Because they needed to keep their budding relationship secret, she felt almost like they were back in the beach house.

"Like we used to?" Kerrigan opened her eyes and lifted her head so she could see his face. His eyes had darkened slightly and the twinkle had changed from impish to a lusty flame that caused her toes to curl.

"Almost," he murmured. "I'm too old to stay up all night."

She laughed out loud as she pulled away from him. When she saw the mock hurt on his face, she only chuckled harder and leaned back against the headboard. He stood and walked to the sink, turned off the light, then sat down next to her on the bed as she wiped the mirth from her eyes. The only light left on was the lamp on the side table beside the bed.

"You're laughing at my advanced age?" He grinned as he sat at her bent knees.

She shook her head. "No, I'm laughing at the idea that you think you're old."

She sat up and leaned toward him, studying his face as she did. Reaching up, she traced the faint laugh lines that stretched from the corner of his eyes, then slowly traced a finger across his temple to his darkening hairline, down and around his jaw, then to the corner of his mouth where the only other sign of age was beginning to form on his face. She met his gaze, now the hunter green she remembered and burning so hot she thought they both might explode. Cupping his cheek in the palm of her hand, she leaned closer.

"You're not old," she whispered, inching toward him as she did. "I wouldn't kiss an old man."

Their lips met and she was consumed by the flame. She closed her eyes as his hands trailed leisurely up her arms, heating her blood as they skated toward her shoulders then shifted to slide around her. His lips moved softly on hers, giving her time to learn and enjoy the pressure before he increased or lessened it. Like their first kiss, this one warmed her and turned her to liquid. She'd never known a kiss could be so all encompassing, could affect every sense she had, heightening some, causing others to shut down. He tasted like mint toothpaste with a hint of sweet tea. She could smell nothing beyond his spicy cologne and cotton T-shirt.

She felt him everywhere.

His tongue lightly brushed her lips and she parted them a fraction. He slowly dipped his tongue into her mouth, teasing hers to join him in play. Gradually she warmed to the sensation and began to tease him back.

He let out a groan and before she realized it, she was on her back and his body was hovering over hers, even as their mouths remained connected. One of his hands slid from behind her and came to rest on her stomach. Her palm flattened against his chest. He deepened the kiss, pressing her head into the pillow and she felt her resistance start to slip. If she wasn't careful, they would take this as far as they could go, and she wasn't sure she was ready for that.

As his hand slowly glided upward from her stomach, she pressed against his chest and pulled her mouth from his.

"Jackson," she exhaled. "I'm not . . ." She was panting for air.

"I know." He sounded as breathless and resigned as she felt. "I swear, I didn't . . ."

"I know," she replied with a smile. "We're getting ahead of ourselves."

Jack nodded as he pushed himself off of the bed. He walked around to the other side of the mattress, pulled back the comforter and sat down on the flat sheet. After he kicked his shoes off, she watched in surprise as he positioned his shoulders against the headboard, then covered himself with the comforter. She realized that was how he planned to sleep, the same way he had the last time, when she'd been too drunk to know he was there.

She stood, pulled back the sheet and comforter, then mimicked him in making herself comfortable. Once she was settled, she looked at him with a grin. "So, what should we talk about?"

"He still watches you," Debra said.

"Hm?" Kerrigan asked, sorting the new bandanas by color on the table. She feigned ignorance, but in truth, she could feel Jack's gaze on her from across the room where the band was setting up on the stage for their first show in Tampa. After having slept beside him two nights ago, she'd become more aware of his watchfulness. The memory of their kiss still made her feel warm all over.

"Jack," Debra clarified.

Kerrigan looked up and immediately met Jack's stare. His lips pursed in a grin he was trying to hide and she felt the heat of his regard down to her toes. She looked away as she felt her own lips twitching upward. Kerrigan bent over and reached into the box of CDs and grabbed a handful.

"Your former science teacher, Mrs. Hylton, says hello," Debra stated and Kerrigan froze.

Her eyes widened as the blood drained from her face. She'd forgotten Debra was an art teacher in Rocky Creek, and was therefore working with most of the teachers she and Jackson had suffered with during high school. Kerrigan realized that if Debra had mentioned the name of the band's new manager, then one of their former teachers could have helped her put two and two together.

"Why didn't you tell me you grew up in Rocky Creek? With Jack?"

"Um," Kerrigan stuttered.

What could she say? She and Jack had never agreed to keep their past a secret from the others, but she hadn't been ready to share that information when she and Debra met. Debra was perceptive; Kerrigan had realized that almost immediately. What if she had figured out Kerrigan's feelings toward Jack when they'd first met? Kerrigan hadn't been ready for people to know then. She wasn't sure how ready she was now.

Kerrigan gently laid the CDs on the table. "I guess I just didn't."

"You should have." Debra's tone held hints of hurt and anger. "From what I've heard, the two of you grew up together and were pretty close. Don't you think that's a pretty big detail to leave out?"

"Maybe." Kerrigan took a breath and turned to look at her for the first time. "But before I joined this band, Jack and I hadn't spoken in six years."

Debra drew back in surprise. "That doesn't make any sense."

Kerrigan's brow furrowed. "Why?"

Debra folded her arms across her chest. "Because everyone I've talked to in Rocky Creek claims they used to see the two of you together so much they were expecting wedding bells."

Kerrigan's eyes widened until they became uncomfortable. "What?"

Debra nodded and shrugged. "Yep. They all talk about what a cute couple the two of you made and how surprised they were that you didn't take him to your senior prom."

Kerrigan sank her hip against the table. "Jack and I were never a couple. He was one of my brother's best friends so we were together a lot during the summer months and whenever Jack was home from college. Another guy friend asked me to prom, so I went." She'd wanted Jackson to ask her, but he hadn't come home from college at the right time.

Debra nodded. "Do you care about him?"

A smile touched Kerrigan's lips. "I do."

Debra bent over and grabbed a few more T-shirts from the box at her feet. She began folding them on the table and Kerrigan thought the conversation was over. She glanced over the table and took stock of what they'd put out for sale to figure out what else she needed to display.

"Kerrigan, Jack's like a brother to me. I'm sure you can appreciate that," Debra said softly as Kerrigan rearranged the keychains they'd recently added to their growing stock of merchandise. "I've seen him at his lowest, I've seen him at his highest, and I've seen the moments where he was behaving so badly I cringed and wanted to pretend I had no idea who he was." Debra grinned as she shook her head. She looked at Kerrigan wistfully. "I've also seen him so sad it broke my heart and watched him act in ways that made me swell with joy and pride."

Kerrigan's smile fell when she realized Debra had seen things she'd completely missed out on. Her shoulders drooped and she looked down at the table.

"If his songs are anything to go by, he's loved someone for a very long time."

Kerrigan slowly lifted her head, turning to face Debra.

"From the stories I've heard, I can only guess that someone is you." Debra's eyes focused directly on Kerrigan's face. "At least I hope so. Because since you joined the band, he's seemed happier than he's been in years. He deserves that kind of happiness. As much as I like you, Kerrigan, if you cause that happiness to go away, I will be more than a little displeased with you."

Debra's voice took on a steely quality that caused a lump in Kerrigan's throat.

"I don't make physical threats—I would never carry them out anyway—but I can promise you won't like what I'll have to say to you if you hurt him." Debra held out her hand to Kerrigan, as if they were making some sort of deal.

Kerrigan exhaled slowly. Since she'd graduated from high school, she had been waiting to further her relationship with Jack. She wasn't about to do anything to ruin that.

"Debra, I have no intention of hurting him," Kerrigan said as she sealed the deal.

Twenty-Four

Two nights later, Jack knocked rapidly on Kerrigan's door. In the past forty-eight hours, they had managed to spend more than two minutes together at any one time. He'd even succeeded in sneaking in a few kisses. It was their third night in Tampa and because Debra had spent the weekend with them, it hadn't been hard to convince Sebastian he was taking Stephen's empty bed. Jack had spent the previous night with Kerrigan.

The problem was, the more time he spent with her and the more kisses he received, the more he wanted. He'd obsessed about her before, but never like this. At least now he knew he had a chance to satisfy his needs, but he wondered if it would ever be enough.

He raised his fist to rap on the door again, but it swung inward and Kerrigan grinned broadly at him.

"Hi," she said as he entered the room and wrapped his arms around her.

He covered her mouth with his and kissed her deeper than he'd been able to since leaving her room that morning. Her lips were hot and sweet and he quickly felt warm all over. The blood rushed to his groin and he groaned as her tongue brushed his bottom lip. He gathered what was left of his self-control and pulled away.

Her lips remained in the post-kiss pout as her eyes slowly opened behind their black frames to look at him. He was momentarily dumbstruck by how beautiful she was. He was growing to love waking up with her every morning and looked forward to these private moments with her all day.

"Hi." His voice cracked.

She giggled. "I was wondering when you might show up." She gently pushed away from him and turned toward the table next to the window.

Jack followed but froze when he saw what was on the top of the table. "What the hell?"

Kerrigan glanced at him as she lowered herself into the chair next to the enormous pile of coins. She chuckled softly as she shook her head. "Apparently, it's someone's idea of a joke."

Jack raised an eyebrow as she separated the coins by denomination. It was clear she intended to sort these coins before they could move on to other things.

Not a very funny joke.

"Let me guess," he muttered as he sat in the chair next to hers. "Sebastian?"

"Probably," she answered simply. "It's the third or fourth time he's done this."

"What, exactly, has he done?" Jack asked as he began sorting as well.

Kerrigan's brows came together as she pursed her lips. "He hands out these flyers and I never see them until customers show me. I don't know when he does it or how I miss them before the show."

Jack frowned and pushed a stack of pennies to the side. "What do they say?"

Kerrigan rose and picked up the folded flyer from the side table and handed it to him. "Here."

Jack took the note from her hands and slipped an arm around her waist as he read it. The general idea was that the fans would "vote" for their favorite band member by paying for merchandise solely in the coin assigned to them. Sebastian had given himself pennies, which constituted the largest pile . . . of course.

"Bastard," Jack mumbled. He'd been assigned nickels, Riley had dimes, and Stephen was quarters. Jack looked up at Kerrigan. "He's done this before?"

She nodded as she moved toward her seat, but he pulled her onto his lap. She landed with a laugh and he grinned.

"The last few times I stayed up for hours wrapping coins, just so I could take them to the bank the next day," she answered, turning herself so her shins were between his knees, and resumed sorting the change. "It's a nuisance more than anything else, but money is money, and right now you guys can use every bit we can get." She looked at him and smiled.

This was one reason why he loved her. She was almost always able to look at the bright side of things and turn lemons into lemonade. He guessed that was how she'd been so successful in Switzerland; he knew it was her key to turning this ragtag band of his around.

But still, his desire for her was growing by the second and he knew that until this mess—Sebastian's mess—was taken care of, he could do nothing about it. His dislike for Sebastian's immaturity was increasing by the day, and more often than not, he was finding himself cursing his bandmate and his foolish actions.

"What's wrong?" Kerrigan asked as she rubbed her index finger between his eyebrows.

He shuddered at her touch as he shook his head. "Nothing."

"Liar," she mouthed with a smile and he tried not to laugh.

He blew out a long breath. "Is there a moment in your life you wish you could go back and change, knowing that it would change the entire course of your life?"

Her smile faded and he wished he could take the question back. He knew what moment she would say and hadn't meant to remind her of it. She turned back to the table and pushed a few coins into their piles before finally nodding.

"That's a rather loaded question," she murmured. "You know it would be the night Mom and Dad died."

"I'm sorry, Kerri. I shouldn't have brought it up." Jack laid his forehead against her shoulder.

"No, it's okay." Her hand began to stroke his arm as it lay across her waist. "It's not like I haven't thought of it a thousand times or more." She began sliding coins around the table again.

Jack knew that, in part at least, she blamed herself for their accident and had considered all the ways she could have prevented it. They'd discussed it the morning of the funeral. But what worried Jack was he was fairly certain she hadn't considered that she could have been in the car, with her father behind the wheel instead of herself, when he had his massive heart attack and crashed.

But Jack always had. And he'd always thanked his lucky stars she had been home safe and sound. Right now, as she sat alive in his arms, he couldn't imagine anyone else in her place.

"What was yours?"

Her words brought him back to the here and now. "Mine?" he asked quietly as he helped her sort coins.

"Your moment." Her voice held a hint of amusement as she placed a stack of coins in a wrapper. "The one that changed everything."

He slid a neat tower of pennies toward her. "There are so many, but they all stem from the day I met Sebastian."

She lowered the full coin wrapper and turned to him with a knitted brow, a curious look in her eyes.

He nodded. "It's true. If I could go back to the day I met him, I'd probably walk away immediately."

She narrowed her eyes. "But then you wouldn't have all this." She gestured at the room around them.

"Probably true," Jack agreed. If he had walked away from Sebastian, they wouldn't have formed Malhypnus. "This was always more his dream anyway. He wanted the rock 'n roll lifestyle, the sex and the drugs, the albums, the tours and the fans."

"You didn't?" she asked as she snuggled her body closer to his and laid a hand on his chest.

"Not at first," Jack admitted with a shrug as he covered her hand with one of his. "I was happy having a band to play in at college and having a band to play in at home." He, Charlie, and Pete had started a band when they were in middle school, but when they'd started college, they hadn't been able to play together as often. "It was fun, but I never expected much from it. I didn't realize how far Sebastian wanted to go with it until six months after we formed the band. That was when I started getting into the lifestyle, but I still didn't believe it would go anywhere until we got our contract."

Her lips had turned down and her focus had shifted when he mentioned the "lifestyle." Slowly she lifted her face, a slight pout on her lips. He wanted to kiss that pout away, to wipe away her disappointment.

"He wouldn't be this successful without you," she whispered, meeting Jack's gaze with determination. "It's your music people react to, Jack. Your songs."

Jack raised an eyebrow at the way she'd shifted the conversation. "They're my lyrics," he agreed, "but the music is his."

"They're *your* words." Kerrigan slid her hand over his shoulder, resting her palm on the back of his head as her frown faded. "It's the most amazing thing, watching the crowd when he sings your lyrics. The songs he's written have them singing along, dancing, bouncing up and down, but your songs . . ." Her gaze softened as she considered her words, and he tried not to become distracted by the warmth radiating from her palm. "Your songs are emotional and heartfelt. I see it in the way the fans look at each other while they sing along. I feel the change in the air. I hear it myself. Even though Sebastian is singing, I can hear your voice, I can hear the passion behind your lyrics."

Jack smiled and gave her a gentle kiss on the lips. He'd written most of those songs about her. Their most popular ballad was one he'd scribbled on a napkin during his flight home from Paris.

She slid her other hand up his chest and behind his neck. "How could you deprive people of that?"

He pulled her toward him, until her hip was resting against his stomach. "I wouldn't want to," he answered with a shrug. "But at the same time, if I hadn't fallen in with his ideal of rock-stardom, then I would have been worthy of you six years ago."

"Jackson," she whispered, bringing her palm to his cheek as sadness filled her eyes. "Maybe you just weren't ready then."

He laid his forehead against hers. "No, you're right. I was lost then, I didn't know myself, let alone what I wanted. But I've missed having you in my life, Kerri." He raised his head until their noses were inches apart. "I know who I am now and I know that what I wanted then was child's play compared to what I want now."

With both hands on his cheeks, her gaze holding his, she slowly brought her lips closer to his until he could feel her breath across them. "Show me."

Twenty-Five

His mouth covered hers before she could utter another word and her entire body became heated as his arms tightened around her. Their lips played at this dance she was quickly becoming familiar with, hardening and softening, shifting and opening, as his hands slowly glided up the length of her back. She tried not to shudder as his fingers wove into her hair and he gently pulled her head away.

He laid delicate kisses along her jaw as her head fell back at his soft tug. "Are you asking what I think you're asking?" he asked between kisses.

She could only nod as her eyes closed and she blew out a sigh.

His response was a low groan as he swept his arm under her knees and gripped her tightly across the back. She threw her arms around his neck and he rose from his seat as quickly as he could and was beside the bed in three steps. Slowly, he lowered her feet to the floor. With her arms still around his neck, she leaned into him and he kissed her again as his hands moved around her waist.

His finger brushed the bare skin between her T-shirt and pajama shorts and her body tensed. Ignoring her own reaction, she slid her hands down his covered chest, to the bottom of his shirt and then under. She felt him tremble when her fingers touched his bare skin and couldn't help but grin. His tongue teased her lower lip as she moved her hands, trailing her fingernails across his stomach and chest as she pulled at the fabric. He broke the kiss for her to lift the shirt up and over his head and her gaze dropped to the broad, muscled expanse of his bare chest.

Her tongue brushed her lower lip as her fingers skimmed the naked skin in front of her. The sparse hairs tickled as she dragged her fingers through them, taking a moment to circle his nipples, drawing a sharp hiss from him.

She looked up and met his deep emerald eyes and her insides turned to mush.

"My turn," he murmured the moment before his lips touched hers again.

His hands had remained still during her exploration, but now they slipped under her shirt completely and she shook with the shock of his warm palms against her back. He pulled her toward him. His lips slowly moved to her cheek, then to her hairline and down her jaw as his hands progressed up her back. Her head fell back as his mouth touched her neck and his hands traveled to her front. He cupped her breasts and she stiffened, mentally preparing herself for the memories to come.

He gently fondled her breasts then lightly pinched her nipples before moving lower on her body, causing a hitch in her breath and leaving a trail of fire wherever he touched her. His fingers stopped on the waistband of her shorts and he lifted his head. Her eyes met his sparkling gaze and she hoped he saw the want and need she had for him, not the fear of the past lingering in the back of her mind. As if willing him to continue, she bobbed her head once and a seductive grin formed on his lips.

He held her gaze as he quickly lowered her shorts over her hips, then kissed her as he hooked a hand behind each of her knees. He lifted her to his body and she felt the hard ridge of his erection press against her core. As he crawled onto the bed with her held against him, the friction between their bodies caused a tingle she'd never experienced. When he set her down in the middle of the bed and pushed himself away, she was almost sorry to lose the contact.

He placed delicate kisses on her face and neck and his hands glided alongside as he moved lower, lips touching her body through the cloth of her shirt. The lower he got, more tautness infused her limbs and mind. She squeezed her eyes shut and forced air deep into her lungs.

"Kerri, look at me," Jackson said softly, between kisses.

She slowly opened her eyes and looked down at him. His shoulders hovered over her thighs, his hot gaze on her face.

"Focus on me." He soothingly pressed his lips to her stomach.

She nodded and he moved still farther down her body. Her eyes focused on the top of his head as he lowered his mouth to the top of her thigh. When his warm breath caressed her skin, she shuddered and her tension slipped away. He continued down one leg then moved up the other. After a final kiss, he placed his hands on the waistband of her panties.

He met her gaze and smiled. "Trust me," he murmured, though she thought she heard a questioning tone in his voice.

Staring at him, she moistened her lips and bobbed her head. "Yes."

His grin widened and he slowly lowered the cloth that covered her most intimate parts down the length of her legs and dropped them onto the floor. Fascinated, she watched as he, instead of standing and taking his own shorts off, settled himself between her legs, a look of anticipation on his face.

He's not going to—

His tongue touched her and she closed her eyes as her hips leapt off the bed. She looked up at the ceiling, trying to steady her breathing as his mouth worked magic on her body. His lips and tongue continued to caress her and her fists clutched the comforter beside her as she pressed her shoulders into the mattress. An entirely new tension infused her body as he kept teasing and sucking and she began to lose control. Her hips seemed to lift and buck with a will of their own. Her breaths came in quick spurts and her arms were no longer content to lay peacefully by her side.

She felt as if she were climbing toward something, but what it was, or how far away, she had no idea. Her head tilted up as her eyes closed, her hands on either side of her head. His tongue darted out and touched her and she exploded. She grabbed one of the pillows and held it to her face as she screamed. Her pelvis pressed against his face and he continued to pleasure her, slowing the caresses until they eventually stopped.

He removed his mouth, her hips fell back to the bed, and her arms went limp by her side. She was vaguely aware of his body brushing against hers until he pulled off the pillow covering her face, a rakish grin on his lips.

"You okay?" he asked with a throaty chuckle.

She ran her tongue around the inside of her mouth, moistening it before she could speak. "Uh huh," was all she could manage and his laugh deepened.

He quickly kissed her lips then pushed himself off of the bed. She turned her head to watch him drop his shorts and underwear to the floor, her eyes widening when she saw his erection spring free.

"Oh my," she muttered breathlessly.

Amusement in his expression, he looked at her and raised an eyebrow. "Are you ready?"

Still dazed and riding the wave of her orgasm, she could only nod.

He quickly covered himself with a condom then climbed back onto the bed. Grabbing the tail of her shirt, he began easing it up her body.

"I want to see all of you," he said as he slowly lifted her so he could pull the last bit of clothing over her head.

Her cheeks burned as his gaze roamed her body, but when his eyes met hers, she saw the desire and admiration in the rich, forest-green depths and all embarrassment disappeared. He stretched out over her, parting her knees with his, and lowered himself to her. His mouth grabbed hers and she could feel his need in the way his lips moved against hers. Slowly, he pressed himself into her, and once again her hips lifted from the mattress despite her best efforts.

She pulled her mouth away, gasping for air as he filled her. Her arms clasped around his neck as she adjusted to the new sensation. Slowly, he began moving his hips, pushing himself in and out of her body. She learned his rhythm and started meeting his thrusts with her own.

He took his time and together they climbed close to the peak before he would change the pace, pulling away for a few moments before charging again. His lips met hers as he sped up and her toes curled. He didn't stop and she pulled her face away from his. She could feel the pressure building and she tightened her arms around his neck as he slid an arm under her back. Her entire body tensed as she exploded, burying her face in his shoulder as she screamed with pleasure. His pace quickened again and he soon followed her into the aftermath.

Jack collapsed beside her on the bed with his eyes closed and his forehead against her head. Under the weight of his arm lying across her chest, he could feel her calming pulse. Slowly taking air into his lungs, he waited for his heartrate to return to normal as well.

A sense of calm settled over him, knowing that when he opened his eyes, for the first time in a long time, he'd see the woman he'd wanted to make love to, not a faceless woman he'd just used as a poor substitute. Kerri was finally lying next to him and he was looking forward to holding her all night.

He opened his eyes, hoping to see a look of contentment to match his on her sweet face. Instead, he saw a tear quietly slide down her cheek and felt as if he'd been doused with a bucket of cold water. Immediately propping himself up on his elbow, he turned to her and wiped the tear away.

"Did I hurt you?" he asked, anxious for her answer.

She laid her palm against the back of his hand, holding his gaze she shook her head. "No, I'm not hurt."

His relief was palpable as he leaned toward her and kissed the next tear away. "Then why are you crying?"

She turned her head and placed a kiss on the palm of his hand. "They're happy tears." She rolled onto her side and grinned up at him. "I never knew it could be like that."

Jack's lips twitched with amusement, but he quickly schooled his features. "Like what?"

"So pleasant," she answered and his good humor threatened to bolt. "So wonderful."

He laid his head down on the pillow and they were face-to-face. "You haven't had pleasant and wonderful experiences?" She shook her head and his mouth fell open. "Never?"

She laid her palm on his cheek. "Jackson, I've only ever wanted to be with you. I was a virgin when I was raped and afterwards . . ." she looked over his shoulder. "Well, afterwards, I couldn't even entertain the thought of being with any man without having a horrible flashback." She visibly shuddered and he pulled her to him.

With her head on his chest, he wrapped his arms around her. He'd noticed the tension infusing her body and had feared it was related to the rape. After all these years, he hated the idea that she might relive that moment, even for a second.

He placed a kiss on the top of her head. "Only wanted to be with me, huh?"

Her responding nod tickled his chest. "I wanted you to be my first."

He wanted to be her last.

"Raoul sort of ruined that dream," Kerri said sadly as her fingers traced light circles on his abdomen.

Jack was silent while he organized his thoughts. Words were his strong suit and he couldn't let them fail him now. She was the most important person to him, and he refused to let her down again.

"That depends on how you look at it, I guess," he said as he caressed her arms and turned her to face him. Her damp cheeks only helped shore up his resolve.

"You guess?" She gave him a small, innocent smile as she shook her head, suggesting she thought she was about to humor him.

He pushed himself up onto his elbow, tipping her onto her back in the process, then rolled toward her.

"Jackson, he took my virginity. That's not something I can get back," she gently argued.

He placed a light kiss to her lips. "No, not physically," he said as he lifted his head. "But, you never invited him to your bed. You've never willingly made love to anyone—"

"Except you," she interrupted with a brazen grin.

Laughter bubbled in his chest. "True," he said and gave the tip of her nose a peck. "And for that, I will forever be grateful." He shifted to place his face directly over hers. "Your virginity was yours alone to give. He had no right to take it, so if you would rather say you gave it to me, I'd be okay with that."

Her clear blue eyes suddenly became cloudy. "Is it that important to you?" she asked with a hitch in her voice.

He quickly shook his head. "No, Kerri, that's not what I'm saying." He raised a hand to cup her face, the warmth of her cheek slinking up his arm and heating the rest of his body. "I love you. I would love you even if you've had a dozen lovers."

Her eyes narrowed in disbelief.

"Okay, I probably would have been insanely, murderously jealous if you'd had a dozen lovers, but then, I have no room to talk." He watched the cloudiness fade from her expression. "What I'm saying is, who you have or haven't been with in the past doesn't matter to me nearly as much as who you'll be with in the future. Namely . . . me."

Hopefully forever.

"I just want you to be happy and never regret anything," he continued.

She beamed at him and the smile lit up her entire face. He lowered his face to hers and kissed her with all of the passion he'd withheld from others over the years. A passion that was, and had always been, reserved for her. Now that he finally had the chance to give it to her, he wasn't going to hold back.

She pulled her head away and he began placing kisses on her bare skin.

"Jackson," she murmured and a shiver went down his spine.

He loved hearing his name from her lips.

"Can we do it again?"

He continued kissing her along her jawline. "Just say the word."

He lifted his head so he could look into her eyes.

"The word," she said with a giggle.

Twenty-Six

As Kerrigan sealed the final tub of merchandise, she looked out over the dawdling sea of people, still drinking and lingering in front of the stage. The band's fourth and final show in the Tampa area had just ended and they were packing up their equipment as she packed up the merchandise. They'd done well in sales tonight, but she was exhausted by the noise and the crowd. Her lack of sleep the night before was starting to wear on her, but a sly smile touched her lips at the memory.

"Are you finished?" Jack murmured as he joined her behind the table. He slid his arm around her waist and she playfully smacked it away.

"Stop it," she hissed, trying not to laugh as she noticed several sets of female eyes focused on the two of them. Kerrigan stepped out of his reach. "You have to behave yourself in public. People can't know about us."

His brow furrowed. "Why? I thought you were only concerned about the band knowing. And we're well past that." He bent over and picked up the tub that sat on the floor, the cash box on top of it.

She placed her hands on her hips. "Sebastian doesn't know yet."

"He's nowhere to be seen," Jack said, placing his tub beside the one on the table.

She frowned, hoping that one of the other two band members was keeping tabs on the troublemaker.

He took a step toward her. Now blocked, for the most part, by the tubs, she let him take her hand. "What's the problem?"

Kerrigan cast another furtive glance over the crowd. The female stares now held a hint of hostility that made her uncomfortable. Turning her focus to him, she raised an eyebrow. "I don't think your female fans like me too much at the moment."

Jack looked over the crowd and shrugged. "They're just jealous," he said casually. "They'll get over it." He took another step toward her. "Maybe we should move this stuff backstage where we'll be away from prying eyes."

Kerrigan tried not to smile as she stepped backward. "Excellent idea," she agreed and released his hand.

They each picked up a container then Jack led the way backstage. He set his load on top of one of the speakers then turned and took hers as Riley came off of the stage with his bass drum.

"Hello," he greeted her as he placed a drum at her feet. "How'd we do?"

"Pretty good," Kerrigan replied. "We need to reorder some things." She made a mental note to take care of that before she called Jacob again.

"Excellent." Riley gave her a toothy grin.

"Are you guys ready yet?" Jack slipped his hand into Kerrigan's and pulled her toward him.

"No," Riley winked at Kerrigan, "but Stephen an' I can handle it."

Kerrigan opened her mouth to offer her assistance but Jack tugged hard on her hand.

"Great," he said. "We'll see you in a bit then." He began moving away.

"Jack, what are you doing?" she asked.

Her answer came in the form of a look—part lust, part boyish mischief—cast over his shoulder as he towed her further backstage toward the dressing rooms.

"No rush," Riley called after them with a hearty, Scottish chuckle.

Jack threw open the first door he reached and swung her into the room. "Don't plan on it," he muttered as he closed the door and pressed her against it.

"Jack—" was all she managed to say before his mouth descended on hers and swept her into the sea of flames she was quickly growing accustomed to.

She threw her arms over his shoulders and his hands came to rest on her waist as their lips hardened and softened against each other. He placed his knee between hers and rocked his erection into her abdomen. She gasped and turned her head away as heat pulsed through her body, emanating from their point of contact. His lips glided across her cheek as his hips continued gently pulsing against her.

Her eyelids lowered as his mouth continued to move over her jaw. "Jackson," she breathed. "Here?"

He laughed against her neck. "Yes, here. Now," he answered, kissing her between words. "I've wanted you ever since I left your room this morning. I can't wait any longer."

Her lips turned up and she slid her fingers into his hair. She couldn't argue. She'd felt the same way all day. Her other hand lowered to the tail of his shirt, but froze when she caught voices coming closer to the door she was pinned against. Jack lifted his head and turned toward the noise as well.

"Let me get my manager an' we'll sort this out," Riley said just before the door vibrated with his knock. "Kerrigan?"

She cast a quick glance at Jack's face, now a cloud of thwarted desire as he scowled at the doorknob. Placing a light kiss on his chin, she lifted away from the door as she gently pushed Jack away.

"Later," she whispered as she turned and smoothed the back of her hair. Reaching for the knob, she hoped the flush in her cheeks didn't give anything away.

Kerrigan opened the door to find Riley directly in front of her, with two men standing behind him, one of them the police officer who'd been monitoring the crowd during the concert. She silently filled her lungs then released the air and gave Riley a large smile.

"Did you need something?" she asked as she stepped into the hall, closing the door behind her.

"Aye," he replied. "This gentleman is looking for his daughter."

The gentleman in question stepped around Riley and toward her. "She was supposed to meet me outside after the concert ended," he said. "I waited for thirty minutes after I started seeing people leave, but she hasn't come out yet."

Kerrigan furrowed her brow. "She's not still in the bar?"

"No," he answered and held up his phone. "This is a picture of her."

Kerrigan took the phone and studied the face of the young blonde woman smiling back at her. There was a hint of familiarity about her. "Is this what she was wearing tonight?" she asked as she returned the phone to the father.

"No. Sorry, I don't remember what she was wearing." He took the phone and stuffed it back in the front pocket of his jeans. "She has a friend with her, but I don't have a picture of her."

Two women, Kerrigan thought with a silent sigh of relief, even as she pushed images of Jack and his twins out of her mind. Wherever they were, they were most likely together and hopefully staying out of trouble. They probably just hadn't been ready to leave and were laying low for the time being.

"I may have seen them during the concert, but not since it ended," she said with a smile. "Perhaps we can take a look in the rooms back here." She released the doorknob and stepped away. "There aren't very many, so it won't take long. They weren't in there." She gestured toward the room she'd just exited. "If you'd like to check that one," she pointed at the door to her left and the officer and the father moved toward it, "we'll check this one." She walked toward the door on her right and reached for the knob.

"So overprotective o' his grown daughter," Riley muttered just over her shoulder.

"All fathers worry, no matter the age of their daughter," Kerrigan replied with a chuckle as she pushed the door open and took a step into the room. The laughter died in her throat as she quickly squeezed her eyes closed and turned away from the scene in front of her. "Gah!"

A naked blonde woman was bent over, gripping the back of the sofa. Sebastian was standing behind her, his lips pressed to the lips of another naked female at his side. They quickly separated and he backed away when the door opened. His pants were nowhere to be seen, but his excitement was clearly evident and Kerrigan struggled to forget that image. She heard two female squeals and a very masculine curse as someone moved in front of her.

"Did you find them?"

Kerrigan opened her eyes and met the anxious father's gaze, a lump forming in her throat as he turned to look inside the room.

"What the hell!" he exclaimed as he burst inside.

Riley now stood in front of her, and looking over his shoulder Kerrigan was thankful to see Sebastian had covered himself with a pillow.

"What did you do to my daughter?" the man's voice boomed through the room as he drew his fist back and took aim at Sebastian.

The officer grabbed his arm just before he was able to land the punch. "Sir, you don't want to do that. Let's just take a step back and calm down."

"Calm down?" The father's face became splotched with red. "Calm down?" He placed his fists on his hips. "You have got to be kidding me!"

"Sir, she's a consenting adult. She's capable of making a decision like this without your approval," the officer stated calmly, stepping between the two men. The woman now cowered behind Sebastian. Her friend had backed into the corner of the room farthest away from the commotion. Both held their clothes to them like shields.

"She's not a consenting adult," the father stated through clenched teeth. "She's only sixteen!"

Kerrigan's stomach lurched and the air completely escaped her lungs.

"Oh shit," she heard Jack curse behind her as Riley's shoulders drooped.

"Sixteen!" Sebastian roared, his face mottled with horror and rage, as he turned to look at the girl behind him. "What the fuck!"

The girl giggled and shrugged a naked shoulder and Sebastian took a step away from her.

Kerrigan's mouth fell open and she quickly closed it as she stepped around Riley toward the father and the officer.

"Yes, sixteen. And don't you dare talk to her like that!" the father snapped. "Arrest him," he commanded the police officer. Kerrigan's stomach lurched again.

"For what?" Sebastian turned his glare on the father. "The little slut came on to me." He glanced over his shoulder at the second girl, who had started to get dressed. "They both did."

"I don't care!" The man took a step toward Sebastian, pointing a finger at his face. "Do they look over eighteen to you, asshole? Maybe you should think with this head," pointing to Sebastian's forehead, "instead of this one," lowering his aim below Sebastian's waist.

The girl closest to Sebastian giggled again.

"Daddy, don't be such a spoilsport." She hiccupped.

"Are you drunk?" her father asked.

When the girl shrugged again, her father's eyes became frighteningly narrow. If her father had looked at her like that, Kerrigan would have crawled under the closest piece of furniture.

This girl just smiled.

"Get. Dressed. Now," the girl's father said through clenched teeth.

"Are you going to do anything about this?" Sebastian snapped. Kerrigan looked at him and caught him glaring at her.

"Me?" she scoffed. "What is there for me to do, Sebastian?"

He stomped toward her. "You told me no one under eighteen would be at the show. You lied, you bitch. Are you trying to get me in trouble?"

"You manage that well enough on your own." Kerrigan drew her shoulders back, hoping to give the impression of a cool confidence she was far from feeling. "I was told by the club manager they would card everyone at the door." She sensed a presence behind her, caught a whiff of cinnamon, and a calm settled over her.

"Why would she lie about that?" Jack growled over her shoulder. "No one wants to see you arrested, you idiot."

The father spun and turned his fury on Kerrigan. "Is that so?" he hissed. "And what were you doing, Miss Manager, that you didn't see this man drag my daughter back here to have his way with her?"

"I was doing my job," Kerrigan snapped. "I'm their manager, not their babysitter. They're all grown men," she glared at Sebastian, "and I expect them to act like it."

"Excuse me?" Sebastian came toe to toe with her. "I trusted that no minors would be in that club based on what you told me."

"Sounds to me like you're both guilty," the father barked. "Arrest them both, officer."

"Like hell." Jack grabbed Kerri by the arm and pushed her behind him.

"Daddy, lighten up," the sixteen-year-old said. "Mom would never throw such a fit over such a little bitty thing."

Kerrigan's stomach began to churn. *Such a little thing?* Really? How drunk was this girl?

"No, your mother would probably strip down and wait her turn," the father snapped. "But she's not here, is she?"

"Sir, calm down," the officer finally spoke as he stepped to Kerrigan's side. "I've called for backup and we will take Mr. Bates to the station."

"What?" Sebastian stared at Kerrigan over Jack's shoulder. "And you're going to let him?"

"I have no choice," she replied, stepping around Jack and approaching

Sebastian. "I told Jacob on my first day that I would not stop you from being punished if you deserved it."

"I want both of them arrested," the father insisted.

"I see no reason to arrest her," the officer said calmly. "She's done nothing wrong."

"She allowed that *rapist* near my daughter!"

The room began to spin the moment he uttered the word and Kerrigan fell back a step.

Had Sebastian forced them? How could she have been so careless and put these girls in danger? She should have been more aware of what was happening.

Jack's hands gripped her elbows and he supported her back with his chest. "Breathe," he whispered and she forced air into her lungs. "Riley, c'mere."

"What the fuck, Jack?" Sebastian's voice drifted toward her. "You're going to back her up and let me get taken in?"

Riley appeared at her side and Kerrigan was juggled from one set of strong hands to another.

"As far as I'm concerned, Sebastian, you deserve the punishment you're about to get," Jack snarled. "Look at the girls."

Sebastian scoffed and Kerrigan watched him drop the pillow and fold his arms across his chest. Her head cleared but her stomach began to roll and she stood a little taller, keeping her focus on his face.

"Look at them!" Jack commanded.

Sebastian's eyes widened as his jaw clenched. He rolled his eyes dramatically then looked over at the girls.

"Do they really look old enough to you?" Jack snapped and Sebastian turned his focus on Jack and shook his head once. "I didn't think so." He turned to the father and pointed his finger in the man's face. "We were told no one under the age of eighteen would be in this club tonight, so my question to you is, why is your sixteen-year-old daughter even here? If you ask me, he's not the only one to blame tonight, but I'll be damned if you're going to try to take Kerrigan down for this."

"What the hell do you think you're saying?" The father straightened to his full height and stood over Jack.

Jack pulled his shoulders back as well and stood eye to eye with the man. "You know exactly what I'm saying. And I will make sure everyone knows my opinion if you continue to press for our manager's arrest." Kerrigan grasped Jack's arm and tugged, but he wouldn't budge. The last thing she wanted was for him to be taken to jail for assault.

The police officer stepped between the two men and put his hand on the father's chest. Another officer entered the room and walked directly to Sebastian. "That's enough. We're going to interview everyone involved and *I'll* decide if anyone else needs to be arrested tonight." He looked at the girls and Sebastian. "Everyone who was in this room originally, get dressed. Everyone else out to the hallway. Now."

"You're not rid of me yet, bitch!" Sebastian yelled as Kerrigan led the way out of the room.

She turned and met his narrowed glare and suppressed a shudder.

"My father will get me out of this," he said coolly. "And I will be back."

Jack gently laid his hands on her back and pushed her into the hallway.

Twenty-Seven

"Kerrigan, how the hell could you let this happen?" Jacob thundered.

She pulled the phone away from her ear and glanced briefly at Jack, who was standing beside her. His brow furrowed and he shot her a questioning look. She shook her head as she placed the phone closer to her cheek. Stephen and Riley had arrived in her room just after her phone call with Jacob had begun. They were all together to decide what the band would do next. Kerrigan had started the conversation with Jacob by laying out the charges against Sebastian.

The statutory rape charge carried up to fifteen years in jail. Sebastian faced two of those charges, plus two more charges for contributing to the delinquency of a minor for the alcohol he'd given them. Another year in jail for each.

Kerrigan felt sure that, despite his final warning to her, Sebastian wouldn't be rejoining the band. The three other members had also felt certain they wouldn't see him again for a very long time.

"Jacob, I was—"

"Not doing your job," he interrupted.

"I told you on day one I wouldn't stop them from being arrested if—"

"You're supposed to prevent them from getting to that point." His volume rose again as her eyes watered with frustration. "Damn it, Kerrigan, do you have any idea what this is going to cost us?"

She swallowed the lump in her throat and avoided making eye contact with the three pairs of eyes she could feel on her.

"He won't be back," she said, hoping to reassure Jacob. "He's looking at—"

"Nothing," Jacob snarled. "He'll get nothing," he continued with a clipped tone. "And do you know why? His father has some of the best lawyers in the country. He'll get Sebastian off."

Kerrigan was thankful she hadn't eaten anything. The thought that he wouldn't be punished for whatever he'd done to those girls soured her stomach.

"And then Sebastian *will* rejoin the band. And when he does, my company's reputation will be shot." Jacob blew a long breath into the phone. "I knew hiring you was a bad idea," he muttered, his words stabbing her in the chest.

On top of everything else, she'd now let her boss down.

"What does the band think they're going to do without a lead singer?"

"We're going to discuss that now," Kerrigan answered, relieved to have him thinking ahead and not about her failures of the night before.

"You have twenty-four hours," Jacob snapped. "If they don't have a plan by then, I'll make it for them."

"Yes . . ." Kerrigan began as the line went silent, "sir."

She put her phone on the bed beside her and placed her elbows on her knees. She closed her eyes as she lightly pressed her fingers to her temples and began rubbing them in small circles.

"What did he say?" Jack asked.

Kerrigan slowly opened her eyes and stared at the floor. "In summary, he wishes he hadn't hired me and has given you guys a day to figure out what you want to do. Otherwise, you'll all be headed home, most likely for good." She lifted her head and met his frown.

Jack dropped into the chair closest to her. "Clearly we'll keep going. We don't have much choice."

"Not if we want to meet the financial requirements," Stephen added.

Kerrigan nodded and looked over each serious face. "I guess the only question now is . . . how? With Sebastian gone you no longer have a lead guitar or a lead singer. Who will replace him?"

"That's obvious," Riley stated, looking at Jack.

Jack's frown deepened and he pressed his hands together between his knees as he avoided Riley's gaze.

"I agree with Riley," Stephen added. "Jack knows the songs; he wrote them."

"An' he's got a better voice than either o' us." Riley leaned his shoulders against the wall. "The real question is . . . what d'we do about bass?"

The answer came quickly to Kerrigan, but she bit her tongue against the suggestion. It was one she'd have to bring up with Jack first . . . in private.

"Nothing," Jack said as he sat up. "We'll have to do without."

Stephen leaned forward in his seat. "We won't sound as good."

"We need the bass to round out the sound," Riley added. "Do any of ye ken anyone who could help on short notice? I don't even care if they're not a pro, they just need to ken how to play."

Jack finally met Kerrigan's gaze. His jaw clenched and she saw the clouds in his green eyes.

"Jack," she said softly. If he agreed, she'd make the call herself.

He shook his head. "No, I don't know of anyone."

They sat in silence for a few minutes before Riley finally pushed himself away from the wall. "Well, we have to be on the road, so we may as well get started."

"Do we have time to rehearse first?" Stephen asked as he rose from his seat.

Kerrigan glanced at her watch. "Yeah. The drive to Sarasota will take about an hour, maybe less. I need to run to the bank first, so you guys have some time while I'm gone."

"Why don't you two go get the instruments from the trailer?" Jack rose. "Let's meet back here and we'll get started."

"We'll make sure we're packed first," Stephen said as he opened the door and he and Riley left the room.

Jack resumed his seat and slid it closer to Kerrigan. "You'll tell me what Jacob said?"

"Later." She pointed to the pastries and coffee sitting on the table. Stephen had come in with them while she was on the phone. "Your idea?"

"Yes," Jack answered as he picked up a chocolate chip scone and handed it to her. "I thought you might be hungry," he added, holding out a cup of coffee to her as well.

She smiled as she took the coffee and popped a piece of her favorite pastry into her mouth.

"A little."

She took a few more bites as she steeled herself for what she wanted to ask. After a sip of coffee, she looked squarely at him.

"I could call Charlie."

Jack held her stare, trying to keep his mask of indifference in place. It had been a long time since he'd seen Charlie. Their most recent meeting was four years ago, when he'd gone to Charlie's house in search of Kerri.

Jack had told Charlie he'd cleaned up his act. Charlie had acted like he believed him but had warned Jack that he had better not slip back into his old behavior if he started dating Kerri. And when Charlie had finally confessed she was in Paris, something in his tone had made Jack think he wasn't sorry she was gone.

They hadn't spoken for two years before that, either, since the day Charlie had asked him to stay out of Kerri's life. That day had been the first time Jack had ever experienced a feeling of inadequacy, and he hadn't liked it. His ego always took a small hit when he looked back on that conversation.

"There has to be someone else," Jack muttered as he sat back in his chair.

"I'll gladly take suggestions," Kerri replied. "But you know he's a fast learner when it comes to music, and next to you, he's the best bass guitar player I know." She turned her body to his but remained seated at the foot of the bed.

"Doesn't he have a job?" Jack covered his eyes with his hand.

He was too tired for this conversation. The previous night's problems had kept them all at the club until the wee hours of the morning. When they'd finally come back to the motel, Kerri had been so upset he'd spent at least an hour trying to convince her that what had happened hadn't been her fault. After she'd fallen asleep, he'd lain awake considering the band's options.

And yes, he had thought about calling Charlie. But he'd pushed that option to the bottom of the very short list. He hoped he could replace Sebastian and no one would notice the missing sound.

A delicate hand grasped his and pulled it away from his eyes. Kerri looked at him with a peaceful smile on her lips. A lump of fear formed in his throat.

What if Charlie found a way to convince her he still wasn't good enough? Jack couldn't stomach the thought of losing her again.

"He'll be with us for just over a month. And, as long as he can check in with his sub-contractors every day, he can do his job from the road," she said softly. "Jackson, he'd come if I called him. But I won't call him unless you ask me to."

"Kerri—"

Her lips met his with a light, feathery touch as her palm cupped his cheek. His arms wrapped around her and he pulled her closer as he deepened the kiss. With her soothing touch, his fears slipped to the back of his mind. The ball was in his court; they could try things his way first. At the very least, he'd have a few days to try to come up with a plan. The longer her brother remained in the dark about Kerri's relationship with him, the better Jack's chances of earning her love again.

She pulled her lips from his and the corners of her mouth lifted a little. "Just promise me you'll think about it."

Jack's upper lip curled slightly, but he nodded. "I will."

Her grin widened and she leaned closer. The second her lips touched his again, there was a knock on the door, followed quickly by Riley's loud, Scottish voice calling to them from the other side. Jack released a growl of frustration and Kerri chuckled as she rose to her feet.

Twenty-Eight

Jack moved between packing up the band's equipment and signing autographs as he strained to hear the conversation Kerri was having with the club manager. He could tell by the man's actions that he was upset, but so far Kerri appeared to have it under control. Jack would rather be the one dealing with the man's anger, but he had his job to do and knew that Kerri would hate it if he interfered with hers.

It didn't help that his thoughts were on the lousy performance the band had just given. Riley had been right. Without the bass guitar, the music didn't have the same depth. They sounded flat and Jack's singing could do nothing to disguise that.

He carried the last speaker backstage and slipped through the door to the club where he could be closer to Kerri and get a better idea what was bothering the manager. She'd placed her table just to the left of the stage, facing the crowd, and he was able to move behind her undetected.

"I understand you're not happy," she stated calmly, "but I've told you I cannot give you your money back."

"That's bullshit." The man placed both palms on the table and leaned over them.

Jack's eyes narrowed on the manager as he studied him. He was at least a head taller than Kerri and twice as wide. He didn't strike Jack as the violent type, but he seemed pretty angry. And irate people didn't always think clearly. Jack edged a little closer.

Kerri folded her arms across her chest and widened her stance. "Did the crowd enjoy the concert?"

"They seemed to," the manager answered.

"And were your bar sales good?" she asked.

"Yeah," he replied slowly.

"Did anyone complain about the music?" Kerri's back straightened. "Because no one said a word to me."

Jack had to admit that watching her in action, holding her own with this burly manager, was surprisingly arousing. He was looking forward to going back to the motel.

"Well . . ." the man stumbled, "that's not the point."

"What *is* your point then?" Kerrigan lowered her hands to the top of the cash box on the table.

"They didn't sound right," the manager griped and a knot formed in Jack's stomach. "You told me we wouldn't notice the missing member. You promised the band would sound just as good."

Kerri let the silence stretch before she waved her hand to the side. "And?"

"They didn't."

The words punched Jack in the gut. This was their second show since Sebastian's arrest, and while the club manager's words hadn't been the same the night before, he'd hinted at a similar sentiment. Kerri had had to refund a portion of the money they'd been paid the night before. Money the band desperately needed to meet the contract requirements. Jack was sure she'd reach some sort of agreement tonight as well and would probably pay back as little as possible, but they couldn't afford to keep doing that.

He slid backstage again. She seemed to have everything under control and he wasn't interested in listening to the negotiations. He knew what he had to do, but he still hated the idea. If they were going to keep this tour on track and profitable, they needed a fourth member. He'd wracked his brain for the past forty-eight hours, trying to come up with a name, any name, for his replacement, without any luck.

Kerri would have to call her brother.

"Stephen," Jack called.

Stephen set the keyboard stand on top of the speakers then looked up and met Jack's stare. "Yeah?"

"I need you to do me a favor."

Kerrigan resumed pacing between the foot of the bed and the dresser in her motel room. Once she had finished dealing with the manager, she'd gone backstage. Stephen had told her Jack had already left and was walking back to the motel, but that he'd left a message for her.

He wanted her to call Charlie.

By Kerrigan's estimation, Jack had left the club about thirty minutes before she had. She'd been in her room for forty minutes and was growing more concerned as the minutes ticked by. It was at most a two mile walk back to the motel along well-lit sidewalks; he should have been there by now. Where was he?

Did the idea of calling Charlie bother him that much?

She heard the card slip into the keycard lock and swiveled to face the door. It opened a crack and her heartrate sped up as she took a few steps closer. Jack walked into the room and she quickly closed the distance between them and threw her arms around his neck.

He wrapped one arm around her. "Hey."

"Where have you been?" Kerrigan asked as she placed her hands on his shoulders and looked at his face, relieved to see his eyes were clear and there was no aroma of alcohol on his breath.

"I made a stop." He held up a plastic bag up between them.

As he opened the bag, she leaned forward to peek inside and her tension slipped away with a soft laugh. He produced two large bags of M&Ms and two of salted cashews as he grinned sheepishly.

"I haven't had this in a long time." Kerrigan laughed as Jack walked to the table and proceeded to open all four bags and dump them into the center of the table. She lowered herself into a chair and began pushing the candies and cashews into a neat pile.

"Me neither," he replied wistfully as he sat down in the other seat, facing her. "I passed a little convenience store and went in to get a bottle of water. When I saw the M&Ms, I couldn't resist."

As she picked up a nut and a chocolate and popped them into her mouth, Jack pulled two bottles of water out of the plastic bag, slid one toward her, and grabbed a handful of their treat.

"How much did you pay the manager?"

Kerrigan's brow lifted. "How did you know there was a problem?"

"I saw him approach you after the concert. He looked angry, so I kept an eye on the two of you," Jack answered with a shrug. "I heard him ask for his money back."

Kerrigan picked up a nut and a piece of candy. "I talked him down to an eighth of what he'd paid us. About one fifty."

"That doesn't seem like much." Jack slid his seat closer to hers.

She swallowed and tipped her head. "No, it could have been worse."

She took a sip of water as Jack nodded and did the same. After lowering her bottle, she focused on his face.

"I called Charlie."

His jaw immediately clenched and he looked at his lap. He remained silent, tilting the sealed bottle from side to side.

"He'll be here tomorrow," she added and he kept his focus on the bottle. "Jackson," she murmured and waited for him to look at her. When he finally made eye contact, she frowned at the dark cloud lingering in his green eyes. "What's the problem? Why don't you want his help?"

The corners of his lips turned down. "How can you ask me that? He's the reason we didn't speak for six years."

"That's not true," Kerrigan murmured as she shook her head and Jack's mouth fell open. "Well, it's not."

"You're already defending him." Jack thumped his bottle down on the table as he stood and began to pace at the foot of the bed.

"I'm not defending him, Jack." Kerrigan rose. "He separated us, I won't argue with that. But let's be honest with ourselves."

Jack stopped pacing and turned to face her.

"I was the reason we didn't see each other in Paris. I was the one who remained in Europe so I wouldn't have to come home. I could have made an effort to find out why you'd been in France, but I didn't," she argued calmly as she walked around the bed.

"Stop blaming yourself for everything that goes wrong," Jack said through clenched teeth.

"I'm not blaming myself for everything." She tried to keep the sly smile off her lips as she continued, "You could have tried again. You could have made more of an effort."

He stomped toward her, his face a mixture of pain and anger. She held up her palm to stop him.

"My point is, we're just as much to blame, if not more so, as Charlie. Yes, he asked you not to speak to me for two years, but anything after that is on the two of us." Kerrigan flattened her hand on his chest and he quickly covered it with his own. "He was your best friend, Jackson," she whispered.

"He said I wasn't good enough for you," Jack growled bitterly.

Her heart ached for him. His face showed how much those words still hurt.

"You said you agreed with him six years ago," she said softly. "Do you still think that's true?"

"Honestly?" Jack asked as he laid his forehead against hers. "Yes. Sometimes." He released her and sunk down onto the bed. "I don't know," he continued and propped his elbows on his knees as he placed his face in his palms. "I just don't want him joining us and changing your opinion of me."

"Oh, Jackson," Kerrigan whispered as she sat beside him on the bed.

She took one of his hands and gently tugged it away from his face. He turned his head toward her and she reached up and rubbed her index finger between his furrowed brows. His eyes closed at her touch.

"In eight years he's not been able to alter my opinion about you," she said softly. "Not that he's tried very hard, but still." Her hand fell to his leg and his eyes opened. "I love you. I've always loved you, and nothing he can say or do will change that."

Jack lifted his head as the tension drained from his expression. "You mean it?"

He sounded so awestruck she couldn't stop the giggle that escaped as she nodded.

"But you said you didn't love me anymore," he said as he turned his body toward hers.

She shook her head. "That's not what I said." The corners of her lips tilted upward and she slid her free hand into his. "What I said was I wasn't sure the man you'd become was the boy I'd loved. The truth is, I never stopped loving you. It just hurt so much to see you so changed."

Jack grinned widely and released her hands as he stood. He walked to the door and turned the deadbolt, then began moving toward her again. His eyes never left hers as he stalked closer and stripped off his shirt, tossing it onto the chair. Her insides turned to mush, just from the look in his eyes and the anticipation of things to come.

"You know what this means, right?" he asked as he leaned over her.

Kerrigan shook her head as she fell back onto her elbows.

"You're mine," he said, his possessive tone sending a thrill down her spine. "I'm never letting you go again."

She eased herself closer to him with a contented smile. "Good," she said, just before his mouth descended on hers.

Twenty-Nine

"You didn't have to come with me," Kerrigan said as Jack led her by the hand through the airport.

He turned to her with a scowl on his face.

She shrugged. "Well, you didn't."

He turned away and they continued their slow progress toward the terminal. When they reached the security gate, Jack found a small table and held a seat out for her. Once she was seated, he sat facing her, his back toward the departing passengers, his fingers drumming on the tabletop.

She laid her hand over his to still his nervousness. "Jackson, I told you last night, nothing will change," Kerrigan said and he met her gaze. "Charlie is here to help, it'll all be fine."

"I haven't spoken to him in four years, Kerri," Jack grumbled. "And the last thing I want to do is ask him for help."

She frowned. "I know." She hated to see him so bothered by Charlie's imminent arrival, and if she were to be completely honest with Jack, she was probably as anxious about this as he was. She had no idea how Charlie would react when he found out she was dating Jack, his estranged best friend.

But she did know that every once in a while, when Jack's name was mentioned, Charlie got a wistful look in his eye. She knew Charlie and Pete had both missed him at Pete's wedding. Neither of them had said anything, but she sometimes managed to catch the look of sadness that passed between them whenever Jack was talked about.

Jackson's absence had been felt by more than just her.

"Did you tell him this was my band?" Jack asked, breaking into her thoughts.

Kerrigan nodded her head. "He knows."

Jack nodded, and looked around quickly. "Did you tell him about us?"

"No," she quietly confessed and he shot a quick glare at her. "As worried as you've been, would you rather he had several hours to mull that over or be surprised when he gets here?"

His expression softened and he looked at their hands on the table. "Good point."

"That's what I thought," she said and looked up.

She made eye contact with a dark-haired man with blue-gray eyes identical to hers strolling through the security gates, and a smile touched her lips. She rose to her feet, tugging lightly on Jack's hand as she did. Her grin widened as her brother got closer. Releasing Jack's hand, she took a few steps and was swept off her feet into Charlie's typical bear hug. Giggling as he put her down, she took a step back to look at him.

"Charlie," she said. "I'm so glad you could make it."

A deep dimple appeared on each of her brother's cheeks. "You needed my help, why wouldn't I come?" He lifted his gaze over her shoulder and his smile slowly fell. "Jackson," he muttered.

Kerrigan suddenly felt Jack's solid heat behind her as his hand came to rest on her shoulder. She turned her head enough to see his expression held the same tension as Charlie's. As she returned her focus to her brother she exhaled slowly.

"Charlie," Jack said tightly. "Thank you for coming."

Charlie's eyes focused on Jack's hand on Kerrigan's shoulder. "Of course."

Kerrigan felt like she was in the early stages of a snowfall. She could only hope it was a few flurries and not a blizzard.

"It's good to see you again," Charlie added. "It's been a while."

"Four years," Jack replied coolly. "I hear you're engaged."

Charlie nodded. "I am. To Olivia."

"Right," Jack said. "I'll bet Pete is thrilled."

One of Charlie's eyes narrowed a bit. "The whole family is."

"Good for you." Jack's mocking tone was unmistakable and a knot formed in Kerrigan's stomach. "Congratulations."

Kerrigan cleared her throat and jumped into the storm before it could get any chillier. "Let's get back to the motel so you can meet Stephen and Riley," she said to Charlie. "And I'll give you a CD so you can acquaint yourself with their music."

"I already know it." Charlie's gaze dropped to her feet.

"Of course." Jack's whisper barely reached her ears.

She nodded. It was obvious now that he was more familiar with the band than she'd thought, even though he had failed to tell her this was Jackson's band. What else had her brother kept from her?

"Good," she said tersely. "Then you'll watch the show with me tonight and rehearse with the band tomorrow after we get to Miami."

"Great," Charlie agreed and gave her another dimpled grin. "Let's go."

Kerrigan had just finished with the last customer of the night and was starting to stack the merchandise into the tub on the table.

"So this is what you do every night?" Charlie asked. He had hovered behind Kerrigan for most of the evening, not saying much, listening to the concert and reading the music Jack had given him for each song.

Kerrigan slid the T-shirts and CDs toward him. "Every night there's a show," she answered, neatly stacking the bandanas in front of her. Charlie had asked her about those and decided he would like red as his color. She would call Debra in the morning and place the order for those, as well as more band keychains.

Charlie placed the T-shirts in the container then picked up a stack of CDs. He put them in the tub as well, then picked the top one up and flipped it over. Kerrigan watched him skim the back of the case as she folded a bandana.

"Jackson told me about your argument," she said and his hand froze in the plastic box. Kerrigan leaned her hip against the table and faced him.

He shrugged his shoulders and looked down. "And you still invited me to join the band." He turned toward her. "Are you sorry you took this job?"

She folded her arms across her chest as she considered his words. If Charlie had told her this was Jackson's band five weeks ago, she probably wouldn't have taken the job. She had thought she'd never see Jackson again. Had thought she didn't want to. But a brief glance at Jack on the stage as he packed away the band's equipment made her heart skip a beat. She looked back at her brother.

"No. Not anymore." She tipped her head. "Did Olivia know this was Jackson's band when she came to Tallahassee?"

Charlie's upper lip curled and he shook his head. "No, she didn't. But she was not happy when she found out I knew."

Kerrigan smiled. "Did you tell her the reason for your argument with Jackson?"

"Yes," he grumbled.

"How did she take it?" Kerrigan enjoyed her brother's discomfort more than she probably should have.

Charlie groaned. "She went back to her parents' house."

Kerrigan covered her lips with her hand to hide her amusement.

"And she wouldn't come back until I went to Pete and asked for his permission to date her." His expression grew more petulant and her laughter became harder to hide.

"I'm sure that didn't take you too long," Kerrigan said through her fingertips.

Charlie raised a dark brow. "It took me a few days. I felt like an idiot. We're already engaged; it was stupid." He shook his head. "But she insisted I needed to know how Jackson had felt when he came to me, so I went to Pete and asked."

"And what did Pete say?" Kerrigan prompted.

"That I was an idiot," Charlie answered bluntly as he shrugged again.

Kerrigan dropped her hand and giggled.

He smiled sheepishly. "He said the reason we'd made that pact was to keep any woman from coming between us, and that by refusing Jackson the way that I had, I allowed that to happen anyway." Charlie resumed packing the merchandise away.

"Oh, the irony." Kerrigan chuckled as she loaded the bandanas into the tub. "Didn't you realize that?"

"I hadn't expected Jackson to stop speaking to me when I told him not to contact you," Charlie answered.

"You idiot," Kerrigan mumbled and Charlie looked at her, feigning offense at her words until they both began to laugh.

Once they had all of the merchandise packed away and stacked on the table, ready to be put in the trailer, Kerrigan picked up the cash box and turned to Charlie.

"Do you have a problem with us dating?" she asked with her heart in her throat. She wasn't sure she wanted to hear his answer, but when he glanced at her with a smile and shook his head, she was able to take a deep breath.

"No, Kerri," he said. "As long as you're happy and he treats you well." His eyes narrowed slightly. "He does treat you well, right?"

Jack held his breath as he waited for Kerri's answer. He had finished packing his equipment and had moved it backstage, then had slipped through the door into the shadows of the bar. Instead of making his presence known, he'd pressed his back against the wall and listened to quite a bit of their conversation. He'd been satisfied to hear both Olivia and Pete were on his side. It also pleased him to hear Charlie might not be as much of a problem as he'd feared, which boded well for his future with Kerri.

"Charlie, he's always treated me well," she answered with a smile that made Jack's pulse quicken.

Charlie nodded as he picked up both of the containers on the table. "Then you have my blessing."

A laugh popped out of Kerri's mouth as she turned away from her brother. "Not like we need it."

Jack stepped out of the shadows and into Kerri's path.

"Oh." She fell back a step and he grabbed her arms. She grinned up at him. "Hi."

"Hi," he responded, holding her sparkling gaze. "Everything go okay tonight?"

"It went splendidly." She gave him a quick kiss on the cheek. "No problems with managers or fans, and sales were pretty high. I'm happy."

"Then I'm happy, too." Jack looked at Charlie. "Need help?"

"Sure," Charlie answered and took a step toward Jack.

Jack took the top tub and, with Kerri in the middle, the three of them strolled toward the back of the building.

"Oh, you know what?" Kerri stopped and backed up a step. "I need to have a word with Stephen, so I'll let you two take those out to the trailer. I'll see you in a bit."

Before either of them could utter a word, she turned and walked back toward the stage, cash box in hand. Jack looked at Charlie then led him out the door into the parking lot. They put the containers into the trailer and Jack sat down on the bumper.

"So you don't have a problem with me dating your sister?" Jack asked, deciding he may as well get it off his chest.

"You heard what I said inside. I know you were listening." Charlie propped his shoulder against the frame of the trailer.

"Did you come to that conclusion before or after Pete called you an idiot?" Jack leaned into the trailer, holding himself up on his elbows.

"Before." Charlie looked toward the door of the club. "After I found out what happened to her in Paris, I felt guilty. She shouldn't have been there at all and I knew she'd left partly because of me insisting on the remodel and partly because of you disappearing." His brows came together and he frowned. "I should have told you how to find her, maybe you could have prevented it. I can't help but think if I'd told her you were coming back for her then she may have stayed home."

Jack sat quietly, mulling over Charlie's words. He'd had the same thoughts himself, but Charlie was being hard enough on himself. Jack didn't need to add to the guilt.

"I should have told you when I found out," Charlie continued as he turned to Jack. "Not necessarily what had happened in Paris—that's her story to tell—but I should have let you know something had happened to her. I should have tried harder to help the two of you."

Jack nodded.

"I should have pushed harder for her to come home sooner. I should have encouraged you both to find the other." Charlie moved to Jack's side and sat down. "There are any number of things I should have done, but didn't. I've known for years that she loved you. I knew it when you asked to date her. Part of me knew you weren't in the right place to be with her at the time," he said and looked at Jack, "and part of me just wasn't ready to let her go."

"She's your sister, not your daughter," Jack stated.

"She's all the family I had at the time," Charlie retorted and looked away.

"Look, I'm sorry I kept the two of you apart. I'd honestly expected you to get together after those two years and ride off into the sunset, leaving me all alone."

Jack grinned at the idea. "That's a bit dramatic, don't you think?"

Charlie chuckled and faced Jack. "Maybe. But I'm sorry that didn't happen. For both of you." He held his hand toward Jack. "Can we just put this behind us and move on?"

Jack looked at his friend's outstretched hand and his imploring expression. Charlie was the most important man in Kerri's life. Next to himself, he hoped. Being at odds with her brother would not be good for their relationship. He reached out and shook Charlie's hand, then looked toward the door of the club. Kerri stood in the doorway, beaming from ear to ear.

That alone made the handshake worth it.

Thirty

Kerrigan held her breath as the club manager stepped up to the microphone to introduce the band. It was Charlie's first show, the room was packed with people, and she was worried how the crowd would respond to him.

After the introduction was made, the band took the stage and the crowd immediately reacted. And not in a good way.

They started chanting Sebastian's name.

Without saying a word, Jack picked up his guitar and started playing a solo he'd written as an addition to their opening song during the ride from Fort Myers to Miami. The noise of the crowd simmered to a dull roar. Kerrigan exhaled, glanced over the mass of people and then back at the band.

Charlie began playing and the crowd fell silent. Kerrigan smiled as she watched the two most important men in her life playing together in front of the audience and a calm settled over her. Charlie was good on bass and had always loved playing but never had the desire to be a rock star, so it meant a lot to her that he'd come. The fact that he and Jackson had made amends almost immediately, and had begun to interact with each other the way they used to, meant even more.

Riley and Stephen started playing as well and it became a tune Kerrigan was familiar with. Jack stepped up to the microphone and began singing.

The crowd went wild.

Kerrigan grinned so widely her cheeks hurt. She turned to face the crowd as her first customer of the night approached the table.

"Good morning, Jacob," Kerrigan replied as she watched the band load their luggage into the van for their drive to Palm Beach. She had called him for their weekly phone conference about the band's progress. It had been just over a week since Sebastian's arrest, but her stomach still knotted when she thought about the last conversation she'd had with Jacob.

She expected this one to go better.

"Well," he said slowly, "how bad is it?"

Kerrigan furrowed her brow. "What do you mean? I just sent you the numbers. Have you not seen them yet?"

"I haven't had the chance."

She heard the tap of keys on a computer.

"We had a few rough days," she filled the silence with the report of things the budget file wouldn't show. "I had to return some of the money the clubs paid because of Sebastian's absence." She paused for him to comment but he remained silent. "Since Charlie joined us though, the band has done exceedingly well. The crowds love the new sound and we are selling out of merchandise. I just placed another order for CDs and T-shirts."

Jacob didn't say anything but Kerrigan could hear a faint tapping, like a pen or pencil drumming against something.

"If things continue as they have been, we're on track to meet the required fifty thousand minimum with a few shows to spare," she finished as she looked up.

She met Jack's gaze and shrugged. She'd been expecting a better reaction from Jacob and her disappointment must have shown on her face. Jack frowned and pushed away from the side of the van. She averted her gaze toward the ground.

"I see that," Jacob said, his words clipped. "Any word from Sebastian?"

Her brow furrowed in confusion. "No, why would I hear from him?"

"Never mind." Jacob's tone was surprisingly dismissive. "Everything looks good, Kerrigan. We'll have to discuss this later, something's just come up and I need to go."

"Okay. Well, if you have any questions—"

"I'm sure I can figure it out. I'll look for your next report in a week," he said and the line went silent.

Kerrigan pulled her phone away from her ear and studied it.

"Everything okay?" Jack slid his arms around her and pulled her against his chest.

She wasn't entirely sure.

"Yeah, it's fine," she answered and turned her face to his.

He smiled and gave her a quick kiss on the lips, filling her mind with memories of the morning's activities, filling her body with the desire to do them again. When he broke the kiss, she pouted and he laughed.

Pressing his cheek to hers, he murmured, "You're insatiable."

She drew away and grinned up at him. "Is that a problem?"

He shook his head and chuckled. "Not at all. I'm enjoying it."

Kerrigan turned toward the van as she slid her phone into the front pocket of her jeans. "We should probably get on the road if we're going to check in and rehearse before the show."

"And then after the show?" Jack asked, pulling her closer as they walked.

"Hmm," she teased as she considered their options. "After the show, we'll see what you can do to curb my appetite."

"Can't wait," he rumbled in her ear and she laughed lightly as they entered the van.

"I think breakfast as a group is a wonderful idea," Kerrigan replied as she walked up the stairs to the second floor of the motel with Debra and Stephen. It was late and she was tired.

After arriving in Melbourne, Florida, earlier that day, she'd managed to find a club willing to book them at the last minute. The manager had wanted to see their show first, and after that evening's gig, Kerrigan had spent an hour in a meeting with him, making the arrangements and coming to a payment agreement for the extra concert the following night.

Luckily, Debra had volunteered to stay with her so the band hadn't had to wait. Kerrigan knew how tired they all were and had wanted them to get back to the motel to settle in for the night. Stephen had come outside when they arrived so he could walk them to their rooms.

Now, all she wanted to do was go to bed, but she figured spending another fifteen minutes to plan for the next morning wouldn't be so bad. Then she and Jackson could be alone for the night, which was quickly becoming her favorite part of the day.

"If you want, we can work out the details with Jack and then let Charlie and Riley know," Kerrigan continued as they reached the walkway outside of the rooms.

"If you think he's still awake," Debra responded with a hint of mischief in her voice and Stephen let out a snort of amusement.

Kerrigan's cheeks warmed slightly, but her smile grew as they walked toward her room. She slid the keycard into the lock and looked over her shoulder at Debra. "Of course he's still awake."

She pushed the door open and turned to look inside her room and her smile fell. Her heart stopped and her stomach dropped to her knees. If it weren't for her vice-like grip on the knob, her body probably would have crumpled to the floor.

In the bed lay Jack, sound asleep, the sheet draped over his waist and hips, his torso naked.

On the other side of the bed lay a sleeping woman.

Kerrigan closed her eyes and slowly opened them again in a long blink as Sebastian's plot popped back into her head.

"Kerri?" Debra's voice sounded like it was coming to her through a long tunnel. "Are you okay?"

Kerrigan pulled her gaze away from Jack as tears began filling her eyes. She looked around the room at the clothes strewn around, some of the articles draped over various pieces of furniture like they'd been tossed in a fit of passion. A nearly empty bottle of liquor sat on the dresser.

"I may kill him," Stephen muttered, his voice only a little less distant.

"Me first," Debra hissed.

"No," Kerrigan protested, unsure what she was arguing against . . . the vision in front of her, or their desire to kill Jack. She felt a hand on her upper arm.

"Stephen, go get her brother."

Kerrigan forced her watery stare back to the couple in the bed. "No," she whispered, the word escaping her throat on a raft of sandpaper.

Jack rolled to his side and his eyes opened. The corners of his lips turned up and he pushed himself up on his elbow. "Kerri," he slurred.

Her heart thudded and her knees weakened as she stumbled toward the closest wall.

He frowned. "Is something wrong?" Jack lowered his feet to the floor then promptly placed his elbows on his knees and put a hand to his temple. "Ow."

"You asshole!" Debra snapped. "Of course something's wrong. Look around you!"

With his head still in his hand, Jack frowned at Debra, then looked over his shoulder. He jumped out of the bed. "What the fuck!"

"Indeed," Debra agreed and pursed her lips as she folded her arms across her chest.

Jack looked down at his nakedness then grabbed a pillow off the bed and covered himself with it. The woman rolled over and sat up, a satisfied grin on her face. Jack turned and stared, wide-eyed, at Kerrigan. He opened his mouth and she held up her hand to stop him.

"No," she repeated, closing her eyes and shaking her head. Her mouth was dry as she tried to swallow the lump in her throat. "I don't want to hear it, Jack. I should have known better."

"Kerri, no," he began.

She lifted her face to his and he took a step toward her.

"Don't," she said, lifting her shoulders and forcing the tears back. "You lied to me. You said you weren't going through with the plan."

"I didn't." He took another step toward her. "I'm not."

"Stop!" she snapped and he froze. "Don't lie to me, Jack. This is exactly what he wanted you to do, isn't it? I may be a little naïve, but give me a bit of credit." Fiery anger was rising up inside of her. "You obviously knew it wouldn't be too hard to convince me you loved me."

"I do." His knuckles were white against the pillow he held. "This isn't what you think."

Kerrigan narrowed her eyes and pushed away from the wall. "You have no idea what I think right now." She could hear the stomp of feet outside and knew Charlie would be there in a few seconds. "How stupid you must have thought I was," she scoffed. "I guess you were right."

Jack reached for her, an arm's length between them.

"Don't touch me," she spat. "Don't ever touch me again. Don't look at me, don't talk to me, don't think about me, Jack. Just . . ." She took a deep, shaky breath. "Just don't."

Charlie stormed into the room, glaring at Jack. "What the hell did you do?"

Debra tugged on her arm. "C'mon, let's get out of here."

Kerrigan allowed Debra to pull her limp body out of the room and toward the parking lot.

It wasn't the fact that he was naked that kept Jack from running after her.

It was that Charlie stood between him and the door with black rage on his face. And that his head was pounding, his stomach was churning, and he was struggling to remember what had happened so he could answer Charlie's question.

"I don't know," Jack answered honestly.

This, apparently, was not what Charlie wanted to hear. He took another step closer.

"Seriously, Charlie," Jack said as he held up his hand. "I don't know what happened here." He turned to the strange woman, naked in his bed where Kerrigan should be, and scowled at her. "Who the hell are you and what are you doing in my room?"

"Don't you remember?" She smiled sweetly at him and his upper lip curled.

"Clearly, he doesn't." Riley's Scottish drawl came from the doorway.

Jack closed his eyes in frustration. Did the entire band have to be here to witness this catastrophe?

He needed to get dressed and go after Kerri.

"After the concert you asked me to meet you in the lobby, so I did," the woman said in a bubbly voice. "We came up here and had a drink," she continued as the smile on her face widened, "and then . . . you know."

Only one drink? So why did his head feel like he'd been hit by a tractor-trailer? He hadn't even felt this bad during his month of binging after Paris.

His eyes scanned the room, searching for the bottle of whatever it was they might have had to drink. They landed on a nearly empty bottle of tequila on the dresser, two glasses turned upright beside it. He couldn't remember buying that bottle, let alone partaking of it. And even if he'd had more than one glass, he shouldn't feel so affected by it. Had she slipped him something?

His vision sharpened as he glared at the woman for a few seconds, until her eye twitched. "You're lying," he barked.

Her mouth fell open and she jerked backward, then quickly pulled her shoulders back and slid off the other side of the bed. "How dare you!" she yelled as she whirled around to face him, holding the comforter against her body.

"Really, Jack," Charlie snarled and Jack glanced at him. "The damage is done, there's no point in trying to deny anything now."

"Where are my clothes? I'm leaving." She made a show of looking around the room.

"You're not going anywhere," Jack argued, searching for his own pair of pants and the fog started to clear in his mind even as the headache was picking up steam. Finding them at his feet, he put his pants on, retrieved his phone from the pocket, and he dialed his brother's number. "You're not leaving until you tell me the truth."

"I've told you the truth," she snapped, her brown eyes shooting fire at him across the bed. "And you can't keep me here," she added loudly.

Holding the phone between his ear and shoulder as he buttoned his jeans, he narrowed his eyes on her as his jaw clenched. "Watch me."

The other end of the line rang several times before he finally heard the connection.

"Damn it, Jackson," his brother Nathan grumbled on the other end. "It's midnight. We don't all keep rock star hours. You'd better be in jail or dead to be calling me this late."

"I need your help," Jack snapped as he looked up at the ceiling.

"Good God." His brother sighed. "You have been arrested."

"Not yet." Jack looked at the stranger in the room, the urge to do her harm surprisingly strong. "But the night is still young."

She glared back at him with a curl in her upper lip, but he could see that just beyond the bravado, she was scared.

"What did you do?" Nathan asked.

Jack frowned as he glanced toward the phone. "Why do you always assume I've done something?"

Nathan remained silent.

"It involves Kerri," Jack stated. "She found me in bed with another woman. I need your help."

"Look," Nathan began after a long release of air. "Unless she's strangled you or the other woman I can't help you. But if she did strangle you, I'd say you deserved it. Can I go back to sleep now?"

"Here's the problem. I didn't bring this woman back to my room," Jack answered.

"That's still—"

"Just listen!" Jack roared. "I think I was drugged and I need your help proving it."

"Hold on," Nathan muttered and Jack guessed he was talking to his fiancée. After a moment, Nathan came back on the line. "Where are you?" he asked.

"Florida."

"I don't have any jurisdiction there; there's nothing I can do," Nathan said with a sigh.

"I'm not asking for police involvement," Jack said and the woman in the room gasped. Jack looked up at her, saw her rounded eyes and her trembling hand covering her mouth. "Yet."

She went white.

Jack took a moment to relish his small victory, then turned his attention back to his phone call. "I just want you to prove I was drugged so I can prove to Kerri I didn't cheat on her."

Nathan blew out a long, low whistle. "I didn't realize you two had progressed to that point." He had another brief, mumbled conversation with the other person. "Okay. I'll do what I can to prove you were drugged, but without being on the scene, the who-did-it may be a little harder for me to figure out."

Jack closed his eyes and relaxed a little.

Nathan continued. "Here's what you need to send me."

Thirty-One

The burly bartender smiled at Kerrigan and Debra as they approached the less crowded end of the bar. "So ladies, what can I—?"

"Two whiskey sours, double shot in each," Kerrigan interrupted as she sat down on the stool. The bartender turned to walk away.

"Wait, I haven't ordered yet!" Debra took the stool next to Kerrigan and when the man turned back to her, she grinned and ordered a beer.

Kerrigan's mind was still in a haze.

Once they'd gotten in the car, they'd put the interstate to their backs and headed east, toward the beach. Kerrigan was thankful for Debra's presence, but even more grateful for her silence. As they'd approached the causeway that led to a barrier island, Kerrigan finally spoke.

"I need a drink."

Debra had obligingly stopped at the first semi-respectable looking bar they'd come to.

Now, sitting in the shadows, facing the door, the noise of the crowd was more like the buzz of thousands of bees. Kerrigan couldn't focus on anything. She wasn't sure she wanted to.

What she wanted to do was clear her mind of the image of Jack in bed with that woman. Since she doubted that was possible, numbing the pain was the next best thing.

She unwillingly recalled Jack and his bottle of brandy in that Parisian brasserie when he'd left the police station. Had he felt as sick and pained then as she did now?

"Do you plan on getting drunk quickly or just sitting here for a while?" Debra asked after she laid her hand on Kerrigan's forearm to get her attention.

Kerrigan shrugged her shoulders. Except for one night a year, she didn't typically use alcohol as an escape. "I'm honestly not sure."

"I wouldn't blame you either way," Debra murmured. "Although, I must applaud your self-control back there. If it had been me, I'd be in jail now for a double homicide." Debra laughed hollowly.

Kerrigan's lips couldn't even attempt a reaction to the humor as she looked at Debra. "Shock, I guess," she replied flatly.

Debra nodded and they sat in silence until their drinks appeared.

Kerrigan placed her cocktail to her lips and tipped the glass up. She gulped down half of the tart mixture before placing the glass down. Closing her eyes, she took a deep breath, letting the aroma of the whiskey tickle her sinuses. The alcohol almost immediately took the edge off, but she knew it would never erase the memory. Deciding these would be her only two drinks of the night, she opened her eyes and took another, smaller sip.

"Let's just sit for a while."

"Sounds good to me." Debra peeled at the label on her beer bottle as she turned her knees toward Kerrigan's seat. "You said something to Jack about 'going through with the plan.' What did you mean by that?"

Kerrigan's brows rose to her hairline as she stared at her drink. "Stephen didn't tell you?"

"No," Debra answered. "He said he could tell there was something going on, but decided he didn't want to get involved."

"Smart man." Kerrigan lifted her glass in a silent toast to Stephen's intelligence, then took another drink before explaining Sebastian's plan to Debra. She placed her nearly empty glass down and turned to look at Debra when she brought up Jack's role in the scheme.

Debra gasped. "You're kidding?"

"Nope," Kerrigan said, popping the "p" sound, then frowned. Maybe the drink was hitting her a little harder than she'd expected. "No," she repeated. "Only Jack told me he'd never intended to carry out the plan. I told him it wouldn't have worked anyway." She propped her elbow on the bar and finished the rest of the first drink, then rested her head in her hand and faced Debra. "I lied."

"You mean it might have worked?" Debra asked.

Kerrigan shrugged her response.

Debra took a swig of beer. "Does Jack know you lied?"

Kerrigan's lips turned up in a self-deprecating smile. "He does now."

Debra frowned. "Are you leaving?"

Was she? Kerrigan had to admit, that was her first instinct. She wanted to run. She wanted to go home, pack all of her things, and leave Rocky Creek for good before Jack could come home.

"I wish I could," Kerrigan answered honestly.

"Why can't you?" Debra grabbed her hand and gave it a reassuring squeeze. "I have a family thing on Sunday, so I have to leave tomorrow. You can come back to Rocky Creek with me tomorrow. I'll keep you company until Charlie comes home and Stephen can manage the band until they find another manager. You don't need to be here to put up with Jack's rotten behavior."

Kerrigan shook her head. "I can't, Debra, for two reasons. First, if I did go home with you, I wouldn't be sticking around. I'd be out of town before they got back and I'd probably only come home for the holidays." Like she'd done for the last four years. "But more importantly, if I leave, there won't be another manager. There won't be a band for Stephen to manage. Jacob made it clear to the band and to me that if I fail, if I leave for any reason, he's nullifying their contract and they're done." Kerrigan slid the full glass toward herself and began stirring the second cocktail with the straw. "I can't do that to them. I can't let my personal problems interfere with the job I was hired to do."

Debra's hand fell from Kerrigan's as the excitement faded from her eyes. "I'm sorry, I didn't realize Jacob had put those restrictions on your tenure." She blew out a long breath and looked toward the crowd. "I also owe you an apology."

Kerrigan froze and focused on Debra. "Why would you owe me an apology?"

"I promised you'd regret it if you hurt him." Debra picked up her bottle and waved it toward the bartender with a nod, then looked at Kerrigan again. "I never imagined he'd hurt you. I thought you meant too much to him."

Tears quickly filled, then overflowed from Kerrigan's eyes. She shook her head as she looked away.

"I'm sorry, I should just stop talking now," Debra said as she slipped a napkin into Kerrigan's hand. "You can be sure I'll let him have that earful I promised you. I won't stop until his ears are bleeding."

Kerrigan giggled through the tears as she turned back to her friend.

"Would that make it better?" Debra asked with a smile.

Kerrigan dabbed at her eyes and frowned. "I'm afraid only time can make this better." She took a sip of her drink, relishing the tart of the lemon and the burn of the whiskey on her tongue as she inhaled deeply through her nose. "But maybe now I can get over him."

"What can I do to help?"

Kerrigan heard someone faintly clearing his throat and rolled over. She slowly opened her eyes to find the fuzzy outline of a man sitting in the chair beside the table. After pushing herself up and grabbing her glasses off of the nightstand, she put them on and saw that Charlie had snuck into her room. She groaned and flopped back down onto the pillow, causing a dull pain to radiate through her head. She'd changed her mind and had two more drinks before they'd left the bar. On top of everything else, she seemed to be experiencing her first hangover.

"How did you know I was here?" she groaned.

When they'd returned to the motel the night before, she'd gone straight to the lobby and booked another room for herself while Debra had retrieved her luggage and things from Jack's room. Kerrigan had asked Debra not to tell him what was going on.

"Debra gave me the spare key," Charlie said, holding up the plastic card as proof.

"Did you have to use it so early?" She closed her eyes and pulled the blanket up to her chin.

The smell of coffee wafted past her nose and her mouth began to water. She rolled to her side and opened one eye. Charlie was holding out a large to-go cup and she slowly pushed herself into a seated position. Once her back was propped against the headboard, she held her hand out for the cup.

"It's almost ten o'clock, Kerri," he said as he relinquished her coffee.

She paused with the cup to her lips, then glanced at the clock on the nightstand to check. Lifting her shoulders in a casual shrug, she tipped the coffee into her mouth. It was her favorite, hazelnut with a hint of chocolate.

She sighed and turned to face her brother but her eyes landed on a white paper bag on the table beside him.

"What's that?" she pointed.

Charlie handed it to her. "A scone."

She opened the bag and deeply inhaled the chocolatey aroma. "Yum."

She reached into the bag and pinched off a piece of the pastry then popped it in her mouth. As she chewed slowly, she noticed the satisfied smile on her brother's lips and her eyes narrowed. She swallowed her mouthful then took a sip of coffee.

"Why are you here?" she finally asked.

Charlie leaned back in the chair and stretched his feet out in front of him. "I was worried about you." He folded his arms across his chest. "How are you?"

Kerrigan swallowed another bite of the scone and scowled at him. "How do you think I am? I wish I could just wash my hands of him entirely, but I'm stuck managing his damn band."

"Jackson thought you might have gone home last night."

"First of all, don't say his name," she snapped. "Secondly, I don't care what he thought or what he thinks." She pointed her finger at her brother and continued, "Or how he feels, so don't even go down that road."

He held his palms up in surrender.

She took a long sip of coffee. "I'm sure he would have liked for me to go home," she added sardonically.

"Don't be so sure about that," Charlie said.

Kerrigan leaned back against the headboard and focused on the wall above the mirror directly in front of her. "Whatever."

Out of the corner of her eye she saw him sit up and place his elbows on his knees.

"Kerri, I really think you should talk to him about last night."

"No." She rolled her eyes. "He's an ass and I don't want to talk to him."

"You're his manager, you don't have a choice."

Kerrigan frowned. Her brother had a point. But she had spent the first few weeks as the band's manager keeping conversations with Jack as short and professional as possible. It shouldn't be too hard to do it again. She shrugged.

"He called his brother," Charlie stated.

"Probably looking for an out in the contract if I leave," she replied.

"Not Mason," Charlie said. "Nathan."

Not the lawyer, the cop. Kerrigan felt sick to her stomach. "Was that girl underage, too?"

Charlie moved to sit on the edge of the bed beside her. "No, not that we know of. He asked Nathan for police help. Would he have done that if he were guilty of anything?"

Kerrigan met her brother's gaze and a seed of hope planted in her chest. No, that didn't seem like something he'd do if he were guilty. But then, what could Nathan do for him? The call had to be for some other bit of advice. Help for what happened between them the night before didn't make sense. Nathan couldn't get him out of that sort of trouble.

The seed was dug up and tossed away.

"It doesn't matter, Charlie," she whispered, taking long, slow breaths to keep her emotions in check and her tears at bay. She couldn't let her brother know how much she was hurting. "It's over. Our relationship will be strictly professional from now until the end of the tour. And then . . ." she forced the corners of her mouth up, "and then we don't have to see each other ever again."

"Kerri—"

"Debra forgot to bring the cash box with the rest of my stuff last night. I would greatly appreciate it if you would retrieve it for me," Kerrigan said brightly, trying to ignore the hurt in her heart and her hangover. "I need to add up the sales from the show and prepare the deposit."

Charlie frowned as he rose and walked toward the door. When he reached it, he put his hand on the knob and turned to face her. "You can't hide in here forever."

"No," she agreed. "But I can hide in here for a few more hours."

"Where's Charlie?" Jack grumbled as he crossed his arms and leaned against the van. More importantly, where was Kerri?

He knew she was still around. Charlie had disappeared several times during the day, once to take her the breakfast Jack had suggested, once with the cash box. Jack knew Kerri wouldn't let that out of her sight or would have entrusted it to Stephen before she left. The problem was that Charlie wouldn't tell him where she was. Jack had even tried to follow him, without success, thanks to Riley and Stephen.

All day he'd had visions of her in a room somewhere, her eyes red and puffy behind the shield of her glasses, her cheeks stained with tears. When she rejoined them, he imagined she'd probably have her hair pulled back again in the tight bun she'd worn when she'd first become their manager. She'd most likely still have her glasses on and her wardrobe would be the no-nonsense, businesslike style she'd recently abandoned for more casual attire.

The thought of her slipping back into that standoffish, professional persona, all because of what she'd seen the night before had his stomach in knots and put him in a foul mood. He wanted to see her. He needed to explain what had happened the night before. Or at least what he could of it. Most of the details were still fuzzy.

"He'll be here in a bit," Stephen answered, leaning against the passenger door as he used one hand to scrape the fingernails of his other hand clean.

He didn't bother looking at Jack. Stephen wasn't convinced of Jack's innocence and was still reeling at the thought that Jack had tried to run Kerri off. Jack was tired of trying to explain himself to Stephen and was perfectly content to let the silence between them remain. He wasn't interested in wasting any more breath trying to enlighten his keyboard player when he was more concerned about Kerri's well-being.

Riley, sitting on the fender of the trailer, remained silent as well, staring in the direction of the motel. Jack looked down at his feet and kicked a piece of gravel away. He wasn't sure where Riley stood, whether he believed Jack's side of the story or not. The only person Jack had received a hint of support from was Charlie, but even that was tenuous.

Not that Jack could blame him. This was the exact scenario that had prevented Charlie from giving his support six years ago.

"Here they come," Riley drawled.

Jack looked up and saw Charlie and Kerrigan headed toward them, and felt a little of the tension leave his body. Her hair was down, she had her contacts in, and she was dressed nicely, but casually in acid wash jeans and a dark blue polo shirt. She hadn't made the changes he'd feared. She looked like the calm, collected manager she'd slowly transformed into over the past few weeks.

This could be a good thing.

As they approached, Jack couldn't help but stare at her. Her lips were pursed together. She held the cash box against her body, resting it on her hip. Her gaze slowly roamed over Riley and Stephen, and Jack frowned when her blue-gray eyes skipped over him completely. His grimace deepened when she lowered her sunglasses from the top of her head to cover her eyes.

The pair stopped at the back of the trailer.

"Are you ready for the gig then?" Kerri asked, focusing, as best as Jack could tell, on Riley.

Riley nodded. "Just waiting on ye for the directions."

A brief smile appeared on her full lips. "Well, I'm here now, so let's go." She turned her head and walked toward the front of the van. "Stephen, it shouldn't take long," she said as she walked toward him. "The bar is about twenty minutes away, but that may not factor in traffic. We're headed toward the beach on a Saturday night, so it will probably take a little longer."

"Kerri," Jack said softly as she walked past him and she straightened.

She turned her head toward him, but didn't looked directly at him. Her body stayed rigid.

"It's Kerrigan," she murmured. "I shouldn't have to tell you that again."

Any hope she'd calmly talk to him about what had happened the night before escaped on the wind her words knocked out of him. She turned and took a step away.

"Kerri, please." Jack turned to follow, but a hand on his shoulder stopped him.

"Live to fight another day," Charlie muttered and stood beside him for a moment. "She needs more time."

Charlie followed his sister toward the front of the van. As she climbed into the front seat, Riley strolled past Jack.

Jack scowled as he forced his feet to follow. If time was what she needed, he'd give it to her.

But he didn't have to like it.

Thirty-Two

Kerrigan stared through her reflection in the mirror as she ran a brush through her hair. As much as she tried, she couldn't forget the previous afternoon and the amount of strength it had taken her to maintain her cool when she'd seen Jack. As she'd walked past him, she'd caught a whiff of sandalwood and cinnamon and had nearly lost all of her resolve. She'd wanted to throw herself into his arms and forgive him for anything and everything. It was borderline madness.

She couldn't forget what she'd seen and no excuse could possibly explain away the vision of him in bed with another woman, naked and intoxicated. That kind of thing didn't just happen accidentally. If he thought she was naïve enough to believe any lie he might tell her, he was in for a big surprise.

"He called his brother," she whispered at her reflection.

Why would he have called his brother, the police detective? She knew how much Jack looked up to his oldest brother. He'd talked about Nathan frequently during their late night discussions at the beach house. Maybe he'd simply been asking Nathan for brotherly advice.

She furrowed her brow. Charlie had given her the impression it wasn't for advice.

He clearly wants to talk to me, she thought with a nod.

He'd tried to engage her in conversation several times the night before. If he had been following Sebastian's plan, then why would he care what she thought? What would he need to talk to her about? And Charlie had hinted that Jack didn't want her to leave. So why had he slept with another woman? Was it out of sheer malice for her rejection of him in Paris? Her hand froze with the brush still in her hair.

The Jackson she once knew, the one she was starting to believe him to be again, wouldn't have done that.

She slammed the brush down on the counter and scowled at her reflection.

"Clearly he's not the man you once knew, you idiot."

A knock on her door made her jump. She swiveled toward the sound and narrowed her eyes on the door. As the knock turned into a pounding, she let out an exasperated sigh. If that was Jack, she'd hurt whomever had told him her room number. She'd told them all she didn't want him to know. It was bad enough that she wouldn't be able to separate herself so easily from him again anytime soon. They were moving on to Orlando that morning, and unless she wanted to continue to pay for her own room, separate from the band, they'd be back to staying in three rooms, most likely grouped together, one of which would have to be hers.

Luckily the drive would only be just over an hour, but she was not looking forward to that much time in close proximity to Jack. She needed more time to build up her defenses so she wouldn't suffer from the same madness that had struck the day before.

She pulled her shoulders back as she walked across the room and grabbed the doorknob, prepared to give Jack a tongue-lashing he wouldn't forget. Turning the knob, she threw the door open and her words died in her throat.

"Charlie?" She tilted her head to the side. "What's up?"

"We have a problem," he answered somberly.

Ice slid down Kerrigan's spine as she pulled her shoulders back. "What's he done now?"

"He?" Charlie shook his head. "Good grief, Kerri, give the man some credit. Jackson hasn't done anything." He pushed past her and walked directly to the dresser and picked up her room key. "You need to come with me."

"What the hell kind of place doesn't have security cameras in their parking lot?" Jack tried his best not to yell at the red-faced manager.

To the man's credit, he didn't cower. He folded his arms across his chest and glared down his nose at Jack. "I'm sorry sir, we've never had a need for them before. Maybe you're the problem."

"Me?" Jack's arms tightened like springs about to explode.

"Your band," the manager clarified. "We've never accommodated a rock band before. Maybe we should avoid it in the future."

Jack clenched his jaw and inched closer to the man. "I don't give a damn what you do in the future. What are you going to do to fix this problem now?"

"Jack! Hey! That's enough," Kerri snapped as she pressed her hand to his shoulder. "Back up."

Jack looked down at her then let his gaze fall to her hand as his tension lifted a fraction. She looked at her hand too, immediately dropping it.

"What's happened here?" she asked.

"Look," Jack said and pointed to the trailer that carried their instruments.

He'd woken up, packed his things, then come out to find their trailer had been vandalized. The tires on both sides had been punctured. The sides had been sprayed with a rainbow of colors. And worst of all, the lock had been cut and the inside ransacked. He'd quickly accounted for his own instruments and at a glance, he'd noticed Riley's, Stephen's, and Charlie's equipment were still there as well.

Stephen was on the phone with the police. Riley was taking a more thorough visual stock of their items. They couldn't touch anything until the cops arrived and Jack was itching to do something.

Punching an arrogant motel manager was currently on the top of his list.

He glanced at Kerrigan and his lips twitched.

Dragging her off to kiss her senseless was a close second.

He shook that thought away. He needed to figure this out so they could be on the road. They had a show in Orlando that evening and needed to leave as soon as possible.

"Jack, I'll handle this," she said calmly. "You go over there and figure out what needs to be done to get us on the road."

The motel manager snorted and Jack glared at him. Jack looked at Kerrigan and she pointed toward the trailer. He turned and walked away, barely resisting the urge to stomp off like the scolded child he felt like.

Charlie was standing beside Riley, peering through the open doors of the trailer and Jack stopped beside them. Charlie glanced over his shoulder at him, then beyond him toward Kerri and a smile touched his lips.

"She decide you weren't handling it well?" Charlie asked with a chuckle.

Jack's scowl deepened. "Yes."

"Catch more flies with honey," Riley stated as he turned to face them. "And let's face it, ye haven't got any honey to spare."

"Shut it," Jack growled since he couldn't really argue. He'd need all his sweetness to convince Kerri she was wrong. He should be mad at her, at least a little, for doubting him, but he couldn't really blame her. When she'd first laid eyes on him after six years apart, he'd had a blonde on each arm. And now he'd been set up to be found in the exact way Sebastian had wanted things to happen.

Jack looked at the contents of the trailer, scattered all over the floor. A stark contrast to the way he typically put them away. It reminded him of the way Sebastian always kept his things.

"Damn it," he spat when the thought struck him.

"What?" Riley and Charlie asked simultaneously.

Jack pointed to the trailer and turned his scowl toward them. "Sebastian did this."

And he was willing to bet Sebastian had set him up with that woman, too.

"Riley." Kerri's sweet voice drifted toward them and all three men turned around. "Could you come over here please?" She waved Riley over.

Jack noted the sing-song quality of her words and an icy wave of jealousy washed over him. Without a word, Riley walked to her side and she grinned at him. Jack's eyes widened and a green-eyed monster began clawing at his stomach as she spoke to Riley. Suddenly she paused and tipped her head to the right.

Jack followed her gaze and saw the woman who'd been in his bed two nights ago standing in the crowd, watching the goings-on. She was wearing a motel uniform and paled when his eyes landed on her face. His lip curled and he turned his attention back to Riley and Kerri.

A few more words passed between them before Riley dipped his head in a brief bow and turned to walk away. As he turned, he said something to her and color rose in her cheeks.

He was flirting with her.

"I'm going to kill him." Jack's hands clenched into fists by his side.

"Kill who?" Charlie asked. "And why?"

"Riley," Jack answered as he turned to face Charlie. "He's flirting with her."

Charlie tried, unsuccessfully, to hide his amusement and Jack narrowed his eyes. There was nothing funny about this.

"I told him she was off limits."

"When did you tell him that?" Charlie asked through a laugh. "You have no right to decide who can or can't date her."

"And you do?" Jack snapped.

All humor left Charlie's face. "Clearly I had good reason," he muttered as Stephen strolled up.

"Cops are on their way and I've been looking for a place to get new tires," Stephen said, waving his phone in front of them. "I've made some calls, most of the places aren't open yet."

Charlie frowned. "Why?"

"It's Sunday," Stephen answered with a shrug. "Most of them won't open until noon. We should probably pack up our rooms and get things loaded so that once they're open we can get the tires and go."

Jack and Charlie nodded and Stephen turned toward Kerri.

"I'll go update her."

Once Stephen was gone, Jack spun to face Charlie. "You had good reason?" he snapped. "I thought you believed me. I thought you were on my side."

Charlie held his palms up. "I'm not taking sides. This is between you and Kerri."

Jack folded his arms across his chest and took a deep, calming breath. He'd been wound so tightly since she'd walked out of their room two nights ago that he was becoming too easily angered by everything. His usual calm demeanor was shattered and he was having a hard time getting it together.

"I wish she'd at least talk to you about what happened, but you know as well as I do you can't force her to do anything she doesn't want to do," Charlie continued as Jack did his best to regain his composure. "I would like to see you work this out."

Jack furrowed his brow. "Why?"

Charlie glanced in Kerri's direction then walked toward the front of the van. Jack followed and leaned his back against the sliding door as Charlie settled his shoulder against the passenger side window.

"Do you know how much the rape changed her? The way she'd been smiling at you, the way she just smiled at Riley," he waved in her direction, "I haven't seen her smile like that since she went to Paris. I have no idea how she lived in England and Switzerland, but for the last four years, she's been spending her vacation time at home, actually staying at home. She doesn't go out unless Olivia needles her long enough, and then it's with Olivia or me, or both of us. And what you took as flirting, well I haven't seen her that relaxed with any guy in a long time. Even the ones she's known her entire life."

"Pete too?" Jack questioned, a knot forming in the pit of his stomach as Charlie nodded. Jack knew what he'd seen in her behavior when she'd joined his band. He could now imagine how lonely she must have been in those four years.

And now she thought he had betrayed her. He looked up at her, surprised to find her focus on him. Their eyes met for a moment before she looked away, but she wasn't able to hide the hurt in her eyes.

He had to fix this.

"For whatever reason, she loves you. She always has," Charlie said. "I want you to work this out so she can either get the happy ending she's always wanted with you, or find the strength to move on."

Jack tipped his head toward Charlie. "She'll get her happy ending."

No matter what.

Kerrigan held back her laugh as she laid the last of the CDs on the table, then dropped the empty tub to the floor.

"You're kidding, right?" she asked Charlie, who was standing at the end of the table, watching her work. "I wasn't flirting with anyone." She shook her head and fanned the CD cases out. "I wouldn't know how," she added under her breath.

"Well, Jackson thought you and Riley were flirting with each other yesterday and he wasn't happy about it." Charlie folded his arms across his chest.

Kerrigan rolled her eyes. "Like I care what Jack's happy or unhappy about." She met her brother's gaze. "That stopped being my problem a few days ago, in case you forgot."

Charlie sighed. "Kerri, I still wish you'd talk to him about that."

"So that's why you came over here then? To plead his case for him?" Kerrigan shoved the tub under the table with her foot. As she watched the empty plastic box slide, her eyes were drawn to a cardboard box, faintly visible through the sides of the other tub under the table.

Jack's box of picks.

A reminder of the man he apparently still was.

She lifted her head and pulled her shoulders back. Taking a deep breath, she met her brother's stare. "There's nothing to discuss. I know what I saw, and I don't need to hear his excuses. Why are you taking his side over mine anyway? I'm your sister."

Charlie pressed his lips together and placed his hands on the table. "I'm not taking sides. The two of you can work this out on your own."

"There's nothing to work out," Kerrigan hissed.

Jack stopped in front of the table.

She straightened and turned to face him. Ignoring the flutter in her chest, she narrowed her eyes at him. "Do you need something?"

Jack held her gaze. "You," he said matter-of-factly.

Her flutter turned into a swarm of butterflies. Flapping at hummingbird speed.

She swallowed the lump in her throat as she reached under the table and grabbed his box of picks from the plastic tub. "Sorry," she said as she dropped the cardboard box on the table. She opened the folds and slid it toward him. Meeting his emerald eyes, she pasted a sweet smile on her face. "Perhaps these can satisfy you."

Jack maintained eye contact as he pulled the box toward him. "Is this my only option?" He reached into the box and the picks fell through his fingers like rain.

"No," she said with a small shake of her head. "It's a choice. It always has been."

Jack's stare dropped to the collection of picks in his hand as he poked through them. He picked one out, dropped the rest back in the box, and slid it toward her. When she reached for the box, he grabbed her wrist. She tried to pull away from his grip but he tightened his hold. He flipped her hand over and slipped the pick into her fist, then lifted it to his lips.

As he placed a feathery kiss on her fingers, he met her gaze and her heart tripped over itself, several times. The look in his eyes spoke of possession and longing and her insides melted from the heat emanating from their point of contact. How much longer would she be able to be near him and not give in to what they both clearly wanted?

He released her hand and glanced at Charlie, then bobbed his head toward the stage before turning and walking away. Her hand remained elevated above the table, she was almost hesitant to break the spell that lingered after he was gone. Charlie pivoted to follow Jack.

"Charlie." She moistened the inside of her mouth as he turned to face her. "Do you believe he's innocent?"

It made sense he might. He was still here. He'd never once tried to convince her to leave, something she felt certain he would have done to protect her from Jack. So it stood to reason that Charlie must believe him, at least a little.

Charlie stood in front of her. "It doesn't matter what I think, Kerri." He looked softly at her. "You have to decide whether you love him enough to trust him. That's only something you can figure out—no one else's opinion matters. Including mine." He gently gripped her arm and leaned in. "But for what it's worth . . . yeah, I believe him."

Kerrigan pulled her hand toward her body and nodded as he walked away. Slowly, she opened her hand and tears filled her eyes. She pressed her palm to the table as her knees turned to jelly.

Jack had laid the pick in her hand with the "U" side up.

Thirty-Three

"No, nothing like this has happened before," Jacob replied. "Was anything stolen?"

As Kerrigan held her weekly phone conference with her boss, she watched the band members loading up so they could move on to Daytona. While Stephen and Charlie packed up the van, her focus was drawn to Riley and Jack as they double-checked the instruments and equipment in the trailer. Nothing had happened during their three-night stay in Orlando, but the band, Jack especially, had become extra vigilant with their stuff after the vandalism of the trailer.

She frowned. "Both of Sebastian's guitars and his amp, but that's it," Kerrigan answered as she watched a shirtless Jack move speakers and sound equipment around.

She felt stupid to still want him, but that familiar ache of lust unfurled low in her abdomen and radiated through her body. She really needed to get that under control. And then get rid of it altogether.

"But no money?" Jacob asked and Kerrigan shook her head to bring her mind back to the task at hand.

What were they talking about? "No," she replied, looking at the ground at her feet. "That was safe with me."

"Really?" he muttered. "Why is that?"

"It was a necessity." Kerrigan shrugged. "Sebastian tried to borrow from the cash box a few times, so I started keeping it with me."

"I thought you were making regular deposits."

"I am, but he was sneaking it out immediately after the shows, after I'd counted it but before I could prep it for deposit." She lifted her head and her gaze fell on Jack as he stepped out of the trailer.

He looked up and met her stare, his chest glistening lightly in the morning Florida sun. Even in early October, it was warmer than she was used to, but the heat wave that rolled through her as their eyes collided had nothing to do with the temperature. She saw the knowing smirk on his face and quickly looked away.

The weasel.

"I see," Jacob said.

She really wished Jacob would say more. A conversation with him would be an excellent diversion.

"Is everything else okay? You seem a little distracted."

Or not.

"Everything's fine," she answered as she pushed away from the wall she'd been leaning against and turned to walk away from the band. "We're just packing up to head out."

"Oh, that's right. Headed to Daytona?"

"Yes." She nodded as she paced and put her hand in her pocket. Her fingers landed on the pick and she pinched it between her fingers.

"Then I'll let you go."

With that, their call ended. Kerrigan wasn't sure she'd ever get used to the way he always simply hung up—no good-byes, no scheduling the next call. When he was finished, their call was over. Still rubbing the pick between her fingers in her pocket, she pushed her phone into the other. She turned her back on the band and took a few deep breaths to clear her head and prepare herself for another lengthy ride in close proximity to Jack.

When she turned around to walk back, she ran straight into the T-shirt clad chest of the man she was trying not to think about.

"Whoa," he chuckled as he firmly wrapped his hands around her arms to prevent her from falling.

"Let me go," she snapped instinctively.

Jack frowned, but slowly relinquished his grip on her and opened his palms out at his sides. "Sorry."

Kerrigan took a step back, willing her heart to slow down before she did—or said—something she'd regret. Like apologize for her abruptness. Or walk back into his arms.

"Is everything okay?" Jack asked as he lowered his arms.

"Everything's fine. Just my weekly call to Jacob," she answered with a forced smile.

He nodded. "Did you tell him about the trailer?"

"I did."

"What did he say?" Jack took a step back toward the edge of the sidewalk and motioned for her to walk.

She took him up on his offer, sticking as close to the other edge of the sidewalk as possible. "He seemed most concerned about the cash but didn't say much after I told him that was always with me."

Jack stayed in step beside her and stuffed his hands in his pockets. "We're ready to go."

She glanced up and noticed the rest of the band was standing around the trailer, looking everywhere but in their direction. She snuck a look at Jack and saw that his eyes were focused directly in front of him.

"I see that," she said.

They took a few more steps before Jack stopped and reached for her arm. Instinct, again, had her move it out of his grasp, even as her body rotated toward him. The look on his face showed how much her reaction hurt him and silently she cursed herself as she blinked the tears away. She was frustrated that her inherent response to men was to pull away, especially when that man was Jack. At the same time, she was angry that she wanted to react differently to him, but he'd broken her trust.

And her heart.

She could almost forgive him for the trust. She was used to not trusting men. And she had been stupid enough to believe he'd changed.

But her broken heart was proving harder to get over.

"Kerrigan, I really want to talk about that night," he said softly, stepping closer to her.

She shook her head and turned back in the direction they'd been walking. "I can't," she murmured with a lump in her throat.

"I didn't do anything with her."

Kerrigan looked at her feet as they started to move. "I'm sorry," she said as she walked away. "I can't."

Jack paced the walkway, his phone to his ear, his eyes on the door of the motel's gym. Before they'd had to tighten the belt on the budget, he'd learned Kerri's daily routine started in the gym. This was the first motel they'd stayed in for a while that had a gym. Of course, he'd tracked Kerri there first thing this morning. He'd peeked in to find her walking on the treadmill, her gaze in the mirror distant and troubled.

He hadn't been able to muster the courage to join her, so he'd decided to stay by the door and make good use of his time with a phone call to his brother.

"What do you remember from that night, Jackson?" Nathan asked.

"I told you already." Jack frowned and cast his eyes on his phone. "The last thing I remember was coming into the room, grabbing one of the glasses, and dipping it in the ice bucket Kerri had filled before we'd left for the concert."

"Why did she do that?"

"So we'd have cold water when we got back." All this talk of "we" was slashing his heart to pieces.

"So, you didn't drink the tequila?"

Jack shook his head and glanced at the door. "No, I didn't. I don't even know how that bottle got in my room." He moved close enough to peek into the gym again and saw Kerri wiping down the treadmill. "You haven't found anything?" he asked as he continued to watch her.

"Not yet," Nathan answered with a sigh. "It took me a while to get the permission I needed to do this for you."

Jack's lips tilted upward. "Don't want to break anymore rules?"

"Not after the last time."

The last time Nathan had bent the rules it had been to protect the woman he loved, Janelle, from her alcoholic, estranged husband. While Nathan's intentions had been noble, he'd still ended up with a suspension. No one on the police force had been inconvenienced, but his unauthorized use of a squad car coupled with the revelations the husband made about Nathan and Janelle's affair had caused his motives to come into question. As a result, he'd found himself off the force for several weeks until things were cleared up.

Jack chuckled then looked into the room again. "Any chance that the setup and the trailer are related?"

"You know anything is possible," Nathan said. "But I can only do so much from here."

"Fine."

Kerri was walking toward the door.

"Gotta go," Jack said hurriedly. "Talk to you later."

"Yup," Nathan answered. "Bye."

Jack ended the call and shoved his phone in his pocket as the door opened and Kerri stepped through it. Her eyes were downcast, but she stopped inches away from him. Slowly, her face lifted to his and he saw her exhale deeply.

"Jack," she whispered. "What are you doing here?"

"I want to talk to you," he answered.

It had been almost a week since she'd found him in bed with another woman. Charlie had said she needed space, but she'd avoided him—and the conversation they needed to have—for long enough. Jack was tired of waiting for her to initiate anything.

"I know," she stated. "But I don't think there's anything you can say that will make this better."

"I didn't have sex with her," Jack blurted.

Kerri took a step back. "Please don't insult my intelligence by telling me I didn't see what I saw," she calmly stated.

"You saw us sleeping," Jack snapped.

"I saw you naked." She closed her eyes and took a breath. "How stupid do you think I am?"

He took a chance and stepped closer to her, gently taking her hands in his. "I don't think you're stupid," he started as she stiffened in his grip. "But I know you've been in a really dark place for the last few years. And I know you've been hurt and that your trust has been shattered." He took another step. "Kerri, I love you and I would never do anything to hurt you or to break your trust. You have to know that."

She lightly tugged her hands out of his and stepped away. Her eyes opened, swimming with tears. Seeing them made him feel like he'd been punched in the gut. Her bottom lip quivered as she opened her mouth. "I thought I did. But now I'm not so sure."

"Kerri—"

She held up her hand. "Jack, clothes don't fall off on their own. People don't just fall into bed drunk and naked," she said, her voice growing stronger. "I can't forget what I saw. I see it again every time I close my eyes. I can't do this anymore, Jack. We tried. We've satisfied our curiosities. It's not going to work between us."

"We were together for two and a half weeks," he growled, taking a step toward her. "That's hardly a fair indication of what could be between us."

"Maybe there can't be anything between us."

He grabbed her arm as she tried to hurry away and she froze. "Why, Kerri? Just give me one good reason."

"We aren't the people we used to be, Jack," she answered, keeping her face turned away.

He guided her body to the wall and pressed her back against it. One hand still gripping her arm, he placed his other on the wall beside her. "Look at me," he demanded.

Her jaw clenched and unclenched as she slowly turned her face to his.

"You're right, we're not the same people," he said. "Six years ago, I thought I knew everything about women, about music, about life. I've learned a lot in that time, and I've learned I don't know everything. But the one constant, in all that time, has been my love for you. It's changed, yes. After you rejected me in Paris, I hated you for a while."

Her chin dropped as her watery eyes widened.

"But that hurt more than your absence from my life, so I let it go and what was left was a longing deeper than I'd ever felt." He cupped her chin in his hand. "Now that you're in my life again, I'm not about to let you go so easily."

She shook her head. "Jack—"

"No, listen to me first." He inched his body closer. "I understand why you don't believe me. I'll prove the truth to you. I just wish you would trust me."

Holding his gaze, she pressed her lips together and remained silent for a moment. She firmly pushed her hand against his chest. He didn't budge.

"What if the roles were reversed?" she asked.

"What?"

"What if you had found me in bed with another man?" she said.

"I'd break his legs," Jack answered with a shrug.

"Would you be so quick to forgive and forget?" she continued, ignoring his attempt at levity. "Would you trust me, without question?"

"Yes." He tried to move closer but her small hand held him at bay.

"Knowing there's a possibility I'm lying, simply to stay in your good graces? Knowing you could forgive me for this transgression, only to have me turn around and do it again?" A tear slid down her cheek and he released his grip on her arm.

"Kerri, you're not like that," he answered tightly, realizing that she thought he was. "But, if that had been the case, I hope I would trust and believe in you. I would forgive you and we would work through it."

Her brow knitted and she frowned. "Why?" she asked with a shake of her head. "Why would you run that risk?"

"Because I love you." His face inched toward hers.

Her face relaxed and he saw the slow rise and fall of her chest. "I . . . I'm . . . I'm sorry," she murmured and turned and walked away as quickly as she could.

Jack slowly turned wooden as he watched her hurry away. The dull ache in his chest grew sharper as the distance between them grew. She was rejecting him again, but this felt different than it had in Paris. This felt worse.

In Paris, he'd had no idea why she'd rejected him. He hadn't known about the rape, he hadn't known she was hurting. He hadn't known then what he was fighting against, hadn't even known he had something to fight, or how to overcome it.

This time, he knew exactly why she was rejecting him. He understood her fear and he knew why she was in pain.. This time, he would fight for her. If for no other reason than to remove the pain from her beautiful blue eyes.

He wasn't losing her again.

Thirty-Four

Kerrigan watched Jack wander away from the group, lifting his phone to his ear. He'd mumbled something about missing a phone call from his brother before hurrying off. Her heart wanted to run after him so she could listen in, but her head told her to stand firm to what she'd told him the day before.

There could be nothing between them.

Even if she wanted to believe him, and she couldn't deny that she did, there would always be a small part of her mind that would never be able to forget the image of him with that other woman. She wasn't sure her heart would be able to truly get past the pain of it, or the fear it might happen again. Yes, he swore he loved her, and she wanted to trust him, but she'd trusted him once before and he'd disappeared from her life.

She'd also trusted Raoul, without as much affection, and look where that had gotten her. For the past four years, she'd avoided letting men get too close to her. After Jackson's abandonment and then the rape, she wasn't one to easily trust any man or give them the chance to hurt her in any way. Her life had been a little lonely, but she'd been safe. She'd be fine now.

"Kerri, you coming?" Charlie asked as she walked toward the back of the trailer.

Kerrigan looked up and he nodded toward the motel. She shook her head. "No, there's something I need in the trailer."

"You want us to help?" Stephen asked, turning toward her.

She glanced at the street lamp directly over the van and trailer, then toward the path she would take to the stairwell that led up to their rooms. It seemed safe enough. And their rooms were on the second floor, looking out over the area they now stood in.

She smiled slightly. "I can do it. It won't take me long," she answered. "You guys go on. If I need anything, I'll let you know."

Charlie frowned as he walked toward her. "You okay?" he asked quietly. "You've seemed a little down the last two days."

She eased her arms around his neck and gave him a hug to hide the tears. "I'm fine," she answered. "You better go call your fiancée." Kerrigan dropped her arms. "She texted me earlier to remind you."

Charlie chuckled. "You're probably right. Otherwise I'll be sleeping on the couch when we get home."

Kerrigan laughed and waved the three men away, then turned back to the trailer. Fishing in her pocket for the key to the padlock, her fingers rubbed the surface of the pick Jack had given her. She'd carried it with her every day since he'd stuck it in her palm. She found the key and quickly pulled her hand out of her pocket.

She unlocked the door and climbed into the dark trailer with a frown. She'd forgotten the inside had no light. Pulling out her phone and turning on the flashlight, she made her way to the merchandise tubs. She was running out of eight-by-ten photos of most of the band members, especially Sebastian. She'd been reluctant to keep his on the table, but fans kept asking for them. If they ran out, they had no way to replace them. Except she was sure there was another box of pictures in the trailer and since they were traveling in the morning, she'd decided it would be better to find them before bed.

And the loneliness in her room was starting to smother her.

She shook that thought away as she shifted boxes and equipment until she found what she was looking for: a small, paperboard box that did indeed hold more photos of the band members. Picking it up, she stepped back and reached for one of the larger plastic tubs. She took the lid off and placed the box of eight-by-tens inside, brushing her knuckles against a larger cardboard box and hearing the rattle of its contents.

Jack's picks.

Her gaze shifted to the half-full box and her hand automatically dropped to her pocket. She traced the outline of her pick through the denim and her chest ached.

"What makes you so special?" she asked aloud. "He's given these things to hundreds of other women." She shuddered at that cold fact. Was she really any different than any of those women?

I love you. His words from the day before haunted her.

She extended her arm toward the box. "You'll get over me."

She should just drop her pick back into the pile. He'd never know she'd returned it. It would simply blend in with all the others, the way she did.

I just wish you'd trust me.

Her hand hovered over the box. He'd slipped it into her fist with the "U" up. He'd picked her. He wanted her.

She closed her eyes and looked up at the ceiling of the trailer. The truth was, she still wanted him. She just wasn't positive she could trust him.

Charlie trusted him. His words to her still rang through her mind as well. Did she really love Jack enough to trust him? Or were these last eight years of her life a lie she'd told herself?

She closed her fist around the pick as she blew a frustrated breath toward the ceiling. "Damn it, this is too hard," she muttered.

Being near Jack was hard. Not being near him was hard. But not knowing what to do was the most frustrating part of all.

In all her life, she'd never missed her mother's advice more.

She replaced the lid on the tub and straightened things up for the trip. She grabbed her phone, picked up the cash box, and walked out of the trailer. Once the padlock was secured, she pushed her phone into her pocket and clutched the box to her chest. She looked left, then right, then glanced up at her brother's motel room and saw him peeking through the curtain and smiled.

Hurrying across the parking lot, she started up the stairs, but slowed when she heard a voice.

"You're kidding me," Jack snapped.

Kerrigan looked up to see if she could spot him as she climbed the steps.

"GHB? And it wasn't in the tequila?"

She frowned. *Wasn't GHB some kind of sedative?*

"Then how did the drug get in my system?"

Kerrigan slowly climbed a few more stairs. Jack was standing with his back to the stairwell. She should be able to get to her room undetected, if she were quiet.

And slow.

She should definitely go slow.

"It was in both glasses? So Kerri could have accidently gotten some, too?" he growled and muttered a curse under his breath. "That's not the point, Nathan. It's a date rape drug, and whoever put it in our room could have done anything to her if we'd both passed out."

Kerrigan's foot froze on the landing.

He had been drugged.

He'd been telling the truth about his innocence, and she'd been too stubborn, or too stupid, to believe him. Her stomach turned over.

What have I done?

"No, Nathan, it's not enough. I want to know who did this to us."

Her legs were like lead as she continued up the stairs. She looked up at him again and breathed a sigh of relief to see him still facing the other direction. He didn't know she was there.

"I have some ideas."

She eased herself around the corner of the wall, toward her room, and inhaled deeply and shakily. She had to fix this. But how?

Admitting she'd overheard this conversation might only make things worse. She'd have to confess she was only willing to believe him because she had proof of his innocence. That was hardly the same as trusting him.

Her mind worked as her feet lightened enough for her to make her way toward her room. She felt nauseous and excited at the same time. It made her sick that she'd doubted him so adamantly. But at the same time, she owed him an apology. An apology that could mend the gap between them.

She'd learned her lesson. He loved her, he deserved her trust. He'd definitely earned it. And Charlie was right, if she loved Jack as much as she thought, he deserved so much more from her than she'd been giving.

Clutching the cash box to her chest like a stack of school books, Kerrigan blew out a slow breath. She'd secure the cash in her room, then find Jack and apologize. She couldn't let him continue to think she didn't trust him; she knew how much her doubt hurt him. If nothing else, before she went to sleep, she'd clear the air with him. She'd fix her mistake and relieve him of some of the stress he'd been under for the past week. The corners of her mouth lifted a fraction as she slid her keycard into the lock of the door and pushed the handle down.

The door flew open, pulled from the inside, and Kerrigan was face-to-face with a man in a ski mask. She screamed in surprise and fell backward as he reached for her.

"What—" she exclaimed as she dodged his grasp.

"Give me the box, bitch," he snapped and lunged toward her again.

Tension and fear infused her limbs and she gripped the cash box tighter. "No."

He reached out and shoved her hard, grabbing for the cash box. She fell backward, her lower back hitting the metal railing. She groaned in pain but held tight to the handle of the box as he began a tug of war.

"Let it go!" he yelled as he slapped her hard across the face.

She cried out again as her head snapped sideways and her eyes watered. She lost her grip on the box as she fell to the ground.

After the first scream, Jack shoved his phone in his pocket and started moving in the direction of the sound. When he heard the groan, a chill ran down his spine and he began running. He turned the corner in time to see the man strike Kerri across the face and his vision turned red.

When the coward in the ski mask turned and began moving toward him, Jack stepped into his path and curled his upper lip in a feral snarl. This jerk wasn't about to get away with that.

"Jackson, the money!" Kerri cried out.

Jack glanced down to see the asshole was carrying the cash box and took off at a sprint toward him. He lowered his shoulder and hit the man squarely in the chest, taking them both to the ground. Jack rose to his knees and ripped the ski mask off, then slammed his fist into the crook's cheek.

The man, pinned to the ground under Jack, tried to grab one of Jack's wrists, but failed as Jack landed another punch to his face. His head snapped sideways and Jack growled. For a week he'd been looking for an outlet for his anger and frustration. This man who'd attacked Kerri seemed like the perfect target.

"Did you think you could hit her," Jack rumbled as he reached for the thief's throat, "and get away with it?"

The man turned his anger-filled eyes upward and lifted the cash box, hitting Jack in the side. Kerri screamed again as he grunted in pain and fell.

Quickly regaining his position, Jack drew back and delivered a punch to the other side of the man's battered face, following it with another swift blow.

As he was about to hit him again, an arm grabbed him around the waist and hoisted him up and backward.

"Stop it," Charlie snapped.

Jack's vision cleared and he saw Riley, his evening glass of scotch still in his hand, positioned over the crook. He glanced toward Kerri and saw Stephen helping her up from the concrete, her eyes wide and focused directly on Jack. Riley put his bare foot on the man's arm.

"I'd stay there if I were ye," Riley drawled, then took a sip of his drink. He bent over and picked up the cash box. "I'll be taking this, thank ye verra much."

"Has anyone called the police?" Kerri asked and Jack looked up again. She was hobbling toward them, wincing at each step.

"Are you okay?" Stephen asked, his hand hovering just under her elbow.

She met Jack's gaze for a second, then turned to Stephen and waved his concern away. "Yeah, he just pushed me into the rail. I'll be fine."

So that was why she'd groaned. Jack glared at the man on the ground and took a step toward him. He wasn't going to get away with that either.

Charlie tightened his grip around Jack's waist. "Don't hit him again."

"He hurt her," Jack muttered through clenched teeth.

"Yes, and now he'll go to jail. Would you like to join him?" Charlie hissed. "There are plenty of people here who saw you assault him when you had reason. Do it again and they might just want to see you behind bars as well."

Jack looked around and saw heads peeking out of some of the doors. A few people had even come out of their rooms.

"Let me go," Jack said, mustering up a calm voice as two police cars, silent but with lights flashing, pulled into the parking lot below.

Charlie took a step back as the doors opened and the officers took off at a run toward the second floor.

Jack watched in growing agitation as the policemen interviewed witness after witness. He wanted everyone to just disappear so he could speak to Kerri, if for no other reason than to verify for himself that she was okay.

After giving his account of the events, he'd watched her deal with the motel's manager then talk to the cops. When they were finished with their interview, they'd waved a paramedic over and he'd put his gloves on, then examined her face. When she lifted her shirt and he'd seen the welt on her lower back, Jack had seen another flash of red.

Standing beside the railing, as she was now, the bar hit her just above her hips. If that jerk had pushed her any harder, she could have gone over. The idea had his stomach in his knees.

Charlie walked over and leaned against the wall beside him.

"That bastard was in her room," Jack snapped. He'd overheard bits of the conversation between Kerri and the police, and seen her gesturing as she'd explained what had happened.

He hated that he hadn't been there to protect her. He'd been so caught up in his conversation with Nathan he'd completely forgotten to watch for her. For the past week, he'd always kept an eye on her until she was safely in her room. Tonight, he'd been distracted.

"I heard," Charlie said, drawing Jack out of his self-loathing.

Jack turned to his friend who was looking at the patrol car in the parking lot. The thief was now seated in the back of the car as an officer leaned against it.

"My question is, why?" Charlie added.

Jack glanced at the police car as well then turned to Kerri.

That was a very good question. This was the third time in a week that they, as a band, had been attacked in some way. Jack still had the feeling Sebastian was behind it all, but he couldn't figure out how.

The investigation continued for another half hour. After the paramedics left, the curious guests meandered back to their rooms, and by the time the police left, the band members were the only ones left to watch them drive away. Stephen and Riley wandered away first, and Jack knew he should follow. He met Kerri's eyes and her steely gaze was narrowed on his face. She still looked a little flushed from the exertion of the evening and he held her gaze as he tried to decipher the look in her eyes.

"C'mon," Charlie said, tugging on his arm.

"Actually," she said coolly, "I'd like to have a word with Jack."

Jack bit back a groan as he followed her to her room. How mad was she and how would he get out of trouble with her this time?

Thirty-Five

Kerrigan tingled with excitement from her head to her toes. She had already been considering forgiving Jack, but when he'd come to her rescue and defense, that had sealed it for her. Her only hope now was that he could forgive her for needing proof of his innocence instead of trusting him from the beginning.

When she heard the door latch behind her she spun around, threw her arms around his neck, and pressed her mouth to his. Jack seemed momentarily stunned before his arms slid around her and pulled her body closer to his. She smiled as his lips began to move against hers, meeting her vigor without question. She moved forward, pressing him against the door as her hands slithered down his torso, coming to the bottom of his T-shirt and slipping underneath.

Her fingers touched his skin and she felt a shudder go through him. She pulled away from the kiss and quickly stripped him of his shirt, meeting his darkened, lust-filled gaze with one of her own as she tossed the clothing over her shoulder. He opened his mouth to say something and she brought her lips back to his. Pinning him to the door with her hips, she felt his erection against her stomach as she went to work on the button of his jeans.

Jack's hands lowered to the top of her pants and he untucked her shirt-tail then pressed his hands to her bare skin. Kerrigan broke the kiss with a sigh of delight at the feel of his hands on her body and he removed the shirt in one fell swoop as she began to lower his jeans over his hips.

"Kerri, what—"

She placed a finger to his lips as she shook her head. She lowered her finger and their lips met again.

As he kicked off his shoes, he grabbed her hips and raised her to him as she lifted her knees to either side of his body. He stepped out of his pants and carried her to the bed, gently lowering her to the mattress. She slid toward the headboard, slowly so their lips wouldn't separate as he crawled along with her. Her head reached the pillow and his lips moved to her jaw then slowly down her neck. He unclasped her bra and kissed the skin surrounding her nipples as he uncovered them. His hands made quick work of her pants and underwear as his mouth played with her breasts.

Panting heavily, she kicked her pants off the bed and grabbed the sides of his head, urgently pulling his face toward hers. Jack grinned with desire and sat up on his knees. She grasped the band of his underwear and quickly lowered it down his thighs, biting her lip with anticipation when she revealed his manhood. He slid the undergarment off and tossed it on the floor as she reached up and pulled his mouth to hers again.

She lay back on the pillow, pulling him with her, and parted her knees as he covered her body with his. In one quick, fluid thrust, he was inside her. Her back arched as her eyes closed and she released a long, slow sigh of relief.

Oh, how she'd missed this. Somehow the week they'd spent apart had felt much longer.

Jack groaned as he moved his hips, seeming to echo the voice in her head.

Kerrigan opened her eyes and met his forest green gaze and the love she saw took her breath away. How could she have doubted him when his affection for her was so clearly written on his face? She pulled him to her and kissed his lips as she lifted her hips and met his thrusts, forcing him deeper into her. He moved faster, harder, and she relished in the feel of his body against hers, the feel of his skin under her lips as she pressed kisses to his jaw, neck, and shoulder.

Without warning, the tremors surged through her body and the heat of her orgasm stretched to her toes. She grabbed the closest pillow to cover her scream and Jack pulled it away as he looked down on her.

"I want to hear you," he breathed as he pushed deeper and faster.

Kerrigan held his gaze until she climaxed and closed her eyes, tossing her head back and releasing the scream of pleasure she usually tried to muffle. Jack's thrusts continued and he moaned, long and loud, then collapsed on top of her.

They lay silent, still connected, as they came down from their peak. Kerrigan's eyes were closed when Jack propped himself up on his elbow. He lightly kissed her cheek and she slowly met his gaze as he smiled down on her.

"So, am I forgiven?" Jack gave Kerrigan a sly grin.

She pressed her lips together and looked away.

"No," she murmured.

His lip curled as he pushed himself off of her. Had she just used him? The thought made him sick. "Then what was that?"

She grabbed his wrist before he could climb off the bed. "That was my apology." Her somber gaze met his and the corners of her lips lifted a little.

His anger quickly deflated as he lay back onto the bed and stretched out beside her. "Your apology?" he asked, gently tugging his wrist free of her grasp as he held her gaze. "What do you have to apologize for?"

Kerri slid closer to him, nestling her body against his, lowering her face. "I should have believed you," she stated, her warm breath caressing his chest. "At the very least, I should have listened to what you had to say." She looked up at him, her eyes wide and full of remorse. "Jackson, I'm so sorry I didn't trust you."

He couldn't help but grin as he cupped her cheek in his palm. "You're forgiven," he murmured as his lips touched hers and he gave her a long, slow kiss, savoring every moment. When he pulled away, his smile widened. "What changed your mind?"

Her cheeks turned pink and she tried to pull away from his grasp. Jack raised himself up on one elbow again and held her tightly. She stopped struggling and blew out a long breath.

"I overheard your conversation with Nathan," she confessed.

He stopped himself from laughing at her obvious distress. "What did you hear?" he asked as he sat up against the headboard. He put his arm around her shoulders.

She turned her body to his and placed her hand on his chest. "That both of the glasses had a date rape drug in them," she answered and he nodded. "And it was in your system, but not the tequila."

Jack nodded again.

Kerri's brow furrowed. "Why would that woman do that?"

He shrugged. "I don't know, but I think she may have had encouragement."

She tilted her head to the side and her lips puckered before her eyes widened and her mouth fell open. "Sebastian?" she breathed then shook her head. "Are you sure?"

"Who else could it be, Kerri?" Jack asked. "By all appearances, what happened in that motel was exactly what he wanted you to see."

Her frown deepened. "But he's still in jail. On the other side of the state," she gently argued. "How could he have done it?"

"That is what we need to figure out."

Kerri nodded as she lowered her head to his shoulder and began tracing figure eights on his chest. "Did you mention it to Nathan?"

Jack closed his eyes, savoring her gentle touch and the feeling of calm that her caress gave him. "I did," he answered.

"Hmm." Her fingers continued their delicate movement along his skin. "Do you think Sebastian arranged the vandalism and tonight's attempted robbery, too?"

Jack's eyelids slowly lifted as he considered. "I think it's possible," he eventually answered.

She pushed herself up and looked directly at him. "Maybe you should call Nathan and mention this to him?"

He laughed out loud and shook his head. "No way am I calling my brother at one o'clock in the morning. I'd like to stay in my future sister-in-law's good graces," he said as he moved his arm from around her shoulder. He slid to the edge of the bed and put his feet on the floor. "But I will text him and ask him to call us first thing in the morning."

He walked toward the door, picked up his pants, and pulled his phone out of his pocket. He quickly sent his brother a message then looked at Kerri, still lying on her side on the bed, watching him with a soft smile on her face. They were together again and he thought his heart would burst from joy. She was his. His to love. His to protect. His to cherish. And he would never again let anything come between them or change that.

Her eyes shifted from his face to his hardening groin and her smile widened. She met his gaze again with lust in her eyes and he couldn't resist their draw. He slowly approached her but stopped at the foot of the bed.

"Maybe I should go get my luggage," he suggested, only halfway serious.

Kerri lifted a delicate shoulder then fell to her back. "You're assuming you're invited to stay." The corner of her mouth turned up in a sly smile.

Jack placed a knee on the bed. "I'm not?" he asked as his other knee landed on the mattress.

Her eyebrows lifted as she slid toward the headboard and laid her head on the pillow. "I haven't decided yet."

He nodded as he lowered his head. "Then maybe . . ." He placed a light kiss on her belly button. "I can help you make up your mind."

He heard her sharp intake of breath as his lips touched her core but he didn't stop until they were both satisfied again. She fell asleep in his arms with a sated smile on her lips.

Kerrigan woke to the ringing of a phone, followed by a groan. As the bed shifted and the warm body left her side, she lowered her head to the cool, soft pillow and pouted.

She heard Jack answer the phone with a groggy, "Hello." As he cleared his throat, she tried to open her heavy eyelids. "Nathan," he said. "Hold on a sec."

The bed moved again and a warm set of lips pressed a kiss to her forehead.

"Kerri," Jack murmured, his breath caressing her cheek. "Are you awake? Nathan's on the phone."

"Mm-hm." She slowly opened her eyes. "I'm awake." She focused on the green eyes staring down at her with concern and love, and smiled widely. "I'm awake," she repeated before stretching her arms over her head.

Jack grinned then gently pressed his lips to hers. "Good morning," he said.

"Good morning." She sat up with her shoulders against the headboard and the sheet covering her chest as Jack put his brother on speakerphone.

"Hey, Nathan," Jack began. "We had another incident last night."

"What happened?" Nathan's tone was serious and he listened as Jack explained what had occurred the night before. "Was Kerri hurt?"

Jack turned to look at her. "She's a little bruised," he answered. "It could have been worse."

"I'm fine," she said reassuringly as she reached for his hand.

"Oh," Nathan exclaimed. "You're there, too."

"Yes, Nathan. I'm here too," Kerrigan said with a light laugh. "Good morning."

"Good morning to you," Nathan replied. "Kerri, did you recognize the man?"

"No, he had a ski mask on," she answered with a shake of her head. "And when Jackson ripped it off of him, none of us had seen him before."

"Hmm." Nathan fell silent as Jack ran his thumbs over her knuckles.

"What are you thinking?" Jack eventually asked his brother.

"When we talked last night, I chalked them up as random incidents. The drugging and the vandalism happened at the same motel, but hardly seemed related," Nathan said. "But this is the third one in a week and the perps seem to be getting more aggressive."

Jack gave Kerrigan's fingers a light squeeze and his gaze became cloudy and full of concern. "I was thinking the same thing."

"Do you still think Sebastian's responsible?" Nathan asked.

"I don't know who else it could be. He was always the troublemaker," Jack answered as he slid closer to her. "But nothing this bad happened until he was gone."

"Does the rest of the band agree with you?" Nathan asked.

Jack's lips pressed tightly together and she knew the answer.

Probably not.

"I agree it's possible," Kerrigan said as Jack's face relaxed. "But we can't figure out how. He's in jail in Tampa."

"You're sure?" Nathan's interrogation continued.

"As far as we know," Jack answered, holding Kerrigan's stare as she nodded.

Nathan was silent again and Jack took the opportunity to lift her knuckles to his lips. The warmth of his mouth eased its way up her arm and caused a pleasant shiver down her spine.

"Let me see if I can head down there and investigate this in person," Nathan said.

Jack's eyes widened and the corners of his lips lifted. "Seriously?"

"It can't be an official investigation, of course," Nathan continued. "But I have information that the police down there don't, so I can work with them and maybe we can figure out what's really going on."

"How can we help?" Kerrigan asked.

Nathan asked them several questions, gathering the names of people and places, and other little details he needed for his investigation. He told them that he hoped to make it to Florida later that day, and he promised to keep them up-to-date on what he learned. Nathan suggested they have Mason take another look at the band's contract to make sure the rest of the band members were protected, just in case this was attempted sabotage on Sebastian's part.

They ended their call and Jack put his phone on the side table.

"Aren't you going to call Mason?" Kerrigan asked as Jack turned toward her.

"Not yet." His lips came together in a flat line and he took in a breath. "Has Jacob said anything about Sebastian?"

She shook her head and slid closer to him. "Not recently. Why?"

Jack's frown deepened. "I was just wondering if his father has told him whether or not Sebastian was out on bail."

Kerrigan tilted her head. "His father? Sebastian's father or Jacob's father?"

His gaze cleared and met hers. "Both."

"What?" she breathed, trying to process what she'd just heard. "They have the same father?"

Jack nodded. "You didn't know?"

Her eyes widened and her mouth fell open. "No."

She was fairly certain Jacob had never mentioned it. If he had, she wouldn't have forgotten that vital bit of information.

"No, he probably didn't bring it up," Jack stated as he released her hand. He leaned back against the dark wood of the headboard and threaded his fingers through hers again. "It's not information they liked to share."

"So . . . Stephen and Riley?" she asked, thinking back to their conversation on her first day.

"Don't know." He lifted the shoulder furthest from her. "At least, I don't think they do."

"When did you find out?" She laid her temple against his shoulder.

"Same time Sebastian did. Our sophomore year in college." Jack told

Kerrigan what he knew about the soap opera. "They've never gotten along," he shrugged.

"So why did Mr. Bates throw them together with the contract?" Kerrigan asked as she digested the new information.

"I guess because he wanted them to have a better relationship," Jack answered. "And to help Sebastian at the same time."

She lifted her head to look at his profile. "What about helping Jacob?"

"Jacob didn't need it." Jack turned his face to hers and placed a gentle kiss on her forehead. "He's always succeeded at whatever he's tried. He excelled at sports. Played football, basketball, and ran track. He always had good grades. I think he got a full scholarship to college."

"And Sebastian?"

The corner of Jack's lips lifted. "Complete opposite. Calls his father for everything. Not athletic and I'm honestly surprised he even got into college or managed to graduate."

Kerrigan nodded as Jack lifted away from the headboard. He moved toward her with a look in his eyes that told her the conversation was over. Her insides began to flutter.

"I suppose you're not going to call Mason now, are you?" she teased with a grin on her lips.

"Nope." He rose to his knees. "I'll text him later and ask him to call when he gets the chance." He placed a kiss on each of her knuckles, causing small waves of heat to course through her body. "I have something else in mind."

Anticipation had caused her mouth to go dry and she watched silently as he straddled her, placing a knee at each of her hips. As he gently tugged on the sheet covering her chest, Kerrigan dropped her eyes to his erection. She slowly lifted her gaze up his abdomen, over his broad chest, and back up to his face. She lifted an eyebrow as she met his emerald eyes.

"I see that," she quipped, then giggled when he pulled the sheet away and their lips met as she sank into the pillows.

Thirty-Six

Jack was backstage, having a quiet conversation with Charlie, when his phone rang. He glanced at the caller ID on his phone, then answered. "Hey, Nathan."

"Can you talk?" Nathan asked as Jack made eye contact with Kerri.

He pointed to his phone and waved her over. "Yeah," he answered. "Just give me a second to collect everyone."

Kerri, cash box in hand, stepped to his side. "Is it Nathan?" she asked as Charlie took the box from her.

Jack handed her the phone. "Can you talk to him while I get the others?"

"Sure," Kerri agreed and put the phone to her ear. "Hi, Nathan."

Jack smiled briefly. It was nice that Kerri knew his brothers and was already comfortable around them. It made Jack feel like she was already part of his family. With a chuckle, he shook the thought away.

He found Stephen and Riley making the final sound check and asked them to join the phone conversation. He and Kerri had discussed the day before that having everyone in on the conversation would be easier than having to relate all of the information afterward. Once they were all together, Jack took the phone from Kerri and put the call on speaker.

"Okay, we're all here," Jack said. "What have you found out?"

"Not much, I'm afraid," Nathan answered. "I was able to talk to the guy who tried to rob you and he was surprisingly forthcoming with what little information he actually had. Whatever he stole was supposed to be the majority of his payday, so he was rather disgruntled."

Kerri frowned.

"What did he say?" Jack asked, not liking the sound of things.

"He said that when they met, the man hiring him stayed mostly in the shadow," Nathan began. "He thought he might have been wearing sunglasses and a hat, but nothing else was clearly visible."

"That's not very helpful," Kerri muttered.

Jack nodded in agreement. "He didn't describe height or build?"

"No," Nathan replied. "The only thing he did say was he thought the guy was a Green Bay Packer."

"A fan?" Riley asked.

"No," Nathan answered. "A player. Either at one point or still playing, he wasn't sure."

"Obviously he couldn't be if he didn't see his face," Jack added with a frown. This didn't make any sense.

"Do any of you think it's possible that a Packer has it out for you?" Nathan asked.

Kerri met Jack's gaze and a blush crept up her cheeks before she looked away. He had a feeling he knew what she was thinking—that perhaps he had slept with a woman who was somehow related to a member of the Packers.

"No," Jack answered for the group. "I'm not sure any of us think it's possible, but we'll put our heads together and see what we can come up with."

"Sounds like a plan. I'll send you my report before I head south tomorrow to see if I can catch up with the girl that was in Jack's room," Nathan continued and Jack watched Kerri's face tighten. "If you guys remember anything else at all, let me know."

"We will," Jack said, looking around at the nods of agreement. They said their good-byes and Jack ended the call. Stephen and Riley wandered back to the stage and Kerri reached for the cash box. Jack took her wrist and gently pulled her closer. "Charlie, could you give us a minute?"

"Sure," he agreed. "I'll just take the cash box out to the table and wait for you there." He gave his sister's shoulder a gentle squeeze as he strolled past her and Kerri's lips lifted a little.

Jack waited until Charlie was out of earshot then lifted her chin so he could look at her. "What went through your mind that made your cheeks so red?" he asked and her cheeks turned a pale shade of pink.

Her eyes shifted over his shoulder. "Nothing," she mumbled.

He tried not to laugh as he placed a light kiss to her forehead. "I can guess," he said and pulled her into his arms. "And I can promise you that none of us have personally given any Green Bay players any reason to hate us. We haven't slept with anyone's girlfriends, mistresses, or wives." He only intended to ever sleep with one wife . . . his own.

Her.

She leaned back and her chin dropped. "How did you know that's what I was thinking?"

He chuckled. "I know you better than you think."

She pressed her lips together and he laughed harder.

"Besides, we've never even played in or near Green Bay," Jack continued after his mirth had passed. She released a long, slow breath. "Better?"

She smiled up at him and placed a long kiss on his lips, heating the blood in his veins. "Now I'm better," she said as she stepped out of his arms. "Now, get back to work," she added with a smile as she turned toward the merchandise table.

Kerrigan leaned back against the headrest, letting the discussion between Riley, Stephen, and Jack wash over her. She'd needed to run to the bank and the rest of the band had decided to take a look around the city of Jacksonville, so they'd tagged along. They'd been in the van for over an hour and she was tired of listening to them debate the whole "Packer" issue. She knew she should pay more attention, but after fifteen minutes, they'd started to repeat themselves.

Jack's current theory was that it was someone that Sebastian had known in high school or college. Stephen tended to lean toward the boyfriend or husband of a woman that Sebastian had slept with, mostly since Riley and Jack vehemently denied ever doing something like that. Riley, an avid soccer fan, mentioned with a grin that he, personally, may have riled up one of the players with one of his anti-American-football rants on Twitter. Charlie sat quietly behind Kerrigan, only adding something to the conversation when he felt they were becoming too outlandish.

Kerrigan could only roll her eyes and try to shut out all the noise.

None of those ideas made sense to her. But she had nothing to contribute to the conversation. She was at a loss as to who it could be, or even if it really was a football player behind the recent problems they'd had.

"Why don't we just stick around until Saturday and we can ask the team ourselves," Riley drawled from the front seat, drawing Kerrigan's attention back to the conversation.

"Riley, you know we can't stay here. We have to be in Savannah this weekend," Kerrigan chided as she looked out the window.

They were sitting at a red light and when she looked up at the billboard, she realized why Riley had suggested they stick around. The sign was advertising that weekend's NFL game, the Jaguars would be hosting the Packers. She stared at the logos on the billboard, trying to figure out what was nagging her about that "G" symbol for the visiting team.

She'd seen it so many times. Another area high school near Rocky Creek used it as their symbol as well. But something about it wasn't quite right.

When she realized what it was, and what it meant, she sat up in her seat and gasped. "Oh no."

"What's wrong?" Jack asked, his hand suddenly gripping her arm.

She turned to look at him. "Did Nathan's report say why the thief thought it was a Green Bay player who hired him?"

Jack's brow furrowed as he slowly shook his head. "I'm not sure. I can check and see." He pulled out his phone and started running his finger across the screen. "Why do you ask?"

"Just an idea," she mumbled and she turned to the window again as they started to move.

She couldn't possibly be right. Her hunch didn't make any more sense than the ones the band members had been tossing around. She silently tried to talk herself out of the anxiety that was the knot growing in her stomach.

"The thief said that the man who hired him wore a large ring with a "G" on it, that he noticed it when they shook hands after they'd made the deal," Jack read from his phone and Kerrigan closed her eyes.

Her guess seemed to be right.

But she couldn't understand why.

"Kerri, do you know who it is?" Charlie asked, his voice closer to her than she had expected.

She opened her eyes and looked over her shoulder at him, then turned to Jack. “It doesn’t make sense,” she stated.

“Nothing we’ve suggested today really does,” Stephen said, glancing at her in the rearview mirror.

“Is one of yer ex-boyfriends a Packer?” Riley teased, turning around completely in the seat in front of her to give her a sly wink.

She shook her head. “The guy is not an ex-anything, and he’s not a Packer.” She looked at them all, letting her focus come to rest on Jack. “He’s a Bulldog. As in, a Georgia Bulldog.”

They were all silent for a minute.

“Makes sense, the symbol’s the same,” Charlie murmured, sitting back in his seat.

“But the colors are different,” Jack calmly argued.

“They wouldn’t be discernable in the dark,” Stephen pointed out.

“Who is this Bulldog then?” Riley asked, still staring at Kerrigan over the back of his seat.

She took a deep breath and blew it shakily past her lips.

“I think it might be Jacob.”

Thirty-Seven

Jack remained silent as he considered her allegation. It didn't make sense.

Jacob was their producer and it was in his best interest for the band to succeed. If for no other reason than the money he'd been promised from his father.

But Kerri wouldn't accuse someone of something without reason or proof.

"How do you know?" Charlie asked. He seemed to be the only one not in a state of shock over her statement.

Kerri turned to look at her brother. "I shook his hand on the day we met. He wore a very large ring with a red stone and a diamond studded 'G' on it."

"We don't know that it's the same ring," Stephen stated. "And even if it is, it's not necessarily a rare piece of jewelry."

"It's probably not widely popular either," Charlie added.

"And what are the chances," Riley slowly drawled, "that two men having very similar rings are related to our band, but not to each other?"

Jack couldn't argue with that. The possibility that it was Jacob, or at the very least someone Jacob knew, also made more sense than some random NFL player that none of them had a connection to.

"When was the last time you talked to him?" Stephen asked.

Jack turned to face Kerri, saw how rigidly she sat in her seat, and realized she didn't like the idea that Jacob was sabotaging the band any more than he did. He reached across and took her hand. She squeezed it in response, but remained stiff as she stared at Stephen.

"The morning we left for Daytona," she answered.

That was five days ago, two days before the man tried to steal their money from her.

"What did you talk about?" Charlie asked and she relaxed into her seat.

"The normal things. How the band is doing financially and any problems since our last conversation," she answered.

"So you told him about Jack and that woman?" Stephen probed and Jack felt the tension infuse her body.

"No," she said. "But I did tell him about the vandalized trailer."

"And that Sebastian's guitars were stolen?" Riley inquired.

She laid her head against the headrest of her seat. "Yes."

"Anything else?" Charlie continued.

Kerri shook her head then slowly stopped as her eyes widened and she lifted her head. "Actually, he asked if any money was stolen."

A chill went down Jack's spine as his eyes sharpened on her. "What else did you say?" he ground out through clenched teeth.

He watched her swallow as she turned to him. Her eyes, still wide, focused on him and she inhaled and exhaled slowly. "That I keep the money with me at all times."

Damn it!

The idea Jacob might have hired someone to do Kerri harm had Jack seeing red. "Stop the car, Stephen," he snapped. "I need air."

His muscles tightened with fury as he waited for Stephen to find a parking lot to pull into. As soon as the van stopped, he flung the door open, hopped out, and stormed away from the vehicle.

He couldn't accept it.

He wasn't Jacob's number one fan, by any stretch of the imagination, but it didn't make sense that he would purposely try to steal from the band. They needed every penny they earned to meet the contract requirements. Why would Jacob try to prevent that from happening?

And the first attack, the one that had separated him and Kerri, had been such a personal one. Was it possible that Jacob hadn't been behind the set-up? Maybe, like Nathan originally thought, the first two incidents weren't related at all.

A small hand touched his back and some of the tension slipped away. Jack turned to find Kerri standing there, a worried look on her face, her lips pressed together as she stared at him.

"I'm sorry," she said quietly. "I didn't mean to make you mad."

He closed his eyes and wrapped his arms around her. "I'm not mad at you," he said as he laid his cheek on her head and she slipped her hands around him. "It's just . . . I've seen the bruise on your back and I can't help but think that if that crook had shoved you a little harder, you could have gone over the rail. And I can't even consider what might have happened if he'd stayed inside your room and trapped you in there with him."

She lifted her head and turned her clear, silvery-blue eyes to his face. "That didn't happen."

"It could have." Jack placed a kiss on her forehead. "And I wasn't there to keep you safe. If Jacob had anything to do with our separation, or the attempted robbery . . ." Jack shook his head. "I'm not sure what we should do about it."

Kerri lifted her hands to his cheeks. "It's just a theory. I'm not sure we can ignore it, but it doesn't mean he's guilty. We don't have any proof yet."

Jack nodded in agreement.

"Let's just call Nathan, tell him what we've come up with and ask him what to do next. What's the worst that can really happen at this point?" she asked. "He shows Jacob's picture to the girl and the crook and neither of them recognize him, so we're back to square one. But at least we can cross him off the list of possibilities," she continued, answering her own question.

"Or they do recognize him and we've been working for an ass for three years," Jack gave his own answer to her question.

"Maybe he gets that trait from his half-brother," she teased with a slight lift in her lips. "We'll deal with that if we have to."

A cool breeze ruffled her bangs, which tickled his chin. He couldn't help the smile that touched his lips. Her calmness was slowly dissipating his tension.

"Why would he do this?" Jack asked as he took her hands in his.

She shrugged. "The only thing I can figure is he's trying to protect his company."

"What do you mean?" He gently pulled her closer.

She looked up at him as they stood toe to toe. "After Sebastian's arrest, he seemed a little bothered by the idea that their father would get the charges dropped. He seemed certain that Sebastian would return to the band and in turn give his company a bad name."

Jack shifted his focus over her head, toward the rest of the band hovering around the van. He had to admit that Jacob may have had good reason to be concerned. But why would he take that out on the rest of them? Had they behaved so badly that Jacob wanted to be rid of them as well as Sebastian?

Kerrigan took a step back and he looked down at her.

"I think we should call your brother, right now," she stated, "then find something fun to do and forget about all of this for a few hours."

He placed his lips to her temple. "I know something fun we can do for a few hours," he murmured.

She laughed and pulled her head away. "I meant all of us. Together. We all need to get our minds off of this." The corners of her lips lifted seductively. "And after the show's over tonight, we can do what you want to do."

"Sounds like a plan," he chuckled, and pressed his lips to hers.

Across the span of the conference room they were using for rehearsal, Kerrigan gave Jack a thumbs-up as she waited for Jacob's assistant to answer the phone. It was time for their weekly call and her stomach was in knots.

They had already spoken to Nathan, who seemed more convinced of Jacob's guilt than he had been of Sebastian's. He'd tutored her on what to listen for and how not to give anything away. He'd emphasized the importance of her staying calm and had reassured her of his confidence in her ability.

Jacob's assistant answered and Kerrigan asked to speak to Jacob, then took a slow, deep breath as she waited for him to pick up.

"Good morning, Kerrigan," he finally said. "How are things?"

She straightened her back and lifted her shoulders, hoping to bolster her confidence and settle her nerves. "Things are good," she answered in a steady voice.

"Great," Jacob replied.

"I sent you the file this morning. We're still on track to reach our goal, most likely before we reach Atlanta," Kerrigan continued. "That will leave us almost two weeks to earn bonus money."

"Good," Jacob said coolly and Kerrigan frowned. She'd become used to his short answers, but he usually had a little more to say. "I'm looking through the numbers now. I see you made a fairly large deposit a few days ago."

Kerrigan quickly recalled that she'd made a big deposit two days after the attempted robbery. "Yes, it was from four shows. I hadn't had time to get to the bank before that."

"So I guess you were able to recover the stolen money?" Jacob asked, his tone businesslike and dry.

The knots tightened in the pit of her stomach and her knees weakened as her eyes widened.

How did he know?

She hadn't spoken to Jacob since the night she was attacked. She hadn't yet told him what had happened. She stumbled backward until she felt the wall behind her, then leaned her hips against it.

With that one simple question, everything came crashing down around her. There had been a reason she was so diligent in her research before she'd taken on clients in Zurich. It was so she knew them inside and out. From day one, she'd wished she'd done more research about this band. Now she realized she should have done most of it on Jacob.

"Yes," she croaked, then paused to swallow. For good measure, she cleared her throat. "Yes, we got it back rather quickly."

"That's excellent news," he stated, still sounding unenthusiastic. "Well, keep me updated. I look forward to seeing the numbers next week." He hung up.

Tears threatened to burst forth. Tears of anger. Tears of betrayal. Tears of frustration and fear. She covered her eyes with the heels of her hands to stop the oncoming flood.

How could he do this?

Jack broke into a trot when he saw Kerri put her hands to her eyes. He'd seen her go pale during her conversation with Jacob and thought something might be wrong. Now, he was sure of it. He stopped in front of her and put his arms around her.

"What happened?" he asked.

She remained silent as she held her hands to her face. When she dropped them, he looked into her stormy, red-rimmed gaze and frowned.

"What's wrong?" he asked again.

She gently pushed herself out of his arms and her upper lip curled. "He knew."

"He knew what?" Jack stepped closer and placed a hand on the wall beside her.

"He knew about the robbery," Kerrigan answered.

A cold wave rushed through him and settled in his stomach.

"I haven't spoken to him since it happened. I didn't send an email about it or anything, Jackson." Her face turned to his and he saw the turmoil deep in her eyes.

"But he knew," Jack muttered in disbelief.

He leaned the side of his head against the wall. He'd have to tell Nathan. He couldn't believe the truth had been so easily revealed. What would this mean for the band?

They had their contract to worry about, and they were so close to reaching their goal. But if Jacob was working behind the scenes to sabotage them, there was no telling what he might do next. For the remainder of the tour, they'd have to be wary and alert, watching for anything suspicious.

He opened his eyes and saw Kerri staring across the room with a determined set to her jaw.

He had to keep her safe from harm. Jacob had already hired one person, possibly two, who had hurt her physically and emotionally. What if Jacob hired someone to strike during a concert? He could only protect her when he was by her side.

"We have to get you all out of this contract," she stated firmly, cool and calm. He was happy to see she was more angry and determined than scared.

"How?" he asked as he pushed away from the wall and stood in front of her.

Her eyes shifted from side to side as she contemplated the options. "You call Nathan and tell him about Jacob. I'll give him more details if you need. I'll call Mason and update him on what's going on. We'll see if we can find anything in the contract that could get you out of it."

"Can ye do that?" Riley asked and Jack turned around to find the other three band members behind him.

"The two of you looked awfully serious over here," Charlie said, cautiously eyeing Jack. "So we thought we'd come check it out. Is everything okay?" he asked as he turned his gaze to his sister. Jack made room for them, moving to Kerri's side and taking her hand.

"I just talked to Jacob," she said. "And it appears our guess was correct."

As she related the entirety of the short conversation to the band, Jack watched their reactions. Riley's eyes remained steady and focused on Kerri, but Jack could see the anger building in their green depths. Riley might always appear to be calm and collected, but Jack had seen him angry a few times and the explosion always started with the look he was currently wearing.

Stephen wore his anger like a mask. There was no hiding what he was feeling. It had always made him an easier target for Sebastian, but at the moment, Jack was thankful to know what his friend was feeling.

The look on Charlie's face surprised him the most. He was newest to the band and had yet to even meet Jacob, but he was clearly just as enraged as the others. Jack had a feeling it was more because Kerri's safety had been compromised. And perhaps Charlie had already realized that if Jacob was behind this, there wasn't much they could do to protect her from a future attack.

"So yes, Riley, it may be possible to get you out of the contract," Kerrigan finished with a deep breath.

"How?" Jack asked.

"Most contracts are entered into with implied good faith, meaning both parties signing the contract will act honestly and in good faith to fulfill the requirements of the contract," Kerri explained. "If, as it appears, Jacob has tried to sabotage our efforts to meet the required minimum, then he has violated our good faith."

Jack had always found her intelligence attractive. As she continued to talk, he took the phone from her hand and entered Mason's number into it.

"Thereby voiding our contract?" Stephen asked.

"Not necessarily, I'm afraid," Kerri answered. "His violation would only hold up in court if we have the proof. We can't guarantee that. However, I want to talk to Jack's brother, Mason, and see what he thinks we can do next."

Jack handed her phone back and she glanced at the screen.

She gave him a smile of gratitude.

"And I'll call Nathan and let him know this new development," Jack added.

"What can we do?" Charlie asked.

Jack shrugged.

"I want you to think of any interactions you've had with Jacob," Kerri continued, "especially during the tour, that might have seemed odd. Now that I think back, there may have been a few things I should have picked up on during our conversations. Especially after Sebastian's arrest. In the meantime though, get back to rehearsal. We have to do everything we can to make sure we can still bring the money in and not give him a reason to let you guys go."

Voicing their agreement, Charlie, Stephen, and Riley walked back to their instruments as Kerri pushed the button on her phone to call Mason. Jack took a few steps away as he pulled his own phone out of his pocket and dialed his other brother's number.

"Hello," Nathan answered after the second ring.

"Nathan," Jackson said. "There's been a development."

Thirty-Eight

Kerrigan released a deep, satisfied sigh as she settled her head on Jack's chest. She slowly trailed her finger through the sparse hair and closed her eyes.

Jack's arm tightened around her. "Did Mason enjoy the concert?"

After their conversation regarding their suspicions about Jacob, Mason had decided to join them in Savannah. Kerrigan and Jack had picked him up from the airport shortly after their own arrival into town that afternoon. While the band had rehearsed for their concert, she and Mason had spent time going over the band's contract.

Mason was her second favorite Harris brother. Not that she had a problem with Nathan, but Nathan was eight years older than her and had always seemed a little intimidating, even before he became a cop. Mason, on the other hand, had always been considered the "good son" and rarely had a harsh word for her, or anyone else. Sure he teased his brothers mercilessly, but whatever mean streak he had was directed solely at his siblings.

He'd gotten married while Kerrigan was living in Europe and now had a baby boy that she couldn't wait to meet. If she had to be stuck going through a boring contract, she couldn't think of anyone better to do it with. Mason made the contract sound interesting and easy to understand. He pointed out a few lines that he'd highlighted, clauses that they could use to their benefit in getting them out of their contract. When they had finished, she felt hopeful that it wouldn't be as difficult to get Malhypnus away from Jacob's company as she'd originally feared.

She chuckled softly. "I'm not sure hard rock is his taste in music."

"I know it's not," Jack readily agreed. "Nathan's either."

Kerrigan leaned on her elbow and held her head in the palm of her hand. "If I remember correctly, it hasn't always been yours either."

"I've always liked a wide variety of music," Jack said as he laid his hand over hers on his chest. "But you're right. I'm not sure hard rock actually is my favorite."

She frowned. It was clearly something else he'd compromised on with Sebastian.

He glanced up at her and gave her hand a gentle squeeze. "Hey, don't worry about it. We can change that soon. What did you and Mason decide today?"

"He showed me a few things that we can use," she answered. "We'll all meet tomorrow morning and figure out what you guys want to do next and what route you might want to take for the future of the band."

Jack placed his hand on the back of her head and pulled her face closer to his. "I just want to think about a future with you," he said. His serious tone made her heart flutter and she tried to contain her smile.

She paused with her mouth inches from his. "We can talk about that once this is all settled."

He grinned widely and met her lips with his, then flipped her onto her back, his chest hovering over hers.

Giggling, she gently pushed him away. "You haven't told me what Nathan said yet," she said breathlessly, and his expression darkened immediately.

"The girl positively identified Jacob in the photo lineup," Jack answered with a scowl. "Nathan has spoken to the PD in Melbourne about what's going on, and they're going to interview her as well and see what they can charge him with. They're also looking more seriously into the vandalism of the trailer to see if they can find the people who did that and if Jacob hired them as well."

"And if the vandals can't be found? Will that affect any charges?" she asked as she rubbed at the crease between his brows.

Jack shook his head. "Not the ones they discover because of the woman. It would simply mean they could tie him to something else and a harsher sentence if he's found guilty."

Kerrigan cupped his cheek and lightly ran her thumb across his cheekbone. "What happens next?"

He blew out a long, steady breath. "Nathan's headed to Daytona tomorrow to talk to the police and interview the would-be thief again. He's going to present him with the same pictures and see if any of them ring a bell. If they do, Nathan will see what Jacob can be charged with there."

"You don't seem happy about this," Kerrigan said with a frown.

Jack lowered his head to her stomach, facing her feet, and she began running her fingers through his hair. "This is not what I was expecting when I asked Nathan to investigate what happened in that hotel room," he confessed. "I just wanted to prove to you that I hadn't had sex with that woman."

Kerrigan felt a stab in her chest. The fact that he'd felt he needed to prove his innocence to her filled her with guilt and remorse. He'd known she doubted him without her having to say it. He'd known she wouldn't believe him.

"I'm sorry," she muttered as she tried to keep the tears at bay.

He lifted his head and turned to face her. She couldn't meet his gaze.

"Hey," he said as he slid up so he was even with her. He laid a hand on her cheek. "You reacted the way anyone would have reacted. Debra probably would have thrown a few things first, but I imagine she wouldn't be so quick to forgive and forget what she saw either."

He kissed the tears off of her cheeks then tenderly pressed his lips to hers. Kerrigan relished his loving gentleness and pushed all of her regret and sadness away. She'd learned that she really could trust him. She couldn't continue to dwell on the past.

When he broke the kiss, she stared deeply into his eyes and gave him a small smile.

"That's better," he whispered.

She nodded then became businesslike again. "You were saying?"

Jack's brow furrowed for a moment. "Oh, that's right. I just never expected that incident to be part of some elaborate scheme to damage us as a band. And I didn't expect that our producer might get arrested for it. I still can't wrap my head around the fact that Jacob's behind it. He was supposed to be the 'good son' and we're making money for him. None of this makes sense."

"I agree," she said. "But it is what it is and we have to figure out how to work around it with as little damage to your career as possible."

"Ugh." Jack flopped onto his back and threw an arm over his head. "My career," he repeated with a curl of his lip.

Kerrigan pushed up onto her elbow again and leaned over him. "Isn't that what you want?"

"Honestly?" He looked her squarely in the eyes, his green gaze cloudy and dark. "I don't know anymore. All I know is I want you to be a part of my life, no matter what I do. Promise me you won't leave me again, Kerri."

Happy tears filled her eyes. "No matter what you do, I promise I will be by your side."

He grinned and Kerrigan found herself in his arms.

Jack was onstage, playing for a large crowd of screaming fans, but his concern was for Kerri. They were still in Savannah and the end of the tour was two weeks away, but Kerri had told him the band should reach their goal before they reached Atlanta. Jacob was running out of time if he was going to stop them and Jack couldn't help but worry he might try something else soon.

Kerri was standing behind the merchandise table, near the side of the stage, with Debra beside her. Mason was closer to the bar, not far from the women. Even so, Jack would have preferred her to be backstage, or better yet back in Rocky Creek, where he could be sure she was safe. They were only halfway through their show and Jack knew he wouldn't relax until it was over.

They finished playing a song and Jack began telling a story to the crowd to lead into the next song. The audience began screaming and cheering. Jack smiled widely as he looked down at his guitar to play the opening chords.

He lifted his gaze and put his lips close to the mic. Glancing around the room as he prepared to belt out the lyrics, his eyes landed on a tall, dark-haired figure near the door. A chill ran through his body when he recognized the man who was scanning the room.

Jacob was there.

Jack's palms began to sweat and his heart raced as he sang and watched their producer wind his way through the crowd. He was moving in Kerri's direction and Jack cast his eyes toward her. She met his gaze with a frown and a tilt of her head. He realized that he'd missed a few notes and his voice had faded, so he focused on the music and made eye contact with Mason.

Mason was no longer leaning on the bar. He met Jack's stare and Jack nodded toward Jacob. Mason craned his neck in the direction of Jack's nod then began to make his way toward Kerri as well.

Jack wasn't sure how he made it through the first two verses and the chorus, but when they reached the drum solo, he stepped away from the mic. Charlie appeared at his shoulder.

"You okay?" he asked in a hushed tone.

Jack shook his head once. "Jacob's here."

"Relax," Charlie whispered. "Mason is with her. She can handle this and we're right here."

Jack pressed his lips tightly together as his gaze bounced between his brother and his producer, anxious to see which one would reach Kerri first, helpless that he couldn't be by her side. Mason was the first to reach her and he stepped into the shadow just beyond the end of the table. Jack inhaled deeply, then blew out slowly, trying to steady his nerves and bring his focus back to the music. He had to trust his brother to keep her safe.

Thirty-Nine

As Kerrigan handed the change to a customer, she noticed a movement out of the corner of her eye. She glanced toward it and saw Mason hovering in the shadows, just beyond Debra and the end of the table. He nodded toward the crowd with a scowl that matched Jack's and she turned in that direction. Her eyes widened for a moment when she saw Jacob approaching and she dropped her gaze to the merchandise table. Her stomach knotted and her mouth went dry. What was he doing here? What would he say? Or do?

"Jacob's here," Debra murmured as Kerrigan pretended to straighten a T-shirt.

"I know," Kerrigan replied tightly.

"Just act normal," Debra reassured her. "I'm here and I won't let anything happen."

Kerrigan plastered a grin on her face and looked at her friend. "I know."

Debra smiled in return, then turned to the next person in line as Kerrigan did the same. Jacob stopped at the corner of the table closest to her as she was making change and she glanced at him for a moment.

"Thank you," she stated as she dropped the cash into the buyer's hand then took a step back and turned toward her boss. "Jacob," she said brightly. "Welcome to Savannah." She motioned around at the crowd and resisted the urge to glance at the stage. "What brings you here?"

Jacob chuckled and leaned closer as he waved to the merchandise table. "I came to see you work your magic."

She forced a musical laugh past her lips. "It's hardly magic," she said. "It's simply good business."

Jacob chuckled heartily as he stood up. "Of course."

As Kerrigan and Debra dealt with the fans making purchases, Jacob stood close, watching and occasionally asking questions. He seemed especially interested in the items they'd added to their stock of goods, not just bandanas and keychains, but magnets with the cover art from the album and pins of the band's logo. Through her nervousness, Kerrigan answered his questions with a smile, and felt slightly pleased when he mentioned, more than once, how impressed he was.

As the line of buyers died down, Jacob pulled Kerrigan aside. "I'd like to speak with you in private."

A chill went through her but she kept the friendly smile on her face. "Of course."

"Somewhere a little quieter," he added as he stepped closer. "Maybe outside?"

Leaving the building with him would be a bad idea and her cheeks felt tight as she quickly tried to find a reason not to.

"It's a major road, it's still pretty loud out there," she finally said. "Why don't we go backstage? It will be a little quieter there."

His jaw tensed momentarily before he nodded. "Sounds fine," he agreed.

Kerrigan patted down her front pockets, checking for her phone, as she turned to Debra. "Keep the money with you and be careful," she whispered as she leaned toward her friend. Over Debra's shoulder, she made eye contact with Mason.

He held up his phone, reminding her he had an app he could use to record her conversation with Jacob in case they needed the evidence, which he'd shown to her earlier. He used it all the time when talking to clients, and they'd briefly discussed how they might employ it. She nodded once then turned back to Jacob.

"Follow me," she said brightly as she stepped past him and through the door.

She led him just beyond the steps leading to the stage, to the quietest place she could find. She could still hear the music and knew they were well over halfway through the concert. Kerrigan stopped and swiveled around, briefly meeting Mason's eyes over Jacob's shoulder. He'd followed them and was once again hovering in the shadows, just behind Jacob. She turned her attention to Jacob.

"What did you want to talk about?" she asked as she clasped her damp palms in front of her.

Jacob stood with his feet apart, mimicking her pose. "I have to admit, I'm quite impressed with the job you've done with this band."

Kerrigan nodded her thanks, but let him continue.

"You've managed to turn them around faster than I could have imagined. It makes me wonder what you could have done had you been with them from the start." Jacob gave her a charming smile.

She remained silent.

"Along those lines," Jacob continued, clearly not noticing her discomfort, "I have an offer for you. I have a band about to start their first tour and I would like you to manage them. And if you're as successful with that tour as I expect you will be, I think I'd like to move you into more of a leadership position. I'd like you to train our other tour managers to do what you've done so well."

Kerrigan's brow furrowed as she considered his offer. She'd never intended to stay on with his company as he'd made it clear from the beginning he was only hiring her to finish out Malhypnus's current tour. Did he really want her to manage another band or was he simply trying to get her away from Malhypnus?

"When does this other tour start?" she asked slowly.

"Wednesday," Jacob answered.

She tilted her head as she folded an arm across her body. "That's in five days."

"Yes it is," he confirmed with a nod. "Is that a problem?"

She pressed her lips together as her blood began to warm. "Jacob, this tour doesn't end for another two and a half weeks," she said calmly, despite her rising temper. "You told them that if I left before the tour was over they were finished with your company."

"That's true," he agreed.

"Now you're trying to lure me away?" She raised an eyebrow and held his stare until he looked away.

Her phone vibrated in her pocket and she ignored it. Over Jacob's shoulder she noticed Mason glance at his phone then meet her gaze. He held the screen toward her and waved it side to side as he mouthed his older brother's name. She slipped her hand into her pocket as Jacob returned his focus on her.

"You're the best person I can think of for this other band and I need to know now that you'll manage them," Jacob stated smoothly, but Kerrigan could see the irritation in his eyes. "I was serious. I won't hire another manager for Malhypnus. But, since I'm the one luring you away and there's so little time left on their tour, I'm willing to give them a chance to meet the contract requirements without your help."

Her vision turned red around the edges. He knew they wouldn't be able to sell anything during the shows if she wasn't there, and the majority of their nightly income came from sales of merchandise. They were less than ten thousand dollars away from meeting their requirement. Her leaving would put them in jeopardy.

"If I allow them to continue their tour, provided there are no behavioral issues, will you agree to my offer?" Jacob asked, holding his arm out for her to shake his hand.

She looked down at his open palm then into his blue eyes. "No," she stated firmly.

His hand dropped and his squared jaw tightened. "No?" he repeated through clenched teeth. "Why?"

"You hired me to manage this band through the end of their tour," she began.

"And it's a miracle they've managed not to run you off," Jacob snapped.

Kerrigan's eyes narrowed. "Regardless," she continued as she pulled her phone out of her pocket. "I won't quit before the job is done. I never have—you can ask my former employers if you need to. Malhypnus's tour is not over, therefore I'm not leaving them."

Jacob's scowl deepened and he turned away. Kerrigan took the opportunity to glance at her phone and tried not to smile when she read the message from Nathan and the response from Mason. She made eye contact with Mason and he stepped out of the shadows and gave her a slight nod.

That was her signal. It was time to bait the lion.

"As for the miracle," Kerrigan began sweetly and Jacob turned to face her. "I really have to wonder why it was so easy for Sebastian to run off four other managers."

Jacob's eyes widened and he folded his arms across his chest. "What are you saying?"

She took a deep, steadying breath. "Sebastian's pranks, his overall behavior actually, seemed childish to me. All Sebastian needed was a little discipline and to be told no. It wasn't really that hard."

Jacob lifted his shoulders. "Well, they also had to contend with Jack's behavior." He studied her carefully. "I wonder why you didn't have a problem with Jack as well."

After the woman in Melbourne identified him, Kerrigan had figured Jacob probably knew about her relationship with Jack, but she didn't need to tell him anything more about that.

"Perhaps Jack wasn't the problem you thought he was," she stated. "A little destructive, maybe. And he certainly liked the ladies," she added with a shrug. "Otherwise, he likes to keep to himself and just let things happen around him." Inwardly she cringed at having to disparage his character, but that was the impression she'd gotten about him from Stephen and Riley on her first day. "Nothing either of them did was enough to make me run for the hills. It does make me wonder why my predecessors gave up so easily. But more importantly, I wonder why none of them stuck to the budget. They all overpaid the band. They all spent way more on hotels and food than they were supposed to. And not a single one of them made the effort to sell merchandise during the shows."

Jacob's face darkened and she saw the rapid rise and fall of his chest. "What are you suggesting?" he bit off.

She swallowed the lump of fear and kept pushing. "If I didn't know any better, I would say it seems like someone was setting the band up to fail from the beginning."

His upper lip curled. "Why would anyone do that?"

"Maybe to get out of a contract," she pulled her bottom lip in and moistened it with her tongue as she held his glare, "with his brother."

Jacob's eyes widened and he looked away. "I have no idea what you're talking about."

Kerrigan glanced at Mason again. He nodded and gave her a thumbs up and she tried to recall all of the things they'd discussed earlier that day. The questions she needed to get Jacob to answer without her having to really ask them. She shifted her focus to his face and took a deep breath.

"It's obvious to everyone that you and Sebastian don't get along," she said calmly.

"That's an understatement," Jacob scoffed and met her stare. "I knew about him. His entire life. But he didn't know about me until we were introduced."

"Why is that?" Kerrigan stopped herself from asking more and tried to keep a mask of indifference on her face.

"His mother is a bitch. He's a lot like her, actually." Jacob laughed once as he took a step back. "She wanted my father to pretend my mother and I were never a part of his life."

A little pang of sympathy struck her in the heart. She could only imagine what that must have felt like.

"Even after they divorced, she didn't want her precious baby boy to know he had a bastard half-brother." Jacob's face hardened as his nostrils flared. "I wish my father had kept it that way. I hated Sebastian the moment I met him and he's done nothing to improve my opinion of him."

She clasped her hand around her elbow so she didn't reach out to try to comfort him. "But you're finally rid of him."

The crazed look in his eyes grew as he took a step toward her. "Do you think that matters? Our father will get the charges dropped and he'll be back with the band. It's only a matter of time."

Kerrigan inched backward as Mason took a step forward. "Is that why you've been sabotaging the band?"

Jacob laughed. "You're kidding, right?"

"I wish I was." The corners of her lips fell and she saw Mason inch closer. The final strains of the last song reached her ears. "We started wondering what was going on all of a sudden with the vandalism and the robbery, so we hired a detective."

The arrogant tilt to Jacob's chin dropped by a fraction as Kerrigan held up her phone.

"He just texted me and said that the man you hired to rob us positively identified you in a photo lineup," she continued and glimpsed the movement over his shoulder as the band members silently descended the steps from the stage.

"That's impossible," he snapped. "I've been in New York until this morning when I left to come here."

"Then there is someone out there who looks a lot like you stirring up trouble," Kerrigan replied casually as she pushed her phone into her pocket. "He also has a ring that looks a lot like that one." She pointed to the large ring on his right hand and he looked down at it.

Jacob's arms unfolded and he held his hands out to the side as he took a step toward her. "Is that all you've got?" he hissed. "No money was stolen so no crime was actually committed. There's nothing to convict me of." He inched closer.

Determined to hold her ground, she simply tipped her chin. "We're looking into that." She raised an eyebrow. "But then there's the woman in Melbourne."

"What woman?" Jacob roared, placing his face inches from hers.

She folded her arms across her chest. "The one who drugged Jack," she replied. "She said you hired her and that you gave her the drugs."

His face turned red. "Do you really think people will believe the word of some two-bit criminal and a motel desk clerk over mine?" he snarled. "You're obviously not as smart as I thought."

Kerrigan pulled her shoulders back. "I never told you she worked at the motel."

The color in his cheeks deepened and he grabbed her upper arm. "If you go public with these outrageous accusations, you will hear from my lawyer. And you can forget any other job with my company, Miss Dodd. You're fired and your tenure with this band ends now."

Her eyes rounded and she froze as he tried to push her backward to the door.

Two hands suddenly gripped her shoulders as Jack, sporting a menacing scowl, took hold of Jacob's arm and yanked him away from her. Jacob's focus turned to the wall the band members had formed between him and the stage.

"What d'ye think ye're doin' wi' our manager?" Riley drawled from Jack's side.

Kerrigan glanced over her shoulder to find Mason, his hands still on her shoulders and his eyes narrowed on Jacob, and breathed a shaky sigh of relief.

"I think you'll be hearing from our lawyer first," Stephen said from Jack's other side.

Mason gave her shoulders a reassuring squeeze then dropped his hands. "Good job," he whispered as she slowly took a deep breath.

"And as of this morning," Jack growled, "she works for us, not you."

Jacob violently shook himself from Jack's grip as he turned and sneered at her.

"Jacob," she said coolly, "I'd like you to meet our lawyer, Mr. Mason Harris. We hired him when it became obvious that you had violated the good faith clause of the band's contract with your attempted sabotage. This morning, he drew up a contract and I became the band's manager, regardless of who their record label is."

"You can't do that." Jacob aimed his finger at her chest. "You worked for me."

"You never had me sign anything." She shrugged. "I guess you expected Sebastian to run me off fairly quickly."

"You have violated the band's trust, so she was well within her rights," Mason added. "And the contract only becomes valid if you fire her or she quits working for you."

Jacob's eyes widened as he turned on Mason.

"So it was really more of an insurance policy," Kerrigan added.

Jacob glared menacingly at each of the band members, but they all looked unimpressed.

"Why did you do this?" Stephen asked. This was a question they'd all asked themselves since they'd figured it out. "You won't get the money from Mr. Bates."

"I would have," Jacob scoffed. "We'd agreed that you all got one more chance." He stared at Kerrigan. "She was it. I honestly did think Sebastian would run you off. I even told him I'd give him a share of the money if he did."

"What happened?" Kerrigan asked angrily.

"I have no idea," Jacob grumbled.

The corner of Jack's mouth lifted and she looked away to hide the smile that was threatening.

"Well," Mason said and Kerrigan turned to him. "I think it's time we renegotiate the band's contract."

Forty

Jack paced outside of the makeshift office like an expectant father. Since Mason had led Kerri and Jacob into the room that had been their lounge before the concert, the band had packed up all of their equipment and loaded everything onto the trailer. Now they were all waiting to see what would come of the negotiations.

Debra leaned against a stack of tables, the cash box clutched tightly in her hands, Stephen by her side. Before going into the office, Kerri had asked the band to keep a close eye on Debra, the merchandise, and the money, just in case Jacob had something else in store for them. Charlie was propped against the wall beside the door and Riley sat on the bottom step leading to the stage.

Jack took his phone out of his back pocket again to read through the texts between his brothers. After Nathan had confirmed the identity of the man who had hired the would-be thief, Mason had responded by letting him know Jacob was at the show. Nathan's reply had been to keep Jacob there as long as possible.

Between wondering what Nathan was up to and how Mason and Kerri were doing, Jack was going crazy. The tension that had infused his body when he'd seen Jacob walk into the club had only worsened since Kerri had disappeared from his sight.

He wouldn't feel better until she was in his arms again.

As he reached to put his phone in his back pocket, it rang the familiar tune he'd assigned to Nathan. Jack stepped away from the door and pushed the answer button as he lifted the phone to his ear.

"Hello," he said.

"What's going on?" Nathan asked in an efficient tone. "Is Jacob still there?"

"Yes," Jack answered. "He's with Mason and Kerri, renegotiating the band's contract."

"Good. Here's what's going to happen . . ." Nathan proceeded to lay out the series of events in store for Jacob. Jack listened as he glanced around at the curious eyes and listened carefully to his brother's voice. "Just stay out of the way and let them do their job," Nathan finished.

Jack rolled his eyes. "Duh," he said and Nathan chuckled.

"I was wondering if I had the right brother. You've been all business and no fun these last few phone calls," Nathan said and the weight lifted a little from Jack's shoulders.

"Can you blame me?"

"No, I'd be the same way if I thought Janelle might be in danger," Nathan agreed. "Just keep me posted."

"Will do," Jack agreed and said his good-byes.

He pushed his phone into his back pocket and looked around the room. The door leading to the club suddenly opened and two uniformed officers came through. Jack walked across the room to greet them as Riley rose to his feet.

"We're looking for Jacob Goldberg," the lead officer stated.

Jack pointed to the door of the office. "He's in there," he said. "But my band and I would appreciate it if you could let our manager and lawyer finish re-negotiating our contract with him before you take him away."

"How long might that be?" snapped the second officer, a younger, rough-looking man. From the look on his face, Jack figured he didn't think what he was currently doing was that important.

"I don't know." Jack lifted his shoulders. "They've been in there for at least half an hour. Maybe longer."

The lead officer turned to his partner and they had a brief, whispered conversation. He faced Jack again. "We'll give them fifteen minutes."

"Thank you," Jack said, and resumed pacing.

Another five minutes passed before the doorknob rattled. Jack froze and swiveled around. The door flew open and Jacob's scowling, dark face was the first one he saw. Jacob met his stare, curled his lip further, and stomped past him. He stopped short when he saw the two police officers waiting for him.

"What the hell?" Jacob hissed.

"Jacob Goldberg?" asked the gruff officer.

Jacob looked over his shoulder and narrowed his eyes at Jack, then turned back to the policemen. "Yes."

"We'd like you to come with us," the younger cop stated.

"Am I under arrest?" Jacob asked politely.

Kerri exited the room with Mason following closely. Both of them wore curious expressions as they watched the interaction between Jacob and the police. Jack took her hand and tugged her closer.

"No." The lead officer shook his head. "We just have a few questions we'd like to ask you."

"If you cooperate, it shouldn't take too long," the younger man said.

"Of course," Jacob said curtly. He took a step forward then looked over his shoulder at Jack. "Don't think this proves anything. You're nothing now and that's all you'll ever be. How far do you really think you'll get without a label?" he hissed.

Riley suddenly appeared at Jack's shoulder. "We'll be fine," he drawled. "We have a kick-ass manager."

"Not to mention an amazing lead singer," Kerri added, giving Jack's hand a squeeze. She narrowed her eyes and glared at Jacob. "I think we'll be just fine."

Jacob opened his mouth as the younger officer grabbed his upper arm. "C'mon, let's go," the policeman grumbled, steering Jacob toward the door.

As soon as the door to the club closed behind them, Jack turned Kerri around and pulled her into his arms. He was so relieved to have Jacob out of their lives. Hopefully the negotiations went well, but for the moment he just wanted to savor the feel of her body against his and inhale her sweet scent.

"What was that?" Mason asked.

"Do we have a new contract?" Stephen asked at the same time.

"What happened with Jacob?" Debra added to the barrage.

Jack exhaled deeply. "One thing at a time," he said as he slid his arm around Kerri's shoulder.

"You first," Kerri murmured and he looked down into her tired, smiling eyes.

"Yes, Jackson, you first," Mason echoed.

Jack nodded. "Nathan called about five minutes before the cops showed up and told me they were on their way."

"I didn't think you were going after him. I thought you just wanted to clear your name with Kerri," Charlie responded with a frown.

"I'm not going after him," Jack stated. "After the woman in Melbourne identified him, she was taken in for questioning by the cops. Given that she drugged me, she was looking at a lot of trouble for herself. She confessed that Jacob had given the GHB to her and she presented the bottle to the police. They tested it and fingerprinted it. The drug had been in the bottle and her fingerprints were on it, along with at least one other set of prints."

Kerri gasped and Debra covered her mouth with her hand.

"They'll get prints from Jacob tonight and if they match, he could be charged with illegal drug distribution and accessory to a crime," Jack continued. "As for the hiring of the thief in Daytona, Nathan has talked to that PD too and they're looking into whether or not he actually committed a crime there."

"So why did they take him in?" Stephen asked.

"Aside from getting his fingerprints, they'll question him to see what, if anything, they can get him to confess to," Jack replied.

"Oh, that reminds me," Mason said as he took his phone from his pocket. "I have a recording to send to Nathan."

"Of what?" Riley wondered aloud.

"Of Jacob's conversation with Kerri before we went into the office," Mason answered with a twinkle in his eye. "He may not have confessed exactly, but to my ears he came pretty damn close." He poked at his phone's screen a few times then looked up with a smile. "Let's see what the police think."

"Yes, let's," Jack agreed then looked down at Kerri again. "Now, how did the negotiations go?"

Kerri took a deep breath. "We got his partners on the phone and told them what was going on. They were not happy about our accusations, but after we laid out the proof their anger seemed to shift to Jacob. When we told them we wanted to renegotiate the contract, they were all ears. After much discussion," she paused and looked around the gathered group, "I'm pleased to say you all are now free from Mattern, Nelson, and Goldberg Records."

Riley let out a whoop, Stephen smiled, and Debra blew out a sigh.

"All the money you've made since Jack was drugged, is the band's money. Everything we earned in profit up to that point goes back to the record company," Kerri continued. "Along those same lines though, they agreed they would cover our expenses only up to the first incident in Melbourne. After that, the expenses are our responsibility." She peeked around Jack at his brother. "Mason and I are going to sit down and figure all of that out in the morning. They're expecting us to have our money out of their bank account by Wednesday."

"Let me know if I can help," Stephen volunteered and Debra nodded in agreement.

Kerri smiled at them. "You're welcome to join us. This is your band, after all." She shifted her gaze to Riley, then to her brother beside her. "There is one thing you all need to do." She looked up at Jack. "Clearly we have to finish this tour as Malhypnus, but after that you have the chance to make whatever changes you want. Whether it's the name, the sound, the look." Her expression became clouded as she looked away. "Or, if you don't want to continue at all."

Jack gave her shoulder a squeeze and pulled her closer. They'd have to talk about their future before he made any decisions about his band. "I think we can talk about it in the morning."

"I agree," said Debra, leaning her head onto Stephen's shoulder. "I think we should call it a night."

"Sounds like a plan," Mason agreed, and they left the club and headed back to the motel.

Kerrigan slowly ran the brush through her hair as she watched Jack strip down for bed. Her mind was on the future of the band. As nervous as she'd been in the beginning, she'd really come to love her job. But she couldn't make Jackson continue if he didn't want to. And on more than one occasion he'd told her this had been Sebastian's dream more than it had been his. If Sebastian was no longer around, what would Jackson want to do?

"Hey." Jack lifted her chin with his finger until they were eye to eye.

"What are you thinking?" he asked, taking the brush from her and laying it on the counter behind her.

She furrowed her brow and pressed her lips together. After a long, slow breath she began, "You said being in a band wasn't your dream. That it was Sebastian who led you down this path."

Jack nodded as he put his hands on the counter on either side of her. "That's true."

"So, now that you have the chance to start over," she continued. "What are you going to do?"

His eyes held hers. "I never told you what my dream was, did I?" One corner of his lips curved upwards. "What I had once upon a time pictured my future to be."

She shook her head. "I don't think so."

He stepped closer. "At one point, after our separation but before this band madness took over, I had thought I might go back to Rocky Creek, start a career in landscaping, and settle down with the most beautiful woman I knew."

She raised an eyebrow. "Oh really?" she teased. "Should I be jealous?"

He chuckled and shook his head then placed a light kiss to the corner of her mouth. "No, not at all," he replied. "I even pictured our children. They'd have my brown hair and her blue-gray eyes."

Kerrigan's heart skipped a beat and she pulled her bottom lip between her teeth to keep from smiling.

"My stubbornness and charm," he added with a twinkle in his eyes, "and they'd all sing like angels."

Tears stung her eyes. "They sound lovely."

Jack nodded. "I can't wait to meet them." He kissed her lips gently. "I thought I'd lost that chance."

She slid her arms over his shoulders.

"The thing is, before you joined our band, I had no direction. I was simply going through the motions because I was convinced I had no other option." His face darkened as he stared over her shoulder. "But you came and that dream started to work its way back into my heart and mind and I couldn't shake it. Then Sebastian left and I began to enjoy myself and the music again. The concerts became fun and the weight of his domination lifted." He focused on her face again and smiled. "I really like being in this band and working with these guys. And now that we have the chance to do things our way, I'm not sure I want to miss that opportunity." Jack moved his hands to her hips. "Are you happy as our manager?"

She nodded. "I wouldn't have signed that contract this morning if I weren't."

"Good." His brow furrowed and anxiety crept into his features. "Because what I want to know is, can I have both of those dreams?"

She cupped his cheek in the palm of her hand and choked back tears of happiness. "You're an amazing musician. I would hate to see you give that up and I'm so excited to start this adventure with you," she replied. "Like I told you a few days ago, I will be beside you no matter what."

"Good," he responded with a smile that reminded her of the boy she'd fallen in love with. "Then let's do this."

Epilogue

Five months later

Kerri smiled as Jackson pulled his Camaro into the driveway of the new-to-them house.

"Stay here," he said after parking under the carport and climbed out before she could argue. He trotted up the steps to the door and unlocked it then pushed it open just far enough to peek into the house. With a grin on his face he hurried back to the car.

She opened her door and stuck out a bare foot. Her feet were tired from all of the dancing they'd done at Nathan's wedding reception and she'd taken her shoes off on the way home. As she put both feet on the ground, Jackson stopped at her door.

"What did I say?" He narrowed his eyes on her, trying to look angry except for the tell-tale smirk on his lips.

She stood, clutching her shoes in one hand and a small purse in the other. "I didn't go anywhere," she stated, then squealed as he scooped her up in his arms. "What are you doing?" she giggled and looped her arms around his neck.

He pushed the car door closed with his hip then turned toward the house. "Carrying you across the threshold of our new home."

"You've been living here for three and a half months," she argued.

The house had belonged to Nathan, but he'd been moving his stuff into his fiancée's home for the past few months as Jackson had been getting settled in and moving his things from his mother's house. Kerrigan had remained at home with Charlie and Olivia, who had now been married for three months. She was more than happy to be out of the newlywed's home for good, but glad it was only a fifteen-minute drive away.

"Yes, but you haven't," he stated. "And now that Nathan has married and moved out completely, the house officially belongs to us." There was a mischievous twinkle in his emerald-colored eyes. "And I think we should christen every room in it before the end of the week," he added with a sultry rumble.

Kerri's cheeks warmed and her body tingled in anticipation. "Why don't we just throw a bottle of champagne at it and be done?" she teased, then laughed as his brow furrowed and he pouted.

He climbed the last step. "I wasn't—"

She pressed her lips to his, cutting off his words with a sweet, loving kiss. "I know what you meant," she murmured, then captured his gaze again and grinned seductively, "and I'm game."

Jackson's eyes glowed with excitement as he pushed the door open and carried her into their living room.

Her heart leapt to her throat. "What is this?" she asked as he slowly lowered her to the floor.

There were roses, dozens of them in a kaleidoscope of colors, sitting in vases on almost every flat surface in the room. As she stood in awe of the color and the sweet smell, Jackson lit candles, of varying sizes, all around the room. She could feel his stare on her and she slowly turned her eyes to his.

"What is this?" she repeated as he stalked toward her, the grin on his face causing her stomach to do somersaults.

He stopped in front of her, took her shoes and purse from her and dropped them on the chair beside the door.

"Surprise," he whispered as he took her hands and stepped closer. "I never realized how much I looked forward to hearing from you or seeing you every day until you weren't in my life anymore. I'm not sure I even realized how dark my life was for those six years we were apart." He dropped one of her hands and she let it fall to her side. "Before you came back into my life, I didn't really care about much of anything. I'd given up on almost all of my dreams."

"Jackson," she stuttered around the lump in her throat.

He shook his head as the corner of his lips lifted. "You are my light, Kerri. You make my days brighter. You make me want to be a better man.

You help me realize all of my dreams." He lifted her left hand and lowered himself to one knee.

Tears filled her eyes when he produced a small box and opened it.

"Would you make me the happiest man? Would you make my next dream come true? Kerri, will you marry me?"

The grin on her lips made her cheeks hurt and she couldn't speak. She nodded vigorously and he slipped the sparkling, round diamond ring onto her finger. "Yes," she finally managed as he wrapped his arms around her waist and kissed her deeply. Giddy with emotion and excitement, she wasn't surprised when the kiss became heated and passionate and his erection pressed against her.

His lips slid to her cheek. "Why don't we take this celebration to the bedroom," he breathed.

Kerri leaned her head back, giving his lips access to her throat. "I think that's an excellent idea," she sighed as she closed her eyes.

He pressed kisses to her neck and had reached her collarbone when she heard the muffled, tinkling ring of her phone. She opened her eyes and lowered her head.

"Let it ring," Jackson groaned as she began to push away.

"It may be important," she argued softly as he tightened his hold.

"Then they can leave a message."

She wiggled out of his arms. "I'll make it short." She hurried to her purse and grabbed the phone. "Hello."

Jackson slipped his arms around her waist and pressed his chest to her back.

"Hi," said a female voice on the other end that sounded a little familiar. "Is this Kerri Dodd?"

Kerri smiled. That wouldn't be her name for much longer. "Yes."

Jackson began to lightly kiss the back of Kerrigan's neck.

"Kerri, it's Claire Finnigan," the woman stated.

Claire was the eldest daughter of the man who owned Finnigan's Pub, the favorite local hangout. Sadly, Mr. Finnigan had recently died in a horrible accident at the pub and now Claire, at twenty-two, had become burdened with putting the pub back together.

"Claire," Kerri replied, stifling the gasp Jackson had drawn from her when he lightly nipped her shoulder. "How have you been?"

"It's been . . ." She cleared her throat. "I have a question for you."

Kerri swatted Jackson's hand as it trailed lower down her abdomen. "Ask away."

"Are you managing Jackson Harris's band?"

In the four months since the tour had ended, all of the band members had returned to Rocky Creek to try to regroup. They'd come up with a new name, a new look, and a new sound, and were currently working on writing songs for their new album. Kerri had been helping the band when she could, but there wasn't much for her to do until she had a sampler or a CD to present to potential record producers.

She'd been keeping herself busy working with Charlie in his general contracting business as his office manager. Stephen and Jackson were currently earning their living working with Charlie as well, Stephen managing the books while Jackson did what landscaping he could during the colder months. They were still trying to find something to keep Riley busy, although he was perfectly content to hang out at Finnigan's on a daily basis.

In addition, the band was playing locally, wherever they could find a gig.

"Yes, I am the band's manager," Kerri answered and Jackson froze. He moved his ear closer to her phone and she turned it slightly toward him so he could listen.

"Well, I'm organizing a fundraiser for the pub and I was wondering if the band might be interested in playing," Claire stated.

Kerri peeked over her shoulder and Jackson nodded. "Absolutely," he whispered and she grinned.

"Of course, Claire. We're more than happy to help," Kerri replied. "When is the fundraiser?"

"At the end of the month," Claire said.

"Great. Why don't I come by on Monday and we can work out the details." Kerri stifled a giggle as Jackson grabbed her waist and pulled her against him. "Let me know if I can do anything else for you."

Claire released a long breath. "Thank you so much. I'll see you on Monday then. Have a good night."

"You're welcome. Bye." Kerri pushed the button to end the call as she turned in Jackson's arms.

He took the phone from her and dropped it in the chair beside them.

"Now," she smirked and slid her arms over his shoulders. "Where were we?"

Jackson put his hands on her hips. "I'm pretty sure we were about to christen the living room."